The Namaste Club

Also by Asha Elias
Pink Glass Houses

THE NAMASTE CLUB

A Novel

ASHA ELIAS

WILLIAM MORROW
An Imprint of HarperCollinsPublishers

THE NAMASTE CLUB. Copyright © 2025 by Asha Elias. All rights reserved. Printed in the United States of America. No part of this book may be used or reproduced in any manner whatsoever without written permission except in the case of brief quotations embodied in critical articles and reviews. For information, address HarperCollins Publishers, 195 Broadway, New York, NY 10007. In Europe, HarperCollins Publishers, Macken House, 39/40 Mayor Street Upper, Dublin 1, D01 C9W8, Ireland.

HarperCollins books may be purchased for educational, business, or sales promotional use. For information, please email the Special Markets Department at SPsales@harpercollins.com.

hc.com

FIRST EDITION

Designed by Michele Cameron

Emojis © Shutterstock_037363962 & 2404572227

Library of Congress Cataloging-in-Publication Data

Names: Elias, Asha, author.
Title: The Namaste Club : a novel / Asha Elias.
Description: First edition. | New York, NY : William Morrow, 2025. |
Identifiers: LCCN 2024029919 | ISBN 9780063425217 (hardcover) | ISBN 9780063425224 (ebook)
Subjects: LCGFT: Thrillers (Fiction) | Novels.
Classification: LCC PS3605.L387 N36 2025 | DDC 813/.6—dc23/eng/20240705
LC record available at https://lccn.loc.gov/2024029919

ISBN 978-0-06-342521-7

25 26 27 28 29 LBC 5 4 3 2 1

For my Laotong, Amy,
because this is her favorite one

Breaking News: Florida Man Partially Eaten by Alligator at Luxury Yoga Retreat

A Florida man was discovered dead this morning at the Namaste Club yoga retreat located just outside of Melbourne, Florida. A resort caretaker notified police early this morning after stumbling upon the body during her morning grounds check. Sources say that the man had several bite marks on his body and was missing an arm, though it was unclear whether the 12-foot reptile believed to be responsible for the injuries attacked him before or after he had died.

According to the Florida Fish and Wildlife Conservation Commission, humans are not typical prey for American alligators and attacks are rare, typically occurring only when the reptile is provoked or mistakes a human for another animal. The alligator in question, who was estimated to weigh between 700 and 800 pounds, has been captured and killed by a nuisance gator trapper. Police have not released the name of the deceased and have said that the case is still under investigation.

The Namaste Club is a private luxury retreat venue that is popular with yoga instructors and students from around the country. According to property manager Martina Shoenfeld, the group renting the space was visiting from Miami, Florida. No other victims have been reported. This is a developing story.

THE YOGA TEACHER

NOW

I'll tell you everything you'd like to know, just please allow me a minute to find my center. No, it's okay. I'm fine, really. Was the incident shocking? Yes. Or, rather, our perception of it was. It is our social programming that tells us how to react.

I never expected something like this to happen during Transcendence Week, but . . . What are expectations in the first place? They are invitations to become disappointed. We cannot control the fluctuations of our environment. We can control only our *reactions* to them.

My studies have taught me that death is only a stop along the way in our cycle of reincarnation. It's a connecting flight from one life to the next. We exit and we enter again. It is a transformation that will come for all of us, and we must learn to be unafraid. Fear of death is an avoidable kind of suffering. I'm sure that Daniel has already re-emerged, like a butterfly, into his next physical form. We should not mourn for him.

Yes, my *legal* name is Alyssa Patterson. But please, call me Shakti.

JESSICA

"Ekam, inhale, arms rise up over our heads," Shakti droned on, half-speaking, half-singing the words. "Exhale, forward fold, swan dive your hands to the floor."

"Psst," I whispered to Indira. "Is she speaking in an Indian accent?" She shushed me without even glancing in my direction, but I was undeterred. "Maybe she did her *studies* in India. Do we know who this guru is that she's always referencing?" I thought that perhaps Indira, as a person of Indian descent, would care to comment, but she just smiled, still without looking over, and shook her head.

Shakti was on a roll with sun salutations that day, which made me feel like I was in some kind of mommy boot camp. I specifically avoided those types of classes. Chaturanga, upward dog, downward dog, jump forward, repeat. Within the first ten minutes of class, I had sweated through my Save Ferris! T-shirt and my face felt rubbery, like I'd fallen asleep in a steam room. It had rained that day, and the yoga studio always kept its A/C off for classes, so the humidity was basically at 3,000 percent.

After our tenth sun salute, I rested back on my heels in child's pose ("it's always an option!" as Shakti says). The mirror was completely fogged up, so I wrote "SOS" on it with my finger. Why was I in the front row? The front row was for show-offs who could flow like ballerinas and balance in yearlong handstands. I cursed Indira for saving me a mat spot before I'd arrived.

Shakti was playing one of her signature playlists, a mix of westernized Hindu mantra, Taylor Swift, and Drake. As "God's Plan" blared from the studio's portable speakers, I looked left and then right. No one was paying attention. I sighed and peeled off my disgusting T-shirt. Underneath, I was wearing a brown and unattractive sports bra that regrettably did not match my black leggings.

Before I could see if anyone had noticed, I popped back up into downward dog, determined to *listen to my breath* and *let go of all external distractions.*

"Psst," Indira whispered to me from her own down dog position, head cocked underneath her armpit. "Nice abs."

I looked down toward my navel before I could admonish her for making fun of me and, lo and behold, there it was. A slight but noticeable line on one side of my abdomen. *No fucking way,* I thought. I mean, there were also some stretch marks and a touch more skin than was necessary. But, come on. Muscle definition? Phase one of my post-divorce *glow up,* as Indira called it, had finally been achieved. This yoga shit was working.

Drake faded out on the speakers and when Krishna Das's "Om Namaya Shivaya" took over, Shakti blessedly moved from sun salutations to standing poses. I lunged forward into warrior I, reaching my hands *for the sky,* as instructed, then opened up into warrior II, reaching my fingers *north and south toward either side of the room.* I was pretty sure that the room was oriented west to east, but close enough.

"Straighten that front leg and stretch the leading arm forward, forward, forward, and then down to your shin, ankle, or—for a more advanced option—take hold of your big toe. Spin your chest toward the sky and straighten your opposite arm all the way to the cosmos. Trikonasana. Triangle pose. And breathe." Shakti was walking between the students, periodically glancing down at our poses like a professor making sure we weren't cheating on our exams.

"As you may know," she said, in her singsongy faux Indian accent, "our fellow practitioner Daniel is apprenticing with me, so he will be making some adjustments during class."

My stomach did a little flip. Adjustments are what they call the yoga instructors' invading your personal space to force your sweaty body into poses it can't naturally do. Then they take the sweat from your body and press it onto the person's body that receives the next adjustment. And then the sweat sharing repeats until, by the end of the hour, everyone is damp and stinks like a disgusting punch of perfume, and natural oils, and body smells. I've always wondered what Shakti must feel like at the end of class, when she's covered in all of our DNA and filth. And then she teaches another class right after?

It's not that I have a crush on Daniel. He's like ten years younger than me and I'm pretty sure he's some kind of finance douche or tech bro (based on the way a cell phone is always attached to his ear when he walks into class). But I've definitely *noticed* him. There were other men in Shakti's power yoga classes, but Daniel was the peacock. The others stayed in the back and kept their clothes on, grunting as they did embarrassingly inflexible versions of splits and heart openers. Most of them were balding and had potbellies and were probably just trying to get a little fitness back into their lives, like I was.

But Daniel, with his man bun and chest tattoos, was youthful and limber, and his shirt came off basically the moment he stepped onto his mat. By real fitness standards, like CrossFit or Barry's Bootcamp, places I wouldn't dare show my face, he was probably fairly average. But in yoga, he was kind of a demigod. Lean, able to do full splits and to hold handstands like a Cirque du Soleil performer. It was hard not to stare.

"Now bend into your front leg, bring your elbow to your thigh or, if you can go deeper, your hand to the floor. Opposite arm stretches over your ear. Extended side angle," Shakti called out from somewhere in the back of the room.

Daniel was walking among the students with his hands clasped behind his back, like he was about to select one of us to play Duck,

Duck, Goose. I tried to *stack my hips* and *open my heart* into my *full expression* of the pose, but my legs were shaking and my pelvis felt like it was going to split open. A few more breaths, and I'd have collapsed into another embarrassing child's pose.

That's when I felt him come up behind me. He dropped to his knees, peeled my hips open, and pulled my buttocks back to rest against his bare abdomen. With his other hand, he leaned my shoulder toward him, bracing my body against his for balance. "Now, breathe," Daniel said, pronouncing the words so slowly that his chest vibrated against my back.

I obliged as best as I could, bizarrely eager for his approval, willing my muscles not to give up and collapse into him.

"Gooooooood," he said, then gently let go of me and stepped away.

My hands fell to the floor, and I quickly sat on my heels and took child's pose, trying to play off the fact that I'd basically fallen down the second he stepped away. I looked up to see if Daniel had noticed, but he was already adjusting someone else. A gorgeous twentysomething in a matching fuchsia sports bra and yoga pant set. He probably enjoys adjusting her better, I thought. Then, What the fuck? Why am I thinking this?

Indira caught my attention and raised her eyebrows. *I know, right?* I mouthed back to her. I snuck a glance over as Daniel moved on to Barbara, the woo-woo seasoned yogi in the back. She's one of those women who could be thirty-eight or fifty-five, or any age in between, and glows from the inside out with enlightenment, or apple cider vinegar, or whatever. Pretty in an age-appropriate, all-natural way (which is refreshing, living in Miami). A real enigma, that one. She looks like a hippie through and through but also is rumored to be the daughter of a billionaire oil baron.

Daniel didn't give me any more adjustments for the rest of the class and I tried not to let the realization faze me. I am a grown-ass woman, after all, not some flitty, horny teenager. The class wound down with us lying on our backs for final relaxation.

"Release your breath. Release all the tension in your body," Shakti whispered. "Allow yourself to melt into the earth, as you meditate on the sacred mantra. Daniel will be guiding us the rest of the way through today's journey."

My body involuntarily clenched at the sound of his name. Then Daniel's deep baritone filled the room like a palm on a hand drum. Round, and full, and soulful. My breath caught in my throat. More than just a pretty face, apparently, the dude had the voice of a minor god. He sang what I knew, based on previous yoga experience, was called the "Gayatri Mantra."

In fact, it was Indira who had named it for me, about a year ago when she dragged me to my very first class. I had been awkward and felt out of place, but Indira flowed naturally and seemed to know the name of every Sanskrit pose and song. It was maybe the most connected I'd ever seen her to her Indianness, something she seemed to have put behind her in many ways. Maybe that's one of the reasons I kept taking classes in the beginning. I loved seeing her like that.

Daniel's mantra lulled me almost to sleep, and I didn't come back to my senses until the mandatory closing "om" stunned me out of my stupor. When I finally sat up and opened my eyes, everyone was already bowing in gratitude to Shakti. I grabbed my mat and half-jogged to the parking lot, where I waited for Indira.

A few moments later, she sauntered over with an otherworldly post-yoga glow and a cheesy, shit-eating grin.

"Don't even," I said.

Indira laughed and squeezed her yoga mat into her chest. "I didn't know that Shakti's classes were going to start coming with happy endings," she said.

"Oh, real professional," I said, even though she knew I loved this kind of banter. "It was an *adjustment.*"

"Really? Because it looked a lot like dry humping to me," she said.

I laughed because, honestly, it's true that yoga adjustments are so ridiculously sexual. They happened in almost all of Shakti's classes, and we had to pretend like it was totally normal and no big deal. While our teacher leaned into the touchy-feelyness, in a post-Bikram-sex-scandal world, most male instructors had become either very careful or avoided adjustments altogether. Shakti probably got away with it so easily because she's young and gorgeous and carries an untouchable air, but also because she's a woman. Is there an inherent power imbalance between male instructors and female students? Not to Daniel, apparently.

Indira looked around to make sure no one was looking and stepped closer to me. "I heard that he's going on the retreat," she said.

Not gonna lie, that gave me a flutter. But I tamped it down. "Great," I said, trying to sound neutral. I knew Indira's ulterior motive. She wanted to go on Shakti's upcoming retreat in the boonies, and she didn't want to go alone.

"We should sign up. Who knows, maybe you'll pop your postdivorce-fling cherry," Indira said. As though that was a reasonable statement and the natural next step in having been adjusted by Daniel once in a yoga class. I hadn't had sex with anyone since Tom, which my friend liked to remind me on a daily basis. But lately, I'd been starting to think that I was almost ready.

"For a million reasons, no," I said.

"Name one," she answered.

"He's too young for me. He's probably not into me. And, you know, don't shit where you eat. I'm actually starting to see results from all these classes, and I mean superficial results beyond the overall mental and physical health part, so I don't know what I'd do if the classes became awkward because of some misguided dalliance."

"I said name *one*." She smirked.

We air-kissed instead of saying goodbye and I spent the entire ten-minute drive home trying not to think about Daniel's warm body pressed against mine, so close that I could feel his heartbeat in my own chest, his warm breath on my neck. How long had it been since I'd felt the touch of a man? Too. Damn. Long.

Sky and TJ were sleeping at their dad's house, which I usually hated, but was thanking god for at the moment. I pulled into the driveway and raced upstairs, tore off my sweaty workout clothes, and slipped under the covers, still smothered in the yoga-adjustment-mix of other people's sweat. *But also Daniel's.*

My fingers found the top drawer of my nightstand, and they searched around a bit until feeling the lipstick-shaped portable electronic device whose batteries had to be changed almost once a week. (I'm too old-school for the USB plug-in kind.)

I closed my eyes and pressed the button on the bottom of the vibrator, then melted into the bed. I pictured Daniel behind me in my extended side angle, tugging on my yoga pants and feeling up my sports bra, then on top of me, peeling my clothes off and kissing my neck, then . . . it didn't take nearly long enough to finish. I stayed on the bed until I caught my breath, then tiptoed quietly to my bathroom, even though no one was home. I washed my vibrator with soap and water and then stepped into the shower, letting the steam fill my lungs and envelop me in its warm embrace. Then I contemplated if this would be a round-two kind of night.

CAROL ANN

I sipped my sugar-free vanilla iced latte and pointed to the stainless-steel refrigerator, trying not to think about the synthetic poisons I was consuming.

"It's brand-new construction with custom Italian floors and counter-tops, and top-of-the-line appliances." It was my third showing of the day with the New York couple and the guilty-pleasure coffee drink had been necessary.

When I was growing up, the New Yorkers sent all their cast-offs and grandmas to Palm Beach or Boca; they didn't settle in Vero. But now, here they are. Soaking up all our sun and hiking up our home prices. (Not that I'm complaining about the commissions.)

The wife beamed like I'd just told her the house was free. "There's so much space!" she said, taking in the kitchen's fifteen-foot vaulted ceiling.

I tried not to laugh. New Yorkers thought that every house was enormous. They'd chosen to live in shoeboxes for so long that they were now impressed by things like garages. It's the exact opposite of when I show houses to Southerners, who think fewer than five thousand square feet is embarrassingly small.

We were looking at a three-thousand-square-foot Mediterranean style home with water views (from the second floor; it was across the street from the ocean), and it is a solid investment if you ask me. Florida real estate is hot. Like August at 12:00 P.M. hot. And with the big urban areas like Miami, Fort Lauderdale, and Tampa getting too crowded, Vero is primed to be the next big town. In fact, it's already happening.

"How are the schools?" the wife asked. She had straight brown hair cut into a neat lob (that's a longer version of a bob) and spoke very quickly, like even her words were in a rush.

I knew that question was coming and was frankly surprised she hadn't asked it sooner. "Well, the public schools here are A rated and just keep getting better," I said. "My kids go to Vero Christian, which is also excellent, if you're looking for a faith-based education."

The couple nodded along and then the husband said, "Our children are three and five. We want them to grow up somewhere they can ride their bikes to their friends' houses and play outside, even in the winter." He had salt-and-pepper hair and was attractive in a George Clooney kind of way. "And I know this sounds ridiculous, seeing as they're so young, but we want to make sure that the high schools here are competitive enough for top-tier colleges."

The New York escapees *always* ask what universities our high school kids are getting into.

"Well, like I said, Florida schools are just getting better and better, and we have some of the best ones right here in Vero. There are so many opportunities for parent involvement, too. If that's something that interests you."

The couple looked at each other with something that might pass for skepticism, but I just bit my tongue. I suspected these were the condescending types who think you can find a good education only up north. Well, something had brought them down here to my doorstep.

"What made you all decide to move down to Vero?" I asked. The wife ran her fingers over the length of the marble kitchen island and brought them to her face for inspection. Not a speck of dust.

"Just looking for a change," she said, with a tight smile that didn't invite further questions. I made a mental note to close the sale and follow up with a bottle of nice champagne and *not* an invitation to dinner with my husband and me. Not every client is meant to become a friend.

Her husband was the better talker. He said, "We'd been thinking about relocating to Florida, somewhere close to the beach, but weren't sure which part. It's like you've got so many states in one here! And then she went to a yoga retreat close by and fell in love with this area. Vero seemed upscale and safe. It ticks a lot of our boxes."

He opened and closed the oven door, followed by the microwave. Both Viking; the developer didn't skimp. "The retreat was close to Melbourne Beach, just north of here. The Namaste Club. Have you heard of it?"

I accidentally groaned. Why do transients always think they can teach you something new about your own home state? "Can't say that I have," I said. "But it sounds lovely."

The wife put her hands into the prayer position, as though it was time to praise Jesus. "It is the most relaxing and grounding place. Very exclusive. You should really check it out. It's about an hour drive from here, but you feel like you're in another world completely."

I like yoga well enough, but what does *grounding* even mean? When I was growing up, it was when you got sent to bed without dinner. Also, I couldn't picture this lady meditating, or burning incense, or any of it. She seemed so high-strung. But who knows, maybe that's why she needed that sort of *retreat*. And hey, she was a client, so I wasn't about to press her about it. The client is always right (as long as I'm able to close them).

"That really sounds amazing," I said. "But I wouldn't last a day. I'd probably have a heart attack if I couldn't be on my phone, and the vegan diet is just not for me."

The husband laughed. "Oh, you'd have to pry the phone out of my wife's cold dead hands."

The wife shook her head. "No, no. It's not some New Age sleep-away camp. It's about mindfulness and being present. But phones are allowed and there's a cook onsite that serves locally hunted wild boar and sustainably caught fish, with farm-harvested vegetables. The food was incredible." She closed her eyes as if trying to summon the flavor of the locally hunted boar.

"And there's a full bar. Food and drinks are all included." The husband winked at me, and I couldn't tell if he was flirting with me or making an assumption about my drinking habits. Either way, it rubbed me wrong.

"My husband and I hunt," I said with a smile, in case he hadn't noticed my ring finger. "The wild boar around here is exceptional. We host a big roast every year for July Fourth. You two should come by, if you're moved in by then." I kicked myself immediately after saying it, but with the way they both tepidly nodded back at me, I knew they'd never take me up on the offer.

"Anyway, let me show you the master suite upstairs. Just *wait* until you see the walk-in closet."

"You mean the primary suite?" the wife asked, because of course she did. Come on, lady. It wasn't like I was showing her some kind of plantation house.

It took every ounce of my patience not to roll my eyes. "Yep," I answered.

I followed the couple upstairs and couldn't help but think that fancy Mrs. New Yorker could probably use a few extra retreats, if you know what I mean. I walk three miles a day and take yoga classes here and there, mixed with weight training at the gym and clean eating on the daily, because I will not let my man pick up a wandering eye. My husband loves to tell his friends how I can still fit into my high school cheer uniform—though it's a little tighter around the bust now—and it's kind of sweet how proud he is of that. (He loves it even more when I actually wear it for him.)

I wondered if this client was still pleasing *her* husband. The way she was strutting around, leading the way like it was her wearing the pants, I thought probably not. Then again, maybe she wasn't even attracted to *him* anymore. What kind of man would allow his woman to take charge of him like that in the first place? Not an alpha.

But it's not my place to judge. I was just there for the sale.

This job used to be such a hustle, but these days you barely even have to try. Florida keeps growing, and there are a variety of reasons; it's not just because we have no state income tax. The weather here is beautiful year-round, it's a fantastic place to raise kids, and we understand business; we don't hate successful people over here like some of those other big states. To all the newcomers I say, "Come on down! I'll sell you the home of your dreams and show you the ropes here in the American Riviera."

Let's just hope all these new residents aren't bringing too much of their woke hipster bull crap to *my* Sunshine State.

SHAKTI

NOW

Transcendence Week is about connecting to our highest consciousness, about being present and mindful in our spiritual journeys, but in a modern way. We don't ask attendees to *cleanse* or be *pure*, even though I personally choose to live my life that way. We don't want to place restrictions on people that will hinder long-term growth.

Imagine, you go on a four-week diet and eliminate carbs, fat, alcohol, and animal protein. You feel better and you lose weight, but then what happens at the end of the twenty-eight days? You begin to erase all the progress you've made. Elimination is not sustainable. If we are going to improve lives, we must create *habits*, not hindrances. When we start small to create meaningful changes, we trickle positive energy into the community. And this positive energy will multiply over and over again until, eventually, we succeed in changing the world.

That is one of the philosophies behind the retreat.

My guru teaches that yoga should be accessible to anyone who desires to go deeper, whether through lifelong commitment or passing curiosity. So no, I do not *vet* our attendees. Signing up for Transcendence Week might be the first step in someone's spiritual journey, and it is our place to nurture, not judge, the students in this process. That means accepting people who might come from complicated backgrounds or possess competing worldviews. I consider it my personal service to provide a safe space for all students. All who are willing are welcome.

It's true that most participants in this group were a little more . . . unaccustomed to the retreat experience. But sometimes that can be a good thing. It's easier to paint on a blank canvas.

There were five students on the trip.

Daniel Rhine had been coming to my class at Om All-Stars for about a year. He frequented my vinyasa flow class, which is known as a strong practice, with lots of chataurangas (which are basically yoga push-ups) and arm balances. I think the rigorousness appealed to him. The young professionals rarely have time to separate fitness from mindfulness, so the combination of the two is popular.

He had a dedicated physical practice but also embraced the spiritual side. You can always tell when someone is holding space for my dharma talks, when I teach my deeper lesson for each class, and also when they aren't. Many of the students are primarily focused on the physical practice, and that's okay. No judgment. Eventually, the body opens itself to the mind.

But Daniel did enjoy it. He would sometimes spend the full relaxation time in full lotus, listening. *Really* listening. He'd recently taken things a step further and started apprenticing for me in class because he was interested in taking my teacher training this winter. That's why I suggested he join the retreat. He was ready to go deeper. Everyone was there for a different reason, but for Daniel, the retreat was meant to open him up to becoming a more spiritual and connected being. I can only hope that he brings that karma into the next life.

Then there was Barbara, beautiful Barbara Babbington. One of my oldest students, both in years and in spirit. A pure soul who cleans the studio in Miami after every evening as her seva, or service, back to the teachings. She also pays for the annual membership because she insists that her sacrifices bring her no financial gain. I would consider her the American version of a Brahmin, especially with her family's background. The retreat presented another opportunity for her to stay connected to her bhakti, her devotion to her practice.

Indira Rao was also there. She's one of my weekend warriors, but despite that lack of commitment, she has a strong asana practice, meaning she is proficient with the yoga poses, and also has a deep understanding of mantra from her cultural background. So she was perhaps a little further on in her learning than some of the others. But like I said, sometimes *experience* can be a bad thing. It makes students less *open*.

I think Indira wanted the retreat to be more of a party week, so she brought along her friend Jessica Herz-Anderson, who is newer to the practice. Jessica enjoys classes but is still blocked in some areas of meditation, manifestation, and dharma. I think it has something to do with unresolved traumas in her past life. I don't know much about her, other than she is middle-aged and divorced and seems to be suffering from some mild to moderate depression. I'd never try to be my students' therapist, but I was willing to coach Jessica along in her healing journey. I don't think she was open to it, though. Only when the student is ready may the teacher appear.

Lastly, there was Carol Ann DeFleur, who was the only attendee who didn't learn about Transcendence Week through my studio in Miami. She'd heard about the Namaste Club venue through word of mouth and selected my experience purely at random. I don't believe in luck or coincidence, so call it what you will, but she seemed predestined to join us.

Carol Ann was the newest to yoga and perhaps initially the most hesitant. However, she allowed herself to release expectations and surrender to the practice in a beautiful and organic way. She might even be on her way to becoming the most passionate follower of all of us. This is a woman who very recently suffered some kind of a public breakdown and faced significant challenges at home. She had the furthest to come, within herself, for healing. Even with the tragedy that occurred, I think we are sending her home a changed woman.

JESSICA

Indira batted her long lashes at me (which reminded me to buy one of those lash-growth serums) and what could I say? The puppy-dog face never works on me from the kids, I'm proud to say, but a grown woman with—I swear—magical cat eyes, apparently I couldn't resist. It didn't help that she was also my best friend/boss.

"Come on, Jess. You need this. It'll be fun," she said. And something about the way she was sticking shipping labels onto the rush delivery orders made her seem wise, sage. Much more so, I imagined, than the twenty-six-year-old yoga teacher who was *curating* the retreat.

Still, I had to bust her balls a little bit.

"A yoga retreat in central Florida? Maybe I'll order a MAGA hat so I can fit in with the locals." I shuddered at the thought and shifted focus to the neat row of velvet jewelry boxes in front of me, waiting to be filled. I dangled a gold ring with a half-carat pink sapphire teardrop on my pinky finger, one of the most popular items from Indira's new collection. It was earmarked for a lucky lady in Santa Barbara, California.

"You should send a couple of pieces to that hot TikTok comedian that the girls are so obsessed with," I said. "She has something like three million followers. I could see her wearing this piece in the videos. It's her style."

Indira rolled her eyes. "Don't change the subject, woman. Melbourne is a laid-back surfer town, not a Confederate stronghold. Are we going or not?" She reached for the ring and gave it a quick polish before placing it in its box. "Besides, you know that Bougie Boho doesn't do influencer marketing."

I stuffed the next jewelry box with an Aries zodiac pendant and looked back at my friend. When you're a single mom, it's important to find at least one partner who you can do the traditional coupley things with, like holidays, vacations, and candlelit dinners. Indira was that person for me. Especially since we'd both renounced our religious backgrounds (mine Jewish, hers Hindu) to marry our misguidedly chosen husbands. The deadbeats were long gone, along with our disappointed families, but we still had each other. Though like with every couple, Indira and I certainly had our arguments.

Maybe I should just try the retreat, I thought, for Indira's sake. The thing is, I don't even *like* yoga. I only go because Barry's Bootcamp makes me want to puke and Pilates is painfully boring. Also, it keeps my mom pooch looking closer to *sad sack of skin* than *is she pregnant again*? Especially now that I have one ab! At my age and being divorced with some hope of having sex again, I think yoga is the best I can do. I'm not exactly a work-out person. Or a spiritual person. Or a green juice and mediation person. In other words, never had I ever pictured myself attending a yoga retreat.

Indira knew all this, but she also knew that I was trying to *put myself out there* and going through a *yes* phase, so . . . I said yes. Or, more accurately, I said, "Sure, I'll ask my boss for the time off. But only if you rethink the influencer marketing hardline. Let me send *one* piece to Allison Kent."

She snorted at me. Actually snorted. But then she smiled. "Okay, Ms. *Fancy Marketing Degree I Haven't Used in More Than a Decade*."

"Until recently," I corrected.

"Until recently," she conceded. "When you reentered the workforce thanks to an unbelievable opportunity."

We both looked around at the detritus of boxes, jewelry, and shipping labels piled into what used to be Indira's fancy dining room and laughed.

"You can send one ring to one influencer this one time. But it must be from the Burgeoning Bougie collection. Not the Luxe." She wagged the box with the pink sapphire ring at me. "And yay. I'm very excited for our relaxing girls' getaway."

Indira is a brilliant designer. Her Indian-glamour-meets-laid-back-LA-cool-girl style has been "can't keep pieces in stock" successful (the company is only two years old), which is how she was able to take me on as director of marketing/e-commerce/order fulfillment at a time when everything else in my life was crashing down. And truly, I'm grateful.

For her, the brand is an opportunity to make a name for herself separately from her successful ex-husband. And she gives back, too. A portion of all profits are earmarked for wildlife preservation in the Everglades. For me, working for her is my second act. My platform to stand on my own two feet after my own horrible divorce. Who else was going to hire me on the spot with a ten-year employment gap? Only a ride-or-die girlfriend.

By the way, I know the LA-cool-girl thing sounds weird, but honestly, no one knows we are from Miami. Our customer base is nationwide. And "Miami cool girl" doesn't have the same cachet. It just doesn't. That's called marketing. That's what Indira pays me a livable wage for.

I scanned the display case that sat above Indira's china cabinet. The Burgeoning Bougie collection was still fine jewelry, all real gold and stones, but made up of smaller and more delicate items than the Luxe pieces. No emerald chandelier earrings or other statement pieces, for example. I selected one of my favorites, the Tara, retail $280, named after Indira's daughter. A rose-gold middle-finger ring with a wispy om symbol in the center. It was simple and elegant, yet unique enough to comment on. And it seemed apropos of my little bargain with the boss.

"Wouldn't it be perfect if the Tara kicked off our new marketing strategy? And brings us a celebrity cult following so we can move out of your dining room and into our own showroom space?" I tried batting my lashes, but Indira just looked at me with some mix of repulsion and pity. I can't pull off the cutesy thing. Noted.

She handed me one of her signature green velvet jewelry boxes and smiled. "We already have a celebrity cult following," she said.

"Kate Hudson wearing the Lucy was lucky. But hardly constitutes an entire cult," I pointed out.

Indira looked around her dining room, which had once been featured in *Miami Interiors* as a "modern art deco masterpiece." Now, display cases lined the cabinets and bar, and the rose quartz dining table (custom cut to seat eighteen) was a de facto shipping operation.

"It *would* be nice to start hosting dinner parties again," she said. "Let's discuss it more at Transcendence Week."

CAROL ANN

They're buying the house. All cash. Thirty day close. We went under contract today and, honestly, they got a solid deal. Two million dollars gets you a gorgeous two-story house with five bedrooms and a huge patio in Vero, versus a shoebox with rats in New York City. It's a no-brainer. Inspections will be a snap because it's new construction. Simple as one, two, three.

"And that is how it's *done*," I told Beau, that night at family dinner, after the seller accepted my buyer's offer.

He pounded his fist on the table. "Kids, say 'Hooray for Mommy!'"

"Hooray for Mommy!" Katie and Kameron said in unison. People always mistake them for twins, but Katie is an older fourth grader and Kameron is a younger third grader.

"Please don't chew with your mouths open," I said. That sort of thing really drives me nuts. I'd rushed home from the office to make lasagna and salad and seeing the combination mid-chew, open-mouthed, was extremely unappealing.

Beau was still in his button-up shirt, but the tie hung loose around his neck. "CA, you know I'm doing paleo. What's with the pasta? We talked about this. No grains, no dairy. You made dinner that has both." He ran a hand back and forth over his head. His usually close-cropped hair needed a refresh, but he still looked devastatingly handsome.

My stomach clenched. I'd been so distracted with the sale that I'd totally forgotten. Last month, he'd been bulking, but now Beau was moving on to a new nutrition strategy. "I'm so sorry, darling," I said. "I saw a recipe online where you don't even need to preboil the noodles and was dying to try it. My bad. But the salad is all backyard to table from our veggie garden. I'll grill you up some chicken to go with it. Wipe your mouth, Kam." My son looked like he was trying to face paint with tomato sauce rather than actually get any into his mouth. "Beau, with the commission from this sale, I thought we could finally get started on the new addition to the house!"

Beau and I have been together since college and still live in our starter home. Why would we move? We bought it so cheap that it's basically free now, and it is *not* a buyer's market these days (but don't tell my clients I said that). We have a full acre just outside of town, so the land is fantastic, and we already put a pool in a few years back. Now we want to renovate the main house, which is currently only one story with three bedrooms, and add three thousand square feet, including a second floor and a mother-in-law suite. We've had the plans drawn up for a whole year but wanted to wait until the cash flow situation was right.

"No money talk at the table," my husband said, without looking up from his salad.

I ran my finger across my lips to show that I was *zipping up*.

"Who makes more money? Mommy or Daddy?" Kameron asked.

I reached across the table and pinched his arm, but not too hard. "Young man, you know better than to ask adults questions like that. You need to apologize."

He hung his head. "Sorry ma'am," he said.

"And?" I pressed.

"And sir," he answered.

I looked up at Beau, but he was slowly chewing his salad and not looking at any of us. That was fine because the majority of discipline is my job. That's how we divide it. I take the small stuff. Etiquette, table manners, those things fall under my role. Bigger things like fighting and name-calling are Beau's area. It's called collaborative parenting.

I finished my salad and wiped my mouth clean with a napkin. "Well, I'm relieved that I don't need to show that New York couple any more houses," I said. "I haven't devoted any time to the Mama Bears recently. The ladies probably think I've lost the passion!"

The Mama Bears is an advocacy group that I founded a few years ago and our mission is to protect children at all costs. With all the shocking things happening in our country right now, we decided to take a real stand and fight back. There are predators lurking all around, everywhere, ready to exploit and take advantage of our precious babies. Pedophiles! The thought of it lights a fire inside me that is so strong, it could burn down the state of Florida.

I saw what was going on and refused to just sit back and complain; I got *busy*. That's how the Mama Bears came about. Because when you attack our cubs, you better be prepared to *run*. We lobby school boards and city council meetings, oversee an informational marketing cam-paign, and host events to educate the community about the issues. It's a lot of work, but really, what could be more important than protecting our own community's innocent youth?

"Carol Ann," Beau said, finally looking up from his plate. "No one would ever *dare* to think you've lost your passion."

JESSICA

My ex-husband is a moron. He thought shared custody was going to be a breeze, assumed that quitting my job and becoming a stay-at-home mom for ten years to watch the kids had been an extended vacation. But now that we're divorced, on Tuesdays and Thursdays, it's Tom's responsibility to pick up the kids from school and drive them to and from their activities. Two days a week. Pick up, drop off, pick up again, dinner, and then back to my house for bed. Simple enough, right? Apparently not. Because this Tuesday, Sky called me crying from the courts at 6:30 P.M. because tennis ends at 6:00 P.M.

I called Tom on my way to rescue her from the Miami Shores Tennis Center, with an uncured coat of chrome gel on my nails, and do you know what he told me? He said our kids don't have grit and reminded me that, when we were kids, we didn't own cell phones and our parents were always late, if they showed up at all. I told him he was gaslighting. He called me a whiny geriatric millennial, and I said he wasn't cool enough to be a real Gen Xer.

"How am I supposed to go away for an entire week?" I asked. Maybe part of me was looking for an out, because the whole retreat idea was starting to give me massive anxiety. Which was pretty contrary to the point of the whole thing. And I wasn't just worried about the kids potentially showing up late to school, in soiled rags, and then brought home, unfed, by someone with the Department of Children and Families. I also didn't know how the hell I'd stay sane listening to Shakti's soft yet condescending voice for seven days straight.

Tom got all savior-y on me. "Listen, I made a mistake." To which I wanted to say, *Oh, no shit, Tom. Just the one, though?* I held my tongue. Then he said, "I'm their dad. We'll be fine and, Jess, you really need this. To be honest, when you told me about this yoga retreat, I was surprised in a good way, excited for you."

Great. Another person in my life saying that I *needed this.* As if he had any clue what I needed. Because I can tell you, not once when we were married had I ever woken up and said, *I'm craving a challenge. Maybe my husband can fuck a bunch of young, hot women so I can work a little harder for his attention.*

Even though it was over the phone, I could almost feel him looking me up and down and feeling a little sorry for me. And hey, it's not like he's in his mid-twenties prime like when we first met, either. But I guess since he can still pull glossy little Kardashian clones (probably even more so than when we started dating), apparently, I'm the sad one. Please. I didn't need his pity. I've been doing fine. Fine-ish. Three Tinder dates. Only one of them a catfish. Only two with unsolicited dick pics. It's a strange new world out there but honestly, I've heard worse stats, and everyone needs to start somewhere.

"Tell me you at least have TJ with you," I said, a little out of breath. How had the thought not occurred to me sooner? Tom was also responsible for picking up our son, whose Tuesday soccer class finished at 5:45 P.M. It was a mad dash every week from Edgewater to Miami Shores in the rush to collect both kids. In other words, pretty difficult to forget one child if you had the other.

"Tommy Jr. and I are at Ciao Pizza," he said, casually, as if we were talking about whether he left his car keys in the kitchen or the foyer. I clenched my teeth. Tom knew I hated when he said *Tommy Jr.* I was against a legacy name from the start. It was considered bad luck the way I was raised and also, why not let your kid be an original? But Tom was the younger brother of a Charles the fourth, and I think he always had a *thing* about that. That's why our son was *TJ*, for Tommy Jr.

"Did you forget you had a daughter?" I asked in the same way I'd discipline a dog if I had one. My therapist says I need to work on being less passive-aggressive and snarky with Tom, for the sake of healthy co-parenting, but really, what does she know?

He sighed and said, "I thought she finished at seven thirty." But his tone told me, *Obviously I have a favorite child. It's too hard to keep track of both.*

"I'm getting Sky," I said. "She can have dinner with me. Drop TJ before eight, please." I hung up before he could halfheartedly apologize. Our daughter was waiting with her coach (who I am sure was not thrilled about sixty unpaid minutes of childcare), and I was still fifteen minutes away.

I white-knuckled the steering wheel of my oversize mom SUV, trying to make up precious seconds during my crawl through traffic, when a gold Lamborghini (definitely a rental—all Lamborghinis in Miami are rentals) pulled right in front of me (no signal) at a stale yellow light. I slammed on my brakes just in time and leaned full force into my horn as the light turned red. The sports car douchebag sped through the intersection with his middle finger out the window.

"Mother fucking piece of shit!" I shouted to no one, slapping my hands on the wheel, which really did nothing for anyone except sting my palms very badly. I bit my lip to keep from crying. God, maybe I did need a yoga retreat for more than just appeasing a friend. Maybe Indira had been suggesting it more as an intervention for me than a girls' trip for her. I guess I had been running on short fumes recently but really . . . how unstable was I?

Come back to your breath. Our yoga instructor's words floated into my head. *When the pose becomes too intense, as with life, we can always come back to our breath.*

Shakti was barely out of college and was probably gifted a Lexus on her sixteenth birthday, but it was good advice. I took a long, slow inhale through my nose, dragging the air down the back of my throat, then released a deep exhale through my mouth. I closed my eyes. *Peace.* Then a horn beeped from behind me. I opened my eyes. The light was green.

Okay, so not *every* moment presented a good time to meditate. Noted. I made it to Miami Shores Tennis Center at 7:05 P.M., which in early October in Miami was just post-sunset and still balmy. Sky stood with her shoulders slumped next to Coach Rivera, dangling her racket loosely in her fingers. Her dark brown hair was pulled into a sticky ponytail that shined in the pale moonlight, and in that moment, like all moments, I stopped to admire how grown up and beautiful she was.

"How's the saddest girl in the whole world?" I asked, jogging up from the parking lot.

At thirteen years old, my daughter's default expression was something between morose and disgusted. TJ and I called it her *resting sad face*, and she took the joke lightly. Generally speaking, her sour moods had more to do with hormones and hating her dad than being disappointed with me. I was a lucky teen daughter mom in that way.

"Fuck Dad," Sky said, her green eyes a blaze of radioactive fire.

I pulled her into my arms. She smelled like the inside of an old sneaker, but she let me hold her, even though we were in public. "Let's make La Scala salads and take a shower," I said.

La Scala salads were something we had ordered in Los Angeles once and then re-created at home at least once a week. They're made with salami and provolone, and parmesan cheese is added to the dressing, making it hard to consider the dish *healthy*. But they're also made with lettuce, so it's still technically a salad.

Sky wiped her mascara-stained eyes on my Covid-era tie-dyed sweater and nodded. How could I leave her all alone for an entire week? She needed me. I was her person. And clearly the most responsible adult in her life. When she pulled away, a drip of boob sweat slid down my body. This was the risk of wearing sweaters in Miami during the fall. It was 50 degrees indoors at any business establishment and 90 degrees and humid the second you stepped outside. Sky and I both needed showers. Stat.

Back home, we rinsed off and I tried but failed to remove the splotchy uncured chrome gel from my nails. Sky called my botched mani ratchet, and I laughed because my aesthetic mishap had put her in a temporarily better mood. It reminded me of when she was a toddler and I'd pretend to fall on the floor or put whipped cream on my nose to make her giggle. I've always been happy to play the clown for her, especially if a smile came as a reward.

I started slicing salami into ribbons and handed Sky the block of provolone to cube. "This isn't very kosher," she said, hacking the cheese into irregularly shaped pieces.

"Don't tell Zadie." I slid the salami to the side of the cutting board and started chopping the romaine. My dad was a modern Orthodox rabbi and therefore not the happiest when I married a gentile and started celebrating Christmas (I still celebrate the Jewish holidays, too). He didn't disown me, but things have been strained ever since I said "I do." That's one of the things that bonded Indira and me when we first met through our daughters' kindergarten class.

She also had a "forbidden" marriage and an unfortunate falling out with her parents. We sniffed each other out, across the tables of coloring pages and nubby crayons. A lonely soul can often recognize a kindred spirit. And this was before either of us were on the path to divorce.

People always ask me if I *escaped* from my orthodox upbringing, as if I spent my childhood trapped in some kind of fundamentalist cult. But it really wasn't like that. Yes, we kept kosher, and my mom wears a headscarf or wig. No, my parents don't have sex between a hole in the sheet (as far as I know), and the men in my community weren't all wife-beating misogynists. I'm sure there are wife-beating misogynists somewhere in my parents' shul, but honestly, show me a community that doesn't have them, and I'll move there tomorrow.

I didn't leave because I was oppressed; I left because it just wasn't *me*. And because I fell in love, but I think I would have left anyway. The other thing everyone asks me is, will I go back to shul life now that I'm divorced? Also, no. I've tasted the glory that is bacon, and I cannot go back. (Sorry, Hashem.) My parents keep in touch with me for the sake of their grandkids, but let's just say that I've sufficiently disappointed them as a daughter.

Sky mixed the dressing all on her own: red wine vinegar, good olive oil, Dijon, garlic, and freshly grated parmesan. We ate while standing over the kitchen island, a little rebellion to Tom's obsession with the immaculate countertops (to show that we were still mad at him for forgetting tennis pickup, even if he didn't live there anymore). Every time a spray of dressing leapt from my fork onto the pristine white and gray Calacatta marble, searing the porous surface with corrosive acid, a petty smile crept onto my lips. We would never have been *allowed* to share a meal on the countertop (with dressing! that had vinegar! which ruins marble!) when my ex still lived here.

The kitchen, with its lacquered white cabinets and unnecessarily expensive finishes, was like a shrine to Tom. A trophy for all his hard work and success as an insurance broker. A testament to his good taste and natural abilities at design. And *not* a place to do too much actual cooking or, god forbid, eating.

People tell me that I was lucky to "get" the house, which I absolutely hate, even though it's true. I'd never be able to afford living in Miami Beach with the current real-estate conditions, even with alimony, but it's hard to feel lucky when I've spent the last decade decorating and cleaning the place, making it a *home*. When Tom moved out, the first thing I did was go to the kitchen to pour a cold glass of water. Then I sliced a lemon on the bare countertop to squeeze on top.

I rubbed the little burn the lemon juice had made, enjoying the memory. "I'm gifting a Bougie Boho piece to Allison Kent," I announced, surprised that I'd waited that long to share the little nugget. One that could potentially earn me some clout with my daughter and her teenage friends. They all love TikTok, and they all love Allison Kent.

My daughter's eyes widened as she swallowed a mouthful of salad. "No way! Do we get to meet her?"

Her excitement was so pure, I was momentarily tempted to say "Of course!" even though I had absolutely no idea if it was true. I hadn't even contacted Allison's *people* yet.

"We'll see," I said, instead. "You know how Indira is about influencer marketing. But I convinced her to give it a shot, just this one time."

Sky has been best friends with Indira's daughter, Tara, since the first day of kindergarten. Back then, their idea of a perfect day was dressing up as *Frozen*'s Anna and Elsa and belting out "Let It Go." These days, they're all about duets on TikTok and ASMR. Times change.

Our salad plates were still sitting on the kitchen island when Tom let himself into the house, a pizza-stained TJ in his wake. "Straight to the shower, bud," he said, as though he still had any authority here. I considered correcting him but instead bit into a chocolate-covered strawberry that Sky had taken out of the fridge and threw the stem into the sink.

Tom looked awful; his once-famously-moppy brown curls were graying and thinning in the front and a paunch where his collegiate six-pack had been settled over his belt. He was fortunate that his above average height and decent posture distributed the middle-aged softness.

Not all of us were so lucky. When he smiled, like he was trying to do for Sky, a mix of hopefulness and apology, a tributary of crow's-feet outlined his eyes. Why was he still so attractive to me, despite everything?

"Sky-bear," he said, approaching our daughter with his hands out, as though showing he wasn't armed, or like he was about to surrender. "I am so sorry about today. There's no excuse."

Spoken like a true dead-beat dad. The thing was, though, Tom isn't a terrible father (as hard as that is to admit). He's an idiot and a cheating bastard, but he loves his kids and tries to be present. He's not always good at it, but he does *want* to be a good dad.

Sky rolled her eyes and tossed her chocolate-covered strawberry stem in the sink. She looked at me and said, "I'll be in my room," before stomping past her dad and disappearing up the stairs.

Tom just stood there, looking like a chastened child. I mean, what did he expect?

INDIRA

Karma. Eating shit. Comeuppance. Paying the Piper.

I don't know exactly what to name it, but calling your estranged mother to *babysit* your adored thirteen-year-old daughter who barely speaks to you is at least some combination of those things. The phone call went a bit like this.

"Indira? Daughter? Has someone died? Why else would you honor me with this call?"

I'm the prodigal daughter. I deserve this. And in that moment, I was also desperate. Tara's father would be out of town for a work trip while I'd be away on the yoga retreat and she's still too young to stay alone. There isn't a babysitter in town that I'd trust to watch her for a full week, and since Jessica's also going on the retreat, I had no choice but to make the dreaded phone call to Los Angeles.

"No, Mata," I said. "No one has died." Only my dignity. "But I am traveling for a week and thought you might want to spend time with Tara while I'm away." It wasn't a stretch of the imagination. Savera Rao much preferred her firstborn grandchild to her only daughter, even though she and Tara had met only a handful of times.

"You think I'm your nanny?" she asked, her voice about as sweet as a serrano pepper. "I should watch your child while you take a vacation? If this is the lifestyle you want, perhaps you should've thought about this before getting divorced."

The irony being, of course, that she'd hated my choice of husband.

"It's a work trip," I lied, because the woman's judgment somehow still gets to me. Then I agreed to send her a plane ticket, first class from LAX, and a driver for the week. (I made a note to research hiring a driver for the week.) She agreed. And though it wasn't quite a deal made with the devil, it didn't give me the warm fuzzies, either. As soon as I hung up, I needed an emotional distraction. Then it hit me.

My best friend needed to get laid. I mean, for fuck's sake, she is probably growing cobwebs down there. My personal philosophy is that female sexuality is a use it or lose it type of situation. You must water that tulip if you want it to thrive.

Jessica's and my friendship is more than just a series of trauma bonds, even though we've technically done a lot of that. We met through our daughters and became attached over how we'd both horribly disappointed our parents with our respective marriages, and then bonded again over the collapses of said marriages. Which is a bit of a sore subject. The end of a marriage is a death, and we grieved ours at roughly the same time. The way mine ended, though. Well, Jessica never seemed to feel that sorry for me. It was as if the most profound way to be a suffering ex-wife was to have been cheated on.

But I've moved on and now it's time for her to do so as well. Enough wallowing. Enough *oh but what if nobody wants me*. She's a good-looking woman and she should embrace her inherent desirability.

I was packing for the retreat, folding most of my standard fare into the mix—some chiffon kaftans, four bikinis, one extremely flattering one piece, workout sets from Alo's new collection—and then it hit me: I was going to give Jessica a little shove on her quest to get lucky.

I'm very good at reading body language and I've definitely noticed the way she retracts into herself whenever that yoga boy, Daniel, is nearby. Like she's trying to disappear so she can stare at him unabashedly. I'm not sure how he feels but am pretty confident he would hump anything with a pulse (and even that might not be necessary; the guy seems horny as heck). He's not really my type, but Jessica isn't too picky at the moment. If that's who her eyes are on, he'll do.

My toiletry bag was already packed, so I grabbed it out of the suitcase and brought it over to my medicine cabinet. Staring at the mini pharmacy behind the mirror, I decided to throw in some Xanax, a handful of edibles, and a bar of psilocybin mushroom chocolate. Jessica was going to need to calm the fuck down if she had any hope of seducing a man. Her natural awkwardness, I can only imagine, would be almost unbearably amplified by the presence of a potential sexual partner.

I threw the toiletries back into the suitcase and took one last scan of my bedroom before zipping the whole thing up. If Jessica couldn't seal the deal, at least we'd have fun with the party favors.

JESSICA

I don't know why packing is such a daunting task to me, but truly I'd rather retake the SATs than pack a suitcase for a seven-day trip. First of all, for no matter how long I'm going, said suitcase will be dangerously overstuffed and have a zipper holding on for dear life. The thought of merely closing the luggage gives me so much anxiety that I'd almost prefer to cancel whatever trip I'd planned in the first place.

And then there's the actual packing, which turns me into some sort of budding stylist who thinks she needs to put together Met Gala looks for all three meals of the day, when at home I just wear denim or leggings with a T-shirt. My vacation MO is to pull out tops from my closet that usually never see the light of day, pair them with *bold* bottoms, and then toss in twenty-five pairs of panties just in case I have diarrhea the entire time I'm gone. On top of all that, I squeeze several pouches, each containing dusty toiletries, into the already full suitcase and voilà! Ostensibly I should be ready for my trip.

At least Transcendence Week was going to be a different type of vacation. No heels. No fancy dinner outfits. Just some breezy dresses and workout clothes. My athleisure wear could use a refresh, but who wants to sell a kidney for one more pair of lululemon? I stood over my half-packed suitcase and surveyed the contents. It was a seven-day retreat, so I'd neatly folded eight pairs of leggings with eight semi-coordinating sports bras. It was my entire collection of workout bottoms, and most of my tops. The color palette wasn't super inspiring: mostly black, a brown, two gray, and an odd yellow (it was on sale, and I was feeling cheery when I bought it). Most of my exercise T-shirts were just old promo/school/freebie things that I'd collected over the years and felt too guilty (or attached to, or nostalgic) to throw away. Like Tom's old Sigma Chi shirt from our University of Miami days.

I closed my satin lingerie bag and shook my head. It contained the typical old cotton thongs, a couple full bottoms for sleeping, and, on impulse, I'd added a few mint-condition lacy panties *just in case*. How pathetic is that? I mean, who was I kidding? But as embarrassing as it was, I decided it was better to be prepared for the extremely far-fetched chance that I might hook up with someone than to be caught pants down, in the moment, with lime green granny panties from the 2001 Victoria's Secret catalog. I threw my trusty mini vibrator into the bag (for emotional support) and zipped it up.

To distract myself from the presumptuousness of the panties, I fell into my bed and opened Instagram. The first image I saw was of my daughter in a new post where she was wearing sunglasses and making a peace sign with the sun shining so brightly behind her head that her features were totally blurred out in the foreground. Was this an artsy thing? Or just a teenager thing? The caption read, "Only in my dreams . . ." and I have no idea what that was supposed to mean. Sky had begged me for the Instagram account six months ago. I begrudgingly complied and, so far, she'd done nothing unreasonable (that I know of).

I switched to the search page and typed in "Allison Kent." Her IG page wasn't as popular as her TikTok, but it still had more than a million followers. Every post on her grid was a reel. In some, she acted out skits where she was buying expensive groceries at Erewhon, the astronomically expensive LA grocery store. In others, she was cooking something sugary and delicious looking while not wearing a bra. She was youthful and gorgeous and funny and dripped confidence. It had been only a few days since I'd ground shipped her the Bougie Boho piece, but I thought *Fuck it*, and slid into her DMs. Yes, it felt creepy. But it was for work.

Hey, Allison! Love your content. My daughter is a big fan! Just wanted to give you a heads-up that I contacted your manager and sent you a rose-gold ring from Bougie Boho (I do all their marketing). It should arrive in the next couple days. I hope you enjoy it!

I hit send and felt a little self-conscious. Partly because I'd just so-licited a quasi-celebrity and partly because I'd *slid into someone's DMs*. I scrolled mindlessly through Instagram for another ten minutes to shake off the ick factor.

That's when I realized I'd never looked up Shakti's social media accounts and, since I had just thrown a pile of money at her to take me to the middle of Florida for a *retreat*, thought I might peruse her page and get to know her a little better. What I knew already was that she was young, mid-twenties, very attractive, and sometimes used a fake accent. I also knew that she proselytized about Hindu gods and goddesses and wore very expensive-looking yoga outfits that were possibly gifted or subsidized, since she couldn't possibly afford all of them on her teaching salary. Maybe she had family money. Or a sugar daddy.

I found her easily under the account name Shakti Yoga Miami. Not the most creative but smart of her because it was simple to locate. She had twenty-four thousand Instagram followers, and her bio read: "Yoga Instructor, Always a Student, Life Coach, Bitcoin Trader." I laughed out loud and then mentally flagellated myself for being judg-mental.

Why stick with Shakti when I could be attending classes with a seasoned yoga teacher, instead? One who smells like carrots and wears

the milky peaceful expression of someone who's either fully enlightened or incredibly stoned? It's hard to say exactly, other than I find
those instructors a little dry, if I'm being honest. And Shakti is fresh
and fun and makes me sweat, and I like her Drake/Taylor Swift playlists. Also, now that I have half of a visible abdominal muscle, there's
no turning back.

I asked Siri to call Indira and then put the phone on speaker. She
answered on the third ring.

"Hey, Jess," she said. It sounded like she was moving furniture or
something similarly taxing.

"Bad time?" I asked, propping up the pillows behind me in case we
settled into a long conversation.

"Nah, I'm just packing. What's up?"

I cleared my throat. "Well, I've been doing some social media
stalking and guess what? If we don't find inner peace on this retreat,
there's still a great chance that we'll get rich. Or, in your case, richer."

There was a contrived laugh on the other end. "Oh, jeez. What are
you going on about?"

Indira likes to play like she's above the gossip, but I happen to know
for a fact that she relishes it. We alternate hosting "family dinners" every Sunday (friends become family when the blood-related ones reject
you), and our food prep time is essentially *Watch What Happens Live*,
but with just the two of us. With the kids out of the kitchen, we unpack
all the school mom and ex-husband/new young girlfriend drama.

"Apparently, our *guru*, Shakti, is also a crypto trader. So I'm looking
forward to learning about investment opportunities. She's also a life
coach. And by the looks of her Instagram photos, her favorite hobby
is getting her hair and makeup done to do handstands on the beach."

This time, Indira laughed naturally. "Jess, come on. Don't hate the
player, hate the game. What does 'crypto trader' even mean?"

"Literally no one knows," I said. "And I'm not hating. I respect the
hustle. Wait a second." I scrolled back up to the top of Shakti's profile.
"You know all of this already. You follow her!"

"Duh, I follow her," Indira said. "Did you think I was going to drop four thousand dollars and travel to the middle of swampland Central Florida with a total stranger?"

"Right, so you looked at this and thought, Ah yes. Very professional and legit." I tapped the follow icon on Shakti's profile.

"I thought she looked exactly how I expected and that was fine with me," Indira said.

I couldn't tell by her tone of voice if she was amused, humoring me, or irritated with the line of questioning. There was a rustling on her end of the call, which sounded like the end of packing desperation where you just start throwing things on top *just in case*.

"I'll let you get back to it," I said. And then, to make her smile, "Namaste."

"Okay, love. Big kiss. Talk to you later."

I pressed end on the call and swung my legs out of bed, figuring I should probably get started on dinner, when a new message popped into my DMs. *No way*. It was Allison Kent.

Hey there! OMG—thank you so much for the merch! I can't waitttt to receive it. Bougie Boho is straight fire. I'm sure you'll be seeing the piece in my videos. Keep an eye out! XX AK

SHAKTI

<u>NOW</u>

Did Daniel have an inappropriate relationship with anyone on the retreat? I'm sorry, but as a teacher I am not at liberty to discuss the intimate details of my students' personal lives.

CAROL ANN

My hands were shaking, but I managed to measure all my supplements and label them on my pill organizer: SHE, for feminine vitality; living collagen, for skin/hair/bones; and grass-fed beef organs, for digestion. Enough for one week. I closed each lid on the container and sighed. Arguing with Beau always makes me jittery.

"Why don't *you* go on a retreat?" I'd suggested when my husband first brought it up. I was just trying to lighten the mood, but he didn't think it was funny at all.

"Trust me, I'd love a solo vacation, but did I bring a gun to school, CA? Did I bring the fake news media to our doorstep? You're the one who got us into this mess," he said. "Not me."

And I felt terrible because it was true. My boldness went against everything my mother taught me about being a good wife. Honor. Obey. Be his peace.

I'd lost my temper, publicly, and brought negative attention onto my household. Now Beau was insisting that I retreat, literally, from the situation. I'd told him about that yoga place the New York wife loved so much and he'd said, "Well there's your opportunity. Take it."

What was I supposed to do? I didn't want to participate in some New Agey group therapy with a bunch of strangers, but my husband is the head of our household, and he was insisting. The thing was, I'd gotten in trouble while fighting for something I passionately believe in. So I honestly wouldn't take back what I did. But Beau said that emotions were running too high, and I should take a breather for a few days until everyone calms down. Come back stronger.

I get it. The local gossip has been a nightmare. The press won't leave me alone.

But this is *my* town. I am *from* here. Born. And. Raised. An original. No one had to teach me that you always choose Publix supermarket over Winn-Dixie, or that the best way to run from an alligator is in a zigzag. Sheesh. I'm not going to let some crazy liberals try to run *me* out of town. They've already tried to take so much from us, even going so far as telling us not to pray on the football field or in the classroom. That's why I put my kids in Christian school in the first place.

The incident involved some other moms at my school, but it's not like anyone got hurt. No one broke the law. I'm the real-life example of a hot-button issue and now am being used as some kind of political talking point. It was just a heated argument, people. So I'm not running; I'm taking a *vacation*. For my own mental health. On Beau's advice, I looked into the Namaste Club place, and it turns out they have a Miami group buying out the property starting on October 20. That's in three days.

The timing is pretty perfect, and I've always said that God gives you exactly what you need, when you need it. I've never done a retreat, but I do like yoga. There are classes at my gym that are great for a nice stretch after weights and cardio. Just don't ask me to chant "om" or bow to some golden idol. No thank you. And I don't really care for Miami people, with all their partying and drugs and fast lifestyles. But I believe in signs, and this is one of them.

Exhibit A: my clients tell me about this retreat that is supposedly relaxing, I can be on my phone, and the food is good and healthy.

Exhibit B: the *incident* happens, and Beau says I need to get out of Dodge.

Exhibit C: the Mama Bears pro bono legal assistant suggests I make a show of being introspective, or some bull like that, so those other moms are less likely to sue. A yoga retreat must be as introspective as it gets. Look at me, everyone! I'm *doing the work,* or whatever.

Like I said, it's a sign, and I'm going to take it.

I paid the deposit for Transcendence Week and am crossing my fingers that it was the right decision. The place is northwest about an hour from Vero in a town that's inland from Melbourne Beach. I figure, worst-case scenario, I can just hop in my car and head back home if I hate it there.

The grounds look beautiful, though. Lots of open green land and lush palm trees, a big lake in the middle. According to the schedule, every morning starts with a hike (which must really be a walk because there are no hills whatsoever in Florida), followed by breakfast, a "strong flow," a "meditation practice," and lunch. After that, there's an "optional wellness activity," a cocktail hour, and something about "a moon welcoming ceremony," whatever that means. A little hippie-dippie, but I can keep an open mind.

The New York lady swore that she felt "rejuvenated" and "at peace" at the end of the week, and I'm hoping that magic works on me, too.

Beau is no Mr. Mom, so I'm leaving everything with the kids and home tied up in a pretty bow for my husband. Meals are prepped and labeled, laundry is clean and pressed, homework and activity schedules are taped up all over the house. It's a huge deal that he's agreed to take on all the domestic stuff while I'm gone. He's not exactly the type (thank God). But since I've made things tense in town for us at the moment, it's for the best. I'll go away so he can breathe and get back to work.

Beau's job is very stressful right now; it's a tough time for mortgage brokers. The Fed hiked up interest rates and basically only cash buyers can afford to buy a home these days. (So much for the American dream.) He needs to hit the pavement to keep his business alive. Of course, I'm nervous about leaving him and the kids. This is new for me. It's a leap.

And I'm not gonna lie. This school mom drama has me *tilted*. Beau is right that I need some distance from the whole thing. I don't want the situation to get any worse, that's for sure. But please don't confuse that with regret. I'm definitely not saying that I went *too far* with the *incident* at school. We have a permitless carry law here in Florida and it's my absolute right to bear arms. This is for the protection of our children for Christ's sake. Honestly, I don't know if I went far *enough*.

SHAKTI

No, I do not believe anyone brought weapons to the retreat. We don't explicitly have a policy about that, but we do teach ahimsa—or nonharming—in all aspects of life. Transcendence Week is a peaceful gathering. Well . . . it usually is.

INDIRA

Matthew ran one of his giant palms over my hip, the fog of sleep still heavy in his eyes. "Do you want a T-shirt to wear home?"

I laughed a little and smoothed out my hair. "And miss the chance for my first real walk of shame?" The blanket was pulled back, revealing his evenly tanned and toned torso, which made me briefly consider staying in bed.

Matthew's apartment is on Brickell Avenue, where all the other young professionals live, and we stumbled there after a night of dancing on tables at the Pussycat Lounge. His home is a slightly more modern version of Bud Fox's apartment in *Wall Street*. Leather sofa (because of course), glass coffee table, art prints from Alec Monopoly and KAWS. It's cute in a way and exactly what you'd expect from a twenty-six-year-old bachelor in Miami.

The sleepover had been an unplanned but welcomed surprise, the perfect distraction from the fact that my mother was arriving the next day. Matthew and I had spooned like the new lovers we were, knowing we'd probably never see each other again. When I woke up this morning, I kissed him goodbye, took the elevator down, passed through the lobby, and stepped into my Uber, all while wearing a cherry-red corset with matching leather mini skirt and five-inch stilettos. On a Wednesday morning 9:00 A.M. I'm loving this version of me.

Young me wouldn't believe what my life has become. I was married at twenty-two, so I like to say that I was a child bride. Greyson and I were college sweethearts at UCLA and had a courtship that both sets of our parents despised. His folks wanted a blue-blooded daughter-in-law with a bold-faced last name; mine wanted a Brahmin son-in-law with a pure lineage. Really, they wanted the exact same thing without even realizing. Maybe that made it all the more appealing to us. Our own taste of forbidden fruit. So theatrical. So tragic. So beautiful. (At least our young selves thought so.)

I wore henna on my arms and draped myself in a custom-made lehenga, Greyson looked dapper in a tux, and we did the courthouse thing. My freshman-year roommate and Grey's brother were the witnesses. We thought we had the kind of love that would last forever, that we'd prove to our parents we knew more than them. Ha! Imagine. But we made a beautiful daughter, and I raised her while he grew his freeze-dried fruit business.

He grew it until his product was in grocery stores in all fifty states, plus Mexico and Canada. And then he sold it. So we moved to Miami to start a new business and enjoy a change of scenery. He started a gluten-free baked goods brand, and again, I stayed home with Tara while he flew around the country meeting buyers. He grew the new business, but not as quickly as he grew to regret having been married so young that we didn't have a prenup. That's the abridged version of my marriage, anyway.

My parents seemed satisfied in being right about Greyson but could also admit that the marriage had been a success because it produced Tara. And because now I'm rich.

After seven years of not seeing each other, my mother flew from LA to Miami to *help me move on*. Tara and I met her at the airport. My daughter, only six years old at the time, had never met her nani. I'm not a naturally nervous person, but the anticipation tied my stomach into a knot. Mother walked out to the baggage claim area and saw us, Tara clinging to me like a baby lemur.

I don't know what she expected. That Tara should have run to her with open arms? That familial love and affection didn't need to be earned? My mother, draped in her fine sari and dripping in diamonds, was essentially a stranger. I'm sure her first thought when taking in Tara was *How American*. Her hair was loose around her shoulders, and she wore a Princess Belle yellow polyester gown. (To Tara's credit, that was because she wanted to look *fancy* for Nani.)

With the coldness of the fucking arctic, she approached us and put her duffel bag on the floor for me to collect. Then she looked my child up and down and said, "What a shame for a child to grow up in a broken home."

She visited three more times after that. And though with each trip she grew colder to me, somehow, she developed something of a relationship with her granddaughter. They even talk on the phone from time to time. Mother likes and comments on her Instagram photos. That sort of thing. My father has never bothered to visit.

Divorce is hard, even when it's the right path. It can taint what once were your happiest memories. Families are ripped apart, holidays divided. You buy two sets of everything so your kid can go back and forth. You try not to disparage your ex, to not say that his physical rejection of you made you feel lonelier than you've ever been in your life.

Divorce is a hard stop. But also a beginning. It can be hard to reconcile the grief with the freedom, but the freedom is there, too.

Here's the other thing. I was a good little Indian daughter who studied hard and kept playtime above the waist. While my high school and college girlfriends were collecting bodies like eyeshadow palettes, I was writing term papers and painting my toenails. I was harder to get into than the Taylor Swift Eras Tour. Eventually, I lost my virginity to Greyson. Because I thought that was what I was supposed to do. Save myself for the right man. And then I married him. Years later, when we stopped having sex, I thought, Well, I suppose that part of my life is over now. And all without ever having experienced a ho phase like the other girls. I was wrong.

Starting in my mid-thirties, I'd wake up in the middle of the night with a tingle, like something I'd felt back in middle school but had suppressed down, down, down with all my other sinful thoughts. As an adult woman, I knew better than to be ashamed of those urges. So I'd roll over and tap my husband. *Psst! Would you mind helping me with a little . . . problem?*

His response? Either none or "I'm sleeping."

That wasn't our only problem, but it did cause a buildup, or a backup. It was like having an itchy foot trapped under a sock while walking in the rain. Torture. I realized that I was too young to let that part of me go. And I didn't want to wait to see if that desire would go away naturally. So now I'm in my scratching phase. At forty-three years old, my ho days have arrived.

On the morning my husband moved out, I asked the universe to send me an abundance of affection. It sent me a tsunami. That same weekend, I met an actor, a restaurateur, and a doctor. And I slept with all of them. Not at the same time; that's a little too kinky for me. I started playing with them one by one. Do you want to know what I discovered? That my divine femininity isn't an old house cat; it's a lion. It roars.

My sexual life with Greyson was quickly cast in a new light. I don't think I ever truly knew what pleasure was in my marriage. Isn't that sad? Sure. I would come sometimes. But almost always because I was learning to understand my own body better. Not because he was becoming a better or more attentive lover. Sometimes, I wonder if I should've been more of a slut back when I was younger. Then I remember how insecure and nervous I was all the time, how unsure of myself and my body, and I realize that my forties are the perfect time to let my freak flag fly.

As the Uber crossed the causeway onto Miami Beach, inching me through morning traffic and back to my house on the Venetian Islands, a text came in from Jessica. I looked at it and rolled my eyes. I know it had been my idea in the first place, but . . . why had I been compelled to invite my most anxious friend on my weeklong escape for wellness and relaxation?

Her constant overanalyzing, I tried to remind myself, was a test for my patience, an opportunity to grow as a person. It was also just annoying as shit sometimes. Our lives were so intertwined that the genuine closeness could at moments teeter into the opposite side of affection. Not into hate, of course. It was all love. But also, we shared the kind of intimacy that was occasionally dripping with irritation.

Back at home, I waited for Grey to drop Tara off before heading out on his work trip and bided my time by tidying up. My house, once a showpiece for the interior designers who curated it, now appeared worn and cluttered to my eyes. Why was I suddenly seeing it with such judgmental eyes? Because that was certainly how Savera Rao would see it. Bougie Boho had hit the ground running, but we weren't yet at the place where we could responsibly afford Miami commercial real estate space. So my kitchen was the office, my dining room was the warehouse, and my spare bedroom was the Zoom background.

That would not fly for Mummy dearest, and I wish that the realization had hit me sooner. I did what I could with the jewelry samples, boxes, and shipping labels in the dining room, which was basically just stacking and shoving them into a corner. Then I collected my notebooks, ring light, and laptop and hid them in my primary closet. Basically, how a ten-year-old cleans their room, but I was tired from the night before and limited in time.

Grey was running late, as usual. Part of my punishment, I imagine, for bruising his fragile male ego when we divorced. Which meant that Tara, beloved daughter and granddaughter, was also late. When the doorbell rang, my heart momentarily stopped beating. The ex and offspring would have just let themselves in using the side door, so I knew it wasn't them.

I took a deep breath, plastered on my long-practiced fake smile, opened the door, and there she was. In her late sixties, my mother was still radiant. Shiny black hair and more diamonds than a Stephanie

Gottlieb showroom. She wore a vibrant orange salwar kameez and crossed the threshold of my house with the air of a maharani. In seconds, I was reduced to a quivering child who'd just spilled milk on the silk Oriental rug.

"No airport pickup this time?" she said not to me, but while taking in the state of my foyer.

I willed my shoulders away from my ears. "Sorry, Mum. I thought I'd just get the house and your room ready before your arrival. Like I said in my text message, I sent a car with your name . . ."

"Seems like getting the house ready might have been done beforehand. Preparation, my dear. Isn't that what I taught you?" She turned around and studied me up and down. "Have you gained a little weight?"

Bitch. I hadn't. I'd actually lost five pounds and gained muscle. "You're right. My mistake." Only one night, I reminded myself. One night and then you'll be relaxing and enjoying your yoga retreat.

She stood up straight and raised an eyebrow toward the door, which made me realize I was meant to retrieve her bags from outside. Which I did, like a cowed servant.

"Where is my granddaughter?" she asked, once I'd hauled them inside and wiped the sweat from my brow.

My stomach knotted. Fucking Greyson. "Her father is just running a bit late with the drop off." I rolled my eyes as if to say: *Men! Am I right?*

She sucked her teeth and let herself into the living room. "How about some chai then? It was a long journey."

As I started toward the kitchen to light the kettle, the side door swung open and in ran my precious teenager. She passed me in a blur and fell into Savera's arms. "Nani!" she said, in the child's voice I hadn't heard for myself in years.

I crumpled into myself as the two of them embraced.

"Tara!" I tried to sound cheerful and unwounded. "How was tennis this morning?"

"Fine," she said, without turning around.

A week alone for the two of them to bond, I thought, my insides churning. What was the worst that could happen? Other than Tara slipping and telling Savera that I'm not, in fact, on a work trip, but rather bastardizing our culture at a Western yoga retreat. Or them becoming closer to each other than either of them is to me. Or that I'd lose my grip on the last person I truly love.

I shoved the thought aside and went to the kitchen to make tea.

JESSICA

After dropping Sky and TJ off at school, I finalized the spreadsheet with their schedules for the week: drop-off times, pickup times, addresses, contact phone numbers, backup contacts, and notes, all in a handy color-coded format that took me the better part of the previous afternoon to complete. It was foolproof. And here I will exercise restraint and not make a joke about how that last qualifier would exclude my children's father.

I emailed copies of the schedule to Tom, the twenty-year-old sometimes babysitter, the sixty-year-old housekeeper, all of the children's teachers and coaches, my parents, and even my former in-laws (who live in Pennsylvania). Then I printed two copies and left them on the kitchen counter to put in the kids' backpacks after school. As I finished these tasks, my mind was stuck on a repeating thought: Why was I even going on this trip? I texted Indira.

Does a week seem excessive for a yoga retreat? I think it does.

When she didn't answer within ten minutes, I sent another message. (It's okay to double-text your best friend, just not a lover/romantic interest.)

What are we even going to be doing all day? Yoga is one hour.
Some pranayama breathing for another hour, and then . . .
meditate? Drink gin-kombucha cocktails? Howl at the moon?
Talk about our periods?

I tossed my phone onto the counter and started chopping onions. Getting an early start on dinner has a magical way of calming my nerves. That night we were having bell peppers stuffed with ground meat and rice. TJ's favorite.

My laptop stays propped up on the kitchen island throughout the day, so I can respond to emails in between prepping, cooking, cleaning, and all the rest of it. Indira prefers that I work from home and come in twice a week to fulfill orders. She likes the flexibility of not being tied down to the house all day. That way she can do whatever it is that Indira does while Tara is in school. Some mix of Bougie Boho business, workout classes (she usually does one in the morning and one in the evening), avocado toasts, ladies' lunches, shopping, who knows.

An iMessage dinged on my computer with a text message back from Indira.

Why would we be talking about our periods?

I rinsed my oniony hands and dried them on a dish towel.

I don't know. Shakti seems weirdly obsessed with them. She's
always telling us not to do inversions when we're on our "moon
cycles." Not that I can do a headstand anyway. But, like, what's
going to happen? Blood will start pouring out of our mouths?

I closed the chat and toggled over to my emails. There were some promos for 15 percent off at every e-commerce site I'd ever purchased from and a few flyers from the PTA. Nothing important. My iMessage dinged again.

Do you even still get your moon cycle? (☺)

It would have been a fair question since, at forty-five, plenty of my friends had already said goodbye to theirs, but it was a little bitchy coming from Indira, who was plenty familiar with my *moon cycles.*

I tried not to let it trigger me. Her comment was a (probably) un-intentional callback to a fight we had last Christmas. Our postdivorce tradition has been for the gentile exes to take our kids for Santa-related merriment while we, the relapsed Jew and Hindu, go for omakase sushi. (Chinese food would've been just a bit too cliché.)

This past year, Indira seemed to have forgotten how quickly the sake can sneak up on her and told the chef that I needed a "holiday miracle" and that he should screw me if he "didn't mind that she's on the rag." It was gross and just not funny. I spent the remaining six courses in silence, trying not to make eye contact with the sushi chef. We didn't speak for a couple days after that, but, like sisters, we made up like we always do.

I sure do. And fuck you very much for asking, I responded, slightly more joking than irritated.

Another message popped up. In that case, I hope you're on birth control. (🧍 ✋ 🧍)

My heart did a little flutter and I shut the laptop quickly, as though the insentient machine could pass judgment about my alleged sexual desires. I'd almost forgotten about my tiny little yoga guy crush. *Almost.* The packing, planning, panicking frenzy had been a bit of a distraction. But leave it to Indira and her witchy spidey sense to read my mind.

It was a completely ridiculous thought, imagining Daniel (whose last name I didn't even know) and me shacking up at the yoga retreat, like we were on *The Real World,* or *The Bachelor,* or, let's be honest, *Love Is Blind.* It was a little fantasy reserved only for me, alone in the dark, and I worried that my proximity to him while at the Namaste Club would ruin the whole thing. The mystery of him, the infinite possibility, that's what kept the appeal going. Spending an extended amount of time with him at a resort would surely chip away, if not completely destroy, that feeling.

What if I walked into one of the public restrooms right after he pooped? What if I had to listen to him speak in some kind of yoga circle talk thing and his pseudo spirituality turned me off? What if I tried to have a normal conversation with him but my face betrayed me and contorted into grotesque shapes? That would be the end of it. And my mental "spank bank" would be empty. Who knows when I'd be able to fill it again?

I wondered if I even knew how to have sex anymore. It had never been an issue in my marriage. We both wanted it often and had it plenty. Well, apparently not enough for Tom, but that's another story. The point is we never stopped having it, until we were *over*. And then just a couple of times afterward. But that was more than two years ago, and I haven't been touched since. Except for getting to third base with Daniel during that one adjustment in Shakti's yoga class.

What if things had changed since the last time I'd been intimate with someone? Like, if people went faster or slower now. Or maybe kissing didn't happen with tongue anymore in a postquarantine world. Or there was *more* tongue because we finally get to touch again. Forget the two celibate years. Before Tom, I'd been with only two guys, and that was twenty years ago! I was a full generation behind on potential sexual trends. Should I start posting thirst traps as a form of preemptive foreplay?

I resisted the urge to text Indira again to ask her what was new in the wild world of sex. She was doing enough field research for the both of us. But I sensed that she was in one of her less patient moods with me, which does happen from time to time, since I can sometimes be a high-maintenance friend. I'm a master of overthinking, and she's more go with the flow. I envy that about her. But I also wish she was less of a bitch about it with me sometimes. Give a girl a break. I've been through a lot.

The retreat was definitely a bad idea, I decided. But with my bag packed, and my spreadsheet sent, and tonight's dinner prepped, I knew I would go anyway.

SHAKTI

NOW

I arrived on-site at the Namaste Club seven days ago, a few hours before the students, so I could set up our sacred spaces for the week. I've done several retreats here already and can tell you that the energy is just amazing. The grounds are surrounded by nature like the goddess Durga reaching up from the earth to wrap us in a hug. Everywhere we look, we find proof of the divine: in the lush green of the grasses and trees, in the peaceful twilight croak of the tropical frogs, in the seductive perfume of the night-blooming jasmine.

Living in Miami, we are deprived of our connection to the living, breathing planet. We come here to remember what we truly are, which is at one with the universe.

When I arrived, the groundskeeper handed me the keys to the villas. Students had reserved their own private spaces for recharging and sleeping, and those lodgings were arranged in a wide circle around the Awakening Fire Pit, which is where we'd meet most nights to reflect on the day or sing to the moon before taking rest.

Once I received the keys, I delivered welcome baskets to each room. It's so important to set the tone for the week with personal touches, to immerse my students in the experience. The theme was "mind, body, spirit," and in each basket I'd included a printout of mantras we'd be reciting, an assortment of healthy non-GMO snack bars, a bottle of Enlightened Tequila from my liquor sponsor, and a bundle of sage for everyone to cleanse their spaces. While I was delivering those, I checked each villa for working locks, running water, and acceptable air-conditioning, and can assure you that they were all comfortable and secure.

INDIRA

FIRST DAY OF THE RETREAT

From Miami, Melbourne is a straight three-hour shot up I-95. Decidedly less boring than the Turnpike (the other way to head north in Florida) and less murdery than Alligator Alley (if you were cutting west across the state). The Namaste Club retreat space is in the unincorporated area just north and west of Melbourne. From east to west, most Central Florida towns will look like this: surfers and beaches, Cracker Barrel, fireworks store, gun store, and, in the center, you'll get to swampy farmlands that have been taken over by entrepreneurial hipsters. Start with the hipsters and work backward to get to the west coast.

I love a long drive. It's a kind of meditation, the way you can get from point A to point B and be totally unaware of the little decisions you're making along the way: speeding up, slowing down, changing lanes. Your conscious mind only latching on to the song playing on Spotify, the breeze in your hair, the openness in front of you. Then you arrive, almost alarmed at having no recollection of how you got there. I was looking forward to the journey almost as much as the destination, and not just because of the "Best of Beyoncé" playlist I'd meticulously curated the night before.

Jessica wasn't thrilled about a three-hour drive with the convertible top down. I could just tell. I picked her up after dropping Tara off at school (my mother mercifully had stayed back at the house to make a more suitable pot of chai and read her book in peace), and there was something skittish about the way she opened the door with her pretty sandy hair pulled into a tight ponytail, the white residue of sunscreen on her face, and a visor strapped firmly to her head.

"The sun shall not touch thy face," I said, kissing her cheek.

She wheeled her bulging suitcase out of the doorway and dragged it down the three steps leading to her driveway. "I heard that Jennifer Lopez's secret is that she never goes out in the sun, she doesn't eat sugar, and she stays away from alcohol. And only one of those things sounds reasonable to me."

"J.Lo said it, and so it shall be done." I opened the passenger door and folded down the seat for her to toss her luggage in the back next to mine.

She looked cute, wearing a tight black T-shirt (that she wouldn't have been caught dead in a year ago), maxi skirt, and leather sandals. I was proud of Jess for making more of an effort recently, and I hoped it was a physical manifestation of her depression lifting. God her ex-husband did a number on her. That guy was such an asshole.

She shut the passenger door and slid sunglasses onto her face, looking me up and down. "I could never pull off the turban look. Good thing I'm not religious anymore."

"You'd totally pull it off," I said. "You've got the bone structure." For the drive I'd opted for a hot pink chiffon headscarf with matching sarong over a white bodysuit.

"You look like a classic movie star, but I'd look like a fortune teller," she said, buckling her seat belt. Jessica is always self-deprecating like that. I used to think it was charming, but honestly, sometimes it just comes off as insecure.

It's like when we go out for drinks. If I flirt innocently with the bartender, she'll say something like "You're so confident with men." And slink down like a sad puppy. Maybe I'm being sensitive, but it comes off as a subtle indictment of how my marriage ended. Like I'm just a slut for attention, while she's a nervous unloved wallflower. Forget the fact that my husband didn't touch me, or so much as look at me, for years before I finally walked away.

I had iced coffees from Panther waiting in the cupholders when Jessica sat down: oat milk and stevia for me, half-and-half and cane sugar for her. She's literally the last person I know who still drinks cow's milk and uses the real stuff, which is kind of badass in an *I don't give a fuck* way. So I can overlook some of her less endearing tendencies.

My playlist kicked off with "Love on Top" (because hearing it always gets me hype), and the gods must have been smiling on us, because we cleared the causeway and made it out of Miami-Dade County without even once slipping into red traffic lines on the GPS. I'm not saying the universe was telling us something, but I'm not saying it wasn't, either.

"Wow, it's a traffic unicorn day," Jessica said. She'd already finished her entire iced coffee, which meant we'd be stopping at a gas station bathroom within the hour. I prefer to drive straight through, but whatever. This week was about openness. Relaxation. Fun.

"Shakti must have prayed to Ganesh to remove all our obstacles." I passed a slow-moving pickup truck and switched back into the left lane.

"About that. I've been meaning to ask you," Jessica said, readjusting her visor. "Seriously, does it bother you how she, and all these other self-proclaimed yogis, appropriate Sanskrit words, talk about Hindu deities and like, I don't know, wear henna on their arms?"

I laughed. There was always this sensation I felt in yoga classes of being watched, especially if the instructor was chanting or telling a story about one of the deities. Quick glances from the other practitioners that said something like *are you okay with this* or *is what she's saying correct?* It was funny.

"Nah," I said. "Although it does make me cringe when Shakti tells us to *nama-slay.*" I-95 opened up and spread before us like an unspooled Costco receipt. I pressed down on the gas.

"Ugh, you and me both," Jessica shouted over the road noise. "Or when she calls us all her *om-eys* instead of her homeys. Though homeys would be pretty weird, too. She needs to *nama-stay in her own lane*."

Truthfully, my parents would shudder if they saw me in a Western yoga class. It would be about as authentic to them as a curried chicken salad sandwich. (Good thing I no longer care what they think.) For the most part, I find the reverence to my mother culture endearing, though sometimes yogis here make mockeries of the words, shorten the mantras, and, in the worst examples, spectacularly miss the point. Their intentions are good enough, though. For me, it's like *Hinduism lite*. I don't need to go back to how I was raised, but the yoga classes give me a shred of nostalgia for it, which is nice.

"Single Ladies" came on and I raised my left hand into the open air and swiveled it for the *put a ring on it* move. "What about you?" I asked. "Does it offend you when Kanye says literally anything?"

"Everyone knows that man is troubled. So no!" She lifted her left arm and synchronized it with mine. "By the way, how is everything going with your mom's visit?"

I pressed down harder on the gas. "Have you ever had your cervix biopsied?" I asked.

Jessica nodded her head. Her own mother may have been slightly warmer and fuzzier, but she was just as disapproving as mine. "Say no more," she said.

I turned the volume up and filled my lungs with sweet, thick, October Florida air, slipping into a Queen Bey trance for the rest of the ride.

SHAKTI

Yes, Indira and Jessica *claimed* to be best friends coming into the retreat. But I think it was said in that Western way in which everyone feigns warmth and a closer relationship than is maybe accurate. Transcendence Week provides space to step into one's authenticity. It breaks down the sociological walls that we build up within ourselves, the artifice that we wear like masks. When that happens, old habits crumble away, like the scaffolding of a time-worn building. What might look like pain, like old relationships dying, or changing, is really the birth of newer, healthier habits. Of clearer, higher vibrational beings.

If you want my opinion, and I say this without judgment or superiority, I think that Jessica and Indira's relationship was built on a trauma bond. From how they both disappointed their parents with their marriages, which is a disruption to the root chakra, the foundation of our identities, the source, where we tap into our feelings of security. Then after that, they bonded again with the collapse of their marriages. An imbalance to the heart chakra.

What happened was that, without strong male figures to guide their journeys—no fathers or husbands—the women lost sight of their divine femininity, they became like Kali, goddesses of their own destruction. We witnessed that at Transcendence Week, and in a way, it was a privilege to watch. In order to rise from the ashes, they first needed to burn their bond into the ground.

They were reborn anew. Without resentments or expectations or burdens or shackles. There was a great intensity uniting these two women. But no, I do not believe that either of them is capable of murder. They were too busy working on their own resurrections.

MARTINA

I let Margaret sleep in while I did my final grounds check. The pre-dawn morning is my favorite part of the day. Quiet. Peaceful. As I blew out leaves from the common area walkways, a shiver ran down my back—one of those Miami groups would be checking in today, which meant the worst possible type of "yogis." The ones who preach about cleanliness and then drink themselves into oblivion, leaving Margaret and me to clean up their vomit. The kind who ask us to make the nature a little less naturey, and that's if they acknowledge us at all.

When Kyle Laughlin bought Grove Orange Farms—excuse me, the Namaste Club yoga retreat—three years ago, his vision was that it would be a "wellness oasis" and "an escape from the distractions of urban life." But if you want to know my opinion, it's an excuse for rich city folks to come party their faces off while pretending to be healthy.

No matter. They don't see the workers here, and we try not to see them, either.

There are things that need to be on hand, though, in case of emergencies:

- **Electrolytes**—I don't care if you're coming from somewhere else in Florida or from Antarctica. People still underestimate how much water you lose in this heat.

• **EpiPens**—because everyone seems to have real or imagined life-threatening allergies.

• **Narcan**—can't tell you how many times we've needed this. Technically, we have a no-drug policy, but we aren't allowed to kick people out for violating it.

I did a quick inventory in the front office to make sure we had enough of everything. It's hard to predict exactly what we'll use, but by the looks of that yoga teacher—with her tiny little outfits and bouncy blond hair—we might have a wild group on our hands.

After locking the emergency kit in my desk drawer, I double-checked the kitchen pantry, the walk-in refrigerator, the full bar with liquor and mixers. Everything had been ordered to perfection, or so I hoped.

As I made my way around Shiva Lake (why'd Laughlin need to rename all these damn places that have been here before him and will survive long after?), I slowed down at a ripple in the water. Looked like Bubba, our resident bull gator and unofficial protector of the grounds, was just finishing up some breakfast.

"You stay out of sight this week," I shouted out toward the lake. "We don't need one of these Miami people getting spooked and calling Fish and Wildlife on you."

I took one last look at the water and sighed. Laughlin didn't pay me enough for this shit.

JESSICA

I wanted to be wowed when we pulled up to the retreat grounds. Gasping and covering my mouth as a secluded secret paradise unfolded in front of me. But it was just like any other plot of land in the middle of the state: green, swampy, buggy, and close enough to a strip mall that you don't have to worry about finding groceries, a dollar store, or outlet shopping. It was *nice* but it wasn't the White Lotus. You know?

The first thing I needed to do, after texting my kids that I'd arrived safely, was shower. We pulled up to the Namaste Club just before 1:30 P.M., so obviously I was starving, since I pretty much eat on a schedule, like a kindergartner. But I couldn't even *think* about enjoying a meal until the three hours of sweating in the subtropical sun was scrubbed off my skin. Who drives with the top down?

Anyway, Indira and I parked outside of the Greeting Center, which is a wooden stand-alone building that smells like nag champa on the inside. A groundskeeper was there to greet us and show us to our private villas (after handing us welcome beverages of spiked Florida orange kombucha. It tasted like spoiled juice but also wasn't the worst cocktail I'd ever had.). Taking in the surroundings, I wondered what "luxury retreat" even meant. It's really just a marketing term that can indicate anything from complimentary butler service to a stale continental breakfast.

The groundskeeper is a real Florida-type lady, the kind that's mostly died out in Miami-Dade. Meeting her was like seeing a native panther in the wild. A real treat. Her name is Martina, and she has skin that is deeply lined and tanned like cowhide. Her hands looked more capable than most men's, and her voice was a smoky rasp that didn't invite bullshit of any kind. How this woman ended up on a New Agey wellness site is beyond me. She must have grown up in the area. I would have asked her if she was local, but Martina didn't seem like one for small talk.

She walked a few feet ahead of us through palmetto grass that was presumably always damp, whether from rains, humidity, or a sprinkler system. "I like her vest," I whispered to Indira, dragging my suitcase as we were led past the Nourishment Pavilion and the Active Room to the largest area of the grounds: the Enlightenment Circle, which comprised a massive fire pit surrounded by six stand-alone villas, each situated about twenty feet apart from one another.

"You like anything with pockets," Indira said. Which was true.

That was when it happened. The moment I had to stop and take it all in. While the approach to the Namaste Club had been nothing special, the Enlightenment Circle presented the breathtaking moment I'd been waiting for. It was Florida nature at its finest. Most of the perimeter was lined with squat but vibrant sabal palms, except just opposite of where we stood, on the path to Shiva Lake, whose entrance was guarded by two magnificent banyan trees, their branches shooting out of the earth like sunbeams. I closed my eyes and let the sweet air tickle my nose. Jasmine flowers must have been in bloom.

When I opened them, Indira was watching me with a look that said *told you*. I answered it with a smile. Already, I could feel my shoulders starting to relax.

Martina turned around and pointed toward the banyan trees. "Shiva Lake is just beyond there." She pronounced it *Shivah* instead of *Sheevah*. "Pretty during the day, but be careful around there, especially at night. Definitely don't walk dogs down at the shoreline." (Neither of us had dogs.) "The lake is home to a lot of wildlife. Native and invasive. There might even be Burmese pythons, which you're welcome to kill if you see them. Would do us a big favor. The gators won't harm you unless you threaten their eggs or bring a tasty little pet for them to eat. Hopefully, no crocs out there. They typically stick to the brackish water but sometimes storms wash them in. That's pretty rare though."

For once, Indira looked like the scared one. I grew up in Florida, so none of this was new to me. When I was a kid and the state was pushing back the Everglades to make way for more residential developments, newly homeless gators would take up residence in our backyard lakes and pools all the time. Or sun themselves on golf courses. We lived in harmony with them; it really wasn't a big deal. But Indira is from LA, so hurricanes and alligators and all the other WTF (What the Florida) weirdness is out of her wheelhouse.

"Don't worry, Indy." I walked over and draped an arm around her. "They're as harmless as a family of mice. I'll protect you."

"I *hate* mice." She shrugged me off. "And how can you tell the difference between an alligator and a crocodile, anyway?"

I straightened my skirt to act like I didn't notice her little snub. She could be so touchy sometimes. "Crocodiles have narrower snouts. And are much more aggressive."

"Like I'm going to know the difference?" She scuffed the dirt off her sandals on a nearby rock. "Okay, Jess. You're on reptile-categorizing duty. Just make sure I don't lose an arm. I need both arms."

Martina looked like she couldn't wait for us to stop talking. I wondered how many times she'd listened to almost identical responses to her welcome lecture, biting her tongue no doubt, while guests panicked and reassured one another about Florida wildlife safety. She handed us our keys to neighboring villas: mine was called Bhakti and Indira's was Dharma.

My room was sparse, and the portable A/C unit looked to be on its last legs, but all together it was still charming and lovely. The floors and walls were covered in pinewood and had a dank smell that wasn't quite moldy, but also wasn't the freshest. Again, not surprising, or unusual given the setting. It reminded me of Jewish sleepaway camp in Orange Springs, but nicer. The queen bed was neat and made up with pressed white sheets and a folded turquoise blanket at the foot. In the corner sat a rustic wooden desk and chair with a vintage-looking table lamp and notebook that said *Intentions* on the top. A round sisal rug covered most of the floor, and the bathroom was utilitarian and clean.

There was a gift basket on the desk, which was hilarious, but also . . . much appreciated. Shakti had gone all out. I mean, it was beautiful: an oversize wicker basket full of spiritual goodies, snack goodies, and liquor goodies, all wrapped up in ethereal white tulle. I snapped a quick photograph to remind myself to laugh about it later (*she has a tequila sponsor!*), and then immediately tore it open and inhaled a gluten-free, vegan, keto, macrobiotic snack bar. It tasted like dirt and fake sugar, but I was fucking starving.

With my blood sugar rising back to acceptable levels, I finally indulged in that blessed shower, while also fully accepting that the subpar air-conditioning and late hurricane season heat and humidity would have me smelling like a locker room again within the hour. Will Daniel notice? God, I'm ridiculous. There was a little window strangely positioned in the middle of the shower that looked onto my villa's backyard. For a moment, I imagined Daniel sitting on the other side, watching me. I pushed the thought away, even though it had been titillating, and smeared on a few extra layers of deodorant. There was no yoga practice today, but I'd probably be sweating regardless.

I wanted to look nice and tried to convince myself it was because I cared about my public image, rather than admitting that I just wanted to impress the one male in the group. My best feature is my hair, which is naturally silky and beachy-looking without products, though I do pay an exorbitant amount of money for my colorist to keep it shiny and gray-free. It's usually in a messy bun for yoga, but the first-day retreat activities consisted of a "welcome meditation," a "welcome cocktail," and a "welcome dinner." The schedule gave me permission to wear my hair down for a change. I threw on a floral sundress and sandals, coated on too much mascara, repeated for myself a quick affirmation in the mirror (*You're a grown-ass woman; don't be weird*), and rushed over to the Active Room for the 5:00 P.M. meditation.

When I arrived, at 5:05 (the cost of having to blow-dry my hair), everyone else was already in seated meditation, eyes closed, arranged in a circle around the room. Fucking shit damn it. That was not how I wanted to make a first impression at Transcendence Week. *Oh, there's the late lady who is clearly a spiritual imposter.* I slipped off my shoes and tiptoed next to Indira, who'd left me a space between her and a platinum-blond woman who looked like a cross between Ivanka Trump and a Real Housewife of Orange County. Who might actually look like the exact same person.

I sat down and crossed my legs, leaving one eye open to follow along with whatever I was supposed to be doing. Everyone but me was sporting athleisure. Why hadn't I asked Indira what she was wearing before I got dressed? The last thing I needed was to stand out even *more.* The very blond woman next to me was wearing a hot-pink tank top and matching leggings that said PINK on the waistband. Her hair was pulled back into a loose ponytail, but honestly, who could even focus on her hair when those boobs were basically in another zip code. Thank god her eyes were closed so she didn't catch me staring.

Indira was sexy and elegant, per usual, in a cream bodycon one-piece that hugged every single curve like water over a smooth stone. Could hotness be contagious? I really hoped so. Shakti was wearing a white sports bra—no shirt—and teeny-tiny shorts. It was basically a bikini. And her less-blond-than-pink-lady but still-magnificently-golden locks flowed like olive oil down her tanned shoulders. At least Barbara, who is such a hard-core yogi that she stays after class to clean floors because, like, she wants to, was sufficiently frumpy in patchwork hippie balloon pants and an oversize OM ALL-STARS T-shirt. Hidden underneath, I knew, was finely corded muscle and a banging body for her age (whatever number that was), but I respected that she had the confidence and class to keep it covered up. (Very un-Miami of her.)

I felt a little queasy, whether from the tardiness, or from being conspicuously overdressed, or because all I'd eaten since breakfast was a disgusting snack bar that could barely qualify as food. But then I allowed myself to steal a one-eyed look at Daniel. He was meditating directly across from me, already shirtless, already glistening, and looked about as peaceful as Siddhartha himself. I squeezed both eyes shut.

An unearthly hum filled the air—I recognized it as the specific siren song that came from Shakti's crystal sound bowls. And I loved it. Whether or not they were *cleansing* or *raised our collective energetic vibrations*, as she claimed, they sounded beautiful, and it was so easy to get lost in the magic.

"Come back to the breath," Shakti whisper-spoke, after a few moments. "Come back to the body."

I was legitimately in the moment, the lateness forgotten.

After we om'ed and bowed, finally opening our eyes, we all smiled at one another, sharing a brief and blissful moment. Maybe I like the yoga stuff more than I care to admit.

But then Shakti will say some shit like she did next (in her fake Indian accent): "Welcome, students. And thank you for gifting me the privilege to guide you through Transcendence Week. I thought we could start by going around the circle and introducing ourselves. When I point to you, please state your name, and then tell the group your canine energy. That is, which dog breed most closely aligns with your personality and why."

She literally said "canine energy."

Shakti pointed to the blondie first. "Hi, there," the woman next to me said, flashing a perfect Miss America smile. "It's nice to meet you all. I'm Carol Ann from Vero Beach, and let's see. I'm probably an American Staffordshire terrier. Because I'm loyal to a fault, strong, and if you threaten my loved ones, I will bite your head off. Ha ha! Just kidding. But I *can* be a pit bull!"

Everyone laughed even though, to me, Carol Ann sounded terrifying. And she looked terrifying. Like the type of woman who would rear-end you for stealing her parking spot, and then smile for the police officers and say it was your fault. Something about her was vaguely familiar, but I couldn't put my finger on it. Maybe she was just a *type*. A hot, God-fearing, Florida Woman type.

It was my turn next. I wasn't allowed to have dogs growing up and Tom is allergic, much to my children's dismay, so I racked my brain to remember all the fluffy and wrinkly and ugly-cute ones Sky and TJ had begged me for over the years. The question reminded me to look into adopting a puppy.

"Hi, umm. I'm Jessica. I think I know most of you. And hmm. I would say that I'm a goldendoodle because of my hair color, and because I'm very affectionate and loving. I like to be playful and fun. And most people aren't allergic to me. Ha ha." Oh my god; kill me. My cheeks burned hot, and I stared at my toes to avoid eye contact with anyone. At least I had a fresh pedicure to gaze at.

"You're totally a French bulldog," Indira whispered.

I turned to answer her with a questioning look, when Shakti said, "What's that?"

Indira sat up straight, breasts forward, chin slightly tucked, and said, "Namaste, everyone."

"Namaste," the group replied in unison.

"I'm Indira and I am delighted to be here with all of you, sharing this space and this experience." She spread her hands out toward the group and then curled her fingers into delicate fists. "I most closely identify with a Shiba Inu. I'm independent and strong-willed but fall madly in love with my people. Also . . ." She looked around the room and gave a little wink. To everyone? To no one? "I've been known to enjoy a good hunt."

Daniel whistled and everyone laughed. I cursed my friend with my thoughts. Why did she always have to be such a goddamn showboat? This was a yoga retreat, not a high school popularity contest.

Barbara went next. "Namaste, I'm Barbara. And I'm an INdog, an Indian street mutt." Her cupid's-bow lips unfurled into a radiant smile. "But from Palm Beach, originally. And I just want to let everyone know that this will be the last time you hear me speak this week. I'll be taking a silent journey for the rest of my time at the Namaste Club. My intention is to search within and live this moment from the inside out." She batted her eyelashes wistfully. Or maybe she was just high.

I bit my lip, begging my face to not show judgment. A *silent journey*? Honestly, sometimes these hard-core followers seem like they're just torturing themselves. Why come all the way out here if you're not going to enjoy the social aspect? I didn't get it, or her, for that matter. If she was a supposed billionaire, or even the daughter of one, it made the whole thing even stranger. I was curious about Barbara and made a mental note to slip a question about her into conversation with Shakti. Or, better yet, Daniel.

Our token yoga bro went next, placing his hands over his heart. "I'm Daniel." I fumbled with my fingers and tried not to let my gaze linger for too long on his nipples. "And I'm a golden retriever. So Jennifer, I guess that means we're related." He smiled brightly at me. Was I Jennifer? "I'm active, friendly, and love to pounce on my friends. Playfully, of course!" He was either funny or a little obnoxious. I couldn't tell. Did it matter?

"And I'm Shakti. Your spiritual guide for the week," said our humble yoga teacher. "A Tibetan spaniel."

It was going to be a very long week.

CAROL ANN

It took me about an hour to get to the retreat from Vero, and I listened to one of my favorite podcasts on the way. Tucker was the guest, and he was making so much sense. All the facts, all the proof about the stolen election. It boggles my mind how many sheeple still don't get it, but people just will not do their research. At least Florida got it right.

My hands were sweating on the steering wheel and not only because it was 90 degrees and sunny. I was *nervous*. I've never done anything like this—leaving my husband and kids, traveling to a crunchy yoga place where everyone was probably a lib. And what if someone recognized me from all the media coverage?

The crunchies actually aren't the bad kind of liberal, though, the ones who hate our country and spam call our legislators to cry about scary guns and sad minorities. Those are the overly educated man-hating lawyer types from up north. The hippie-dippie ones just care about the environment and preservation, and so do I! I love everything on God's green earth.

And the thing is, I probably know more about natural living than anyone else there. I listen to Liver King, I take organic supplements for optimal health and virility, and I've read all the ancestral diet books. I know how God intended us to eat, which is mostly off the land. I figured at the retreat I'd at least find some common ground on the topic of clean living with the others. As long as they weren't perverts, that is, but I honestly don't think the Namaste Club is that sort of place.

Okay, maybe the people there wouldn't be *my* people, but the retreat ticked enough of my boxes. It was set in nature; the food was all organic and biodynamic; the mission behind it was about purity or oneness or something like that, and those things sounded nice. Also, there'd be no lamestream media knocking down my door and no indoctrinators trying to peddle their garbage, like at *my* babies' school!

As soon as I arrived, the nerves disappeared. The Namaste Club felt like home even from the parking lot. The smell from the wood-burning oven meandering all the way from the Nourishment Pavilion to the Greeting Center, the mosquitoes buzzing—which may sound strange but to me that's as comforting as a blanket in winter—and those gorgeous banyan trees greeting me hello and then popping up again all around the property. It was a beautiful place.

Martina (who reminded me so much of my aunt Marcie I had to show her a photo and say *Meet your twinsie!*) showed me to my villa. It was a sweet little escape. Perfect for my *rejuvenation,* or whatever Beau said I needed. And the best surprise was that there was an absolutely gorgeous gift basket in the room packed with all the essentials: healthy foods, some spiritual mumbo jumbo I didn't understand but felt appropriate, and even some organic booze made from 100 percent sustainably farmed agave.

I could tell that I would like Shakti based on her organizational and presentation skills alone. Ladies like her are exactly who we try to cultivate for the Mama Bears. You can *never* have too many helping hands.

Timeliness is next to godliness. (Or is it "cleanliness is next to godliness"? I always get that confused.) Well, either way, I showed up to the Active Room, showered and dressed, at 4:45 P.M., a full fifteen minutes before our scheduled start time. Just like my father always taught me. And that's where I met Shakti.

She was setting up her crystal bowls when I walked in, and I thought she was absolutely adorable. A young little thing, with a sweet face and collagen for days.

"You must be our fearless leader," I said, removing my sandals and leaving them in a shoe bin by the door.

She walked up to me, barefoot, and placed her hands on my shoulders. "You must be Carol Ann," she said. "Thank you for trusting me with your journey."

"Thanks. I am *so* looking forward to it," I said. It meant something to me that she knew who I was before I introduced myself. Proved that she wasn't flaky, like some of these yoga types can be.

We got to talking a little bit and immediately clicked. I told her that I didn't feel comfortable with all the chanting mantra stuff that was mentioned in the welcome basket—that it wasn't really aligned with my religious beliefs—and asked her if that would be a problem. But she said it was absolutely fine, and that we wouldn't be worshipping gods so much as raising our vibrations with our voices. I'd have to get Beau's opinion on the whole thing, though honestly that sounded fine. Harmless enough.

What we really got going about, though, was Big Pharma and the global conspiracy that doctors like to call *vaccines*. I told her that I really appreciated Transcendence Week's commitment to natural foods, because I avoid poisons of all kinds and we kind of snowballed from there. I mean, this woman could not have been more aligned with me on the subject. I was impressed. She was doing her own research, not following along blindly like most people. I thought, Hey, I might even be leaving this retreat with a new friend.

The other guests started arriving, so I sat next to Shakti and zoned out while she welcomed everybody with a sound bowl performance. It was *divine*. I found myself closing my eyes to feel the reverberations even deeper, swaying my body a little left and right. This instructor might be young, but I could tell that she is an old soul, full of heavenly wisdom. I felt that something bigger than myself had guided me to that moment.

When I opened my eyes, most of the spaces were full. There was an empty spot next to me (What, did I have cooties?), and beside the vacancy sat a dark-skinned woman wearing lots of expensive-looking jewelry. She looked *very* Miami, with her overly trendy clothes and earrings crawling all the way up her cartilage. These types—and you can't blame them for it—usually come over from countries that are very *showy*.

Then there was a cute hippie lady who could have been thirty-five or fifty. It was hard to tell, with the baggy clothes and lack of makeup and hair color. I respect her type, even if I couldn't go that far into my own natural journey. I've been blond since high school, and I plan on staying that way! I have to keep Beau interested. And after two kids, I wasn't gonna hang it up with saggy boobs and stretch marks. It's my duty as a wife to please my husband and that is more important than living 100 percent chemical-free. Sorry, Jesus. Priorities can be contradictory and that's just a part of life. We all must do our best to balance the scales when we can.

There was also one man in the group, and if anyone was going to give me a hard time, I could tell it was him. Good lord. He sat next to the hippie lady, shirtless, with this creepy no-teeth grin on his face. And let's just say he wasn't looking anywhere near my eyes. I'd jujitsu his ass to the ground if he so much as tried to lay a finger on me but, honestly, I'm used to his type every day at the grocery store, the gas station, you name it—nothing I couldn't handle.

Then the last attendee sauntered in and sat in the empty space next to me. I could tell she was my least favorite kind of person, the disrespectful type who shows up late, like the world should rotate based on her schedule. The rest of us had no problem being on time, but this one lady—a little older than me, looked like she was trying too hard with her makeup and outfit—snuck in ten minutes after the meditation had already begun. What made her so special? Miss Latecomer waltzed in dressed like she's going to an afternoon tea, instead of a welcome meditation. I'm not even a part of this yoga world and I knew better! When she walked in, I shut my eyes and made a note to avoid her as much as possible. Not because she would try something per se, but because she looked like the type who would trigger me. I did *not* need a repeat of the school incident.

BARBARA

When one quiets a single sense, the others awaken.

That was why I decided on taking the silent journey for Transcendence Week. If I restricted myself from speaking, how much more would I hear? How much better would I listen?

As soon as I took the vow, my third eye opened. The grounds sang to me. The leaves on the banyans whispered to me about the ancient power that lies in their roots. The fire roared of its love for the moonlight. All the earth below me was in harmony with the creatures at my feet. Except for, that is, the creatures who had lost their way. The human animals, who were burdened with suffering, who had forgotten their divinity.

I was like them once, though. Saddled by my own privilege. Blinded by comfort and luxury and material pleasures. These external binds kept me asleep to the truth of our sacred divinity, our essential oneness.

That is why I honor Shakti, the one who brings us back to the path of light. We must be grateful for the teachers in this world, for they are few. They deserve our loyalty.

I've been studying Bhakti yoga, the practice of devotion, for longer than Shakti has been alive. But that doesn't matter. Gods and goddesses are reincarnated every day. To seek one is to find. To find is to accept. To accept is to follow. To follow is to serve. That is what I believe.

My first guru was a barefoot prophet who took me from my castle, where I was a Palm Beach princess, and placed me in a humble abode, where he made me a goddess. I renounced all my worldly possessions to follow his teachings. In doing so, I became more than I ever could have imagined. A complete soul. When he disappeared two years ago, like an apparition that pixelates and fades, I found my next teacher. Shakti.

On the first day of the retreat, I quickly realized that the others there were lost and needed to sit in the stillness of this place. To absorb it. To connect with its energies, both earthly and cosmic. So I decided to discreetly guide them without judgment. That would be my service. I knew it would be the most difficult part of my practice.

For when I saw that the loud and jittery one from our yoga studio had joined us on this retreat, the one who drinks out of single-use plastic bottles during practice and then tosses them away afterward, my heart ached for our oceans and our sea life. But that was her burden, not mine. And perhaps one day she will evolve. Until then, I decided that I wouldn't let her pollution harm my spirit. I'd let it wash over me like rain.

And the woman who speaks the mother tongue but would rather take selfies in the mirror than meditate on the names of the gods and goddesses she knows so well—I vowed to not let her disrespect affect me personally, for her disconnect from the divine was through no fault of my own.

And finally, to the one who joined us from outside our sacred studio, who is chemically enhanced of hair and surgically enhanced of body, I told myself, "Let me not mourn her hatred of the natural form."

My silence allowed me to absorb these observations, but then let the judgments pass above me like clouds. They became as useless as wallpaper and wisdom teeth and bras.

INDIRA

The singing of the crystal sound bowls was an elixir to my spirit, like honey on my tongue and ecstasy to my flesh. I drank it in and let it fill me up. This was why I was here. To refuel my spirit and reconnect with my essential being.

In equal parts pleasant and unpleasant ways, the meditation and Shakti's Westernized Hindu chanting sent nostalgic pangs through my bones. I was born in California, but my Delhi-born parents held kirtan every Friday at our house growing up. The sounds of drums and mantra, their heavenly, soul-filling vibrations, were the sounds of my childhood. Maybe immersing myself in this watered-down American version of Indian culture is a kind of masochism. It feels good to re-member, but it hurts, too, to remember how disappointing I am as a daughter.

If Savera saw me sitting in that circle, eyes closed at the feet of a white woman who mispronounces the names of Shiva, Krishna, and Parvati, what would she say? *Tsk, beti. What is this? First you marry a foreigner, now you worship in this way?* Forget that my ex and I are both American. Foreign means only *not Indian descent.*

To make matters worse, my family are Brahmins, and to this day can't conceive of how I'd denounce that sacred privilege to coexist with the lower people. To eat meat. To drink alcohol. When I first told my mother I was pregnant—which was over the phone at thirty weeks along—her response was "What will your child be, beti?" Which really meant, how can you do this to me? And yet now I've left that child in her care, and neither of them has so much as responded to my text messages.

I shook away the thought.

After the welcome meditation, we broke the peaceful spell and stood to greet our fellow retreat attendees. I could feel Jess's eyes on me, but I wasn't in the mood to latch on to the one person with whom I was already close, so I pretended not to notice and crossed the room to speak with Shakti.

"That was fabulous," I told her, bowing a little bit to show my gratitude.

A woman I'd never seen before but who might as well have been called Florida Barbie joined us next, clasping her hands and appearing to be on the verge of tears.

"Wow," she said. "Just wow."

"I'm so happy you enjoyed." Shakti bowed back to us both. "Carol Ann, have you met Indira?"

Florida Barbie shot out her hand and said, "Hi there! I'm Carol Ann. So nice to meet you."

She stretched out the last sentence slowly, as though I were a small child or nonnative English speaker. Even though she'd just heard me speak in front of the entire room. I smiled and nodded.

"I'm Indira. Nice to meet you." I accepted her extended hand in both of mine and gave a little squeeze.

Like an eager puppy (or goldendoodle, apparently), Jessica joined the conversation.

"Great class, Shakti. And sorry I was late," she said, tugging on her dress. Why was she wearing a dress? "Hi! I'm Jessica." She turned to Carol Ann and shook her hand vigorously. Maybe it was me, but I sensed a slight recoil from the new woman.

I love Jessica but the last thing I wanted to do was babysit her for the week. She can be a little socially awkward around new groups, which I have compassion for, but it's also hard for me to relate to. She's forty-five years old, for fuck's sake. The forties are supposed to be when you shed the insecurities. But I get it. Tom did a number on her.

As a group, we all walked the grounds back to the Enlightenment Circle, where welcome cocktails and a welcome dinner were being served. Shakti and the Namaste Club staff were going out of their way to make us feel *welcomed*. That was for sure.

It was a balmy Florida evening, but the firepit was lit (for ambiance, no doubt). The blaze cast an eerie but beautiful light against the smoky autumn dusk, flames dancing and chasing away the buzzing mosquitoes. I was grateful to be wearing a bodysuit, otherwise my clothes would be clinging in odd places like poor Jessica's dress.

Martina and another woman who could have been her sister or partner or even daughter met us with trays of cocktails: blush pink palomas with sage garnish, made with Enlightened Tequila. A buffet table was stationed at the far end of the fire pit, with the banyan trees as their background. Even from about fifty feet away, I could smell the intoxicating aroma of charred meats.

I've never shied away from being the first person at a buffet—someone needs to get it started—so I sipped my delicious (and strong!) cocktail and headed over to grab a plate.

Jessica showed up behind me. "I'm so glad Shakti isn't into the kind of ahimsa that says we can't kill animals."

"As long as we kill them humanely and then eat or use as much of the animal as we can." I slipped a fork and knife under my fingers and reached for the first dish, a gorgeous salad with fresh greens, cut grapes, pine nuts, and a white cheese.

"Oh my God. That's exactly what I always say. Literally, what I always say." Carol Ann had appeared behind Jessica and was helping herself to her own plate and silverware. "It's so nice to find like-minded people in a group of strangers. Hey, do you ladies hunt? You mentioned something about it with your canine energy."

Jessica made a face, but I answered before she could. "Actually, I've always wanted to. I briefly dated a guy who came out to this area for wild boar hunts. He was supposed to teach me, but we didn't last long enough. It just seems so primal. So fulfilling."

"Oh, that is exactly what it's like." Carol Ann was smiling widely, revealing an almost blindingly perfect set of teeth. "And they're an invasive species, so really it's our duty to hunt them. I can teach you, if you're still interested. I think we can even rent rifles on the property. It was on the optional activities list from the grounds."

I smiled back and told her I'd love to do that, which I meant. Hunting has been on my list for a while. If you can eat an animal, you should be able to kill it. In theory, anyway. Even if I only try it once and then realize that it isn't for me.

I finished filling up my plate with the fire-roasted boar, wild rice, and a big scoop of plantains. It was all perfect and delicious, and though it was heavy, it was also clean. High-quality food hits differently.

After eating, I pulled Jessica to the side so we could speak privately.

"Are you really going hunting with Marjorie Taylor Greene over there? And why does she look so familiar?" Jessica asked, in between bites of the boar.

I waved her off. "Never seen her in my life. Give Carol Ann a chance. She seems sweet and is also way hotter than MTG. But that's not why I pulled you over here." I opened my tote bag to reveal the little stash of party favors I'd brought along.

"You brought drugs to the yoga retreat?" She bugged her eyes out at me as if the two things were mutually exclusive.

"Don't be judgy," I said. "I did it for you. So you could get out of your own way and make a move on Daniel. Have you even spoken to him?"

She blushed, which was enough of an answer.

"I knew you'd need a little help getting over yourself. Even though you're beautiful and smart and fun, and in the best shape of your life.

Besides, the weed gummies and shrooms are organic. And the pills, whatever. Pharmaceutical, but since when do you care about that?

"Take half a gummy," I said.

Jessica looked around to make sure no one was watching us, as if we were surrounded by undercover cops. "Not tonight," she said. "Weed makes me paranoid and I've already had a drink."

"Fine," I said. "Pick something else then. Choose your own adventure. Why don't you layer a little edible with a little mushroom chocolate to balance out the highs? Think of it as a drug lasagna."

She shook her head. "Okay, if you insist. More for me." I shrugged, popped a square of mushroom chocolate into my mouth, and rejoined the group.

After that, things took a turn. Not because of the microdose. If anything, that probably improved my mood about the whole thing.

While everyone else was laughing, eating, and drinking, Jessica was unsubtly eyeing Daniel and sharply turning away whenever he seemed to notice. Shakti and Carol Ann were glued together like old friends. Barbara was dancing under the moonlight like a sexy whirling dervish, and Daniel was filling what must have been his fourth plate of food. He was still shirtless from meditation class but had seemingly recoiffed his man bun.

I joined him at the buffet because I'd skipped on turmeric potatoes the first time around. The yellow-tinged tubers and scent of my childhood beckoned me. My elbow bumped Daniel's while we were filling our plates, so he turned to me and we made small talk about the grounds (so peaceful), the food (delicious and nutrient balanced), and the welcome meditation (inspiring).

"Everything here is so tactile," he said, while taking a slow bite of dripping meat. "So sensual. The colors, the sounds, the flavors. I feel like we have found the whole essence of life here on these grounds."

I had no idea what that meant, so I nodded along.

"Sensual. Huh. Okay." I tried the potatoes. They were oversalted but cooked perfectly.

"Do you believe in tantra?" he asked.

"Like believe if it exists? Like Santa Claus or the tooth fairy?"

Daniel laughed all the way from his diaphragm, his abdominal muscles tightening from the effort. I was beginning to see the appeal.

"You're funny. I guess what I meant to ask was, do you follow it? Tantra is all about engaging every sense in the present moment, to fully participate in life. Forming a living connection with everything around us. It's transformational."

He widened his stance like a football coach giving a pregame speech.

"There are different camps of thinking in yoga philosophy. Shakti, for example, is all about purity and abstinence. But I believe that we are here on earth to derive as much pleasure as we ethically can."

His weird tantra lecture was painfully boring, and I found my focus wandering around the Enlightenment Circle. My gaze landed on Jessica, who twitched when our eyes met. At first, I thought she was jealous I was talking to Daniel. But that would have been beyond juvenile and, if anything, me starting a conversation with him made it easier for her to walk up and join us. No, she looked worried. Guilty. Afraid. Like a mouse in the path of a Burmese python. She had her phone in her hand and kept scrolling, covering her mouth, shaking her head.

Daniel droned on about how tantra isn't just about sex and how all anyone knows about it is that Sting and his wife like to practice. I tuned him out and reached into my purse for my phone. I'd been so locked into the present moment that I hadn't checked it since before the meditation. Now there were fifteen missed calls and more than a hundred unread text messages. Most of them from a group chat for Bougie Boho. *My* business. I opened the chat and scrolled to the beginning—though it was impossible to miss the oh shit! and what is the strategy? and How the fuck did this happen? messages along the way.

"What the fuck?" I said, cutting Daniel off midsentence.

He cocked an eyebrow and then groaned in recognition. "Ohhh, I meant to ask you about that but didn't want to bring it up in case it was a sensitive topic. You just seeing that Bougie Boho shitshow?"

I glared at him with what must have been pure disdain. "What did you say?"

He shrugged. "It's blowing up on my IG stories. I've followed that chick for ages but had no idea she'd say anything crazy like that. Assuming you didn't either, since you sponsored her page or whatever."

A sick sense of disaster passed over me and I looked back down at my phone. At the beginning of the Bougie Boho message thread was an article. "Allison Kent Canceled? Influencer Compares Covid Lockdowns to the Holocaust."

What a fucking idiot, I thought. Then my blood ran cold. On the imbedded Instagram video, Allison Kent was leaning her chin into her palm, the Tara ring featured prominently on her middle finger. *The one Jessica gifted her.*

I swallowed hard and opened the video. The influencer's awful vocal fry attacked my ears.

"Hey, fam! It's your girl, Allison Kent, here. You know what I've been thinking a lot about lately? How we all just basically lived through a damn war together. And now we're on the other motherfucking side. We survived the Holocaust, you guys! We lived through concentration camps of isolation! So next time you're feeling down, or inadequate, remember what you have overcome. Real talk. Anyway, thanks to my sponsors, as always, and special thanks to Bougie Boho, my *favorite* new jewelry line, for gifting me this gorgeous middle-finger ring. The Tara! Bye, y'all!"

A wave of nausea threatened to expel turmeric potatoes all over Daniel's bare feet. This couldn't be real. It was a joke. A prank. A dream. I thought maybe I'd taken a macro- instead of a microdose of shrooms and was having a bad trip. I marched over to the garbage can and threw the rest of my plate inside, then covered my face with my hands, willing the nightmare to end. *A million followers.* It was offensive, mind-numbingly stupid, and borderline narcissistic. And she was wearing the fucking ring named after my *daughter.*

She even said her name, Tara. The sweetest sound in the universe, bastardized on Allison Kent's tongue. In Sanskrit, it means *star*, or *light of the soul*. And that's exactly what my daughter is. She's the last person on earth who deserves her name associated with ignorance and filth.

I designed the ring for her as a symbol. When my mother came to visit and met her that first time, she admonished me for raising Tara without any culture. For having an American child. I reminded her that I, too, was an American child. But when she left, I'd felt guilty and began teaching Tara some Hindi words, some stories about our deities. I taught her about om, the sacred sound. Then I designed a delicate ring with its symbol and named it after her. I marketed it as for the middle finger, to make it cheeky. A little salty and a little sweet, like my child.

Seeing it on that influencer's finger, someone who clearly knew nothing of our culture or a mother's love, sent me into a rage.

Bougie Boho is my second baby. When we were married, Greyson was the business mind, and I was the creative one. I designed all our packaging and branding, and it was my idea to start a business in the healthy food space. But, in reality, the companies were *his*. Once we separated, I wanted to create something that would be *mine*. I started it with the seed of an idea, a fantasy, a passion, and turned it into a booming business. The company is the center of my world, other than Tara. I've poured my whole heart into it. And I knew this negative association was more than just an offensive embarrassment, it was a potential career killer.

Jessica had the nerve to show up behind me and put a hand on my shoulder.

"Indira, I'm so sorry. I had no idea . . ."

"That what?" I turned around and shrugged her off. "That your brilliant marketing plan included sending free jewelry to an idiot and possible anti-Semite."

Jessica stepped back. "Well, I'm Jewish, so obviously . . ."

"Don't even right now, Jess." I put my hand up to separate us. "I told you I don't believe in influencer marketing. And it's because of shit like this. They're all morons! They aren't businesspeople. They don't have marketing degrees." I gritted my teeth. "Unlike you."

Tears were in her eyes, but I didn't care. I half listened while she said that she'd strategize a response and a plan to minimize the damage, but I was in no mood to hear it. This is what I got for hiring a friend. A fucking rookie mistake that could ruin everything I'd worked for.

Anger transformed into something else, something tingly and fuzzy. I took a few steps back, giggling. The mushrooms were starting to hit. The situation wasn't amusing but something about the pathetic look on Jessica's face was becoming absolutely hilarious. I doubled over in laughter.

Daniel came over with a cocktail in each hand, asking what was so funny.

The thing with mushrooms is, they give me the biggest body high. They make me want to be touched. Or to take a long shower. It's intense and amazing. And Jessica was ruining it.

I needed to get out of there right away.

JESSICA

It must have been a sixth sense that drew my hand to my phone after not having checked it all afternoon. A sense of dread I felt even before having seen the messages, missed calls, and voicemail notifications. The screen was basically screaming at me: *Something very bad happened. Where have you been for four hours?*

I sifted through the alerts and landed on the link, my heart in my throat before it even had time to load. Whatever this was, I had a feeling I was somehow at fault.

We survived the Holocaust, you guys!

Was she fucking kidding me? And really? Another non-Jewish person comparing literally any modern discomfort to the Holocaust? From my many relatives who survived the actual war, and especially from those who didn't, we say fuck you very much, Allison Kent.

This was bad. Both because it was a disgusting thing to do and because I'd aligned the Bougie Boho brand with an absolute moron. And it was all over the internet. Indira was going to kill me.

I looked over to find her engrossed in conversation with Daniel. Good. She clearly hadn't seen the message yet. My thinking was irrational. Maybe I could stave off the inevitable by grabbing her phone and flinging it into Shiva Lake beyond the banyans. *Let's embrace this experience and live in the moment!* I could use the extra time to formulate a solution. I'd have the whole thing fixed before she even found out about it in the first place.

Then she checked her phone. It happened in slow motion, like a glass of milk falling off the counter. The confusion on her face. Then registering the shocking news. I froze in place with a sick combination of terror and guilt.

My bad decision had caused this, just like, as my mother loves to remind me, my poor choice of a husband caused me to be cheated on relentlessly and dumped. When I'd called her to explain that my marriage was over, the first thing she'd said was, "Well, what did you expect?" I prayed that Indira would be more understanding of this new fuckup. But I somehow doubted it.

Finally, my feet carried me over to Indira, where she was chucking a plate of food into the garbage, her face twisted into an angry mask. My heart pounded in my ears. I tried to reason with her, to apologize, but she was obviously not ready. Then she started laughing at me. Hysterically, mockingly, in my face. Like I was some kind of joke to her. I reminded myself that she was on drugs, but the malice seemed so much more calculated than that. Indira looked like she *hated* me.

Then, as if to prove my suspicion, she left . . . with Daniel. The backstabbing bitch. I watched their backs as they giggled, bumping shoulder to shoulder, back toward Indira's villa. The truth of it slapped me in the face: I was unattractive, unfuckable. Who would want me? A pathetic, delusional, sidekick of a woman. I felt so stupid. And my supposed best friend was the one who proved the point.

It was almost too much to process, the levels of hurt and betrayal. Not because of the guy. Fuck no. Because of what he represented—an opportunity to wound me. Which had been successful. Not because I cared about Daniel, even though I sort of did, but because my best friend had *wanted* to bruise me.

And I felt like a failure. A friendless, loveless, terrible-at-marketing failure.

I'm not sure how long I stood paralyzed by the garbage cans, but eventually Shakti showed up and placed a warm hand on my shoulder.

"I couldn't help but notice that the energy between you and Indira is off. Is everything okay?"

I bit my lip to hold back the tears. Never had I so badly wanted to leave a place. The last time I could truly remember wanting to flee was when I was nine years old and had just arrived at sleepaway camp, realizing I had to sleep on the bottom bunk under Talya the bedwetter. I begged to call my parents to pick me up, even though the counselors told me not to. But this was worse. Way worse.

"It's nothing." I wiped an errant tear from my cheek. "Just a work misunderstanding." I hated euphemisms and hated myself for casually throwing one out.

"Remind me again what you do for a living?" Shakti tilted her pretty head in an almost faux-looking attempt at sincerity.

"Oh, I work for Indira's jewelry line. Bougie Boho? Mostly marketing. Some order fulfillment."

Shakti nodded like she was taking it all in. "I see. And does that work make you *feel* fulfilled, Jessica?"

This girl was really about to pitch me on her *life coach* services while I was in the midst of a massive personal and professional meltdown. Which was arguably an opportune time to do it, but in that moment, I really hated her.

I turned toward the banyan trees and sulked away from Shakti, away from the welcome dinner, away from the Enlightenment Circle. The grass was wet between my toes, which meant my leather sandals would forever be stained, but I didn't care. I needed to be alone with my misery and shame. The farther away I got from the group, the easier it was to cry. First the tears flowed in fat drops, then eventually devolved into convulsing waterfalls.

As I passed through the banyans, grasping their veiny branches along the way, I had the distinct feeling of passing through a new portal of existence, like walking through the wardrobe and into Narnia.

Night had fallen, and the air was thick and inky. The specific darkness and grass scent reminded me of sneaking out with friends at our childhood sleepovers, when our bustling Miami Beach neighborhoods took on an almost eerie quiet. When magic and mischief loomed just along the edges of what we could perceive. We'd walk over to the intracoastal and crouch down in front of the water, watching the transient effects of the moonlight on its surface, glimpsing the fish still barely perceptible just inches below.

The nostalgia calmed me down a little bit. I closed my eyes and let the last of the tears fall, then filled my lungs with the hot, damp air. When I opened them again, a smile crept onto my lips. Shiva Lake was stretched out in front of me with the moon shining overhead. Little ripples broke the stillness of the water. It was beautiful.

"Doesn't get old, does it?" a voice called out from behind me.

I turned around to see Carol Ann, one hand jiggling a cocktail and the other holding the purse strap on her shoulder.

"It's Florida at its finest." I agreed.

Carol Ann stepped toward me and tilted her head in almost the exact way Shakti had earlier. "Hey. You okay, hon? I saw you get heated with your friend and then storm off."

And then, for some reason I cannot understand, I opened up and told her everything. About the influencer/Bougie Boho debacle. About how I went to school for marketing and once had a vibrant career. How I gave all that up to be a mom, but now was finally back to it after a bad divorce. I think I just needed to say it out loud. To hear and understand it for myself and let it out. What I'd done wrong, but also what had been out of my control.

Carol Ann was a good listener. She maintained eye contact and nodded her head to show she was engaged. When I finished talking, she sucked her teeth. "I'm sorry. That is just *awful*. I am so tired of cancel culture. It's the *worst*!"

She jiggled the ice in her glass again and took a sip, shaking her head.

"Well." I scrunched my face. "I mean, Allison Kent deserves to get canceled. What she said was objectively horrible. Even if I wasn't Jewish, I'd be mortified by the association with her."

She stretched her lips into a pinched smile. "Right, of course. Bless your heart."

Her eyes snapped away from mine and focused instead on something in the distance, just behind my feet, like she'd fallen into a sudden trance. Maybe I'd lost her with my statement. I continued, though again I wasn't sure why. Maybe just to break the awkward silence.

"I mean, influencer marketing is a fairly new thing and it's hardly an exact science. But I never thought Allison Kent would say something so atrocious. She seemed kind of smart and *with it*. You know?"

I was gesturing with my hands and about to make my next point when Carol Ann slowly reached for something in her purse, her eyes still fixed on the ground behind me. She quietly placed her cocktail glass on the ground. I wanted to turn around to see what she was so focused on, but I froze when I saw what she'd pulled out of her bag. A gun.

My feet planted into the earth, an itch forming on my feet from the grass and bugs. I tried to think of something to say, but my mind had become terrifyingly blank.

She pointed the gun toward my shin. I gasped but didn't move. Was this lady really about to shoot me? And then . . . bang! The shot was so loud I fell to my knees, covering my ears. I must've been screaming but I can't remember any sound coming from my mouth. Had I been hit?

I looked down at my legs, which seemed fine. Then back up at Carol Ann.

"Got 'im," she said, fiddling with the gun before putting it back in her purse.

I turned around and, this time, there was no question as to whether or not I was screaming. Sprawled out, just behind me, was an enormous—maybe six-foot-long—leopard-printed snake. With a gaping mess of a hole where its head used to be.

I covered my mouth and turned back, wide-eyed, to Carol Ann, who just shrugged.

"It's a Burmese python," she said. "Invasive species."

BARBARA

When one cannot speak, one hears, one feels. One senses what others cannot, because they are too immersed in their own voices and on how they are being perceived. Self-centered. Selfish. *Me, me, me.* It took everything within my soul to not weep. Should we not be better than this?

The evening started out joyously. Eating, drinking, and enjoying one another's company. And though I do not eat carcass, the mood was light. But as the sun rises, it also must set. And with that comes the darkness. Yes, the women were behaving vilely. All of them except for my dear Shakti. But that's not what I mean. I'm referring to what happened *after* the immature catfight.

When the evening wound down, I tucked Shakti into bed and crept back outside to enjoy all of nature's splendor, which was so much more alive after everyone had retired for the evening. At least, that's what I'd thought.

It was a still night, and my rural surroundings were devoid of the toxic car fumes and synthetic noises of the city. I spread my arms wide like a heron's wings and circled the Awakening Fire Pit, watching the last embers fade to dust. Tiny sparks like fireflies flashed and died in the coals. What once was fearsome and dangerous became harmless as soil. I buried my arms in the faintly hot ashes and let the soot seep into my skin. The coals are known to be energy-rich and detoxifying.

I imagined myself as the dancing god, Nataraja, and shed my shoes to tiptoe through the magical banyan trees and pirouette around Shiva Lake. As I passed through, my bare feet spinning in the dirt, I heard women's voices, which stilled my dance. I hid behind sturdy branches, listening.

Plastic-water-bottle woman was upset about social media. How oddly unsurprising. Unnatural-looking woman was there, too, commiserating. They were loud, then quiet. Then . . . POP! I made no sound, but tears sprang from my eyes. A weapon! On these sacred lands. Where we come for peace and worship and service. The sight of it tore my heart in two. And in its wake, a serpent, slain. Even the beasts of this world possess a soul and serve a purpose. That is why I don't eat flesh, unlike the others on the retreat. Not that I judge.

The snake was an innocent, unlike us humans. There he lay, mutilated and dead. The sight was too much to bear. I felt as though all the evil of the world was creeping up against my feet, a blackness threatening to enclose and suffocate me. I turned and ran, not stopping, back to my room, where I burned a bundle of sage, prayed to Durga, and sang my mantra. I begged for the safe passage of the serpent's soul. That he may be born again as a frangipani, for all to admire and love. For it is easy to love a flower, and hard to love a snake. Take these women's unholy souls instead, oh goddess. Finally, as the sun rose, I took an hour's rest.

MARTINA

The knock was like an insistent woodpecker or a dog aggressively thumping its foot, pulling me out of what had been a well-deserved sleep. We hadn't even spent twenty-four hours with this group, but it was already apparent that we'd be seeing, hearing, and doing more than we'd care to while they were on property. I rolled over and kissed Margaret on the cheek. She'd told me before bed that the Miami people had already polished off two and a half days' worth of the week's booze, which meant I'd be making a Costco run in the morning on top of everything else.

"I'll get it," I said. "You sleep."

The clock read 10:30 P.M. Not the middle of the night, but not appropriate, either. I'm not saying it was the first time a guest had roused me after hours, but that didn't make it less irritating.

The knocks grew louder, and a screechy voice sounded from the other end. "Martina, hon. You in there?"

Christ. Not even one of the Miami people. It was the chatty Vero lady who honestly stuck out from that crowd like an abscessed tooth. I threw a robe over my T-shirt and shorts and opened the door.

On the other side, Carol Ann was lit up, her eyes glistening and her tight clothes damp with sweat. She smelled feral, like my dog when he's on the chase.

"I got one," she said.

I shook my head. She didn't seem the type, but it seemed pretty clear that she was on some kind of hallucinogenic drug.

Then she said, "A Burmese. Down there by the lake. Sorry to bother you, but I figured we should dispose of it and notify the state before anyone stumbles on it tomorrow."

Her Cheshire cat smile told me she was both proud and teeming with adrenaline. I sucked my teeth. If she was hallucinating, she was having a pretty weird one, even for this place.

"I'll call the Invasive Species Hotline," I said. Then, second-guessing myself, "But maybe I'll have a look at it myself first."

The night was too humid for a robe, so I shrugged it off and slipped into my outdoor sandals. Carol Ann trailed me like a triumphant toddler, and I'll be damned, that lady was telling the truth.

A few feet from the Shiva Lake shoreline, a freshly shot python lay lifeless in the grass. It had to have been a nine-footer. Easily. A pro trapper would've cashed in more than gas money for that sucker but, unfortunately, amateur hunters can't claim compensation. No matter, though. The bragging rights were prize enough.

"Congrats," I told Carol Ann, realizing that maybe she wasn't on drugs, after all. Or maybe she was and also got lucky running into a Burmese during her night walk. I didn't bother asking about the firearm she used, which obviously hadn't been borrowed on-property. None of my business, really. We don't have a policy on the books about it.

"What now?"

A shaky voice cut through the dark. Jessica, one of the Miami women. First impression wasn't too bad. She seemed like the people-pleasing kind. Someone who's over the top with staff so that everyone likes her, which is fine with me. Weird bedfellow for Carol Ann, though. I wouldn't have pegged those two as bonding.

"Now I bag him and call the state. You all can head to bed, though. I'm sure you have a full day of . . . yoga . . . tomorrow."

Jessica looked relieved and shuffled back toward her villa. Carol Ann, though. She wanted to stay and watch. Definitely on drugs, I decided.

SHAKTI

NOW

I wasn't aware of the Burmese python or the gun. This is the first I'm hearing about it, but I can tell you that I absolutely support the humane execution of an invasive species. When an animal with no natural predators is allowed to proliferate in a new environment, it wreaks havoc on the local ecosystem.

I went to bed before the others that night, shortly after dinner. It had been a long day and I needed to replenish my energy for the rest of the retreat. How could I hold space for my students if I was depleted myself?

We began our rigorous yoga practice the next day and I spent the early morning hours setting up the studio and preparing my sequences. Daniel, as my apprentice, arrived shortly after me and we went over the flow together so he could be ready with demonstrations and adjustments.

The tension was thick that morning as the students trickled in, as I knew it would be, given how some of the women had been arguing the evening before. But it wasn't my place to pry or judge. Only to listen and spread light.

Daniel seemed peaceful and grounded, as usual, focused on the yoga practice and on his role of assisting me. He did not appear to be involved in the women's griping.

I believe in the healing power of yoga. And that morning in practice, everyone was able to shed their outside distractions and embrace their essential oneness. We raised our vibration as a group and lifted our hearts and our voices in the chanting of *lokah samastah sukinho bhavantu*, may all beings everywhere be happy and free. When they went back out into the world after class, however—well, I can't really speak to that. I wasn't there.

All I know is this—by the time they showed up for my meditation class, they'd lost all of their morning yoga glow.

JESSICA

After Carol Ann executed the invasive python (with terrifying efficiency, I might add), she ran off to wake up Martina so the animal could be reported to the state and disposed of. That left me alone with the dead snake and other potential creatures I couldn't even see in the dark. I'm no stranger to Florida wildlife, but come on.

I backed away from the carcass (you know, just in case it, like, wasn't dead) and then spotted what was either the moon's reflection glinting off the lake's surface or two large reptilian eyes assessing the situation. Thank god I hadn't taken those mushrooms.

By the time I made it back to my villa, I'd expended enough adrenaline for a lifetime. I didn't even bother with a shower. Just texted a quick *good night* to my Sky and TJ group chat, stripped off my stupid sundress, and slipped under the covers, allowing the wall-mounted A/C unit to whir me to sleep in seconds.

You would have thought I'd suffer a fitful night's sleep after the horrible fight with Indira and the existential threat to my reputation and career (thanks to a truly moronic influencer). And, oh yeah, the giant snake. But no. I slept like I'd taken Ambien and fallen into a luxurious bed at the George V in Paris.

Mind you, the Namaste Club mattresses reminded me of my college futon and the thread count on the sheets was comparable to single-ply toilet paper (so much for "private luxury experience"). But I was exhausted all the way into my bones, which negated all the discomforts.

When I woke up the next morning, with a slight headache and smelling like I'd just played tennis, it was after 9:00 A.M. Meaning I'd missed the morning "hike" and breakfast, and was in danger of being late (again) for the morning yoga practice. I was killing it on this retreat. Literally.

The awkwardness of seeing Indira didn't seem as bad as the shame I'd feel from flaking on the entire day, so I quickly popped two Excedrin and rinsed off the previous day's sweat. I riffled in my underwear bag for a workout thong and felt a stab of embarrassment when I accidentally grabbed one of the lacy ones I'd packed in case things got handsy between Daniel and me. So. Cringe. (As my daughter would say.)

Damage control on the Allison Kent scandal would have to wait. For one, I was still feeling bruised by Indira and wasn't in the mood to do her any favors, even though it was my *job* to handle things like that. One I take seriously, I should add. But also, couldn't it wait until after yoga? Surely I'd have a clearer marketing brain after vinyasas and ujjayi breathing.

I dressed, slathered some SPF on my face, called Sky and TJ and told them I was having a wonderful time, and grabbed my mat, miraculously making it to the Active Room before opening *om*s. Of course, after "hiking" (walking! The grounds are flat!) and breakfast together, Shakti and the participants all seemed chummy and comfortable with one another and were chatting in the front of the room. Whatever. I kept my eyes down and set up toward the back.

Carol Ann placed her mat down next to mine and gave me a smile that was so broad and sympathetic, I regretted judging her so harshly with my first impression.

"I hope I didn't scare you off last night." She patted my knee. "I'm always carrying, especially out in nature. You never know what you're going to come across." Her overprocessed hair was pulled back into a high bun, and she looked cute in a Fox News kind of way.

Was she saying that she kept a *gun* on her at all times? I shuddered at the thought. But maybe she had a point? I mean, what would have happened if she wasn't there last night? That giant snake was right behind me. And god knows what else was back there. I wasn't sure if snakes eat humans, but I'd heard somewhere before that they can eat deer. So it definitely seemed possible.

As if reading my mind, Carol Ann said, "Don't worry. Pythons haven't been known to kill people. But they disrupt our local ecology. They're apex predators, you know."

I nodded, even though I wasn't positive that I knew any of those things. "It was an impressive shot," I said.

She shrugged and waved it off, which made me think she knew exactly how good of a shot she was and, honestly, good for her.

Shakti called out for us to *find our mats* and *take a comfortable seat*, and I took that as my cue to scan the rest of the room. Barbara was next to Carol Ann, already with her eyes closed and swaying to some unknown melody, her impressively rosy nipples peeking through an airy cheesecloth-looking tunic. I wanted some of whatever she was drinking. Indira and Daniel were in the front with their mats placed closer than was necessary, she in full lotus for no apparent reason, and he in half lotus. Why did she have to look so goddamn stoic all the time?

I crossed my legs and squeezed my hands on top of my knees. Indira was being such a bitch. But why? Yes, the influencer marketing play was an epic failure, but I wasn't the one who publicly embarrassed the brand. Technically, I was vaguely responsible for it, but again, I had no idea that Allison Kent was going to do something so bizarre and gross. There were no clues to suggest she was capable of it. It was like when Britney Spears shaved her head, and we were all like "what?"

I'd made an honest mistake. But Indira's reaction was both disloyal as a friend and unprofessional as a boss. What? Was she going to rake me over the coals, too? Or just flaunt how much hotter she is by dangling my secret crush in front of me like Regina fucking George.

But maybe this is what I should have expected all along from someone like her, someone who cheated on her husband while their young daughter was waiting for her back home. I mean, what does that say about her character? Meanwhile, Tom was doing the exact same thing to me, and she knew that. She held my hand and watched me cry and didn't speak a goddamn word—like "What a piece of shit" or "How awful"—because what could she even say? She was just as fucking bad.

I was seething, but then before I knew it, I was flowing through sun salutations and breathing and sweating and it felt *good*. I was in control of my body, not distracted and thinking about other people and how they'd disappointed me. I was letting that shit go. Like a damn yogi.

CAROL ANN

I've gotta *nama-say*—the retreat has been blessed from the moment I stepped on-site. Seriously, what were the odds that I'd come across a Burmese python my first night, and just by accident? Beau and I have gone on guided hunting trips in the Everglades and come home with zero. Zip. This had to have been more than luck—this felt like destiny.

There's an electric kind of feeling to the air here, and I picked up on it right away. Who knows, maybe I even had a sixth sense about it when my New York clients first mentioned the place. I didn't particularly love *them*, but something they said about the Namaste Club stuck with me. And I do not believe in coincidences. Our Father gives us exactly what we need, when we need it, as long as we stop to *listen*.

My husband goes to sleep on the early side, so I texted him a little love note before I went to bed the first night and called him when I woke up the next morning.

"You won't believe what happened, Beau," I said. "Hold on. Let me send you a couple of pictures."

I had been dying to send them overnight but wanted to hear the surprise in his voice when I told him about the kill, so I waited.

"Babe, slow down," he said. "Where is Kam's lunchbox? It's not next to Katie's. It's not where your note said it was going to be."

I cringed. I'd tried to leave everything perfect, so it would be easy for Beau to handle the kids while I was gone but damn, I must've made a mistake.

"Shoot, honey. I think I washed it. Check the laundry room."

I heard him rustling around on the other end of the line and my stomach sank. I'd put him in a tricky position having to fly solo. He wasn't used to all the childcare responsibilities, and here I was eating delicious food, blissing out on meditation, and shooting snakes.

"I'm sorry about that," I said.

"Found it. Laundry room." He sighed. "So how's the retreat so far? Are you clearing your mind and all that?"

"Honestly, yes!" I said. I put the phone on speaker while I laid out my gym clothes for the day: a tangerine-colored set with a white tank top. "The ladies here are a little *different,* but they seem nice. And I love the yoga teacher. There's one guy here, which is a little weird, but whatever. But Beau, you won't believe what happened last night . . ."

"Excuse me, CA. Did you say there was a guy there? Wasn't this supposed to be a ladies' retreat?"

I pinched my nose. Of course he would feel uncomfortable with that. I'd feel the exact same way if the roles were reversed. If he was on a work trip and there was some female waltzing around, I'd be there in a heartbeat, wearing something classy but flattering to let her know that my husband was more than taken care of.

"Oh, honey. Don't even worry about that. He's not an alpha. He's not even a beta. Nothing worth talking about."

But he wasn't letting it go easily. "That's just great, babe. You're out in your tight spandex for a week with some dude and I'm making lunches and lining up for school pickup. We're going to have a talk about this when you get back home."

I'd prepped all the lunches and dinners for him and the kids before I left, so it was a little unfair of him to throw that in my face, but he did have a point. I was having a great time, and he was holding down the fort.

"I'm so sorry, Beau. I honestly had no idea about the man. And

I really appreciate everything you're sacrificing for our family this week." It was quiet on the other end, and I could tell he was cooling. "But seriously, check out the photos I just sent you."

There was a pause and then Beau gasped. "Is that what I think it is? How the hell?"

"I know, a nine-and-a-half-footer. We measured. Pure luck. I was just standing there down by the lake, and it caught my eye." I started pulling my clothes on so I wouldn't be late for the morning hike but was glad to hear Beau's awestruck reaction on the phone.

"And you hit it between the eyes like that? One shot?"

"One shot, baby." I'm sure he heard the smile on my lips.

He hmphed on the other end. "That's my girl. Wow. Maybe I should come on down there if they've got a python issue. Hey, you want to talk to the kids?"

I felt a twinge of guilt. Beau had always dreamed of nabbing a Burmese and there I was bragging about it. But before I could apologize, I wanted to talk to the kids. I missed them badly. This week would be the longest I'd ever been away from them, and it was breaking my heart to picture them dressed and ready for school without Mama ready to drive them.

I told the kids about the python, too. About how afterward I helped the groundskeeper collect it and bag it for the state. They were adorable, so giddy about the whole thing, asking for graphic details about how it looked and smelled postshooting. A kid's curiosity is boundless at their ages. Then I wished them a beautiful and blessed day and told them how much I loved and missed them.

I hung up the phone and stole one last look in the mirror before heading out for the day, excited to start in on the retreat itinerary. Everything so far had been such a pleasant surprise. The classes. The food. Even, surprisingly, the company. It was already taking my mind off the situation at home. A literal breath of fresh air.

I met the rest of the group for the morning hike in front of the Awakening Fire Pit. Well, everyone except for that woman, Jessica, who was late the day before, too, so that wasn't too much of a surprise. I wondered if maybe she was avoiding her fancy ethnic friend (not that I'd blame her).

The fire pit was still smoldering with last night's embers, and I was tempted to breathe in the char and smoke. It's an aroma that always brings me back to my childhood, reminding me of s'mores and sleep-away camp.

Daniel led the hike and was already shirtless for some God-known reason. He reminded me of those boys in high school who'd try to get girls' attention by flexing in the hallway out of absolutely nowhere. Those were the same guys who went dateless to prom.

We toured the Namaste Club grounds, even hiking through the banyan trees and around the lake a little bit. As we passed the area where I'd shot the snake, a smile overtook my face. The memory of the surprise kill came like the perfect dream, vivid and exhilarating, except it had been real. I could even spot some blood stains still dotting the earth where it had died and thought about telling the others what had happened. I didn't want to seem braggy, though, so kept it to myself. At least for now.

The hike ended with breakfast at the Nourishment Pavilion, where a whole spread was waiting for us inside the covered patio: fresh yogurts, homemade breads and sausages, and local fruits like papayas, bananas, and oranges. I was in heaven, which made me feel even worse for Beau, who was probably letting cereal and milk congeal in bowls in the sink while he was at work. I drew the long straw this week and I'm totally aware of that.

Shakti and Daniel left the meal early to set up the yoga space, so I found myself talking to Indira while Barbara watched us and smiled. They seemed nice enough, even if the Barbara lady was a few grapes short of a bunch. Great body, though. For an older lady. Indira and I discussed our wellness regimens and supplement routines, and it turned out we had a lot of common ground there. By the sound of it, we might single-handedly be keeping the collagen industry in business. Even

Barbara was nodding along. None of us are twenty anymore, and these old skin and bones need all the help they can get!

The day seemed destined to pass in the idyllic manner of a Sandals commercial. Utterly indulgent. I couldn't remember the last time I didn't have to make meals, answer clients, and chauffeur children on repeat. This was a true vacation.

I went to yoga and sweated my butt off. It was a *strong* class, with lots of arm balances and push-ups. Shakti really knows how to keep everyone moving and grooving. Lots of people were taking little breaks here and there but I kept up, even though I'm not a die-hard yogi, thanks to all my hours in the gym.

After class, we had some free time and I used it to cool down with a jog around the lake. With my muscles warm and pleasantly sore and the mourning doves fluttering overhead, it felt like nothing in the world could spoil the day's splendor. When I came back, though, Jessica and Indira were blowing up at each other again around the Enlightenment Circle. There were lots of raised voices and hand gestures, and I was momentarily triggered back to that awful day at school with those woke moms. The day that sent me to the Namaste Club in the first place.

Whatever was going on with those two, it wasn't my battle. I decided to talk to Shakti about it after meditation. Someone needed to keep an eye on those ladies to make sure they didn't ruin it for everyone. But then in the next class, before I could even have the conversation, Indira and Jessica aired all their stinking laundry for the whole group to smell.

We were sitting in a circle and had placed ourselves in the same arrangement as the day before, like we'd given ourselves assigned seating. Shakti started the class by playing her crystal bowls, the otherworldly hum of it practically lifting my body off the floor. I deepened my breath and committed to releasing my distractions and my ego and all my outside worries.

Shakti welcomed us in her teacherly way and asked each student to state our intention for the week. I went first.

"Hi, again, everyone. Carol Ann here. My intention for the week is to be less judgmental, to let go of things that aren't serving me, and to balance a handstand. Can I say all that?"

Shakti made an *mmm* sound and nodded. "That's great. Well, technically you said three things, but I think it's wonderful that you have so many goals for this journey. I hope we can guide you to realizing each one of them."

Jessica went next and I could tell that the woman was on edge. Between all the lateness and crying and fighting with her friend, my spidey senses told me to keep my distance, *but* I'd also just said I intended on being less judgmental so—I needed to at least try to keep an open mind.

Her hair was still dripping from the shower and her yoga clothes looked a tad too big, but maybe she'd recently lost weight. "Yeah, I'm Jessica. As you know," she said. "And my intention is to be strong within myself and not let others affect my happiness." She sniffed a little and paused. "And to not be a whore."

We all gasped. I looked around the room and everyone looked equally shocked. Well, everyone except Daniel, who was kind of creepily smiling. Ugh.

I thought Shakti might step in and moderate, but Indira spoke first.

"I'm Indira. And my intention is to keep being my own woman and not throw little pity parties for myself whenever any minor thing doesn't go my way, and to not play the victim every time I make a mistake. Because that shit is pathetic." She smiled in that no-teeth way people do when they want to act unfazed but are clearly fuming inside.

"Okay, ladies . . ." Shakti tried to take the reins, but Jessica swooped back in.

"Sure. It must be easy to do all that when you're morally bankrupt and don't care about the people you are hurting."

This must be what it felt like to be on a prank show or an episode of the *Real Housewives*. I wouldn't have been surprised to turn around and see a camera crew. It was almost like they *wanted* the attention.

Indira didn't let Jessica's comment slide.

"This isn't about me, and you know it. This is about your husband not loving you enough and then leaving you. And now you're project-ing all of that on me, like some sad old spinster."

I covered my mouth and glanced again at Shakti, who looked too stunned to speak. Barbara appeared to be in deep meditation, and Daniel was still smiling, like he was *enjoying* it.

"Right, I wouldn't expect you to know anything about that." Jessica was practically foaming at the mouth. "Considering you were so bored with your own husband, you decided to start fucking everything in town with a heartbeat. Do you have any idea how much it hurts to be cheated on?"

"Oh, hell no," I accidentally said out loud. It just slipped out. I know I vowed to be nonjudgmental, but cuckolding? Adultery? What kind of *woman* is even capable of that?

Indira looked like she'd been slapped, so at least she had the good sense to feel ashamed by the accusation. Then, with the way she stut-tered in response, I knew what Jessica had said must be true. And Indira was a mother? Her poor child. Growing up with a role model like that.

"You know why I called you a French bulldog?" Indira said, teeth gritted. "Because you're either stupidly affectionate or misguidedly ag-gressive, with no in between."

Shakti finally found her voice. "That's enough ladies. This is a meditation. Let us clear this negativity by being mindful together."

But it was too late. Jessica stood up and stomped toward the door, both hands covering her face. She'd almost made it outside when In-dira called after her. "Go ahead and leave. I doubt Daniel will want to fuck you after he's seen how pathetic you are, anyway."

A tiny part of me was exhilarated to see I wasn't the only one with lady drama, but this was so damned inappropriate. In a soothing med-itation, of all places! Those women needed Jesus.

INDIRA

Jessica stormed out of group meditation because she's basically an attention-seeking toddler. And yet, I knew I was the one who had gone too far. First, with my reaction to the Allison Kent scandal, but even more so when I took Daniel to my room in front of her face. We didn't have sex. I just wanted a back massage, but it was a low blow, and I can't even blame the mushrooms. I had known what I was doing.

Honestly, it had been a shit evening in more ways than one and I had been feeling angry, and raw, and weak. And high. Before dinner, I'd called Tara, who of course didn't answer. So I tried Mother, who answered right away, with a curt, "We are cooking dinner together. Call you later." Then she hung up. I could practically smell the daal and paneer and chana, Savera's signature at-home dishes. And it made my heart ache.

That was before the stupid influencer comment and the dustup with Jessica, which were honestly the last straws. Sometimes the people you love are the ones who scrape your nerves the most, and that's definitely the case with Jess. She's bright, and funny, and a great mom. A loyal friend. But man, she can get my blood pressure up.

Maybe her crazy outburst at the meditation pressed on the thing that really bothers me. The thing I don't like to admit to myself. Which is that all her sadness, and her marriage exploding, was caused by the very same thing I'd done to my ex-husband. I was the Tom in my relationship. And seeing the fallout from that type of betrayal written on her face every day . . . I don't know. It sets me off.

When my husband stopped having sex with me, when the writing was on the wall that our connection had been broken, I should have been strong enough to leave. But I didn't think I could do that to Tara and be responsible for ruining her childhood. Obviously, what I did was worse. I'd taken Grey's disinterest in me as a wholesale rejection and begun to believe that no man would ever want me. That I was past my prime. But then my Pilates instructor, Manuel, started paying extra attention to me, keeping me to talk after class, squeezing my arms before I left. We started sneaking around. He was romance-novel-cover hot and had a deep understanding of the body. Very deep. I told myself it would be a one-time deal. Then once a month. Then once a week. You get the gist. But I started getting sloppy. My therapist thinks it's because I wanted to get caught, but I don't buy that at all. I think it was more like temporary insanity. None of my decisions during that time period were rational.

My husband found a fucking condom wrapper in my bathroom wastebin and that was it, our marriage exploded like a birthday party piñata. The worst part of the whole thing is that Tara knows about the affair, though I have no idea who let it slip, and if I did know, Lord, have mercy on their souls. She may never fully forgive me, no matter how much I overcompensate. Which I do with designer clothes, expensive vacations, and effusive praise. It's okay. I know I don't deserve her absolution.

And all while this was happening in my life, Tom apparently was fucking around with Jessica's dermatologist, Sky's elementary school guidance counselor, and god knows who else. It absolutely destroyed my friend. Of course it did. She'd given up her career, identity, and youth for that man and he tap-danced all over her heart in return. Jess knew what had broken up my family, but I obviously couldn't talk to her about it. It would have been morbidly insensitive, even though

I was also suffering. Everywhere I turned, the devastating effects of infidelity loomed.

I need her to pick up and move on with her life to prove that what I did can be okay in the end. That people can move on and fuck shirtless yoga bros, and start new careers, and discover that their remaining years can be their best ones yet.

I had hoped Jessica would carpe the damn diem on this trip but when she seemed incapable of doing that, I dangled Daniel in front of her face instead. Yuck. When I took him to my room, I knew exactly what he must have been thinking. But there was no way I could have gone through with it. Can you imagine the awkward squeezing and thrusting and grunting with that one? Daniel probably fucks like a teenager who just listened to a Blink-182 song (judging by his *sk8er boi* tattoo).

Everyone was staring at me following Jess's dramatic exit, which wasn't surprising. Throwing in that extra bit about Daniel not wanting to fuck her was pretty awful. And it wasn't even true. I'm sure that guy would hump an anthropomorphic goat. But she'd taken aim at me and hit a bull's-eye with her infidelity comment. What came out of my mouth next had been almost involuntary.

Shakti struggled to conjure words in the wake of the fight. With her mouth agape and hands fidgeting, her stunned silence was painful to watch.

Thankfully, Carol Ann cut the silence. "Well, then? Should we get on with it?"

Everyone closed their eyes and put their hands on their knees. Shakti snapped back into teacher mode and went into some inspirational talk about clearing blockages and *accepting all thoughts, even negative ones, before releasing them*. What I really wanted to do was run out of the room and track down Jessica. Maybe even apologize. But I sat in stillness instead.

Someone should've handed me an Oscar, because my quiet reflection face might have looked calm, but those forty-five minutes stretched out like an all-day Saturday detention. Shakti guided us through a full-body relaxation in her best soft guru voice, but I was screaming on the inside the entire time. I tried to maintain my composure while vacillating between being angry at myself, at Jessica, at Allison Kent, at all the ex-husbands in the world, and even at Shakti, because her voice was getting on my nerves.

We all took corpse pose—lying down, face up on our mats—for final relaxation, while Shakti chanted *om namah shivaya.* I tried to melt into the floor, hoping it would swallow me whole and deposit me anywhere else. It felt good to be lying down, though, and I was relieved the class was almost over.

Then I felt two hands pushing down on my shoulders, pinning them to the floor and then gently rocking them back and forth. I peeked one eye open and smiled. Daniel. He was apprenticing, but it still seemed intentional that his focus was just on me. Even if I wasn't physically attracted to him, I can't pretend I didn't enjoy the special attention. I closed my eyes again and allowed him to take me deeper into the Savasana. He slipped his fingers lower down my chest and I clenched to keep the wetness that followed from staining my yoga pants. Hadn't I just been regretting bringing him to my room, given what it had done to my friendship with Jessica? God, I was a bitch sometimes.

He stepped away from me and I bit my lip to hide the smile on my face. Shakti had gone silent, allowing us to spend the final moments of class deeply immersed in our own relaxation. I couldn't help it; I felt a little giddy. Then I heard a deep moan. Trying to be subtle, I turned my head and parted my eyes. Barbara was in savasana, heaving her chest, as Daniel stood directly on top of her like a creepy disbarred chiropractor, pressing into her chest and rubbing circles from her lower pecs to her shoulders. So. Gross.

I squeezed my eyes closed and tried not to throw up in my mouth. As it turns out, I'm not just a bitch. I'm also a complete idiot.

SHAKTI

Fighting. Jealousy. Those things are always related to the ego. It's the inflated sense of self that causes people to compare themselves with others, to allow someone else's words or actions to mirror back what we dislike about ourselves.

The only way to overcome that kind of suffering is to embrace our *lack* of individuality. We must become one with the universe's energies. From the tiny ant to the mighty elephant, we must recognize our sameness. Only when we embrace this collective consciousness may we shed the burden of human suffering.

That was the last blowup, at least that I saw, between Jessica and Indira.

CAROL ANN

Evil begets evil, you know. That's why, after Jessica and Indira tussled at the beginning of meditation, a whole can of rotten beans was opened. Sweet baby Jesus.

Poor Shakti seemed off her game, but who could blame her? Even a professional, a spiritual healer, is allowed to get rattled in the face of inappropriate behavior. But I made the most of it and found my happy place while sitting there, legs crossed and eyes closed. I was thinking about that perfect shot, over and over. How the Glock became an extension of my hands, and the bullet was like a laser that shot from my heart and into the python's brain. It was really just so beautiful when I stopped to think about it. As perfect as my babies on the day they were born.

At the end of meditation, we all lay down like we do in yoga classes, and I was so relaxed and at peace that I woke up snoring a little bit. Something had startled me, and not just the sound coming from my nose. Someone had their *hands* on my feet. Giving them a *massage*. At first, I thought it was Shakti, with one of those weird but sweet yoga touches she does, but I peeked my eyes open, and it was that *man*. Daniel.

Thank God my husband wasn't there or this perv would have been the next invasive python at the Namaste Club. I made a face at him and kicked my feet a little bit. He walked off, looking unperturbed, and started putting his hands all over Indira instead. I knew he was suspicious from the second I saw him.

When we were released from class, I knew two things for sure: I was going to stay away from Daniel and also avoid Indira like the China virus. Those lusty heathens had no business in a spiritual place such as this, and I wasn't inviting *any* more drama into my life.

Maybe I'd judged the chronically late woman too harshly. It's an annoying habit, for sure, but not exactly a deadly sin. And I wasn't in the mood for a *silent* journey, like that kooky Barbara. I needed someone else to talk to while Shakti was busy setting stuff up. Also, Jessica seemed like she could use a friend.

We all washed up and met for cocktails and dinner at the Nourishment Pavilion, which was a pretty old-Florida indoor-outdoor space with a big, open dining area and an outdoor patio with a tiki-style bar. It reminded me of a small-town wedding venue for young couples. Kind of like the one Beau and I rented out for ours.

I found Jessica by the bar, ordering a drink from Martina's helper lady.

"Hey there." I slid next to her and put a hand on her shoulder. "Glad to see you out and about, enjoying a nice drink." I turned and waved to Martina's friend. "I'll have a Moscow mule, please."

"One double spicy margarita and one Moscow mule," the bartender repeated, then turned around to get started on the drinks.

"Double, huh?" I said, impressed. "Let's not waste any time tonight."

Jessica laughed. "At this point, I could use an IV of tequila." She shook her head. "I can't believe I melted down like that in front of everyone. At meditation practice, no less!"

I waved it off. "You should have seen the meltdown that sent me here in the first place. Yours was *nothing*. And by the way, I don't know all that happened between you girls, other than the silly work thing. But I can just tell it wasn't your fault."

What I wanted to say is that Indira seemed like a loose woman but decided to keep it to myself. It obviously wasn't a detail Jessica didn't know, anyway.

Jessica looked relieved. Her shoulders relaxed as she reached for the fresh double marg. "Thanks, I really appreciate that. Honestly. I should probably apologize to Shakti, though. How was the rest of the class?"

"It was a little weird," I said. "But don't worry. Shakti is a professional. And she doesn't strike me as the judgmental type."

My drink came out next and I lifted the glass. "Cheers! To a peaceful rest of the week. Meltdown-free." I winked.

"Meltdown-free," Jessica repeated and clinked my glass with hers. She took a long sip and coughed. "Damn. That's strong."

"Hallelujah!" I said. "By the way, you look really nice tonight. I love that color on you."

She flushed a little and tugged on her dress. It was a fitted maxi in a vibrant teal, with spaghetti straps and a low-cut neckline. "Oh, thank you. I don't usually dress so *boldly*. Actually, Indira bought me this one."

"Hmm," I said. I guess that wasn't surprising. Not that I have anything against suggestive clothing. God gave us our bodies to rejoice and celebrate. Not to share with whoever comes along tickling our feet, but it's important to look good while out in the world.

Shakti joined us at the bar and beckoned to the bartender. "Enlightened Tequila and soda, please. Extra lime."

"Hey, girl," I said, squeezing her arm. "Great day today. Practice really got me sweating."

She folded me into her arms and, I swear, I felt the heat of pure love in her embrace. I could tell I was in the presence of a special woman. A healer.

"Thank you," she said, releasing me.

Jessica took another sip of her drink. "Shakti." She shifted on her feet a little. "I am so embarrassed by what happened at meditation today. I'm sorry about it."

"Nooooo." Shakti shook her head vigorously. "Never be sorry. Never apologize. You must accept your surroundings exactly as they are, even when they appear to be painful or challenging. Only when we release those tensions may we become cleansed." She wrapped Jessica in a hug. "I'm glad it happened. Congratulations. On your growth."

Jessica stumbled back. "Oh, great. Thank you," she said.

"Go in light," Shakti said. She took her drink off the bar. "Ladies, dinner is served. I'll see you inside."

Jessica and I sat together in the dining room, getting to know each other better over braised cabbage and freshly caught mahi-mahi. It was funny. The dynamics between her and her friend, or frenemy to be more accurate, had clearly shifted from the day before. At that dinner, Jessica had appeared to be pandering to Indira, seeking her approval, and later, begging for her forgiveness. But on this night, Jessica didn't so much as peer in her direction, while Indira kept stealing hopeful-looking glances at us. She was sitting with Barbara, so there was nothing for her to talk about there.

"The food here is fabulous," I said. "I love how fresh everything is."

"It really is. I think most of the produce comes from a garden over by Martina's residence." Jessica wiped her mouth. "The fish is really good, but I have to say. Kinda miss the boar tonight."

A lightbulb went off in my brain. "Hey!" I slapped the table. "We have some free time tomorrow. Let's take out a couple of rifles from the Activities Center and do a boar hunt. They have a bunch of them living here on-property."

I had been planning on taking Indira, but after I learned what kind of person she was? Hell no.

"It'll be fun," I said, reaching out for her hand. "You don't have to shoot if you don't want to. But if you love the meat, you might as well see where it comes from."

Jessica chuckled like a nervous schoolgirl. "No, you're right. And I have no doubt you're a pro, after what I saw yesterday. But . . . is it dangerous?"

It was my turn to laugh. "It can be," I admitted. "In the wild, these hunts are done with tracking dogs and can be pretty dramatic. But on a property like this? It's like Disney World. Point. Shoot. Dinner."

"Let me sleep on it," Jessica said. "Though it might be cathartic to do something like that after everything that's happened the last two days."

"Absolutely." I took my last bite of fish.

"Hey." Jessica drained her cocktail. "You said you had some kind of drama before you came here. What happened? From one meltdowner to another."

I really didn't want to get into all that. You never quite know where people's sensitivities lie, and I didn't have a solid read on exactly where Jessica would fit on the spectrum. But I also wasn't ashamed of anything I did, and she wasn't in any position to judge, so whatever.

I tapped a finger to my lips. "Tell you what. If you come on a boar hunt with me tomorrow, I'll give you the whole story."

BARBARA

The cosmotini made me feel silly, like I wanted to play jokes and laugh with the other yogi and yoginis. But that was proving impossible, since the selfie-taker, Indira, had claimed most of my evening, ranting on and on about her jewelry business and what it meant to her. I suspect she wanted me to absolve her from the plastic-water-bottle friend's accusations. The cheating and the sexual things. But I didn't care about any of that in the first place. I'd never shame someone for their desires.

In fact, if I hadn't taken my vow of silence, I would have told her that the real problem was with her socialized thinking. There's no reason that someone cannot enjoy a husband, a lover, and a friend, all at the same time. Society has told us that sex is dirty, but all we need to do is look at the animals to understand our own nature. They don't limit themselves to the humping of only one partner, so why should we?

Since I couldn't say all that, I nodded along and periodically touched her hand, so she'd know that I cared. Even though her endless self-centered chatter was making me weary.

Sometimes, alcohol unearths the child inside me. The one who wants to play and not listen to trivial adult problems. I waited for Indira to yawn and took that as my cue, pretending it was contagious and stretching my arms overhead. It worked. She looked at me and said, "Well, I guess it's getting late."

I smiled and patted her on the shoulder, excusing myself from the table. But who should I choose to have a little fun with? Shakti was in a serious mood. She's not one to take her spiritual responsibilities lightly, which I do respect after what I learned reading her emails. I'm assuming she left her computer open in her room as a kind of confession, knowing that I'd come to empty her trash and make her bed and see them. Of course, she knows I wouldn't judge; everyone has a past. But it wasn't a time to seek her for play.

I could have tried with plastic-water-bottle Jessica and unnatural-looking Carol Ann, except they wore their energies too heavily for my taste. I wanted to be light and free. Then I saw Daniel, leaning against a highboy table, watching his phone. I giggled to myself and crept up to his back, tapping him on the shoulder.

When he turned around, I pointed and dashed off toward the woods. The trees and grasses became a verdant blur in my peripheral vision. My whole body felt light and alive, ignited with excitement and possibility. If we aren't on this planet to find connection with one another, then why would the gods have put us here together in the first place?

I ran until I was far away from the group, somewhere in an unexplored area by the groundskeeper's home. I heard the snorts of wild pigs in the distance, and they sounded like joyful friends.

Daniel is a like-minded creature. He understood my game and took off after me, peering behind the building structures and around bushes for my hiding place.

"Ready or not, here I come," he said, as he searched.

It was hard to stay silent with the thrill of being sought. I bit my lip, my whole body quaking with the effort to contain my laughter. Suddenly, I heard soft footsteps rustle near the corner where I lay crouched.

I held my breath. Closed my eyes. Then, "Gotcha!" Daniel jumped out in front of me, arms over his head like a happy monkey. I couldn't help it then, I spilled onto the earth, shaking with joy.

Daniel fell down beside me, and the two of us gazed up at the stars. Quiet for a moment. Then he spoke.

"You know, Barbara," he said. "I've always admired your practice, both physical and spiritual. I aspire to deepen my own understanding to one day be more like you."

We both turned our heads, our eyes meeting with a flash of soul's recognition. His jewel-toned irises sparkled like the stars overhead. A tear slid down my cheek. I knew he would achieve what he was wishing for. Pure wisdom and love were radiating behind his eyes.

He smiled beatifically and slowly rolled over, pulling his knees under him. Then, with a mischievous Hanuman smirk, he jumped to his feet and said, "Now you're *it*!" And ran off to his hiding place.

I counted to one hundred and readied myself for the hunt.

JESSICA

My phone blared with the 6:30 A.M. alarm, but my annoyance from being jolted awake was quickly replaced with terror for what lay ahead of me that day. Had I really agreed to go *hunting* with Carol Ann? Who even was I on this retreat? First with the public catfight and now this. Next thing you know, I'll be bleaching my hair and watching Newsmax.

Carol Ann was being over-the-top friendly to me. Actually, she might've been the only person who was being nice to me on that whole Gilligan's Island. Unless you counted Barbara, but I didn't want to be playing charades for the rest of my vacation. Of course, after my embarrassing fight with Indira, I could've just left. And maybe I still would. But for that moment, I was loving the food and the classes. Also, the retreat was four thousand fucking dollars, and I might not have a job when it's over, so I figured I'd at least attempt to enjoy it.

My crisis management strategy for Bougie Boho was already being executed. We were making public apologies, distancing ourselves from Allison Kent, disavowing her statements, and writing donations to the Jewish Federation (as if they weren't calling me enough already). I'd answered media requests, talked to upset customers, you name it. And can you guess who'd been noticeably absent for all of this? Indira.

You'd think she'd want to be front and center, since the brand is *her* baby, as she always says. But she couldn't seem to be bothered. She was cc'ed on all the emails; it's not like she didn't know what was going on. Indira either didn't care as much about the faux pas as she'd initially let on or she hated me so much that she was unwilling to engage with me even about business.

At least there was an apology. It came after dinner when I was walking back to my villa. I felt a tap on the shoulder and turned around to see Indira, looking sheepish for maybe the first time in her entire life.

"Listen, Jess," she said, looking at the ground, over my head, anywhere but in my eyes. "I know things have gotten a little out of hand these past two days, and I just wanted to say I'm sorry for my part in it."

Her part in it? It was a narcissist's explanation if I'd ever heard one. If the tables had been turned, she'd have expected me to beg for mercy on my hands and knees. I wasn't in the mood to be gaslighted.

"Thanks. Me, too," I said, then turned and headed back to my room.

That was the other thing about my hunting day with Carol Ann. Sure, I'd agreed to it in a moment of weakness, but it wasn't lost on me that this outing was originally supposed to be for Indira. She might have claimed Daniel in a petty fit of bitchiness, but I could take . . . a wild boar away from her? Maybe it wasn't as sexy, but it was something.

Indira is the kind of woman who always gets what she wants. And if it doesn't come to her naturally, she takes it. It never used to bother me. Before our divorces, when we'd meet for mommy wine hour on random Wednesdays, guys would always be sending her drinks. Maybe it gave me a little pang of jealousy, but then she'd ask for a second one, and by the end of the night we were just blatantly drinking for free. It's not just men, either. People in general are drawn to her like mosquitoes are attracted to my thighs. If not for Indira, my social circle would be pitifully small. I benefit, I suppose, from her magnetism. But sometimes, I wonder what it would be like to live outside her shadow.

Because I'd set an alarm like a proper grown-up, I actually made it to the morning "hike" that day. It was really a walk, as I'd suspected, around the retreat grounds that ended at breakfast. We walked together as a group, Indira and I frosting each other enough to be noticeable but without making everyone too uncomfortable (I hope). It was like when you break up with a boyfriend/coworker but still have to sit at meetings with each other, so you just avoid eye contact and laugh loudly at everyone else's jokes.

At least my kids had been having a great time while I was away, which made me both happy and a little jealous, if I was being honest. Tom was working overboard to impress them as the "fun parent" with cheap ploys to delight TJ and win back Sky's affection. Despite my protests, he'd pulled them out of school for a surprise Universal Studios vacation. I'm not opposed to playing hooky for forced family fun. I was just miffed that he got to do it on his watch. The irritation melted away on FaceTime, however, when Sky's and TJ's beaming faces lit up the screen, jubilant after telling me that Tom had thrown up after stepping off the Hulk roller coaster.

I shuddered as we passed through the banyans and around Shiva Lake, remembering the gigantic snake that nearly ate me (hey, you never know) on the first night. At least we were in the light of day, so the creatures had lost the element of surprise.

A scream rang out behind me, and I turned to see Indira covering her mouth and pointing to the lake. In the middle of the water, floating along the surface, was an average-size American alligator. Its brownish green skin was almost camouflaged in the murky lake, but as it slowly swayed its tail, ripples followed in its wake. Almost reflexively, Carol Ann and I looked at each other and laughed. Maybe we were more similar than I had thought.

"That swamp puppy is just enjoying a little morning bath. Nothing to worry about. Trust me. It's more afraid of *us* than we are of *it*," Carol Ann said.

Indira had gone pale. "Is that . . . an alligator or a crocodile?"

"Oh, don't be ridiculous." I swatted the words away. "You're not going to see any crocodiles this far from saltwater. I don't know why Martina even said that. That is just your basic bitch Florida gator."

People who aren't from Florida will never fully get it. You don't get out of bed for less than a Category 3 hurricane, and you definitely don't need to be spooked by an alligator having a swim in a lake. Indira was fooling herself. This was the same woman who had thought she'd enjoy spending the day *hunting*? Nature's splendor didn't seem like her thing, so it was good she wasn't coming on the wild boar adventure. Carol Ann hadn't flat-out said that Indira was disinvited, but it was pretty obvious that she'd chosen me instead.

Breakfast was so good that it made me wonder if my outbursts in meditation the day before were caused by hanger, since I'd missed breakfast that morning. Setting an alarm had been the right call. It meant I was treated to fresh banana pancakes, an acai bowl, and home-made chicken sausage. It was possible I'd become the first person in history to *gain* weight while on a yoga retreat.

At morning practice, we all found our same spots as the day be-fore, though I noticed Indira pulled her mat a little farther away from Daniel's. Guilt? Trouble in paradise? I didn't really care. She could have him.

Shakti chanted Hare Krishna to start the class, which is actually one of my favorite mantras. I looked over and Carol Ann had her eyes closed but her face was scrunched like she was smelling a fart. I tried not to giggle. At least she was open-minded enough to be there and participate.

I let go. My breath synchronized with my movements, and I al-lowed Shakti's dreamy Hindi-tinted cadence to carry me through the flow. The class was almost balletic. One pose melting into the next, shorter holds so it felt like we never stopped moving. In the middle of the practice, Shakti announced that we were going to slow it *down*, and instructed us to take a long downward dog.

I spread my fingers wide and pressed my hands into the mat, lift-ing my hips to the sky and stretching my heels to the ground. Was I getting good at this?

As I slowed my breath and tried to release deeper into the pose, I felt strong hands come onto my upper buttocks. I lifted my eyes and then tried to stifle a tiny welp. Daniel's feet were directly in front of my hands. He pushed down harder and then replaced his hands with his entire body, laying his hips on my back and his torso on my hips. Like, he could literally smell my butt if he wanted to, and if I lifted my head, it would graze the bottom of his balls. Okay, apparently, I was still a little into him.

He hadn't put his hands on me at all the day before—something I noticed with a combination of embarrassment and annoyance. But now? It felt good. He rooted me into the pose, but also, the touch was exhilarating. My mind flitted to a jumble of images: the sexy panties in my lingerie bag, the moistness forming between my legs, the smell of his sweat mixed with something coconutty.

Maybe Indira was wrong. Maybe Daniel *did* want to fuck me. Was that even something I could go through with? He was my teacher's assistant and in a position of service. Would having a physical relationship with him be taking advantage of a power imbalance, like that Anusara guy turning his students into a sex cult or Bikram generally being disgusting? Did my desire for Daniel make me a yoga predator?

The questions swirled in my head for the rest of class. After the downward dog adjustment, Daniel took a break from assisting to practice on his mat, demonstrating the more advanced postures with strength and grace—an effortless flying lizard, a pretzel-like standing backbend. I gazed at him with what I hoped was closer to respect than creepy leering. Then, when we took final rest on our backs, I felt him rubbing my feet. He lifted them off the ground, bringing my legs up, too, and swayed them back and forth as I surrendered my weight into his able hands.

He was strong yet gentle. His touch was simultaneously light but commanding. Neither hesitant nor intimidating. It felt amazing.

When the class was over, I gathered my mat and found the courage to approach him on my way out. He was in a corner of the room, stretching in a forward lunge.

"Hey, thanks so much for the adjustments." I hugged my mat for security. "They were really amazing today."

Daniel stepped out of his lunge and bowed. "I'm so happy you enjoyed them. Your practice is really coming along." He made a muscle with his biceps. "Getting strong."

I laughed nervously and shuffled my feet. "Thank you. I think the consistency is really helping."

We were holding eye contact the whole time. Didn't that mean something? A universal sign of mutual attraction? Daniel looked especially handsome, shirtless and with his man bun pulled tightly back, which highlighted his boyishly handsome face.

A hand flicked my ponytail. "Jess. We better get going if we're going to make the hunt. Martina is waiting for us."

I turned to find Carol Ann smiling, but with a look that said *hurry up*.

"Right!" I said, too brightly. "We better get going."

Daniel lifted an eyebrow. "Hunting, huh? Cool." He winked. "Bring me back something tasty."

I blushed and giggled like a schoolgirl, resisting the urge to run out the door as fast as I could before embarrassing myself further. Instead, I grabbed my belongings and walked out, pretending to be interested in my phone.

"Don't tell me you've got a thing for Creepy McTouchy over there," Carol Ann said, once we'd left the Active Room.

I feigned surprise. "No! Nothing like that. I know him from our studio in Miami. That's all. He's nice. Completely harmless."

We skirted around the Enlightenment Circle and picked up the pace toward Martina's residence at the edge of the property. "Oh okay. What does he do for a living, anyway?"

I had no fucking clue. But I assumed he had money based on his clothes and grooming and the brand-new Tesla he drove to and from the studio. Though in Miami, that didn't really mean anything. You never knew who was draped in luxury goods while also saddled with piles of debt.

"Umm, hedge fund, I think. Or commercial real estate development. Something like that."

Carol Ann turned to me and nodded like she was fake impressed.

"Okay. Sure." She skipped a few feet ahead. "Just let me know if you need any help with that one."

I'm sure she thought he was a huge player. Daniel definitely came across as a flirt (and had probably just banged my best friend, if I could still call her that). But I was an adult and not even looking for a relationship. Just a good time. Was that allowed? Indira certainly thought so.

Martina was waiting for us outside her residence, wearing full-body camo and a vest. She had three rifles leaned up against her porch railing and a dog sitting patiently at her feet. My stomach did a flip. Why do I get myself into these situations?

The funny thing is, I grew up in a household that considered swine to be unclean. We weren't hunting it and we most certainly weren't eating it. The consuming part changed for me with my first pregnancy (since I'd married a gentile anyway), but never did I think I'd be out in Central Florida, rifle in hand, procuring one for myself.

Carol Ann reached into her tote bag and then dropped it on the floor so she could pull a long-sleeve camouflage shirt over her green yoga outfit. *Smart,* I thought. She'd dressed for both the practice and the hunt. I was still wearing my soft pink yoga pants and bra set with an OM ALL-STARS T-shirt on top. At least I'd remembered to wear sneakers.

Martina nodded toward her deck, where a couple of clipboards with waivers were placed on a table. Ah yes, signing our lives away, whether to jump at a trampoline park or shoot deadly weapons at wild animals. At what point does one become desensitized to the dangerous world we live in because we are so used to literally signing our names in acknowledgment of possible death?

Our guide must have sensed my greenness, because after our requisite greetings and small talk, she asked me if I'd ever shot a gun.

"Haven't even held one," I said. I knelt down to pet the dog, a medium-size mutt-looking thing with a happy, sloppy tongue.

"That there's Scout and he's going to help us on the hunt." Martina smiled, revealing a mouthful of stained but strong-looking teeth. "He's a real good boy."

She looked me up and down. "You're along to watch only for today. If I'd known you were a first timer, I'd have set you up with shooting practice, but we're already running late. That okay?"

I exhaled a huge sigh of relief. "Yes! Perfectly." Knowing me, I'd Dick Cheney my first ever gunshot and hit one of the other ladies in the head.

We left our mats and tote bags at the residence, then Martina, Carol Ann, Scout, and I walked over to the Namaste Club's on-site boar preserve, which was in an area I hadn't yet explored. We passed a sawgrass field that was much less manicured than the retreat grounds and had little storage sheds littered along the way. Carol Ann and Martina discussed their experiences with "feral hogs," which is another term for the boars apparently, and their various hunting highlights while we walked.

I followed a few feet behind them, out of the line of fire, just in case a target jumped out in front of us. Scout trotted along ahead of the group, tail wagging.

"Hey, if the hogs are invasive and we need to kill them, why do they have a preserve here?" I asked, the question suddenly occurring to me as they went on and on about our responsibility to eliminate invasive breeders.

The women turned around and looked at me like I'd just asked if we should consider nonviolent mediation instead of shooting the boars.

"So we can hunt them," Martina said, as though that was the most obvious answer in the world. "It ain't like we're breeding them."

Carol Ann nodded authoritatively, and I pretended like that made total sense. "Right. Great."

I decided to keep my curiosities and opinions to myself for the rest of the adventure and pivoted to something less dangerous. (At least, I thought it was.)

"Didn't we make a deal, Carol Ann?" I asked playfully. "I come on this wild ride with you, and you tell me the real reason you came on the retreat."

We had just crossed through the sawgrass and into another expansive field. This one with shorter grass. Even though I was wearing sunglasses, I had to shade my eyes with one hand. In the scorching midday sun, the field was almost glowing.

Martina and Carol Ann stopped to load their guns.

"Oh, Lord. You really want to hear about that?" She snapped the rifle shut and took a few steps backward so the three of us were standing in a circle.

"It can't be any worse than calling out your boss's marital infidelity in the middle of a meditation class."

Carol Ann laughed. "All right, then. You better buckle up for this one."

CAROL ANN

The retreat was supposed to be an escape. Meaning, I hadn't wanted to tell anybody about the *incident*. But sometimes the truth will set you free, or so they say. Also, Jessica is a Florida girl, like me, so there's a certain level of understanding there. She and I were speaking plainly and hearing each other. Maybe she'd lend me a sympathetic ear about the whole thing.

I took a big breath and closed my eyes, bringing myself back to that day. It was a dreary, early October morning. Dark clouds threatened heavy rain, but it didn't come down until later that day. If God had seen fit to wash out the morning, maybe the thing never would've happened in the first place.

I had dropped the kids off at school, kissing their cheeks and handing them their lunch boxes, when one of my Mama Bear sisters grabbed me by the elbow outside of Kam's classroom and dragged me into the hallway.

"CA," she said, "did you hear what the woke mom brigade went and put in our library?"

I shook my head, blood already boiling. Vero Christian was supposed to be a sweet and inviting place, but it had been almost unbearable for me ever since those groomer nutjobs had been giving us hell. I have to believe that most people quietly appreciate the work we are doing; it's God's work after all. But can you believe that some of the Christian school moms were loudly *against* our good deeds in the community? They were so damned *triggered* by our organization.

My fellow Mama Bear squeezed my arms, her eyes watery with tears. "They filled it with those same books we got pulled from the public schools. The same damn ones. It's like they're *trying* to start a fight with us. What did we ever do to them?"

I was at a loss for words. I couldn't have been hearing her right. It was just too malicious. Some people just need to hate for the sake of it. It's sick. It's the devil's work.

"You've got to be kidding me," I said, finally.

She shook her head. "Unfortunately not. Go see for yourself." As if those lib moms hadn't already taken so much from us. They just do not stop.

So that's exactly what I did. I marched over to the Vero Christian school library and tore through the stacks. It didn't take me long to find the books. They weren't even hidden. Nope. The completely useless, America-shaming, indoctrinating books I had worked so hard to remove from public school shelves were front and center on a display table. Which meant that these other moms at *my* kids' school had the librarian put them there. The first books the children would reach for. They *wanted* me to see them. It was a clear provocation.

My inner Incredible Hulk busted out of my skin. Why would anyone do this? There are millions of age-appropriate elementary school books in the world. Why fill my children's library with *these* books?

Because the woke moms wanted a fight. That's why. Well, guess what? That's what I gave them.

They must have been waiting for me to discover their little prank, because little by little, the moms who were responsible started congregating in the library, arms crossed over their chests, like they'd proven some kind of point.

I was mad. Nuclear explosion mad. But I was smart, too. I knew my rights and I knew the law.

I burned a hole through their smug faces with my eyes, then snatched up all of the contraband books in my arms and stormed outside. I knew they'd be dumb enough to follow.

The morning's final image in my memory is almost beautiful, like the scene in that old pedo movie with the plastic bag floating in a breeze. Except, in my climactic moment, it was ribbons of paper, strewn on a concrete pavement.

JESSICA

The silence was becoming uncomfortable, as was the image of Carol Ann holding onto a rifle with her eyes closed. Finally, she spoke.

"Okay, so I founded an activist group in my hometown, Vero."

"Wow!" I said, genuinely impressed. I hadn't taken Carol Ann for the socially conscious type. "What type of activism do you do?"

She rested the trigger of the gun on her hip and pointed the barrel away from us.

"Well, we are wholly committed to protecting children." Her voice rose in tenor. "There are all kinds of sickos out there who are trying to sexualize kids. And then there's the indoctrination. Our youth are under attack! So I formed a group of the fiercest women I know, the Mama Bears. To combat child abuse in all its forms."

My throat tightened, not that I would have spoken even if I had the words. Carol Ann's speech was becoming more animated by the second, and she was carrying a deadly weapon. I swallowed hard.

"One of the most effective things we do is attend school board meetings and petition their members to remove pornographic and noneducational material from school libraries."

I don't know if I imagined it, but it looked like Martina took a step back. A bell rang in my head. Carol Ann was a *book banner*. And probably a lot of other horribly prejudiced things. Like one of the Gilead wives in *The Handmaid's Tale*. What. The. Fuck.

"We've been successful!" Carol Ann flipped her head, tossing her bright blond ponytail onto one shoulder. "So many delicate minds have been protected from the absolute *garbage* they stock in these classrooms and libraries. And it's *hard* work. People come and protest us all the time and we just have to suck it up and keep working. Listen, Jess. I don't know where your political sensibilities lie, but trust me, these books are trash. We aren't out there being willy-nilly with what we object to."

"Oh. Of course not," I said, because I'm a fucking coward. Something about the story was starting to sound familiar, but maybe just because book bannings in schools were becoming such a *thing* in Florida.

She shifted her weight. "What we do takes a lot of time and passion and love. And my kids don't even go to public school. I'm doing it for other people's kids. Children who are less fortunate and need someone to stand up for them."

I prayed for a feral hog to show up and distract everyone, but not a creature was stirring in the vast open preserve.

"My kids go to Christian school." She looked at Martina, who was stone faced, and then back to me. "And some crazy libtard moms heard about all the success we've had within the district. And do you want to know what they did?"

I really did, so I nodded.

"Those little she-devils stocked *our* private school library with some of the very books I had removed from the district."

It required every ounce of restraint in my body not to laugh at that.

"What . . . what were the books?" I asked. Maybe on some level I hoped she was taking *Hustler* magazine out of elementary school libraries, but I worried that probably wasn't the case. However, the truth was worse than I'd even imagined.

"Oh, just CRT bull crap," she said, her voice teetering on hysterical. "Like *The ABC's of Black History* and *Antiracist Baby*. Zero educational value! Just teaching kids to hate their nation." She groaned.

The lightbulb finally went off. I knew exactly who she was, had seen her face in a Breaking News alert in the *Herald*. The story had even been picked up by CNN. Carol Ann represented the absolute worst that Florida has to offer.

Part of me wanted to call her a stupid bigot to her face. I grew up in a modern Orthodox Jewish household where we weren't even allowed to watch PG-13 movies. My family may not have loved my decision to step away from religion, and I have issues with that, of course, but my parents and my community would *never* attempt to make rules or restrictions about how non-Jewish people should live their lives. I'm not saying that they aren't conservative or even closed-minded in some respects. But our rules were for our community, and we didn't prose-lytize to people outside of it. We didn't tell people how to live or what to read.

Carol Ann hadn't even gotten to the *incident* yet. And even though I knew what it was, I wanted to hear it from her own mouth.

It was actually Martina who spoke up. She had her rifle balanced between her legs and sounded the same as she had when she showed us to our rooms. Difficult to read, that one. "So what did you do?" she asked.

Carol Ann shook her head, a wild look in her eyes. "Well, I showed those moms what happens when they try to *mess* with my kids. I stormed into the library and grabbed all those books, then marched back to my car to get my gun. After concealing it, I asked them to follow me across the street from the drop-off area and threw the books down onto the sidewalk in front of me. They went berserk! Shouting like the wild animals they are. But they were messing with the wrong Mama Bear. I lifted up my pants leg and gave them a good look at the Glock on my ankle."

I couldn't help it. I gasped. Reliving the story from the source's mouth felt like walking through an ultra-realistic haunted house. Scout started barking and ran off. I wished I were a dog so I could take off, too.

"It's perfectly legal," Carol Ann continued. "I have a concealed carry permit, not that I even needed it. I made sure not to show them the gun until I was more than a thousand feet from the school."

She seemed to misunderstand the part of the story I found offensive, which was all of it, but I didn't care if her actions were legal or not. They were absolutely horrific, regardless of the law.

Carol Ann smiled proudly. "Those snowflakes all started backing away with their hands up, like I was a robber or something. And that just triggered the hell out of me, no pun intended. I saw red. They were acting like I was the crazy unstable one! So I took my gun out of the holster and *pop, pop, pop*. Shot up their precious books like they were Fourth of July fireworks."

I stuttered, the shock of her words too intense to process, and then realized I was supposed to say something. How could I possibly tell her how I really felt? That I'd already heard everything she'd said and had forwarded the press coverage to my blue state friends with a note saying, "This is what we are dealing with here!"

But before I could say anything, a shot much louder than the one from the other night broke the silence. What was with all the fucking guns? I felt like I was in the damn twilight zone.

I uncovered my ears and cautiously looked up; Carol Ann's eyes were as wide as mine.

"Good boy, Scout." Martina patted his head and took her rifle by the barrel.

Maybe twenty feet ahead of us, a black wiry-haired boar with yellowed tusks lay supine and panting. Its huge belly was undulating rapidly. I had the sudden feeling that I'd woken up in a *Game of Thrones* episode. It was gruesome, and the beast was clearly in pain, squealing and wheezing in a way that made me want to cover my ears and cry.

We silently followed Martina to the wounded animal and watched her place the gun on the grass, take a large blade out of her belt, and slit the hog's throat. It immediately went quiet.

Carol Ann whistled. "Nice work, Martina. He's a beaut."

Martina wiped sweat beads from her forehead with the back of her hand. "It wasn't a clean shot." She shook her head. "He suffered too much."

My heart was still racing. This day was testing my nerves more than I could handle. "What's that smell?" I asked, my voice shaking. I wasn't sure what feral hog was supposed to smell like, but this animal seemed to be reeking of death far sooner than it should have.

Carol Ann and Martina exchanged a glance, then Martina dug her blade into the top of the hog's belly and split it open all the way down to its genitals. Its entrails spilled open onto the carcass, revealing blood, and guts, and something else, white and writhing. Worms. With it came an even more fetid smell. I turned away from the women and vomited onto the grass.

"You never know when they're gonna be like that," Martina said.

"Not until they're dead," Carol Ann agreed.

The smell crept up my nostrils again and I pressed a hand to my mouth and tried to hold down the bile.

"You ladies go back to the main grounds," Martina said, waving us away.

It was the most grateful I'd felt since leaving the nice safe yoga class.

Carol Ann shook her head. "We should stay and help," she said.

"No, it's messy. You didn't pay all that money to come here to clean up worms and guts. I'll have my wife come help me with the cleanup."

I couldn't help but smile. The helper lady/bartender was not Martina's daughter. She was her *wife*. I stole a glance over at Carol Ann, who was making her fart face again. Sometimes the universe hands you little gifts like that. Thanks, Hashem.

I couldn't wait to get the hell out of there, even though I'd be walking back with Ms. Pizzagate Carol Ann. I needed a shower. And some ginger ale. But all I kept thinking about was how badly I wanted to tell Indira every detail of what had just happened.

MARTINA

I thought I'd seen it all in hospitality, but I was wrong. Goddamn. Carol Ann's dumpster fire, MAGA-reeking story was hands down the worst thing I'd ever heard at work. Maybe even in life. And that's saying a lot. I once had a yoga guy from Colorado ask if I would stuff a *healing elixir of herbs* into his anus. That was a hard pass.

I felt bad for Jessica, taking in all the poison from Carol Ann's story *and* losing her breakfast at the sight of the sick boar. For a Miami person, she seemed all right. I didn't need to subject her to any more nastiness, so I sent the women away to deal with the carcass on my own. When I made it back to the house to fetch Margaret, she took one look at me and held her nose.

"What the heck happened to you?" she said. "You smell like road-kill."

She pulled her hair back into a neat ponytail and slipped on her shoes before I'd even told her we had a cleanup to handle. Good woman, that one. She grew up on a dairy farm in Vermont, so is no stranger to the less glamorous parts of this life. Her Tinder profile photo had been of her birthing a calf, her arms elbow deep in blood. You could say it was love at first sight for me.

"Carol Ann's crazier than a rabid dog at a fish fry." I wiped the sweat off my forehead with my shirtsleeve. "Also, the hog was sick. Totally infested."

Margaret shook her head. "I hate when that happens."

"The crazy or the worms?" I asked.

She laughed. "Both. You wanna tell me what happened?"

I thought about it. Carol Ann's whole twisted, disturbing tale was nastier than what was inside that wild boar. Did I really need to ruin Margaret's day, along with mine? You'd think we'd be used to it by now, living in Florida. Though my wife was still getting used to it all, five years after I convinced her to move in with me at the Namaste Club grounds. These kinds of stories surprised you and didn't surprise you at the same time.

"Later," I said. "Dear lord. This week really can't end soon enough."

INDIRA

I'd brought a week's worth of party drugs for what was turning out to be a completely solo mission. It was depressing. After yoga class, when Jessica ran off with her new best friend, Carol Ann, and the others dispersed to "talk to the banyan trees" (whatever the fuck that meant), I slipped back into my room. Alone. And ate half an edible to get me through the rest of the day.

A text came through from my mother, a photo with no caption. It was of my beautiful daughter wearing a radiant smile that hadn't shown itself to me since I divorced her father. Tara was painted in intricate henna designs up and down her arms. Her wrists sparkled with twenty-four-karat-gold bangles. My mother had a new doll to play with. I swallowed a mix of pride and jealousy and closed my phone.

The solitude reminded me, with an unfortunate pang of longing, why I'd wanted Jessica to come on the trip in the first place. Because when she's not whining or being a victim, she's a hell of a good time. She gets me. There are few people in the world with whom you can enjoy sound bathing, meditating, and saluting the sun all while simultaneously getting tipsy and throwing shade on all the funny things you hear along the way. Jess is one of those people.

Every relationship has its ups and downs—every real one, anyway.

Yes, Jessica and I have had our fights. Big ones. About important things. But that bitch is my sister, too.

The night Greyson packed up his old Tumi roller and checked into a hotel room, never to return to our marital home and bed, Jessica was there. She picked up Tara for a sleepover with Sky, left both girls with a babysitter, came back to my house, and opened an expensive bottle of Napa cab. We sat on the living room floor in sweatpants and T-shirts and drank the whole thing while crying in each other's arms. It was one of the worst nights of my life, and I would have been totally alone if not for Jess.

Without her, the whole retreat experience was turning out to be a bust. Before the THC hit, I promised myself that I'd find a way for us to be normal again by the time the sound bowl rang on the last day of the retreat.

But, as it turned out, I didn't need to wait that long.

About an hour into my sweet buzz, there was a frantic knocking on my door.

"I didn't order room service," I shouted, then giggled uncontrollably at my own joke.

"Indira, open up." It was Jessica, sounding like she'd just discovered a dead body in her villa's closet.

I tied my kaftan around my waist (because for some reason I'd been lounging with my breasts out while watching *Ted Lasso* on my laptop) and ran to the door. I must have been smiling ridiculously, because Jess made a strange face at me before asking if she could come in. "We have to talk," she said, barreling past me and over to the little desk in the corner of my room. "And Jesus, I need a drink."

"Have some Enlightened Tequila." I gestured to the bottle, which was still in its gift basket. "Pour me one, too."

Jessica pressed her hands over her heart as if willing it to slow down. Then she grabbed two water glasses and poured a hefty amount of tequila into each. "By the way," she said. "How have we not discussed the fact that Shakti has a *tequila sponsor*."

I shrugged and accepted my drink from her. It wasn't clear what Jess was all riled up about, but I was happy she was there and apparently ready to gossip. "She's a hustler."

Shakti's tequila was surprisingly good, smooth and sweet, almost like a Clase Azul. The woman had taste.

"Well, anyway." Jessica took a long sip of her drink and closed her eyes, sighing. "You won't believe what just fucking happened out there." Her eyes were bloodshot, and she smelled like sweat and fear and something else that was musty and feral.

I sighed a breath of relief. She wasn't there to hash it out with me.

"Don't tell me I won't be seeing you on the cover of *Garden & Gun* magazine anytime soon. I had high hopes that you'd find a fun and exciting new hobby." I patted the bed for her to come and sit down next to me.

Jessica kicked off her sneakers and climbed onto the bed, crossing her legs in front of me. "Remember when I said something like 'Carol Ann is Marjorie Taylor Greene, but hotter,' and you told me stop being judgy and give her a chance?"

Great, she was trying to prove a point about how she was right, and I was wrong.

"And then *you* went off on a best friend girly hunting trip with her?" I pointed out.

"Yes, well it turns out"—she took another big sip and shook her head—"she's worse than I thought. She's a fucking crazy book-banning vigilante."

I spit tequila out on the comforter and started laughing. Fucking edibles. Jessica looked horrified. I coughed and composed myself.

"That's terrible. What did she do?"

"Don't you remember that story from the news? I forwarded it to you on Instagram." Jessica held her hands out like she was about to catch a basketball. "That was her! I knew she looked familiar!"

I shrugged. "No offense, but I don't have time to look at *every* meme and article you forward to me."

Jessica rolled her eyes but then told me the whole story. About how Carol Ann was removing books about diversity from public school libraries, even though her kids go to private school. About how some anticensorship moms bought those same titles and put them in her kids' library (poetic justice?). Then the confrontation, Carol Ann's meltdown, potentially threatening people with her gun? And meanwhile, Martina was shooting a wild boar who was rotting from the inside and infected with worms.

It was quite the tale.

"What an absolute psycho. I didn't realize that people like her actually existed outside of clickbait news articles." It was terrifying, really, how someone could look so relatively normal on the outside but possess such crazy dark personality traits on the inside. "Jess. Holy shit, you could have died out there."

She scrunched her eyebrows. "It got my adrenaline pumping for sure, but I can't say I was in any real danger. Anyway, I signed a waiver. So you wouldn't have been able to sue to avenge my death if I didn't make it back."

I laughed. "Carol Ann's crazy story makes us look better, at least. With our harmless little fight."

Jessica rolled her eyes. "Little? I don't remember it being so little. You're right, though. We can feel somewhat superior knowing we weren't the firemen from *Fahrenheit 451*."

"What else happened?" I asked, steering the conversation away from our argument. I didn't want to mess up the vibes, since we were finally slipping into a comfortable space and making jokes again.

"That was the climax, really. The far-right extremism and the disgusting pig." She shivered. "I wish you'd been there to see it."

"Me too," I said, honestly.

"Oh, and Martina's gay. The helper lady is her wife." Jessica drained her drink and stood up to pour a new one. I handed her my glass for a refill.

"Cool. You mean Margaret?" I asked. "She's pretty. Young. Good for her."

Jess handed me my glass back. "Cheers to Martina and Margaret."
She lifted her glass, and I clinked it with mine.

I took a tiny sip and put the glass down, weighing what to say next.
I'd been holding on to something that could speed up the whole kiss-
and-make-up process, and maybe now was the time to use it.

"Hey, I'm sorry about Daniel. I know how it looked, but I swear we
didn't hook up." I looked down at my hands, then back up at her eyes.
It might have been a weird time to pivot, but she looked amused.

"Yeah, right." She rolled her eyes. "You can be such a whore, I
swear."

I stretched my arm out and patted her knee. "Seriously, Jess. Nothing happened. Other than a very erotic back massage and I even feel
terrible about that. I had no business going near something you wanted."

Jessica snorted, then lifted an eyebrow at me. "We aren't in high
school. It's fine." She swirled her drink around in her glass. "But that
was pretty bitchy of you. Though not as bad as when you told the
whole class that Daniel would never want to fuck me. I mean, ouch,
Indy. Did you really need to go there?"

"Are you really playing the moral-high-ground card? You called me
a whore and a cheater in front of the same group, Jess. Listen, I'm sorry
I said that about Daniel. It obviously isn't true."

I couldn't tell if we were fighting or making up, but just the fact
that we were talking seemed like at least a small improvement. We
were working through it.

"So you didn't mean it?" she asked, not making eye contact.

Oh, that little hornball. She was still into him.

"Are you kidding? He'd probably lick the worms and guts off your
tennis shoes. If you still want it, I'm pretty sure you can have it."

She tapped her glass. "Would that be weird?"

"Why, because of a back massage? Who cares. *We* won't be weird
about it." I could feel Jessica warming back up to me a little. Also, I
still wanted to get her laid. As soon as she opens those floodgates,
she'll find a whole new world of experiences waiting at her feet.

"Here," I said, and walked over to my toiletry bag, removing a tiny plastic baggy containing my last two edibles. "Take these with Daniel. They won't make you paranoid, promise. They're an indica-sativa hybrid that I got in LA. Giggly, happy, body high."

She looked at them skeptically and put the baggy in her sports bra. "Maybe." She smiled.

We clinked glasses again and I was suddenly grateful for Shakti's random swag bag, especially because of the Enlightened Tequila— *100 percent organic agave!* Mixed with my edible and the possibility of salvaging my friendship with Jessica, it was turning the afternoon around nicely.

"Wanna watch *Ted Lasso* in bed and drink more tequila?" I asked.

Jessica sighed heavily and let out a little laugh. "There's literally nothing else I'd rather do."

SHAKTI

I believe in cleanness of the body, but we weren't hosting a puritanical retreat. Alcohol and other organic, well-sourced substances were acceptable, and sometimes encouraged. They can help us break down walls, crack our hard exteriors, and reveal our vulnerabilities to one another. Of course, sometimes, it can go the other way, too.

CAROL ANN

I had to take three showers after that hunting mess. One to rinse off the yoga sweat; one to wash away the blood and gore that splattered on me when Martina slit the beast's belly; and one to cleanse myself of that smug judgmental look on Jessica's face when I told her my Mama Bears story.

Shame on me though, because I had a bad feeling about her from the get-go, and my sixth sense is *strong*. I've been trying to keep an open mind out here but not everyone is worthy of grace. The Lord sends us angels, but He also sends us demons, and He sends us challenges, so I need to keep my eyes open. Which led me to the question: If the Burmese python was a gift from God, well, then who sent us the infested hog?

Signs.

After my triple shower, I sat in front of the mirror, applying my evening makeup, and stared at myself right in the eyes. *Remember who you are and why you are here on this earth*, I said. *Be the light. Be the protector of the weak.*

I didn't need to make these people like me; I needed to be unapologetically myself. To believe in my ideals so fiercely that it didn't matter what other people thought. Because I'm not out here serving man. I'm serving something higher. And I bet Shakti would understand that in her own way, since she's also living a life of devotion.

Perverts. Adulterers. Weak-minded haters. Those were some of the characters I was faced with on the retreat. I could see that clearly now. All I could do to combat that was make my presence there be a source for good.

I finished my makeup and dressed for cocktails, slipping into a little midi dress that Beau got me for Christmas last year. It's fitted and orange like a blazing sunset and he's always said it looks nice on me when I'm freshly tanned, which I am now thanks to the recent stretch of sunny days.

There was another thing worrying me. What was I supposed to tell Beau? That I was on a trip with a man, a cuckolder, and a lesbian (even though Martina was just a worker)? He was really going to hate that. And the thing with the diseased feral hog. I almost didn't want to bring it up after he'd seen me so excited about the python. I didn't want him to start thinking about bad omens.

I FaceTimed the kids to say good night and decided to save the unsavory details of the day for when I arrived safely back home. There was no reason to make Beau worry.

Kam and Katie looked sweet as can be in their matching koala jammies, blowing kisses to me on the screen and telling me about school. Daddy had swapped their lunches by accident so they both came home a little hungry—Katie is more of a clean eater and Kam is an organic chicken nuggets kind of kid—but it was okay. There were plenty of snacks in the kitchen, and they ordered pizza for dinner, which was a special treat.

I was telling them not to eat too much dessert after they had junk for dinner, but Beau snatched back his phone and hissed at me.

"Are you saying I'm not feeding them properly, CA? What am I supposed to do after a long day at work? Come home, put on a little apron, and prepare a four-course meal? Wear rubber gloves and scrub down all the dishes when the kids go to bed? Must be nice to be shooting pythons and relaxing all day while I'm over here with a dirty house and mouths to feed."

He was right, of course. Beau was doing his best and I had no right to criticize, especially when I was enjoying a restful vacation and not contributing my fair share.

"I'm sorry, baby. I didn't mean it like that. I'm just a little stressed, I guess. I miss you guys so much."

"What do you have to be stressed about, Carol Ann? Aren't you doing yoga and dancing in the moonlight or whatever? This is supposed to be making you *unstressed,* so you can come home and continue to be an active wife and mother. That's your real job, babe."

He'd walked into our bedroom and closed the door so the children couldn't hear, which I appreciated.

"You're right," I said. "'Stressed' isn't the right word. This place is heavenly. And the classes are amazing. I'm so grateful to be here." I was.

"Why are you dressed like a slut?" he asked. His face was cold and unblinking. Beau could be a little jealous, but he loved when I dressed up for him. That's why I always took care to look my best when he came home. I guess this was different because we weren't together.

"Oh, I just love this dress so much because you gave it to me. It reminds me of you." I smiled to betray the fact that my heart was beating out of my chest. I hated disappointing my husband. Hated when he wasn't proud of me.

He sucked his teeth. "I can see half of your tits."

I peered down. The neckline *was* a bit low-cut. I tried to tug it up a little but worried it would keep falling back down. "I'll change," I said. "No problem."

Beau sat on our bed and tousled his hair. "You look beautiful," he said, and I blushed like it was the first time he'd ever said it. Even though he says it every single day. Beau still gives me butterflies. "I just don't want that man there to see just how rich of a man I am, if you know what I mean."

"Understood, babe." I nodded. "I've got a little jumpsuit that I'll put on instead."

"Yeah, that's nice," Beau said, clearly softening. "I like how you kind of look like a prisoner in that one." He smiled.

"A prisoner for your love," I said. "Can't wait to see you in a few more days."

BARBARA

THIRD DAY OF THE RETREAT

It's so easy to make yourself invisible. When people think that you aren't listening to them, they'll forget you can still hear what they are talking about. Then they'll say all kinds of things as though you aren't even there.

I found it amusing at first, like how Jessica and Indira would banter about the other yogis, me included. I'm the *weird* one, they said. How original. I know their words were merely a mirror, reflecting their own blurry images, so I didn't let it alter my mental equanimity or sense of self. Is it *weird* to strive for existence in a higher vibration? I don't think so.

But then what I started overhearing became uglier. Gunshots. Fighting. Angry words. Another beautiful creature slain on these sacred grounds. As soon as I heard about what happened to the feral hog, I ran to the safest place I could find. Daniel's cabin. After three knocks, he answered, towel wrapped around his waist.

"Sorry, I was showering," he said. "Are you okay?"

I threw myself into his arms and soaked his chest hair with my tears. The image of the slaughtered pig was too much to bear. So many animal sacrifices had happened in just three days, when the real animals were the women on the retreat. I'd heard the whole sordid tale when I was weeding in front of Indira's villa. Jessica had entered just minutes before. Even from the outside, I could hear that their voices were raised, and I wanted to make sure they were okay, since only one day before they'd tainted our meditation practice with their superficial catfighting. No more blood needed to be shed. Not on my watch.

I pressed an ear to the little window at the bottom of the villa shower and closed my eyes, straining to make out the conversation inside. That's when I heard the whole, evil tale.

"What happened?" Daniel asked. He rubbed my shoulders and had the softest look in his eyes. For a moment, I wished I could break my vow and tell him what I'd heard. Instead, I just shook my head.

He seemed to understand, taking my hand and leading me to his bed. My heart quickened, but I knew he wouldn't try to take advantage of me, even though part of me wanted him to. My emotions were too raw in the moment.

"Lay back and relax," he said. So I did. He sat at the end of the bed and began to sing "Om Namo Bhagavate Vāsudevāya," sounding like Krishna himself had landed from the heavens. My tears shifted from mournful to hopeful. Then he took my feet into his hands and slowly, lovingly rubbed out the last of my grief.

JESSICA

THIRD DAY OF THE RETREAT

I left Indira's room feeling less traumatized than when I entered it, and not just because I was tipsy. She'd put a bandage on me. It didn't get her off the hook completely and I was probably just using her for comfort in the moment, but so what? How often had that woman done the exact same with me?

My worst fear growing up was that I'd end up old and alone, like an unfortunate great aunt of mine, and it seemed like I was now about halfway to being both. To avoid that fate, I'd stayed in my marriage longer than I should have—months after I'd seen the credit card evidence and found a pair of cheap red lacy panties in Tom's BMW. I couldn't imagine losing my spouse along with my parents (who had already relegated me to B status within the family for marrying a goy in the first place, so that support system was effectively gone). I wasn't shunned by them, but I was a massive disappointment, unworthy of their inner circle. There were no more weekly Shabbat invitations for me.

Yes, I have a beautiful relationship with my children but, in a handful of years, they'll be off to college, and I'll be lucky if they remember to call once a week. (Though I'm hoping my overcompensating parenting will inspire enough guilt for them to reach out to their sad old mom more often than that.)

In short, I needed Indira. And not only because I was lonely, though that was part of it, but also because I love her. And love isn't something I have an abundance of these days. She *gets* me. She had me at *hello*. It's complicated. Not making up with her would be like chopping off a limb, and I'd already lost too many.

We drank half a bottle of Shakti's unusually delicious sponsored tequila and then I slipped into my room to shower and change for dinner. I smelled like death. Literally.

After towel-drying my hair, I blushed and put on one of the lingerie sets I'd reluctantly packed. A black mesh matching set with underwire and a little pushup on the bra. Two kids and a combined three years of breastfeeding had helped gravity along earlier than I'd have liked, but honestly, I still have a great rack. Standing in front of the bathroom mirror, I had to admit it to myself. I looked good. Maybe even better than I had in years. A strange impulse took over (maybe tequila or osmosis from Indira), and I took out my iPhone, stuck my butt back and my chest forward, and snapped a selfie. Part of me wanted to send it to Tom without comment. *Look what you're missing* would be the subtext. But the prick didn't deserve the attention. At the very least, I'd save it for myself, for a day when I wasn't feeling quite as confident.

I put on a high-waisted ombre lilac skirt I'd purchased three years ago but had never worn because it was too daring and—I must have had a lobotomy on this trip without realizing it—a crop top that Indira once made me buy. I looked like one of those moms at pickup who would just casually show up to school looking like socialites at a fancy luncheon. And I loved it. YOLO.

Indira passed by my villa on her way to cocktails and catcalled as I walked out the door.

"Damn, sexy mamacita. You got a number?"

She looked like Elizabeth Taylor, wearing a chiffon headscarf and flowing frock. Seriously, only Indira could make a damn muumuu look sexy.

I did a little spin for her, letting the light breeze catch my skirt as I twirled.

"I'm no expert, but is asking for someone's number even a thing anymore?" I asked.

"Not really," she said. "People usually just follow each other on Instagram and then slide into the DMs."

"Oof. I really need to edit my grid. It's all photos of my kids."

Indira waited for me to catch up to her, and we walked together toward the Nourishment Pavilion. "I've been telling you that!" she said.

The night was warm and sticky, but the breeze kept the boob sweat at bay. In other words, it was a perfect Florida autumn night.

We were the last ones to arrive for cocktail hour, but this time I didn't mind. Barbara was already silently sipping her cosmo (talk about a *Sex and the City* throwback) and smiling at everyone. Shakti and Carol Ann were leaning against a highboy table and appeared to be locked in a deep conversation. Probably trading conspiracy theories about who in the group was a secret Illuminati lizard person and how everyone who had gotten the Covid vaccine was now microchipped in preparation for the zombie apocalypse.

Carol Ann caught me looking at her, so I gave a little wave while elbowing Indira in the ribs. My prodigal best friend, who was probably still as high as Snoop Dogg on a cooking show and also half-drunk, doubled over giggling. I gave her a stern look, but as soon as I saw the hysterics on her face, I also erupted into uncontrollable laughter. We were like a couple of immature teenagers caught making fun of our science teacher during a sex-ed lecture. I tried to find Carol Ann's gaze again to feign an apology, but she just rolled her eyes and reengaged with Shakti.

"Those two are *so* funny to me," I said. "It's like crunchy meets QAnon and there's this weird alchemy that turns them into one combined substance."

Indira wiped happy tears from her face. "Jesus, Jessica. What's with the chemistry talk? Have you been doing Sky's homework for her?"

"Yes, it's science," I deadpanned. "Something neither of those women believe in."

Indira burst into laughter again and squeezed my arm. "I'm so glad we made up," she said, looking at me with pure warmth in her eyes.

It was on-brand for her to assume everything was fine just because she was ready for the fight to be over, but I wasn't about to forgive and forget that easily. The woman had publicly shamed me two days in a row out of sheer spite.

"I wouldn't go that far, yet," I said. "But I'm glad we're not trying to kill each other."

Indira looked stunned, because since when did I ever stand up to her? I sighed, the people pleaser in me wanting to make it better. Was it time for a hug? Why not? We stopped in front of the bar and I wrapped my arms around her. She smelled like the spa at the Four Seasons in Surfside, and I say that, I hope, in the least creepy way.

"Now that's something I love to see," said a male voice. Daniel. He was wearing tight pants—yes, tight enough to see a substantial bulge—and a thin white collared shirt. He wasn't topless! His man bun gleamed in the golden hour glow.

"The girl-on-girl or two friends making up?" Indira put a hand on her hip.

Daniel laughed. "I guess both, actually. But truly, I'm happy to see you two making your peace. That's what this retreat is about. Unity. Can I buy you beautiful ladies a drink?"

The drinks were free.

"Two spicy margaritas," I said, and almost surprised myself with the confidence in my voice. I thought back to the edibles Indira had given me, which were tucked away in my room, and wondered if tonight would be a good time to offer them to Daniel.

Margaret was behind the bar and started on our drinks before Daniel could turn around and make a show of ordering for us (which he did anyway).

"Heard you had quite the adventure this afternoon," she said to me, lifting an eyebrow.

Daniel looked curious. "Right. The hunting trip. How did that go? Did you procure our meal for tonight with your own two hands?" He leaned an elbow against the bar, his piercing blue eyes burning a hole right into my soul.

My cheeks burned. "No. They didn't even let me hold a gun." I turned to Margaret. "But Martina is an incredible shot. Wow."

She garnished our drinks with orange wedges and slid them across the bar.

"Eh, she wasn't too pleased with the kill, actually. Said the animal suffered too much. Guess she at least put it out of its misery, being diseased and all."

I shuddered at the memory. Merlot colored blood, ivory slithering worms. "Yeah. That's an image that will live forever in my nightmares."

"Why didn't you shoot?" Daniel asked, apparently unperturbed by the suffering diseased boar comment.

"Oh, I just don't know how to. We were more of a *pick some meat up at the kosher butcher* type of family growing up."

I drank a sip of the margarita. It was perfectly balanced, a little sweet, a little tangy, just enough spicy. It would take restraint to not have four more of them. "This is delicious." I smiled at Margaret.

"I can show you tomorrow, if you'd like," she said. "How to shoot. Technically, we aren't supposed to. But if you're interested, I have a little target range I built behind our lodging."

It was such a sweet and generous offer. I wondered how much Martina had told her wife about that afternoon. If she was as offended as I was by Carol Ann's bigotry and book banning.

Or if she just thought I could use some protection. Learning to shoot was probably fairly low on my totem pole of new things I wanted to try, but my ability to say "no" is even lower.

"I'd love that," I said.

SHAKTI

NOW

The third night, that was when Carol Ann started opening up to me about her marital problems. I think I've mentioned this before, but I'm a life coach in addition to being a yoga instructor. I like to consider myself a spiritual healer; my areas are the mind, the body, and the soul.

Carol Ann was distraught with the state of her marriage and didn't know who she could trust with talking about it. She's a good, traditional wife, with her priorities properly aligned. Therefore, the problem wasn't that she was trying to dominate her husband. So many women of our time make that mistake. She and I agreed that the divine masculine and the divine feminine each have their distinct places in nature, and it is our duty to honor that. Husband is king and wife is queen. These are our roles, as simple as how mother is nurturer and father is protector.

Of course, there is room for divergence, but for the majority of us, this is the truth. Women trying to control men have caused the mass emasculation of the American male. It has fostered a hatred of women, which is one of the reasons society is suffering so much right now.

Carol Ann confided in me that her husband has been detaching from her, belittling her, and not honoring her as a divine goddess. He's become angry and dismissive with her. She is worried that it's because she's not as attractive as she was when they met, but also speculated that he was intimidated because she makes more money than him. Perhaps his ego had turned him cold to her.

I didn't fault Carol Ann for her success. No. She is doing an admirable thing. But I reminded her that it is also her responsibility to make her husband feel secure again in their partnership. To let him know how deeply he is needed. I suggested she ask for his advice more in financial and business matters. To let him be the man.

She was so overcome with hope for a path forward that she wept in my arms. It was a powerful moment.

Barbara had been standing close to Carol Ann and me, nodding along serenely with our conversation. No doubt sending love and positivity through her generous heart. We were fully present in the conversation. Which is why I didn't notice that Indira, Jessica, and Daniel had left sometime during cocktail hour. They must have slipped away. They didn't return to join us for dinner that night, either.

I don't like to speculate, but it *had* been a long day of spiritual cleansing. Everyone had shared and given fully and openly in their meditation and yoga practices, so maybe they went to bed early. Personal growth is tiring work.

JESSICA

It was a hard no for me. Margaret told us wild boar was on the menu that night, and the thought of it sent a rush of bile into my throat. I could practically taste the fetid pig that had laid before me earlier that day, its insides already decomposing from the infestation of worms.

"I can't say that I have much of an appetite, either," Daniel said, tapping his empty glass on the bar. "I'm used to fasting at least two full days a week, so all these meals are compromising my gut flora."

Indira smiled tightly. "Fasting? Cleansing? Can't we all just go back to calling it a starvation diet?"

We all laughed.

"I'm very much against depriving myself of food," I said. "But there's just no way I'm going near a buffet with one of those animals on it tonight."

Daniel raised his glass toward Margaret. "How about another round for the three of us?" He turned to Indira and me. "What do you say we skip dinner and go for a night walk around Shiva Lake instead?"

My stomach started turning again, but with excited nausea instead of disgusted nausea. "As long as it doesn't upset your delicate gut flora," I said, proud of my newfound ease in talking to an attractive man.

I was happy to skip dinner and spend more time with Daniel, but was also slightly terrified of going back to the lake at sundown. After my run-ins with the python and diseased pig, who knew what else was lurking in the night. But the cocktails and our strength in numbers shored up my courage. I was relieved to have Indira by my side, too, even though she wasn't completely off the hook.

Margaret gave us flashlights from behind the bar to light our way, but we barely needed them. The moon glowed like a spotlight overhead, illuminating our path through the Enlightenment Circle and towards the banyans.

When we reached the other side of the trees and the lake spread out in front of us, Indira turned her flashlight to me and froze. Her face was twisted with worry and pleading, which was such an unusual thing for her.

"What's wrong?" I asked, stepping forward so I could reach out and squeeze her arm. "Did you see something?"

She shook her head, but her eyes remained huge, like giant charcoal-colored glass beads. "It just gives me the creeps. I don't like it back here."

The air was thick and still hot from the day. Jewels of sweat lined Indira's nose and the top of her lip. She shined her flashlight toward the lake. I felt a rush of affection for this version of my friend. The vulnerable one, capable of fear and uncertainty, which was so unlike her normal confident facade. It also made me feel brave.

"It's totally safe," I said, though that was probably a lie. Nature is unpredictable, which is part of what makes it so beautiful.

"Come on. I'll hold your hand." Daniel stepped to the other side of Indira and traced circles on her back. A flash of jealousy jolted through me, but she quickly brushed him off.

"You two go on without me," she said. "Too much weed and alcohol. I'm feeling paranoid."

She stepped backward away from the lake. "Have fun," she whispered in my ear. Then she was gone, disappearing through the banyans and out into the night. And it was just Daniel and me. Alone. I turned my flashlight to him and saw he was smiling widely. I hoped he didn't notice my flush.

"Shall we continue on?" he asked, waving his arm like a maître d' ushering me to my table.

I followed along beside him as we crunched the damp grass under our feet on our way to Shiva Lake. Frogs croaked their throaty songs in surround sound all around us. It was mating season, and they'd be loud like that all night.

For a few minutes, we didn't speak. We just walked side by side, sipping our sweating cocktails and watching the water.

The moonlight's reflection made his eyes almost exactly the same dark blue of the lake. He really was a great-looking man. "It's awesome that you two made up." He broke the silence, glancing over at me as he slowed his pace.

I smiled despite myself and looked away. His attention was almost unbearable, but in the best way.

"Yeah, I hate fighting with her. She's my best friend. Even though we can really go at it like sisters." I forced myself to look back up and make eye contact.

"Did she really cheat on her husband, like you said?" Daniel broke the gaze and walked to the water's edge.

I winced. The memory of my outburst was embarrassing. I still couldn't believe I'd called her out like that in front of everyone.

"It wasn't my place to say that." I put my flashlight down and pulled the elastic out of my ponytail, letting my hair fall down onto my shoulders. "I mean, we all have secrets. Right? It's nobody else's business, really. What we do in private."

Daniel smiled wider and placed his flashlight and cocktail on the ground. Then he stood up and put his hands out. For me to take? I wasn't sure what I was supposed to do, so I took one step closer and let him close the gap. He grabbed my drink and put it next to his.

"What are your secrets?" he asked, taking my hands into his. "I want to get to know you better."

We were holding hands. It sent a flash of excitement through my bones. But why were we holding hands? Was it flirting or some kind of weird yoga ritual? Either way, I didn't want it to end.

"Oh, I don't know," I said, my voice shaking a little. "Probably nothing exciting. What about yours?"

"I asked you first." He pressed his fingers into my hands and made little massaging motions on my palms. "Like . . . have you ever had a threesome?"

My heart did a little leap. Is that why he wanted to bring Indira and me on a quiet night walk? So we could all hook up? If so, it would have been insanely presumptuous and borderline predatory. But, at the same time, kind of a weird compliment? It wasn't something I'd ever done or even wanted to do, but for some reason in that moment it seemed like the sexiest thing I'd ever imagined. Though I didn't think it would be good for Indira's and my friendship. Why make things awkward?

I shook my head.

"No?" he said. "You're so sexy, though. It's hard to imagine you haven't tried one. I feel like you would be able to teach me a thing or two."

Was he joking? I was the most awkward person on the yoga retreat. Literally even silent Barbara probably seemed more outwardly fuckable than me.

"I guess there's a first time for everything," I said, and immediately cringed.

I hadn't been expecting him to be so forward, even though I'd desperately hoped that our walk would lead to something. But now that we were there and all of that seemed possible, I froze and said the least sexy thing I could think of. "Carol Ann has secrets, too. You should have heard what she told me when we went hunting today. About the reason she really came to Transcendence Week."

Daniel scrunched his face but also looked amused. "Oh yeah? What's that all about?" He was still holding my hands, massaging his fingers into the meaty part of my palms.

"Well, she runs this group called the Mama Bears," I said. And immediately I knew that I'd ruined whatever momentum we had going. The only thing less sexy than pivoting from dirty talk to random shit talk was adding the word "mama" to the mix.

I could see his eyes glazing over as I rambled on about book bannings and pedophiles and open carry laws. It was definitely diarrhea of the mouth. Good one, Jessica. You're finally about to get a little action from an attractive younger guy, and you go and start talking about elementary schools and alleged sexual predators.

He stopped massaging my hands and, honestly, I deserved that.

"Wow. That's super messed up," he said.

I nodded.

"Well, it's getting kind of late." He released my hands and scratched at his man bun. It was painfully obvious that I'd lost him. Painful. And obvious. Because I have zero game. I mentally flagellated myself. *Stupid fucking idiot.*

"Yeah," I said. "You're right. Well, it was nice walking with you. Thanks for saving me from the PTSD I'd have gotten from eating that wild boar."

"Anytime." Daniel smiled and picked up my flashlight and nearly empty glass, handing them back to me. Then he grabbed his and starting walking back toward the banyans.

I followed a few feet behind, defeated by my own awkwardness. As we walked, I shined the flashlight across the surface of the lake, letting the light dance on the gently rippling surface. That's when I saw it.

I gasped and jumped back, spilling the last drops of margarita onto my chest. Daniel turned around and followed my gaze and the beam of my flashlight into the middle of the lake, where two giant bulbous eyes and a broad back with a slithering tail were skimming toward us. "Holy fuck!" he shouted, then grabbed my elbow as we ran together to the other side of the trees. We kept sprinting until we passed the Awakening Fire Pit and made it all the way to my cabin door. Then we stopped and panted, catching our breath, sharing a glance that said, *What the hell was that?*

We looked back in the direction from which we'd run, but the path was empty. No people. No monsters.

"That was the biggest alligator I have ever seen," Daniel said, still breathing heavily.

I nodded. "Easily a sixteen-footer. A bull. I'm not usually afraid of them, but . . ."

Daniel interrupted, reading my mind. "But that boy looked like a man-eater."

CAROL ANN

Before bed, I swallowed my usual supplements, but added a little extra magnesium and melatonin for sleep. My mind was racing with a
mishmash of thoughts. Like about how I was stuck for three more
days with these nasty women, and how Beau—if I was being honest—
hadn't been his best self lately.

When we were first married, everything had felt so easy, and our
lives looked like a yellow brick road spread wide open ahead of us,
right down to counting down to our golden years with grandbabies
at our feet. I still feel that way, but there are speed bumps, too. Sometimes Beau just needs his alone time; other times, I feel like I can't
breathe without his affection. But he's going through a lot, and it's my
job to be understanding and supportive. Even if that means giving him
space. Maybe that's what this retreat was about, too.

I half wanted to pack up right there and then and leave the Namaste Club, get back to my real life, but I am no quitter. No sirree,
Bob. I'd committed to a week away for my own wellness, and I was
going to take it. Besides, Shakti had proven herself to be a blessing.
She is wise beyond her years, and I could tell her heart was made of
pure gold. Even if we didn't follow the exact same god, our devotion
sprung from a similar intention. Goodness. Faith. Service.

Though we'd just met, I'd trusted her with confidences I wouldn't have shared with my best friends. Not my mother, not even my minister. My worries about my marriage are so deeply personal that frankly, I don't even like to admit them to myself. I'm scared that thinking about them will give life to the worries and threaten the very foundation of my family unit. Which is *everything* to me.

I'll never lose Beau; I know that. But he's just been so angry and disappointed with me lately and I can't for the life of me seem to crawl back into his good graces. A lot of it is my fault. Sometimes it's because I make mistakes, like calling attention to myself with the Mama Bears incident. Times like that when my intentions are good, but I end up embarrassing him somehow (even though it was those *other* women who should have been embarrassed).

But also, there's the money thing. There's nothing grosser than talking about money, even with your spouse. Is there? But there it is anyhow, controlling every aspect of our lives. For most of our marriage, I had nothing to do with the finances. I stopped working after we said "I do," and at that point, the home became my sacred domain. I went all in. Matching linens and tablecloths for a perfectly set table, even when it was just dinner for Beau and me. Pressed sheets for our marital bed. Healthy and delicious meals every evening. Then the kids came along, and I doubled down. Homemade baby food in the food processor. Matching seersucker overalls for Easter.

Beau was the provider. And I was happy to care for the home while he built the fire, if you know what I mean. We had a beautiful lifestyle. But then a few years back, his business started to lag. He was in construction at the time, and no one was building. So he jumped over to mortgage sales, which is a lucrative and growing business. Plus, he could be behind a desk instead of working in the hot Florida sun all day. He's a very smart man; I knew he'd be wildly successful. But it takes time to build these things.

What happened next was almost an accident. I wanted to help my husband kickstart his career, and sales is all about networking. Between the two of us, I am the social one, so I figured I could use those skills to his benefit. I talked an old friend into buying a new house.

Time to upgrade! I told her. I knew she'd need a new mortgage and I also knew exactly who could sell her one. But first, I needed to find her a house. I got my real-estate license and she and I started looking. Within three months, she was under contract on a beautiful new three-bedroom, three-bathroom house close to downtown and Beau handled the mortgage like a champ.

We were a little team. I reeled them in, and he took them off the hook and filleted them. At first, Beau seemed proud of me, bragging to his friends about what a natural I was. Then word got out and more and more people started calling me to look at houses. I was picked up by a big real-estate brokerage. Then other clients started asking me to manage their listings. I never meant for it to turn into a career. Really, I didn't.

For a while, I pushed all the mortgages to Beau, but then something funny happened. The market picked up and got so hot that the mortgages went away. I know that sounds counterintuitive, but the sellers wanted cash buyers. And these buyers had the money to do it. No need for a lender in the middle.

Beau's business tanked while mine boomed, and that would really be hard for anyone. I get it. But honestly, I was just trying to help my family and I hate to admit it, but my husband's income couldn't fully support us anymore. What was I supposed to do?

Shakti understood my predicament completely. A man needs to feel like a man. And it's my responsibility as his wife to make sure Beau knows he's the king of his castle. Which he is, of course. Shakti and I brainstormed a plan for me to prove how much he was needed. Maybe that sounds silly or even deceitful, but it was just an innocent game to restore the power balance in my marriage and to please the man I love. To show that I still needed him as my hero.

After I took my supplements, I sent Beau a text, knowing he'd already be asleep. Babe. This is getting really hard because I miss you so much. These people are as immoral as they come and it scares me a little. Wish you were here. Love you to the moon.

The next day, I'd lay it on thick.

INDIRA

My idea of a natural paradise is a manicured botanical garden or a white sandy beach, not a bug- and reptile-infested swamp. I guess I'm still quite the West Coaster in that way. It's not that I wasn't enjoying my time at the Namaste Club. I was all for the food and drinks and Hare Krishnas. And Shiva Lake was pretty and serene enough during the day. But at night, there was too much that could go wrong. Snakes, gators, spiders. No thank you. Besides, I wanted to be a good wing woman for Jess. It felt like the least I could do after our dustup.

I left her with Daniel basically wrapped up in a nice little bow and slipped back into my villa. As a rule, I try not to work on vacation, but the Allison Kent situation had thrown a wrench into that intention. After taking a moment to breathe and process the social-media debacle, I was ready to get my hands into the muck. To her credit, Jessica was managing the crisis like a pro. She deserved the retreat cock she was hopefully in the middle of receiving.

Only she wasn't. I had already passed out when the text came in. (Edibles tend to give me the deepest, most dreamless sleeps.) The next morning, I checked my phone and saw Jessica's message, sent a mere thirty minutes after I'd left her by the lake.

Saw a monster, but unfortunately not in Daniel's pants. Ironically, almost getting eaten by a giant gator was less traumatic than me attempting to flirt. Explain later. Xx

Oh, Jessica.

I met her the next morning for group breakfast. (Who needs to do the same damn "hike" around Shiva Lake every morning, especially after learning about the alluded-to monster that lurks within?) Jessica told me the whole story over Florida orange kombucha (virgin, this time) and house-made yogurt with fruit.

And it was fucking funny. Well, the botched flirting part was. I almost wished I'd stayed to watch it in person. Poor Jess. I'd have felt bad for her if Daniel was anyone special enough to be embarrassed for. But since he just happened to be the closest fuckboy in our vicinity, it really wasn't a big loss. You win some, you lose some.

"What about this gigantic alligator?" I asked her. That was the more serious issue. "Is it safe for us to even be here? Should we call Florida Wildlife or something?"

Jessica snapped the waistband on her yoga pants. "Shit, are these things getting tighter?"

"Pay attention, woman!" I snapped the shoulder of her bra strap. It was the first time I'd ever seen her outside of a yoga class wearing only a sports bra and leggings, even though everyone else in Miami does it all the time, and it made me a little proud of her.

"I was getting to that part of the story," she said. "He scared the shit out of me last night, but apparently that's just Bubba. I saw Martina on my way over here today, and she says that he lives here. He protects the lake."

And that is why Floridians have a weird reputation, in my opinion. Only people from this phallic-looking state would think an explanation that preposterous was acceptable.

"Bubba?" I asked.

I looked around to see if anyone else was catching the conversation. Shakti and Carol Ann were holding hands with their eyes closed and, possibly, I don't know—praying? Daniel was stretching languorously in the screened-in patio. And Barbara was watching us and smiling. Again. I'd pay to know what was going through that woman's head.

"He's a bull gator." Jessica shrugged, as if that explained anything.

I chewed a fingernail and reminded myself that I was trying to be nicer to her because our last fight was still too fresh for my usual snark.

"And we know he isn't dangerous because?"

Jessica laughed. "Listen, I wouldn't do anything stupid, like take a swim in the lake with a fish under my arm. But gators really know to stay away from humans. We're the apex predators. Not them."

Daniel finished his stretching and walked into the Nourishment Pavilion, shirtless and glistening. Jessica stood up straighter and sucked in her stomach.

"Martina said he's been here for years, and no one has ever gotten hurt," she continued. "I wouldn't worry. Maybe Bubba is the reason we don't see any stray cats around here, but other than that, he's probably harmless."

I felt dizzy. How could a prehistoric beast with daggers for teeth be considered *harmless*?

Daniel put a hand lightly on Jessica's back, and I saw her skin immediately goose bump.

"Morning, ladies," he said, wiping the sweat off his forehead with his other arm. "Jessy, did you tell her about our lake friend from last night?"

I might have blushed on her behalf at the mere hint of *last night*. Also, *Jessy*?

Jessica smiled and ever so slightly leaned back into his hand. "His name is Bubba. And he's basically a pet here at the Namaste Club."

Daniel took a step closer to her. "I bet he keeps the other gators in line."

God, flirting is so gross when other people do it. I took that as my cue to head to the Active Room for morning yoga.

SHAKTI

NOW

There was a point when I pulled Daniel aside to gently remind him of our responsibilities as teachers and mentors. While we do want to forge strong bonds with the people who take our classes, it is important to keep a clear line between them and us. We have a duty to nurture and guide, and that becomes difficult if we grow too intimate with our students.

Daniel was only an apprentice, so it was an informal and open conversation. Not an admonishment. It was my job to guide him on his journey to becoming a yoga instructor and I was trying to do that in an authoritative, yet gentle way.

It was calm and collaborative. I mentioned that I'd noticed him being casual and friendly with many of the students at the retreat and asked that he just be mindful of that. I reminded him that purity is an essential component of spiritual guidance.

He understood.

CAROL ANN

It was already working; I could feel it. I woke up to a sweet message from Beau. Miss you too babe. You don't ever have to be afraid because I'd never let anything bad happen to you. Sweet man. That was the Beau I married.

I dressed quickly to meet Shakti for the hike and to let her know I could already feel the tide turning. The night before, when I'd told her about everything that had made me uncomfortable at the retreat, like Daniel trying to tickle my feet and Jessica's totally unnecessary judgments, she'd said, "Use it. Use those things to pull your husband closer. Let him know you need him to protect you."

It was brilliant. What I originally wanted to keep from him so he wouldn't worry was exactly what I needed to win him back.

It had become crystal clear to me that *this* was why I was meant to be at Transcendence Week. Not to escape the Vero Christian woke mom army, but to save my marriage.

Society has taken so much from people like Beau and me in the last couple decades. It has tried to make us ashamed of our forefathers, guilty for the color of our skin, embarrassed to raise the flag. Liberals have stolen our country and are turning it into a godless land of sin. Pushing hardworking people out of their jobs. Taking knees at our national anthem. Removing the Lord from our holidays. Blaming violence and crime on my *privilege*, instead of on the people who are actually breaking the law. But I'll tell you one thing. They can take, and take, and take, but they'll never steal my family.

I was almost giddy when I met Shakti that morning at the Enlightenment Circle. She was dressed in an all-white sheer robe over her workout clothes and looked like an angel. Which is really what she was for me.

"It's going to be okay. I can feel it in my bones," I told her, and pulled her into a tight hug. "Thank you. So much."

She released me and squeezed my shoulders, her eyes as blue and calm as a cloudless sky. "Keep your intentions directed to him and manifest the marriage you seek. All is coming."

"Amen," I said. She covered her mouth in a girly cute way, and we shared a little laugh. Maybe she was expecting me to say *namaste*. Even with our differences, we'd found such a deep understanding.

"I brought you something," she said, reaching into a pocket in her robe. She pulled out a little pill bottle and handed it to me. It looked like a lot of the small batch supplements I like to buy, with a white homemade label affixed to the front: *Skinny Genes, by Shakti.*

"It's pure ashwagandha, sourced from the Himalayan mountains, and is good for your stress and anxiety."

I must have beamed, because it was just so thoughtful. She'd picked out the perfect gift. "It's also good for fat-burning and lowering blood sugar." She pointed to the label. "This is just a prototype, but I'm going to have them available for subscription around the holidays. You're the first person to try it."

What a doll. I held the bottle to my chest. "Thank you. I love it," I said. "And I'm sure I'll be purchasing more of these as Christmas gifts for all my Mama Bears."

We walked together to breakfast and continued to manifest healing energy for my marriage. At one point, we closed our eyes and chanted a little mantra. *I am love. I radiate feminine energy. I surrender to my husband and accept my womanly duties. I allow him to wrap me in his masculine embrace.*

By the time morning yoga started, my soul was full of hope. I rolled my mat out and took seated meditation, waiting for class to begin. One of the best parts of meditating was not having to make eye contact with any of the other retreat people, who I'd been ignoring all morning (other than a smile and wave for Barbara, the strange one).

The class started off slowly, with focus on our breathing. Shakti's voice floated into my ears, as smooth as water in a glass.

"Inhale peace."

I filled my lungs.

"Exhale pain."

I felt my anxieties melt away.

"Inhale calm."

My shoulders relaxed.

"Exhale chaos."

I cleared my mind.

INDIRA

I held a handstand in the middle of the room. For three whole seconds.

It was magical, like I'd embodied the goddess Kali herself, fearsome and powerful. We were in downward dog when Shakti asked me to walk my feet forward and kick into adho mukha vrksasana, which had been my goal pose for years. I'd only ever attempted it at the wall (which is one of the reasons I prefer to practice in the front of the room). But I'd set my mat up next to Jessica's, instead of in my usual spot, upsetting the unspoken order we'd all agreed to on the first day of the retreat. It seemed like the thing to do, though I can't explain why. Maybe it was because I wanted to be closer to her, even physically, after our fight.

I'd always been too afraid to kick up in the middle of a room. But when Shakti cued me, there was no disobeying. Because, for some reason, when a yoga teacher instructs you to do a pose, you listen. They're all part-time hypnotists or cult leaders, I swear.

Gingerly, I tiptoed my feet toward my hands as I rooted my palms into the mat. When I felt my hips stacking over my shoulders, with my hamstrings quaking, I lifted my left leg as high as I could, bent my right knee, and launched my feet into the sky. Shakti was there to catch me, aligning my legs and guiding my hips into the perfect position.

Then she stepped away, and I balanced. On. My. Own. It felt like freedom, or an orgasm, or how I imagine the sensation of flying. For a few glorious moments, my body was capable of the impossible. My mind's parameters for what I was capable of blew wide open. Who knew? Maybe tomorrow I'd levitate.

And then it was over. It wasn't quite falling but it wasn't quite controlled, either. My feet landed on the mat, and I allowed my knees to follow. Gently. I looked up to see Shakti maybe two feet away. Close enough to intervene, if necessary, but far enough to give me the chance to achieve the pose on my own. We exchanged a smile.

"Good job," she said, before turning to guide the rest of the class, who were all waiting on hands and knees for their next instruction.

The serotonin rush was incredible. Yes, I loved Shakti's validation. I can admit that. But also, the best feelings I've ever experienced have always come from accomplishment. In school, in business, in parenting. Some people seek out a soulmate and others strive to reach the limits of their own potential. The latter is me. I'd rather free solo El Capitan than fall in love. And the freestanding handstand gave me that rush. I'd done something new and hard that I couldn't do the day before. That meant something. A small superficial something, but also a nice justification, if nothing else, for taking the trip.

Then I thought about Tara. About how I'd disappointed her as a mother with my infidelities. How I tried to compensate for that with gifts and compliments and faux cheeriness. How all of those efforts were just a kick against the wall, a cheap way of feeling accomplished when in fact I'd achieved nothing. I deserved the spite she was throwing at me. It was time to step away and do the hard work. I made a vow while resting in child's pose. When I got home, I would take Tara to dinner and listen, let her eviscerate me, let her tear me to shreds, and then I'd work on building us back up from the foundation. Take that, Savera.

At the end of class, even my oms sounded clearer and brighter, at least to my own ears. I sat in full lotus and kept my eyes closed for several moments after bowing and saying *namaste,* wanting to stretch the moment out as long as possible. When I finally opened them, Jessica was giving me a thumbs-up.

Shakti was facing us in the front of the room, her hands in prayer.

"Thank you for sharing your light and your practice with me this morning," she said, stretching the words out like someone doing an impression of a very stoned Valley girl. "There will be no meditation class today as I have a lot of work to do for tonight's full moon ceremony."

The Active Room was still and quiet, with everyone vibrating from a strong class. We listened respectfully to our teacher. The moment broke when Jessica scooted her butt next to me and whispered, "I bet she needs to cleanse her aura, or maybe sage her vagina."

Carol Ann and Shakti gave us matching sharp looks and I stifled a laugh, smacking Jessica's knee. The room was way too small for hushed shit talk.

"As I was saying," Shakti continued. "You are welcome to practice meditation on your own or to try one of the other wonderful activities offered here at the Namaste Club. Daniel will be leading an adaptogenic cocktail class as another optional activity. And as a reminder, drinks and dinner will both take place around the Awakening Fire Pit tonight."

"Oh, how lovely," Jessica said, clearly trying to make up for being caught making a snide remark.

Shakti smiled politely. "Yes, it should be. And one more thing." She opened her palms in what I've been told is the *gesture of receiving*. "I'd like us all to show gratitude to Barbara, who has been tidying our rooms every day as part of her seva, or service back to the practice. Thank you, Barbara, for keeping our spaces clean, as we cleanse our bodies and minds."

Shakti returned her hands to prayer and bowed deeply as the rest of us looked confusedly at one another. In unison, we said, "Thank you, Barbara."

Of all the odd things to happen at a yoga retreat, one of our fellow practitioners was scrubbing our toilets? Our silent friend put her hands on her heart and closed her eyes, bowing back to each of us in turn.

I don't know Barbara that well. Back in Miami, she didn't really hang out with us after class and I'd never thought to ask her about her background or family or career. Rumor had it that she came from serious money, which I bought based on her perfect American orthodontia and annoyingly effortless elegance. But also, she was such an old-school diehard yogi, and just seemed happy to share space with other practitioners. I wondered what it must be like to be that devoted to something. Anything. Did I love anything (other than Tara) as much as Barbara loved yoga?

Maybe she was the only one of us who really *got* it. The whole yoga thing. The goal, if I understand it correctly, of the eight-fold path of yoga is to quiet the fluctuations of the mind, both good and bad, so that one can be unaffected by external events. To achieve such a state of balance and equanimity that both winning the lottery and losing a limb would bring you the same sense of calm.

But who is actually in it for that? Honestly, I just like how it makes me feel and enjoy the small nods here and there to my Indian heritage. I've never had delusions of becoming a monk or a stoic.

But Barbara? Hmm. Maybe she had reached that nirvana-like state. She was paying for a *luxury* retreat, and then mopping our floors to stay humble. Meanwhile, I was flirting with my best friend's crush and getting an ego boost from a handstand. I suddenly remembered, with a flush of shame, the weed roach that was emptied from my garbage bin two nights before.

Hopefully Barbara's devotion means she's also nonjudgmental.

BARBARA

Here are some of the things that I've found (and cleaned) in the yogi's and yoginis' bedrooms:

1. Dirty magazines (Indira's room)

2. A very heavy steel gun that emits a terrible, dark vibration (Carol Ann's room)

3. An unclean and recently used personal pleasure device (Jessica's room)

4. Drug paraphernalia (Indira's room)

5. A personal laptop containing pornographic images in a desktop folder (not that this is anything to be ashamed of) (Daniel's room)

6. Wads of crumpled-up toilet paper and a small unlabeled bottle of oil (Daniel's room)

7. More makeup than a Sephora store (Carol Ann's room)

8. A journal full of mournful recollections (Shakti's room)

It is amusing how people will leave their private things out, the objects they'd hide from respected friends and family, for service workers to easily discover. It suggests a lack of respect for those deemed *lower*.

But this is part of the reason I serve. To humble myself. To throw myself at the feet of fellow practitioners and teachers alike. It does one well to remember our place in this world, which is to give, not to receive.

JESSICA

Twelve hours earlier I could have died from embarrassment, but after the morning yoga session, it was clear I was so back in the game.

Daniel was basically my personal adjuster for the entire class. We flowed together as we stretched, and balanced, and breathed. His breath was warm on my neck as he cradled me in chair pose. His hands left prints on my body as he peeled my hips open into extended side angle. I finished the class hyped up and wet in more ways than one.

Was anyone else noticing this? Did Shakti find it unprofessional?

To be clear—it was *highly* unprofessional. But I didn't care. Also, it was baffling to have that much attention after I'd blown my chances so spectacularly the night before. Men are confusing. Maybe he'd thought I was rejecting him in some weird way when we were down by the lake, and that made him hot for the chase? Maybe I had accidental game? All I knew was that I'd been celibate for too long and was finally ready to break my streak.

But first, I had a date with a hunting rifle. I met Margaret down by her residence, where she and Martina were sitting on the porch with Scout. The women nodded as I approached, my heart beating like an incessant morning alarm. Their four-legged helper trotted up to me and barked a hello.

"Hey there, Scout," I said, bending down to scratch behind his ears.

The pup pressed his head into my hand and rubbed it back and forth and I thought, Maybe I really should get a dog.

It was unseasonably hot for October. Which is to say, it was scorching. More of an August heat than a mid-autumn one. Mosquitoes hummed in every direction and the air was thick like a mimosa with pulp. Between the yoga, the erotic adjustments, and the two-minute walk from the Active Room to Martina and Margaret's house, I was drenched in sweat.

"You ready to learn something new today?" Martina stood up from her Adirondack chair and fixed her ponytail. She had the kind of hard lined face that looks more beautiful and interesting than weathered. She probably wasn't much older than me (just used fewer serums and Botox and SPF).

I scratched my shoulder. "I guess?" Truthfully, I wasn't thrilled about holding a deadly weapon, but Margaret's offer had been so kind. And hey, when at a meat-eating, firearm-loving yoga retreat, why not?

Margaret looked surprisingly chic with fashionable-looking hunting gear and her shiny dirty-blond hair in a topknot. She was the outdoorsy Barbie to Carol Ann's Bratz doll. If I had to guess, Margaret was probably ten years or so younger than her wife. Roughly the same age difference between Daniel and me. Did that make cougars of us older women? I smiled at the thought. I'd always wanted to be a cougar.

"Good luck." Martina kissed her wife goodbye and then waved to me. "Remember, always keep the muzzle pointed down when you aren't shooting." I must have looked like a lost cause.

Margaret hoisted a backpack onto one shoulder and grabbed a rifle that was leaning against the porch.

"She worries too much," she said, with a smile in her eyes. "Don't worry. Everything will be fine." She nodded at the dog. "Let's go, Scout."

He trotted along after her, and I fell in at the back, becoming stickier by the second as the late-afternoon sun burned my bare shoulders.

We made small talk along the way, and I learned that she and Martina had met, long distance, on Tinder, and then Margaret—lovestruck and brave—left behind her family farm in Vermont to manage the Namaste Club with her now wife. There was hope for me yet.

Margaret led us to a part of the property I hadn't yet seen, where there was a clearing and a wooden fence-looking structure set up with targets nailed to it. My breath caught in my throat. This was fucking real. I was going to shoot at something.

In general, trying new things gives me anxiety. It's twofold: fear of the unknown and performance anxiety. I typically suck at things on my first try, and I hate that feeling. But this was even more intense, since I'd be wielding a deadly weapon. Something I grew up crazy opposed to. Though I can now admit the utility of hunting for food or even shooting targets for sport is probably fine.

We stopped at a pavilion area with homemade benches and a ledge that faced the targets. Margaret leaned the rifle against the wood frame and slipped her backpack off.

"Martina and I built this range for practice." She smiled proudly and handed me a pair of protective glasses and earmuffs from her bag.

I accepted the gear, hoping she didn't notice my sweating palms.

"I've been wondering. Who are the owners of this place?"

Margaret laughed as she unloaded a box of bullets from her pack.

"The land has been in Martina's family for generations. Before all this"—she gestured with her chin—"it was an orange grove. There're still some trees out past the boar preserve, but most of them died off with disease. Citrus greening. Poor Martina was forced to sell during Covid. Now a hedge-fund guy owns the grounds. Turned it into a *private wellness escape*. We just manage it."

So a finance guy owned the pseudo-crunchy yoga retreat grounds. Why was I not surprised? "I'm so sorry," I said.

Margaret shrugged and loaded the rifle with practiced precision, her fingers slipping the bullets into their cartridge as if loading batteries into a TV remote. Then she pulled on her earmuffs and eyewear, picked the gun back up, and posted up against the wooden ledge. She stepped her right foot forward, brought the rifle to her shoulder, paused, and pulled the trigger, releasing a bullet directly into the head of her paper target.

This time I didn't fall to my knees, but my mouth did gape open in admiration. I didn't know anything about guns, but this woman could *shoot*.

"Holy shit, Margaret! I'm guessing you've done that once or twice." I shouted so she could hear me with her ears covered.

"Let's give you a try," she shouted back.

I surprised even myself by stepping forward eagerly, securing my protective gear into place.

"Which is your dominant foot?" She put the safety on her rifle and leaned it back up against the wood frame.

"I have no idea!" I shrugged unhelpfully.

"Turn around."

I obliged. Then, out of nowhere, she pushed me hard from behind. I lurched forward with my left leg and was about to spin around and ask her *what the hell*, when I realized what she'd done.

"Okay. Right foot forward then. Let's build your shooting stance like we're building a house. From the ground up."

She helped me space my feet shoulder width apart with my dominant foot back, then showed me how to angle my body slightly forward with a micro bend in my knees. It felt exactly like learning proper alignment in a yoga pose.

After some safety warnings that seemed painfully obvious but would have been irresponsible not to say out loud, she readied the rifle and hoisted it on my shoulder.

Holding it steady, she said, "Look here" and "aim there."

Beads of sweat rolled down my face. This was it. A pulse was throbbing in my shooting finger. The target was in my sight, blurry and seemingly moving, even though I knew it to be stationary. Tamping the nerves down, I inhaled a full breath through my nose and pulled the trigger on the exhale.

Everything went dark. Then Margaret pulled the rifle off my shoulder and said, "Okay. Next time, keep your eyes open."

I scanned the target. No hit.

"Where did the bullet go?" I wiped my dripping hands on my yoga pants, my heart sinking.

"Somewhere out by the trees over there." Margaret said it without judgment, which I appreciated. Scout lay down in the shadiest part of the pavilion and rested his head on his paws. I tried not to think that he was giving up on me.

"Let's try again." Margaret returned the rifle to my shoulder.

It was heavier than it looked, but she kept it in place for me, like she had last time. All I had to do was point and shoot.

I tried to quiet my mind, focusing on the chest of the paper man in front of me. I willed my heartbeat to slow. This time, my gaze was steady, the target was unswaying. Once I knew I had it perfectly in my sight, I pulled the trigger and BAM.

Not a direct hit, but not too off, either. The bullet went through the paper, about six inches from the chest's center. I resisted the urge to jump up and down in celebration.

Margaret removed the rifle and patted my back. "Not bad, newbie. You're looking like a natural."

Of all the things in the world I could have a natural aptitude for, I never once imaged it would be shooting. And succeeding at it was one of the best highs I'd ever experienced. We stayed out at the range for another hour, practicing over and over using different targets. Who would have thought? The most fulfilling event so far at the yoga retreat was learning how to shoot a rifle.

But then again, I hadn't had sex yet . . .

CAROL ANN

After yoga class, I gathered my mat and stepped out into the steamy Florida air. The humid blast covered me like a bear hug and squeezed me all the way to my villa. When I reached the door, Barbara appeared behind me like a middle-aged Cinderella with a mop and a bucket, but I told her to please come back in an hour, which she agreed to by nodding her head and moving on toward Daniel's cottage instead.

We had extra free time that day and I knew exactly how I was spending it. For starters, I was going to stop blaming myself for the mistakes I'd made with my home life. I'd promised Shakti—no more negative self-talk! And also, I was going to work on fixing it. Being proactive instead of reactive.

The modern blessing of air-conditioning had kept my room cool and inviting, and I felt grateful for a break from all the heat and humidity. I closed the door behind me and locked it for maximum privacy. After ditching my yoga mat, I grabbed the chenille throw blanket from the foot of my bed and threw it over my shoulders, crumpled into the pillows, and mussed my hair a little bit. I wanted to look a little disheveled but still pretty. There's a fine line there. Then I took a deep inhale through the nose, exhaled it completely, and FaceTimed my husband.

Beau answered from work. It was 11:30 A.M. and he was sitting at his desk, impossibly handsome in a checkered button-down and a crisp red tie. My faux-distressed face betrayed a smile. I couldn't help it when he looked so cute. The phone must have been leaned up against his computer monitor, because the camera showed him from his waist up and I could see his eyes trained just above me on whatever he had on the screen and his fingers below, working the keyboard.

"Hey, babe," he said, without looking down at me.

I checked my face in the camera and adjusted my features to read more solemn.

"Hey, honey bear," I said in my smallest voice.

Beau's head snapped down to the phone.

"You okay?" He lifted his hands off the keyboard and pushed his chair back, leaning down closer to the screen so that we were eye to eye.

"Sorry, I know you're busy. It's just been really hard, and I miss you and the kids so much." I lowered my eyes and tightened the throw blanket around me with my free hand. I was laying it on thick, but men aren't that great with the art of subtlety, so I had to.

Beau picked up the phone and studied my face. I met his eyes and half-smiled, then looked back down.

"Well, we miss you, too. You'll be back in a couple days, right? I thought you were having the time of your life over there."

I sighed and shook my head. "I was. I thought I was. I really tried, babe. But these people are just too much. You won't believe what I'm dealing with here. It just makes me miss home, and you, so badly."

He sucked his teeth. "What, are they a bunch of yoga hippies? I thought this was a different kind of retreat. You nabbed a Burmese python, for Christ's sake."

"I know. I know." I rearranged myself on the bed and let the throw blanket fall down a little, revealing a bit of cleavage inside my sports bra. "But other things have happened since then that have me spooked. You'd know how to deal with it but it's becoming overwhelming for me. I'm trying to be as strong as I can. Maybe I should come home early. My place is with you and the kids."

Beau's gaze drifted from my eyes to my chest, so I let the blanket drop a little more and squeezed my arms around my breasts to make them look plumper.

"No, we paid for the week, and you need to stick it out. What do you mean 'things have happened'? What kind of things?"

"Remember when I said I was going on a boar hunt?" I tried to make my face look as anguished as possible, not that he was looking there. He nodded. "Well, that should have been my warning sign. Our lady guide got to it before I did, and when we opened it up, it was full of disease and worms."

"That does happen," Beau said, leaning back in his chair and looking up at my face, but this time with a hunger in his eyes.

"It does," I agreed. "But there was a darkness to this one and I could feel it. A darkness to this whole place, really." I explained how I was surrounded by perverts and enablers. Women who don't care about children; married women who cuckold their men; women who have sex with other women; men who try to sleep with anything that moves.

Whatever spell Beau had been under immediately broke.

"What did you say?" His eyes filled with rage. "Is this that man who's flitting around your yoga retreat? Around all you women in your sweaty skintight clothes?"

I closed my eyes and nodded.

"Did he touch you? Because I will kill him."

I shook my head.

"No, baby. He knows to stay away from me. I'm protected by a forcefield of righteousness. The only ones he doesn't bother are me and the yoga teacher. I swear. But I am surrounded by sinners, and it is disgusting."

"I don't know what you ladies expected. You're out there like a bunch of sheep to the slaughter, letting a wolf into your *sacred spaces*. A rooster into your damn henhouse." He looked back down at my sports bra. "Carol Ann, you are crazy if you think that man doesn't have his eyes on you."

I slipped the blanket completely off and lay on my back with the phone directly on top of me.

"I don't feel safe here, Beau. I wish your hands were around me right now. I can't wait to come home so you can take care of me."

He glanced over at his office door and then unbuckled his belt and started working on his pants buttons.

"Oh, I'm gonna take care of you."

I smiled and, with my free hand, slipped the sports bra off from one shoulder and then the other. Beau took himself into his hands, and I pulled the bra down and squeezed my right breast.

"I need you," I said, narrowing my eyes.

Beau held the phone at his eye level, but I could see he was working himself with the other hand.

"I won't let anyone hurt you, baby. Now show me what's mine."

I held the phone up higher and slipped off my yoga pants and panties.

"It's all yours, baby."

Beau shut his eyes for a second and bit his lip, then looked at me again. I spread my legs and slid my hand down slowly.

"That's my good girl." His words came out choked and I could tell it wouldn't be long.

I arched my back and moaned. "Oh, Beau. Promise you'll take care of me no matter what."

He breathed heavily and looked like he was trying to find the words.

"Of course, baby. I'm your man. I'll protect you." He winced and bit his lip, straining for a few more seconds, then grunted. And it was over.

I knew we were on our way back.

SHAKTI

NOW

Preparing for the full moon ceremony required a lot of time and dedication. I wanted it to be perfect for the guests, and that meant first cultivating the proper mental state within myself.

After yoga class, I meditated on my own to quiet my mind. Then I practiced an ancient Tibetan body flow to align my chakras and prepare my body. I fasted for the day, as a sacrifice, and journaled a gratitude list. Then I wrapped individual bundles of sage for all my students to cleanse their energies under the full moon.

I didn't see the group again until just before sundown, so I'm not exactly sure how everyone else spent the day.

JESSICA

Daniel was leading an adaptogenic cocktail-making class in the afternoon, and I decided it was finally time to manifest my desires. To *dress for success,* in other words.

My lingerie bag beckoned to me, a siren call from the skimpy white lacy set that had just days ago seemed like a mistake to pack. I put it on and stood in front of the mirror, remembering the selfie I'd taken in the black bra and panties. How sexy and empowered it had made me feel. Why not take another one?

If the black lingerie was vampy and seductive, the white felt virginal and kittenish. Like I was a maiden waiting to be deflowered. I posed with one hip out and pinched a nipple with the hand not holding my phone. And snapped. Who was I? This sultry and confident roleplay version of me was new, and I loved it.

Part of me expected the photo to be unattractive and cringey, an immediate delete. Imagine my surprise when I checked it and, actually, I looked pretty hot. Why hadn't I ever seen myself this way before? Surely, seductive Jess must have always been there. Albeit buried deep. My mind started to drift, imagining men seeing me this way, reacting to my body, wanting to touch me. The thoughts sent an all-over tingle down my skin. Then I remembered what else was in the lingerie bag. And I had time to kill.

Masturbation is nothing new to me, but this time was different. I wasn't turned on by the thought of a man, I was turned on by the thought of *myself*. I was the sexual object in my fantasy. And the men were just lucky to be in my presence. Yes, there were more than one. My brain, my rules.

Afterward, I showered and blow-dried my hair, spent a little extra time applying natural-looking makeup, and put the lingerie back on. The fact that I had just come in it made it feel even sexier. Maybe I'd take Daniel back to my room that night, and maybe I wouldn't. But I was going to channel my inner Indira and be ready for either possibility.

I threw on a fitted olive-green tank dress that showed off my cleavage and hugged my curves in all the right places, for once not caring that those curves might be wider than they were in my twenties and thirties. Then I slipped the edibles from Indira into my tote bag and was ready for whatever came next.

The cocktail-making class was optional, but everyone except for Shakti ended up participating. Even Carol Ann, who didn't seem to want anything to do with me, or the rest of us, since our ill-fated hunting trip, showed up.

We met outside of the Nourishment Pavilion, where Daniel had set up a long table and covered it with various fruits, herbs, and liquor bottles. It looked like he was preparing a science experiment for alcoholic witches.

The sight of him gave me a shiver, a little secret thrill, and instead of tamping it down, I walked right up to him and kissed his cheek. No big deal. In Miami, that's how we say hello. But I'd always been too nervous to close the gap between us before.

"You look beautiful," he said, gazing from my face down to my chest. It excited me to be so blatantly objectified.

"Thanks, you don't look so bad yourself. And already shirtless again, I see." I let my eyes scan his body, lingering down by his taut and toned abdomen.

Daniel was wearing elaborate mala necklaces that night. Some with crystal beads, some with carved wood. It struck me as funny, because Daniel—other than his man bun and *sk8er boi* tattoo—had seemed more finance or tech bro–ey than yoga dude to me when I first started seeing him in class. But people do change. And sometimes quickly when they get into culty wellness things. I wondered if the same would happen to me. Did I want it to?

"The best way to harness the full moon energy is through direct skin contact." He stretched his arms out; I suppose to take in more of that moony energy.

"Oh, okay," I said, trying not to imagine myself having direct skin contact with Daniel. And then, because the question suddenly occurred to me, "Hey, what is it that you do for a living? When you're not giving world-class adjustments and leading craft cocktail classes."

He shifted his weight a little bit and tilted his face up. "This and that."

So he was unemployed. No big deal. It's not like I was ready to pick out china patterns with him.

"I was in tech, but it was too soulless for me, you know? Everything was so literal and numbers driven."

I was pretty sure he'd just given the definition of a job, but I let it go.

"Yeah, that sounds awful," I said.

Daniel was no brain surgeon. But men pursue women all the time based on looks alone, so why couldn't I?

Indira, Carol Ann, Barbara, and I gathered around the table and Daniel changed the cadence of his voice from flirty to teachy.

"What are adaptogens?" he said, standing back from the table and projecting his voice.

Carol Ann raised her hand. "Adaptogens are herbal and other plant-based ingredients that assist with brain function and relaxation."

It sounded like she was reading labels at the Vitamin Shoppe.

Daniel snapped his fingers. "Very good," he said, which made me irrationally annoyed. "Also known as euphorics, adaptogens are a category of substances that have been proven to relax the nervous system and encourage optimal cognitive function."

Okay, so he didn't sound like a total idiot.

He pointed to the little glass jars on his table. "Ginseng, mushrooms (unfortunately not the magic kind), CBD, and kava. On their own, these drinks can make you feel fantastic, even causing a natural high. They make a great replacement for alcohol. But today, we are going to take them one step further, and use them to actually create cocktails *with* alcohol."

Indira leaned into me and whispered, "So we can get double fucked up." It was like she was on college spring break all over again. I respected it.

I covered my mouth to laugh, and Daniel said, "Hey, you two. I've got my eyes on you." He winked, and I blushed, enjoying the naughty-professor vibe a little too much.

Barbara laughed joyfully and wagged a finger at us. That woman always appeared to be happy. What was her secret? I'd gladly try whatever adaptogenic Kool-Aid she was drinking.

Carol Ann, on the other hand, looked like she'd rather be anywhere else. It was an optional activity. I wondered why she would torture herself if she wasn't into it.

We spent the next hour experimenting with different combinations, like a ginseng old-fashioned (not bad), a kava negroni (fucking disgusting), and a CBD margarita (pretty good). The unanimous winner, though, was Carol Ann's creation—a reishi-mushroom espresso martini. It was bitter, and sweet, and earthy, and perfect. After tasting it, Barbara dropped to her knees and kissed Carol Ann's feet (which was gross).

All the sipping gave me a healthy buzz, whether from adaptogens or hard liquor, or the combination, and part of me wondered how I'd get through the rest of the night.

I felt a hand on my waist and, thinking it was Indira, playfully swatted it away. Spinning around, I realized it was Daniel.

"Sorry, didn't mean to . . . " he said.

"Oh no!" I blushed. "I thought you were someone else."

He looked around as if to say *who exactly could that be?*

"I just came by to say that I'm looking forward to seeing you at the full moon ceremony later. After I clean up over here."

I hugged my arms around my body and took a step closer to him.

"Oh, me too. I actually have a little something, if you're interested." My boldness surprised me, and I met his eyes, both of us smiling.

He raised an eyebrow.

"Yeah?" he said. "I'm intrigued."

I tapped his stomach, his tanned hard stomach. "Nothing like that. Just a couple edibles, if you partake. Not that we need them after these drinks. I'm already feeling pretty good."

"I'm definitely interested." He ran a rough hand down my arm, leaving goose bumps in its wake. "See you in a bit."

CAROL ANN

There was full moon energy in the air. Like a low-level humming in the atmosphere that pierces all the way to your blood. That's how I felt, anyhow. Even the trees looked more alive, lit up and sparked from the inside out. It was the kind of night when anything could happen.

Earlier that day, Shakti had told me I should purify for the full moon in order to fully receive its power. This isn't hokey; it's proven stuff. The moon controls the tides in the seas but also the blood in our body. There doesn't have to be a rhyme or reason to it; God works in mysterious ways. So after my phone call with Beau, I prayed to the good Lord for all I sought to manifest: a happy husband, a peaceful home, a fruitful career, a healthy body, and a sound mind. Then I drank two shots of pure castor oil to eliminate all the toxins in my body. It went down easily, with its nutty taste coating my throat, and I could feel it going to work. Castor is a natural laxative, and also how I initiated labor with both of my children. The cramps brought me right back to the delivery room, but this time at the end it wasn't a brand-new baby, but an empty stomach, ready to receive.

I'd been trying to learn more about the healing properties of adaptogens ever since one of my favorite podcasts, *The Primal Woman*, had devoted an entire episode to the topic. I'd already started experimenting with maca smoothies for breakfast, but the alcoholic versions offered a great way to make social drinking more healthful. At the cocktail class, the adaptogens soothed my nerves and coated my whole body so that it was an empty vessel.

I was relieved when it was over, though. I didn't need to spend one more second looking at Daniel's bare flaccid torso. It took every ounce of my strength not to say, "Put a shirt on, Bucko!"

The next part of the evening was what I'd been waiting for.

The Awakening Fire Pit was majestically ablaze, its flames licking the thick air like they were reaching out for the moon. All around me, I breathed in the earthy aroma of the char mixed with Shakti's sage. The combination made me dizzy, but pleasantly so. I could already feel the power of the moon pulsating in my bones.

Shakti wore an airy tunic that stuck to her in several places. She kneeled on a woven rug in front of the fire and beat her hands on a bongo drum, the vibrations pulsing through the back of my throat. The heat was made more oppressive with the roaring fire, but she seemed immune to it, even as sweat poured down from her face and onto her dress, which became translucent with the moisture. She had brown dots painted around her eyes in three concentric lines, and her luscious blond hair tied into two braids spilling down her back.

Night was beginning to fall, and the moon shined bright overhead, like a Florida orange in the sky. It was breathtaking to behold. The force of nature so powerful and almighty. God's creation in all its splendor. A light breeze blew in from the banyan trees, rustling their leaves and then catching Shakti's tunic, puffing it out like an ethereal balloon. She banged the drum.

And some people claim to not believe in a higher power.

I was rapt, like being in church for an especially moving sermon. But other than Barbara and Shakti, I appeared to be the only one.

Indira, the fallen lady, was tapping away at her phone, oblivious to the magic right before her eyes. And Jessica, barf. She was canoodling with Daniel, all lips to ears and giggling. Not for the first time that trip, I thanked the heavens for giving me a husband like Beau.

Thinking about my husband, my eyes became watery. I imagined him next to me, gazing up at the full moon in the pitch-dark sky. He'd love it as much as I did. And I remembered how, when we were just twenty or twenty-one, we'd drive down to the beach at night and sit in the abandoned lifeguard stands and just watch the stars with the swoosh of the Atlantic Ocean below us. Those were some of the best moments of my life. We could get back to that place and do that again. So easily.

Without realizing it, I had started weeping uncontrollably while simultaneously laughing, because everything in my life was so perfect and beautiful. And really it always had been. I'd just stopped noticing.

Shakti sang one of her hauntingly beautiful mantras and I didn't even care that it was about Shiva or whoever. I translated it to Jesus in my own heart and let my body carry me, swaying back and forth like Barbara was doing. I let it all wash over me. The night, the moon, the whole universe at my fingertips. The special awareness and connection with nature.

SHAKTI

NOW

Sometimes, to receive the full moon energy, one must eliminate all the toxins in the body, from the inside out. That's what happened to Carol Ann. What might have looked like crying, and vomiting, and other bodily functions wasn't sickness, but healing. It was her subconscious literally eliminating what no longer served her.

Carol Ann experienced a profound spiritual awakening that night, and I was proud of her. It was like watching your child take its first steps. But the process took a toll on her physically, so I had to end the full moon ceremony early to take care of her.

I'm not sure what the other students were doing at that moment, as I was focused only on how Carol Ann needed me. The expulsion of tears and other fluids had weakened her, and as I sang "Ma Durga," I noticed she had collapsed onto the earth.

With Barbara's help, I gathered her into my arms and let her lean on me while we walked back to her villa. I helped her bathe and dress and then tucked her into bed, waiting with her and singing mantra until she fell peacefully to sleep.

Healing is not a solitary or linear journey. We all need guides to light our path.

JESSICA

It was hot as Hades outside. Really, Shakti. A fire pit?

A single bead of sweat slid off my cheek and down my cleavage. I didn't usually consider boob sweat to be sexy, but the way Daniel was tracking its journey, my mind imagined him sticking his tongue out to taste it.

"Those edibles you mentioned earlier . . ." His breath was steam on my ear and smelled like mushroom espresso martini. "Should we take those and get out of here?"

I looked around at what had to have been the saddest full moon ceremony in history. One silent yogi hippie dancing, one right-wing nutjob crying, and my best friend, who couldn't wait to get the hell out of there.

Two nights in a row without dinner would have been a record for me, but also, I couldn't imagine sweating through another minute of Shakti's full moon ceremony before our specified mealtime.

I rooted around my tote bag until I found the little pouch containing the gummies. Was this a bad idea? I'm not a big drug person, though I do partake from time to time. And Indira assured me that these were a *hybrid* and therefore would be mellow but also social, with no paranoia. I chewed off half of one and handed a whole one to Daniel. He took it from my fingers with his teeth.

Shakti's sound bowl playing and chanting grew louder. I coughed from the fire smoke in my lungs.

"Did you want to stick around for this?" Daniel asked, eyebrow raised.

I weighed my grumbling stomach against my neglected vagina and decided that the latter was hungrier.

"Not particularly."

Daniel and I locked elbows and headed back to my villa.

The crisp air-conditioning welcomed us inside like a glass of ice water after a hike. Daniel, still shirtless and wearing muslin cotton balloon shorts, stretched his arms and breathed it in.

"The energy is so pure in here." He turned around and pulled me into his arms, lowering his nose to mine. My stomach fluttered.

"I'm so glad we left the group," he said. "Something about you has been calling to me ever since the first day." He breathed in deeply, as if trying to inhale my face.

"Was it my goldendoodle energy?" I let my hands slide around his strong back. It was sticky but I didn't care. It felt good to touch his skin.

Daniel laughed. "It might have been that. What did your friend say? That you have bulldog energy? I don't see that at all."

I cringed but tried to let the comment wash over me. Fucking Indira. But then again, she and I had both said regrettable things. Unraveling myself from the hug, I took his hand and led him to the bed. This mating dance/ritual, now that I was in it, was going easier than I'd anticipated.

"A French bulldog," I corrected. As if that made me more sophisticated. "A dog who eats croissants instead of biscuits." It was the worst joke I'd ever told.

A tingle formed behind my eyes, and then pulsed in my hands, chest, and throat. I giggled. There it was . . . the edible was kicking in, and quickly.

Daniel's cobalt eyes sparked and locked with mine, a wide grin taking over his face. We fell into each other's bodies, laughing. And there it was. The feeling I'd been missing for so long. An electricity. A playfulness. A joyfulness. The knowledge that we probably had only this one moment together, but that it was okay. Because we were currently inside that moment. Living it.

I felt like a teenager. Uninhibited and free.

We sat up and scooted a little closer to each other, both of us wearing huge, cheesy grins. I fiddled with my fingers a little, which he stopped by placing one of his hands on top of mine. I loved how much bigger his body parts were compared with mine. How one of his hands could cover my two.

"I didn't want her, you know," Daniel said. "Your friend."

The comment bristled, and I silently begged him to stop there, to not ruin what we had going. But he continued.

"I mean, I could've hooked up with her. But I didn't want to ruin my chances with you." He reached his other hand out and caressed my knee.

Instinctively, I didn't believe him. And I realized that I'd probably hate him later for the comment. It also reminded me of how Indira had paraded him in front of my face on the first night of the retreat, and I bristled all over again. But in the moment, I took the bait.

"She thinks you'd go after anyone." I hoped it came out teasing instead of insecure. "Is that true?"

He slid his hand farther up my thigh and squeezed. Any higher, and he'd feel how wet I already was.

"I have standards," he said. The desire in his eyes was palpable, and I was sure that mine was just as intense.

"What about Shakti?" I asked. "She's young and beautiful. And you two are obviously really close. You two never?"

I'd always wondered about it. How did two young, hot, single people spend that much time together and not cross a line? It seemed unlikely. I almost regretted asking. Did I even want to know?

He shook his head, easing my mind. Not that I had any right to care in the first place.

"Trust me. I'd love to."

I swallowed the jealousy.

"But nah. Shakti's celibate. You knew that right?"

Now *that* was a surprise.

"Umm. No. What? Isn't she like twenty-five years old?"

Thankfully, he resumed the inner thigh massage. I had been starting to wish I hadn't switched topics right before things turned steamy. Again.

"Something like that," Daniel said, pressing his fingers into my flesh and making deep imprints. "She's taken a vow of purity." He shrugged. "But I haven't."

"That doesn't add up," I said, though I should have just let it go and leaned into his inuendo instead. "She trades Bitcoin. She has a tequila sponsor. She wears teeny-tiny yoga outfits. But she's taken a vow of *purity*? Something is off-brand there. Also, she could have any man in Miami that she wants."

Daniel stopped his massaging. Shit.

"What do you mean?" He raised an eyebrow, and I couldn't tell if he was confused or somehow disappointed.

I leaned in closer to him. Somewhere, I'd read that this body language gave unequivocal permission for sexual relations.

"Nothing. Forget it. I just think she can be a hustler sometimes. I mean, we all can be. But I like her; don't get me wrong."

I slid my hand up his balloon shorts, ready to pivot the conversation back to the task at hand.

Daniel sat up straight but didn't stop my hand from wandering.

"You think Shakti is a false guru?"

I sighed. "No. I mean. She's a great yoga teacher. But she wasn't born some guru. Like, she must have been someone before she was Shakti. Like we were saying yesterday. Everyone has secrets."

"Hmm," he said. I felt him harden just above my hand.

"Or maybe she's just from LA. There are lots of Shaktis in LA, probably." I teased my hand just below his bulge.

Daniel tensed then relaxed. "Maybe she just doesn't like sex. Do you like it?"

"Mmm-hmm," I said. Something inside me felt alive and powerful, like when I'd held the rifle earlier, steadied it, and shot my target.

Daniel ran his hands over my still-clothed chest and lightly tickled a nipple. I tried not to gasp.

"What do you like?" he asked. "Can you tell me or is it a secret?"

"Everyone has secrets," I whispered.

"You want to know mine?" Daniel thrust his hips so that his erection landed in my hand. He leaned forward and put his tongue in my ear. "I have a crush on you."

It was the cheesiest pickup line I'd ever heard, and I went completely weak at the words.

Daniel pulled down my tank sleeves and exposed my breasts, cupping them with both hands as he put his tongue in my mouth and used the weight of his body to lay me down on the bed. I moaned into his mouth and found myself hyper receptive and alive to his every touch. This was what I'd been waiting for. And I accepted it greedily.

He kissed his way down my body, taking one of my nipples between his teeth. I yelped in pleasure. An actual yelp, like how I imagine a frightened Chihuahua would sound. He pulled off the rest of my dress and worked his fingers around my clitoris. I hadn't been this wet since seeing *Interview with the Vampire* for the first time as a teenager.

I pulsated into his hands, his mouth, his pelvis. He brought his mouth back to mine and pinched a nipple hard while pushing himself inside me. I came immediately. How embarrassing. Was this how incredibly horned-up teenage boys felt?

Moaning into his ear, I pushed harder to let him know I was still good to go. He reached down to my hips and pulled them in deeper, his sweat dripping down onto my chest and mixing with my heat and musk and pheromones. Then he squeezed his eyes shut and gasped. "Oh my god. Fuck."

He was into it. Me. The thought was thrilling.

"Oh, Daniel." It was put on at this point but who cared. I wanted him to explode in ecstasy like I just had.

"Oh, fuck." He thrust faster and deeper. "Oh my god. Jennifer."

BARBARA

The moon is my mother. When she is full, her love radiates through me like electricity conducted through a wire. I danced for her, with my vibrations lifted in her honor, her life force coursing through my body and inspiring my movements with pure freedom. Arms. Legs. Breath. Intention.

Shakti sang as though possessed by the mother Durga herself. If I allowed myself to speak, I would have chanted back to her. *Hey ma Durga. Jay jay ma. Jay jay ma.*

Just as the moon guides the tides, my blood rose and fell under her glow, coursing like lava through my veins. I closed my eyes and breathed the super-charged air. It was alive with energy. Time washed over me like a breeze.

When I opened my eyes, everything had changed, like I'd woken up in a new plane of existence, a different version of the same earth simulation. The dreamlike chanting had ceased. Jessica, Indira, and Daniel were missing. Disappeared into the night. And Shakti was kneeling over Carol Ann, wiping vomit from her filler-enhanced lips.

I froze for a moment, trying to recalibrate my senses to the reality before me.

"Can you help me get her to the villa?" Shakti asked, her eyes laced with fear.

Something uncomfortable pressed on my chest, a sensation I hadn't felt in a long while. Jealousy. To my surprise and disappointment, Shakti's maternal care for Carol Ann triggered something deep within. For a moment, I hated them both. How could this newborn yogini who slaughtered sacred creatures with her own dirty hands be worthy of my dear teacher's love? I balled my hands into fists and fought the urge to scream. Then I hung my head in shame. This was why I need to serve. Devotion sets fire to the ego.

I walked over to my teacher and the semiconscious woman and grabbed the latter's legs. Shakti took Carol Ann from under her arms, and together we carried her safely to her villa.

I left Shakti there to care for her student and stepped back into the moonlight. As the lunar energy pierced my skin, it awakened my third eye. I realized that something had been troubling me. Over the past few days, in my quiet and reflection, I'd overheard many disturbing conversations from my fellow practitioners. There were immature squabbles and ideological differences. There was life stolen from animals in the name of hunting. There were unattained desires and matrimonial disharmony. These people reeked of suffering in ways both seen and unseen to even themselves. And they were destroying our sacred divinity with their negative lifestyles.

By the time I reached the door to my villa, I knew what I needed to do. It came to me as clearly as when Sanjaya received his divine visions. This was my *divya drishti*. In order for these people to truly evolve, everyone on the retreat needed my love and my service, my care and my loyalty.

For Shakti, I would act as silent servant and anticipate her needs before even she did. I'd soothe her aching soul with my loving presence.

For Carol Ann, I would provide her with food and drink so she wouldn't again become weak of body. I'd pray for her gun to mysteriously disappear, so that no more blood need be shed on these grounds.

For Indira, I would act as a role model for how a spiritual woman should act.

For Jessica, I would gift a reusable BPA-free water bottle, which would be a good start.

And for Daniel, what more could I give than my playfulness, my friendship, and my body?

MARTINA

Margaret refilled the ice buckets on the buffet and frowned at the platters of food that had gone untouched. She'd spent all day preparing her most extravagant meal of the week: a mélange of roasted meats, three vegetable salads from our garden, a tray of homemade dips, and her famous dairy-free cornbread. All for nothing. Tomorrow some of it would be feed for the chickens.

"How long do you think we need to stay?" She swiped a stray blond curl behind her ear, and I couldn't help but smile. Even sweating and exhausted and frustrated, my wife looked movie-star gorgeous.

"You go on and head home. I'll start clearing this up. These people aren't eating tonight," I said.

Margaret shook her head.

"We're gonna need to burn the sheets when these people leave." She nodded over to Daniel and Jessica, who were touching and giggling like lovers at a high school dance. "That guy gives me the creeps. How many of these ladies here is he trying that with? Jesus Christ."

I shrugged.

"Definitely seems like an opportunist. But I'm more concerned with that one." I tilted my head at Carol Ann, and Margaret groaned. When I'd finally told her about the boar hunt, the full story of it, she'd taken it hard. Carol Anns are a dime a dozen here in Florida, but where Margaret's from, they do things differently.

Margaret winced. "Does she look all right to you? Her skin is a little . . . gray. And her legs look wobbly."

Now that she mentioned it, Carol Ann did look half stricken with the flu. But Shakti seemed to be on top of it. She might be young and kind of out there—I definitely didn't peg her for some kind of guru—but Shakti was fine enough. She seemed to care for her students, or clients, or whatever she called them.

I sucked my teeth. "Nothing about that woman is all right. I'll keep an eye out for a bit. You should head in. Only two and a half more days, babe. Then we'll never have to see these people again."

INDIRA

I tied a duster around my waist and snuck over to the Nourishment Pavilion, filling a tote bag with breakfast pastries and fruit to bring back to my room. Sometimes it's important to follow instructions before asking questions.

The text had come in at 6:30 A.M., but I didn't see it until I woke up an hour later.

Jessica wrote: Get food and meet me in your room ASAP! Please confirm.

At 7:45 A.M., I responded: On it. Meet you back here in 20. Ps, love the cryptic morning text.

The early hours were bright and sunny, again, and I wondered when it would finally start to feel like fall, or at least a Florida version of it. Underneath the cloudless sky, I could already tell that the day would be another scorcher.

As I hustled back to my villa, in anticipation of juicy gossip, something stole my attention near the Awakening Fire Pit. It appeared to be human, male, in an extremely odd position. On his back with his knees around his ears and his rear end in the air, to be exact. Naked.

Daniel, of course. Possibly the weirdest person on the yoga retreat, and that's really saying something. I paused for a minute to make sure he was breathing and, therefore, in that strange position on purpose.

When he reached around the outsides of his glutes to spread his cheeks out farther, I took it as my cue to leave and jogged the rest of the way back to my room.

A few minutes later, Jessica arrived, looking freshly showered but somehow still tousled. Her workout clothes were mismatched, and her hair was damp and chaotically brushed.

"Ooh, you okay there?" I asked, as she blew past me and started stuffing her face with the breakfast assortment I'd laid on the nightstand.

"No. I'm fucking starving," she said, with a mouthful of pineapple muffin. "I skipped dinner again last night."

I sat down next to her on the bed and waited for her to swallow. "Don't tell me you blew it again. I just saw your lover boy, sans clothes, outside with his butthole in the air. Is that some sort of remedy for his never-ending blue balls?"

Jessica helped herself to a sip from my water bottle.

"Perineum sunning," she said. "He says the sensitive anal membranes absorb vitamin D faster than other skin or some bullshit like that."

I exploded into laughter, which Jessica met at first with a dirty look, but then quickly joined in with me.

"So you fucked." I patted her on the back. "Congratulations."

"Ha. Thanks," she said. "Why do I feel so dirty?"

Jessica told me how he layered on cheesy pickup line after cheesy pickup line, and how it was like she went temporarily insane and fell for them because she just wanted the sex to happen.

I smiled, understanding that feeling all too well. "You slut. Well. How was it?"

She sipped her water and shook her head. "It was actually great. Until he called me the wrong name. It all went downhill quickly after that."

I couldn't help it. I started laughing again, but even harder this time.

"Screw you," she said, throwing the muffin paper at me. "It was like a hypnotist's spell suddenly broke, and I could finally see him for the horny yoga bro he's always been. Honestly, I want to shower again just thinking about it. Why was I so into him? He's a total douchebag."

"A fuckboy," I agreed. "But sometimes we need that. And honestly, you were just blinded by your vagina. You weren't thinking straight."

Jessica frowned and combed her fingers through her hair. "Is it always like this? Sex in this stage of life?"

I shrugged. "It's definitely different. But if you're a woman who's looking to get off, there's a good chance you'll find yourself a Daniel. It doesn't have to be a bad thing."

She bit her lip and smiled. "I did come at least."

"Score!" I said, lightly punching her on the shoulder.

It felt nice to be gossiping with her and I wondered if this meant we were over the hump of our awkward postfight phase. Conversations like this, analyzing the previous night's events, had been one of the things that had brought us together in the first place, even if the whole sexual experience thing was new for Jess.

After we unpacked her dalliance with Daniel, I told her what she'd missed last night after sneaking away with him. How our Bougie Boho chat kept pinging because our disavowal of Allison Kent had actually garnered us positive press, and how I was being interviewed by *Women's Wear Daily* about our response. Of course, Jessica had already known about that. Then I told her about how Carol Ann had been dancing under the moonlight like a tongue-speaking revivalist before suddenly throwing up and passing out in front of everyone.

"What the hell? Is she okay?" Jessica was wide-eyed and eating a yogurt parfait.

I grabbed the jar from her and spooned out a bite. "Not sure. Shakti and Barbara carted her off. Said it was all part of her cleansing. Something like that."

Jessica shook her head. "That sounds dangerous. Do you ever think that maybe there's such a thing as too much wellness? I mean, these *gurus* aren't trained as doctors or therapists. But they're telling us how to live and feeding us medicinal plants and asking us to spend long hours suffering blazing heat, and we're not even stopping to question it?"

I handed her back the yogurt. "I question it within reason. Shakti's a great yoga teacher, though. I feel good after classes and meditation. I don't really take it much deeper than that."

"Agreed," she said. "I do love her classes. But that lady is an enigma. You know what Daniel told me last night? She's *celibate*."

"Huh. Weird. Maybe it's a trendy thing in the spiritual community. She's so young, though. No sex? I don't know how people live like that. Sorry, no offense. You were basically celibate before last night."

She pinched my arm fat. "Don't remind me. It was awful. But so is this morning after ick. Shit. Do I really have to talk to him today? I'm so skeeved out by him calling me Jennifer. And, oh. He said something gross about you, too."

I shouldn't have cared, but my stomach clenched. "What?" I asked.

Jessica looked guilty. "It's stupid. He said something about how he definitely could have *had* you."

That asshole. I mock gagged myself with a finger. "Vom. Absolutely fucking not true. I asked him for a back massage. But then I told him to get the hell out so I could sleep. It was unequivocal."

Jessica rolled her eyes and said, "He's probably the type who thinks that any attention is an invitation. And I fell for it."

"Who cares." I waved it off. "You had fun for a little bit. And now you're done. You don't owe him, or his tanned butthole, anything."

Jessica leaned over and gave me a hug for what felt like the first time in ages.

"Thanks," she said.

I accepted her embrace gratefully, silently chastising myself for not telling her the whole truth.

CAROL ANN

When I woke up that morning, category five headache pounding my brain, I was briefly reminded of the awful hangovers of my twenties. Like kids do, Beau and I used to drink beers at a bar, singing "Friends in Low Places" at the tops of our lungs (this was before Garth Brooks got all PC) or we'd sometimes have a cocktail too many at a club.

I've never believed in the evils of alcohol. Jesus himself turned water into wine. It's all about moderation. There's no reason not to enjoy life's pleasures, as long as they aren't sinful and you aren't negatively affecting your health. A glass of wine or two. A cocktail or two.

Of course, as youngins, we didn't know our limits, so a night out ended up with 4:00 A.M. pizza at best and my face in a toilet bowl at worst.

This morning was different. If I was hungover from anything, it was from the mistakes of my past. My hubris as a working mom. Forgetting my role as a traditional wife to a traditional husband. Those poisons had left my body and, though the exorcism had been painful, I was ready to start fresh.

Despite how sick I'd been the night before, I didn't wake up disheveled, with vomit crusted in my hair and drool streaming down my face. No, I'd been lovingly bathed and dressed, my skin rubbed with rose oil, my hair brushed and tied back into a neat ponytail. I was wearing clean pajamas, and a glass of water with two Tylenol and a ginger candy were laid out on my nightstand.

Like a mother nursing her child, Shakti had fed my soul through its spiritual awakening, and for that I will be forever grateful. She was my angel.

There were only two and a half days left in the retreat and I was going to stay there for her. To absorb every drop of wisdom I could before heading home to my husband and children. New. Awakened. Who knows? Maybe I'd even quit my job, refocus on my duties as a wife and mother. We'd find a way to manage financially because our marriage is more valuable than money.

I texted Beau before running out for the morning hike.

Morning sunshine! Missing your strong arms and million-dollar smile. Let me know when's good to facetime you and the kids. XO

The Tylenol and ginger were helping, and by the time I walked out the door, I was already feeling fresher. And just a little hungry, because I'd missed dinner the night before.

Beau texted back as I was leaving.

Well someone sounds chipper. What happened to the scary Satan-loving women and the pervert? You all better now?

Of course. How could I have been so stupid? I was still supposed to be miserable and scared.

Just looking on the bright side, babe. Trying not to wallow in despair because I know I'll be back with our family in just a few more days. You're my rock.

That was a close one.

When Beau and I were first married, I'd known exactly how to play it. I let him open my car doors, climb the ladder to change lightbulbs, make the money, and pay the bills. My mother taught me well; she knew exactly how to get the ring. She'd say, "Carol Ann, men are looking for a lamb, not a lion. No suitable husband type is going to be attracted to a woman who is stronger than him, mentally or physically."

It's easy to forget that as the years go by, especially when we have babies and our mama instincts teach us to grab the reins and take care of business. Sometimes, it's just easier to do things on your own. But my mama's voice is whispering again in my ear, *Humble yourself.*

I skipped toward the Enlightenment Circle but had to slow down halfway, realizing I was still dizzy. Shakti met me there with a big hug. It seemed only her, Barbara, and I would be hiking that morning, which was probably for the best. I was going to make nice for the next few days, I'd decided, but I didn't miss the other retreaters one bit in that moment.

"I want you to take it easy today," Shakti said, taking a hold of my elbow as we walked. "You lost a lot of fluids last night, and your spirit went through a major transformation. Your body is going to be tired."

I nodded. "I feel it already."

"Coconut water, turmeric shots, nothing harsh or overheating. Be gentle on the body."

Barbara smiled and bobbed her head in agreement. For the first time, I noticed how the older woman appeared so vibrant and healthy. The natural shine in her hair caught the light in an almost mystical way, and her face, finely lined, was bright with alert eyes that radiated kindness. I wished, in that moment, I could talk to her. Ask for her secrets. I'm sure she had knowledge to share, a hidden well just waiting to be tapped.

We passed through the banyans, enjoying their brief shade from the already full sun overhead and walked down to the lake. Its steely blue was broken up by a family of mottled ducks floating along the surface, leaving soft ripples in their wake.

On the far end of the lake, near the cypress trees, three gators rested with their snouts poking out of the water. Two of them were your normal variety, the kind you see sunning themselves on the golf course, like ladies tanning at the beach. But the third one, good Lord. That was one big boy. He was the alpha male of that lake for sure.

As we crossed back through the banyans and into the Enlightenment Circle, a realization hit me. I was going to miss this place (not that I'd admit it to Beau). The immersive nature. The spiritual clarity. The healthful living. It had all done good work on my soul. I'd be leaving revived and refocused.

We were heading to breakfast, me still blissing out on the moment, when something horrible caught my eye. Next to the Awakening Fire Pit, pasty white ass cheeks were in the air, with a ding-dong hanging upside down toward a man's face. I gasped and stumbled back.

What a way to ruin a perfectly beautiful morning. I wondered if it was some kind of perverted satanic ritual. Why else would there be a man's penis out in public for everyone to see?

And wouldn't you know it, it was that filthy foot rubber, Daniel.

"I'm sorry, but I cannot be looking at this," I told the other ladies.

Shakti looked concerned but Barbara was just smiling, like she always was.

"You need to eat," Shakti said. "Just cover your eyes and I'll walk you to the Nourishment Pavilion."

I placed one hand over my eyes and Shakti covered it with one of hers. Barbara took one of my hands to guide me. Together, the three of us walked slowly to breakfast.

When we arrived, Shakti removed her hand and I turned to her.

"What the heck did I just witness? Because I feel like I need to bleach my eyeballs to get them clean again."

Shakti nodded. "I see how that would be uncomfortable to stumble upon. I'll talk to Daniel about choosing a more private location next time."

"Next time?" I asked. "You're telling me this is a normal thing?"

"Actually, I think it's something you might want to try. In the privacy of your own home, of course."

Shakti explained to me that Daniel was perineum sunning and

then told me all about its health benefits, like how it maximizes the life force in our bodies. I vaguely remembered Tucker Carlson talking about it on one of his shows so, surprisingly, Daniel was actually in good company, though I still fully judged him for doing it out there in the open. It's like he *wanted* people to see him. At least he wasn't doing anything crazy or ritualistic.

"Oh, I'll definitely try that out when I'm back in Vero," I said.

We walked inside the Nourishment Pavilion and headed straight to the breakfast spread, where Margaret had laid out the morning's selections. That's when the dizziness struck me again. I hadn't realized how starving I was until I laid eyes on the assortment of fresh pastries and parfaits. The sight and scents immediately sent my stomach growling, and I reached for a still-warm cinnamon bun.

Barbara poured two cups of coffee and stirred in almond milk, handing one to Shakti and one to me. Apparently, she knew my order better than most Starbucks baristas. I accepted it gratefully and patted her shoulder.

"You're a doll," I said.

That woman might have been on a silent journey, but she was definitely paying attention.

JESSICA

After scarfing down two hundred grams of carbohydrates in Indira's room, I realized that I looked like a woman who'd just stayed up late having drunk and stoned sex. My hair. My haphazard clothes.

Still, I wanted to make it to yoga. To hold my head up high and enjoy the last days of the retreat. Indira had a Zoom interview with *Women's Wear Daily* about our fallout with Allison Kent, and though I technically should've offered to stay in and help her prep, I opted to join the class instead. Not my most professional move, but I felt it was more important to prioritize my mental health. Self-care. Even if that also meant walking into my first awkward postcoital reunion with Daniel.

The funny thing was, for once, I wasn't even nervous about seeing him, even though the potential for uncomfortableness was so much higher than it had previously been. After all my pining, I'd finally seen underneath his sexy man bun and glistening torso, and what I'd found there wasn't all that special. Certainly no more special than what I had to offer. I felt strangely empowered. Like Beyoncé or Jamie Lee Curtis.

Back in my room, I transformed into something more presentable. Smoothed my hair out and tied it back and changed into a pair of workout clothes that actually matched. If I had a goal for the next two days—an *intention*—it was to be like water and flow from one experience to the next without pain, stress, or judgment. That seemed like a better ambition than *get laid*.

There was a stainless-steel water bottle on my nightstand with a note that read, *From the Universe*, which was a little weird, but I grabbed it, filled it with filtered tap water, and headed toward the Active Room.

I was the last person to walk into morning yoga, again, but that was fine. In just a handful of days, the energy in that room had shifted significantly. Where on the first day we'd all been buzzing with a mix of nerves, excitement, and hesitance, by now we'd settled into a kind of group rhythm, despite our differences.

Of course, I spotted Daniel first, momentarily holding my breath and avoiding eye contact as I walked past him. He was in the front row, solo today in Indira's absence, sitting gingerly on his knees instead of in his normal half lotus seated pose. Maybe he'd sunburned his taint? Other than that, he practically vibrated with toxic masculinity. He was shirtless, obviously, and his always semi-erect penis bulged out of his white lululemon performance shorts. How had I not fully noticed his doucheyness before? Hormones really are a helluva drug.

On one side of me, Carol Ann, in her brightly colored skin-tight clothes, seemed to block out all of us around her and home in on only Shakti, like a Padawan learner to her Jedi. On my other side, Barbara sat so comfortably in her crossed-legged position that she could probably fall asleep if she wanted to. She wore a loose cotton T-shirt with no bra and balloon-style patchwork pants. Her eyes were closed, which they almost always were during yoga, while she, along with her impressive breasts, swayed to the beat of something only she could hear.

And there, in front of us all, our divine leader, Shakti, sat with the calm of a Buddhist monk. She looked radiant, with her glowing hair spread over her shoulders, a teeny blush sports bra that highlighted her perky, youthful cleavage, and matching short shorts. Okay, she looked like a sexy white young female Buddhist monk. One who was also celibate and traded Bitcoin and had a tequila sponsor. We all contain multitudes.

"Before we begin today," Shakti said, pressing her hands over her heart and clasping her fingers together. "I want to talk a little bit about respect."

Did I sense her glaring over at Daniel?

She continued. "This is a diverse group and it's important that we acknowledge our differences and boundaries."

My fellow practitioners nodded their heads. Reflexively, I wondered if she was talking about me, though I had no reason to believe that was the case.

"It has come to my attention that some of us, whether intentionally or not, have been engaging in insensitive activities."

I looked around the room. Who the fuck was she talking about? She looked at each of us in turn.

"This saddens me, as the mission of Transcendence Week has always been to embrace our essential oneness with the universe. If we are not unified as a group, how can we be unified as a collective soul?"

Carol Ann made an "mm-hmm" sound and Barbara bowed to her feet. Daniel turned around and winked at me. Oh shit. I hoped the whole charade wasn't because of our public flirting.

"That is why," Shakti said, making mudras by touching her thumbs to her forefingers and placing them on her knees, "I have decided to add another item to the itinerary for this evening. Instead of cocktail hour, we will be having a group trust-building workshop, where we can manifest our collective harmony."

I accidentally grunted out loud. Everyone turned around to stare at me.

"Sorry!" I tried to recover. "Something in my throat."

Shakti winkled her nose. "Anyway. Don't worry. There will still be cocktails. Margaret will set up the portable bar by the Awakening Fire Pit."

She looked at me with an unreadable expression. "Jessica, will you let Indira know? And tell her we missed her in practice."

Group trust-building exercises? The thought of trust falling backward into Daniel's erect penis made me shiver. But a weird part of me also agreed that would be nice to leave the retreat on good terms with everyone. Carol Ann and I had barely acknowledged each other since our hunting fiasco, and even though we had nothing in common and I found her morally reprehensible (a feeling that was clearly mutual), I wanted to say my goodbyes without animosity. Also, it would be nice if Daniel and I had some bridge between sex and seeing each other back in Miami at the yoga studio. A *that happened but let's never speak of it again* moment. And Barbara. Well, it would be nice to spend more time with her, too.

Before I could analyze the new event any further, Shakti said, "Downward dog," and I pressed into my hands and lifted my hips to the sky.

It was a much slower class than Shakti usually taught, which was fine, because I was exhausted and probably dehydrated from the night before. We melted into long lunges, languorously opened up into side stretches, and took indulgent breaks in child's pose.

By the end of class, I suddenly realized that Daniel hadn't been adjusting me, which I should have been grateful for since I truly did not want him to touch me. But for some reason, the implicit rejection stung. All my empowered Beyoncé-ness threatened to melt away.

Shakti guided us through some energizing backbends before final relaxation and I tried to put him out of my mind. My shoulders opened and stacked over my wrists, and my full wheel felt more rainbowlike than usual. The effects of daily practicing, no doubt. To recover from the intense posture, we sat up and forward-folded over our legs. My nose reached for my knees, and as I inhaled a few final deep breaths, a deep moan sounded from next to me. An orgasmic, guttural moan.

I turned my head to the side and quickly snapped it back, vomit threatening to suddenly rise and spill onto my legs. To my right, I'd glimpsed Barbara in her forward bend. Daniel had his entire body draped on top of hers. Pelvis to butt. As in, if they'd both been naked, penetration could have been possible. And by the sound of it, whatever they were doing was just as pleasurable. Ugh. Thank god my blinders for the man slut were finally off.

INDIRA

I riffled through my villa closet, which was futile because of course I knew exactly what was in it. It wasn't like I could will something professional to magically appear. This wasn't just a print magazine interview; we were going live on the *Women's Wear Daily*'s Instagram page. Normally for something like this, I would've hired Glamsquad for camera-ready hair and makeup and pulled out something expensive but understated to wear, my mother's voice whispering in my ear, *Try to look smart, dear.* But all I'd packed for the retreat was athleisure and resort wear.

Luckily, I'd at least brought my Dyson Airwrap and makeup bag. After taming and curling my hair and applying my best daytime lip and eye combo, I settled on an emerald green frock with gold embroidery. The color made my skin glowy, which was tricky to achieve in the subpar villa lighting (you'd think I would've learned to travel with my ring light by now). I positioned my laptop so that the natural light was in front of me and the camera was facing the weathered-wood-paneled wall behind me, secretly hoping the background made me seem charmingly down to earth. After all, the Namaste Club was *nice*, but it was not the Four Seasons.

My interviewer was a young and chic-looking woman who wore a fuchsia tailored blazer and styled her hair tastefully pulled back in a messy high bun. I forced down the pang of jealousy at her more professional look and instead playacted at being overly cheerful to meet her from our respective Zoom squares.

"Good morning, Ms. Rao. I'm Caitlin Adderley with *Women's Wear Daily*. Thanks so much for going live with us today." Her tone was friendly but clipped. A savvy choice in case I went down in flames in the face of controversy. "For those of you watching at home, Indira Rao is the chief designer and CEO of Bougie Boho, the cult fine jewelry line that has caught the eyes of all the *first to know* fashionistas."

I was sure that was hyperbole but, from her lips to God's ears, let it become true.

"Thanks so much for having me. Please, call me Indira." My smile said *I'm friendly but I'm also older than you and a boss-ass bitch so please don't fuck with me.* Truthfully, I was a little worried that the interview would go south. That I'd slip with some perceived microaggression, and that Gen Z IG would jump all over it and get me canceled à la Allison Kent. Public scrutiny is brutal these days.

"Let's get right to it," Caitlin said, and I appreciated her cutting to the point. "By now, I'm sure that most people listening have heard about the epic rise and fall of TikTok and Instagram darling Allison Kent. Just a few days ago, Kent seemed poised to ascend to the ranks of D'Amelio and Kardashian. That was, of course, until she made the inappropriate and insensitive comparison between Covid quarantine and the Holocaust. Ms. Rao . . . I'm sorry . . . Indira is here with us today because Kent plugged her jewelry line immediately after making that comment. Indira, is Bougie Boho a paid sponsor for Allison Kent? I'd love to get your reaction to the whole scandal."

"I'm so glad you asked me that," I said, meaning it. And not only because my business was involved. How often are we able to really publicly disavow the dumb, ignorant shit that comes out of people's mouths? I was grateful that *WWD* was giving me the platform. "First of all, let me say just that I was disgusted and disappointed with Allison Kent suggesting that we lived through anything nearly as horrible as the Holocaust. Was quarantining difficult? Yes. Did people lose lives? Yes. Was it an existential threat to any of us because of how we were born?

Absolutely not. To even mention the two events in the same breath shows an almost unfathomable lack of judgment and understanding."

Caitlin nodded along, and I paused, suddenly wishing I'd begged Jessica to skip yoga and join me for moral support. Not because I needed her, but because I wanted her to be proud of how I was handling the situation. Even if I was bombing, which for all I knew I might have been, I wanted the friend she'd always been behind the computer smiling and giving me a thumbs-up.

I cleared my throat and finished. "Second, no. Bougie Boho does not sponsor Allison Kent in any way. We gifted her a ring from my collection, but that's it. And honestly, I wish I could take it back. That ring, the Tara, was named after my daughter, someone who would never stand for her name to be associated with the garbage that came out of that influencer's mouth."

We spoke for about twenty minutes about the scandal, the fallout, my feelings about influencer culture, and, yes, my jewelry line. Afterward, I was more than ready to put Allison Kent and her ignorant statements behind me. It felt almost dirty to suddenly be the beneficiary of all the attention. That wasn't the way I wanted to grow my brand. But honestly, I wasn't turning down the opportunities, either. After the interview, I slipped in my ear buds and went for a solo walk around the property to clear my head.

The Namaste Club grounds were straight out of an eerie children's story. It was like walking through *The Jungle Book,* but without the talking animals.

I'm not a Florida girl by any stretch. I'll accept that I've become a transplanted Miamian, but that's where it ends. And as people in this state understand, Miami and Florida are *not* the same thing. They're two different matrix simulations that live close to each other: the city, a haven for sin, excess, and very small articles of clothing and the state, a dystopian fever dream with book bans and prehistoric swamp monsters. Though some overlap does exist.

To be honest, when I agreed to this retreat, I had no idea that I'd be stepping into an anthropological and ecological study. But everyone had been telling me that it was totally safe to walk around Shiva Lake in daylight. So with Tupac in my ears to steel my heart, I passed through the banyans, imagining myself as one of my ancestors in Northeast India, trudging through a dank rainforest to bring back fresh water. Mosquitoes buzzed in my ears and feasted on my bare arms, leaving red welts in exchange for my blood. Unseen creatures rustled the leaves and bushes as I passed. What was the appeal of all this nature? I wondered. I preferred the manufactured kind of great outdoors that one experiences in luxurious ski towns.

I wish I were the type of person who embraced all this Florida splendor, and sometimes I fool myself into thinking I am, which is one of the reasons that I was so eager to sign up for Transcendence Week in the first place. As I pondered this particular folly, a small black snake slithered across my feet and into a nearby bush. I screamed, a panicked bloodcurdling sound, and hopped backward as though my feet were on fire. *Nope.* Definitely too much nature for me.

Doubling back to the Enlightenment Circle in a jog, I was grateful that in two days I'd be going home to concrete buildings and highways, a boutique jewelry business, and adequate water pressure. I'm a woman built for modern comforts and it's time to own that. Meaning, if the apocalypse is coming and the only ones who survive will need to live off the land, then please let the horsemen take me first.

I slowed my pace after passing back through the banyans and almost immediately ran into Jessica, yoga mat under her arm. I popped out my ear buds.

"Hey!" I stopped directly in front of her. "How did practice go? I need every detail. Was it weird seeing Daniel?"

Jessica rolled her eyes and shrugged. "It was honestly fine. Hey, you missed meditation. Did the Instagram Live go long?"

Lurching forward, I threw my arms around her, almost knocking her over in the process.

"I'm so proud of you, Jess. I should really tell you that more often." She hugged me back with one arm and then shook me off.

"Stop being weird." She half smiled. "How was the interview?"

I told her about how *Women's Wear Daily* wanted to know if Bougie Boho had a previous relationship with Allison Kent (no) and how we felt about her comments (disgusted). And then how we'd discussed that influencers are basically just people who are good at social media and leverage the platforms well but aren't necessarily experts in anything.

Jessica rested her yoga mat against her leg and fixed her hair.

"I never should have sent her one of your pieces. You always had a bad feeling about influencer marketing."

"No, I'm sorry I made you feel so bad about it," I said. "It was a solid strategy, and you couldn't have seen this coming. How I reacted to you was way over the line. Also, I hate to say this, but we are kind of getting tons of free press from Allison being a total idiot."

"Kind of a guilty silver lining," Jessica agreed. She pointed toward the banyan trees. "Hey, what were you doing out by the lake? I thought you hated it over there."

"Just confirming I still do," I said.

Jessica picked her mat up and we fell into step back to our rooms to change for lunch. On the way, she told me about the new trust-building workshop we'd be having that evening. "I shit you not" were her exact words.

I shook my head. "Who cares whether or not we're a cohesive group after we all leave? It's not like we're going to be meeting up for reunion dinners."

We stopped in front of Jessica's door.

"It makes no sense! Shakti says she wants us to embrace our collective oneness or something like that, but I think she's just worried about us leaving a bad review on her website."

"What are you going to wear to that?" I asked—clearly the most important question.

"Something light. It's in front of the fire pit again." She opened the door. "I don't need to be the next person who throws up and passes out on this trip."

SHAKTI

NOW

When we dislike someone, it's usually because we see a mirror of ourselves in that person. A quality we possess but cannot accept. Rather than address that which upsets us, we project our disgust for self onto others. Furthermore, it is preferable to hate another person than to hate ourselves.

I witnessed a lot of this mirroring phenomenon during the retreat. Reproach for one woman's boldness because another has acted in ways unfeminine. Embarrassment for one person's nudity because the other is ashamed of her own.

It was my job to address these prejudices, so we could come back to the truth. The reality that we are all the same and vibrate on one celestial frequency.

The group trust-building exercise was meant to salve our anger and bring us back into the light. But sometimes, when the darkness is so heavy, that's what can take over instead.

JESSICA

FIFTH DAY OF THE RETREAT

The Awakening Fire Pit was raging again, despite the subtropical heat. Barbara held a handmade straw fan in each hand and walked around fanning the group. We hadn't even started yet, but Carol Ann sucked on her water bottle greedily, already looking dizzy and unsteady on her feet.

It felt like we were in some kind of sweat lodge ritual, though I'm sure the comparison was unintentional. Shakti may have been running a smorgasbord of spiritual and wellness traditions, but in this case, I honestly think she simply loved the vibeyness of fire.

Dressing for the impromptu occasion had been a challenge. I'd opted for a sports bra and tennis skirt (which I had no recollection of packing). It was something I wouldn't have been caught dead wearing back home, but retreat me was apparently a completely different person than Miami me. Also, it was fucking hot out.

Indira was wearing a bikini under a sheer cover up. Smart.

"I'm so humbled that you've all joined me here this evening for our special group activity."

Shakti was suddenly there, walking toward us from around the fire pit like some sort of apparition. Had she planned that? Her hair was braided like a Kardashian's, and she wore an elaborately beaded bra with matching little shorts. I exchanged a glance with Indira. Shakti looked more like she was headed to Coachella than leading a yoga retreat of middle-aged women and, well, Daniel.

"Tonight, we will come together as one consciousness, one soul." She spread her arms, revealing sweat beads that shined like diamonds against her honeyed skin. Barbara knelt in front of her, braless in a light spaghetti-strap dress, and rapidly waved her fans.

I leaned toward Indira. "If she pulls out paper cups of Kool-Aid, I'm outta here."

Indira put her mouth to my ear. "Don't be ridiculous. Kool-Aid has too many chemicals. She'll probably kill us with Florida orange kombucha."

I bit my lip. Why were we always the inappropriate ones? Also, I wondered what compelled us to keep coming back and submitting to Shakti's weirdness in the first place. Were we just extremely compliant? Nah. I think we were motivated, more than anything, by basic human curiosity.

"To begin, let's join hands."

Shakti continued toward us with outstretched arms. I wondered how she seemed so calm and comfortable. The fire must have been blazing on her back. This was real Mother of Dragons shit.

Carol Ann pinched the bridge of her nose, then reached for Shakti's hand with one of hers, and Indira's with the other. I linked with Indira to my left, and Daniel—who was, as always, shirtless with a partial hard-on—took my right. Barbara and Shakti rounded out the rest of the circle.

Daniel's hand was cold and clammy. I shuddered, desperately wanting to drop it and wipe the dampness on my skirt. But I didn't. It was crazy how just one half of a day could so drastically change my feelings from intrigued to ick. I almost felt guilty for my abrupt change of heart toward the man. *Almost.*

We opened the session with an *om.*

"Now open your eyes," Shakti said, gently. "For our first activity, I want us to truly see each other. To use our eyes as portals into one another's souls. To see beyond the artifice and superficial. In groups of two, we will gaze into each other's eyes. No blinking, no breaking eye contact, for sixty seconds. Then immediately after, we will tell everyone what we saw. Jessica, why don't you and I go first."

Great. I could think of literally nothing more awkward.

"Okay," I said, dropping my neighbors' hands and stepping toward her.

Shakti and I stood about a foot away from each other, then creepily gazed into each other's eyes. It was the most uncomfortable staring contest of my life. At first, I was rigid and tense, nakedly self-conscious. What could she be seeing? She looked so serious. I tried to focus on her eyes instead of what she might be perceiving in me. They were shockingly blue. Intense. Strong. But then, the longer I looked, the more fragile they seemed. More like a shield than the jewels they so closely resembled.

Barbara clapped her hands to call time and I snapped out of it. Shakti spoke first.

"Beautiful. Bold. Able. But insecure. I see fear and doubt, but more than that, I see strength."

My eyes stung. Was I crying? Whatever opinions I've had about Shakti, I couldn't deny a certain inner beauty and intuition. Tequila sponsor or no, there was something special lying underneath. And I felt in that moment that she had *seen* me.

I swallowed hard and spoke next.

"Angelic. Powerful. Scared. Sad. I see a little girl inside a goddess. One who is still trying to heal."

Indira gasped. Did those words really just come out of my mouth? I had no idea where they came from. It was like I'd just been speaking in tongues. Shakti flinched but quickly recovered.

"Let's have Indira and Carol Ann go next," she said, stepping back and guiding the other two women forward.

Indira pinched my leg before taking her place. Neither woman looked thrilled to be sharing sustained eye contact, but they did it anyway. For the first time that day, I noticed how frail Carol Ann seemed to be looking compared to her vigor on our hunting trip. Her platinum-blond hair was matted against her forehead, and her eyes were bloodshot red.

At the end of the minute, Indira spoke first.

"Rigid. Closed. Cagey. Lonely. I see a woman who is searching for meaning but coming up short."

Oh damn, I thought. Indira was really going for it. That woman truly gave zero fucks.

"Let's try to keep it positive," Shakti reminded us. "This exercise is designed—"

Carol Ann cut her off. "Slut. Whore. Godless. Jezebel. This woman might as well have a penis between her legs because femininity has never touched her."

Something in my gut ignited. Indira and I had had our fights, but she was still *my* person. And no one was else was allowed to attack her. It was like when your friends called your parents crazy, but that comment was only okay coming from you. I wanted to pipe in and remind Carol Ann that jezebels were actually feminine by definition but held myself back. Poor Shakti looked vexed. Her trust-building project was already going down in flames.

Carol Ann must have noticed the same thing because she turned to her and said, "I'm sorry. That's just what I see."

"She's right about everything except the dick," Indira shot back. God, I really do love that woman. Carol Ann squinted into her fart face. I was starting to wonder if it was some sort of tick she had.

"Let's do Barbara and Daniel," Shakti said, too quickly. "Barbara can't speak, of course. But she can fill her partner with her radiant energy, nonetheless."

The two of them stepped forward and what happened next could only be described as eye-fucking. With sly smiles on their lips, they seemed to be boring into each other's souls. At one point, I thought Daniel was going to lick his lips.

After Shakti clapped for time, they held the gaze for at least ten more seconds. Then Barbara stepped back and pressed her hands to her heart, then to her lips, kissed them, and pressed them into Daniel's chest.

She was nice, but painfully strange.

Daniel spoke. "Sensual. Womanly. Durga. Passion. I see Venus, goddess of love, masquerading as a mortal."

Oh, come the fuck on. Could this guy be any more transparent? Not that I was anyone to judge. Indira and I shared a quick glance and turned back to the group. Shakti looked exhausted. Carol Ann appeared as nauseous as the last display made me feel.

Surely, our leader would pull the plug on this fool's errand. But no. I had to give her props for the determination.

"Okay, next," Shakti said, "we are going to share a meal and reflect on some memories, to get to know one another better."

Eating was a good idea. We were all looking a little weak and dehydrated, if I was being honest. And this group combined with low blood sugar was a recipe for disaster.

Margaret had laid out a beautiful spread for us, mercifully away from the heat of the fire pit. Carafes of iced fruit water sat ready to be drunk, and an assortment of refreshing salads and freshly caught grilled fishes lined the buffet. No wild boar, I noticed.

We filled our plates and cups and sat in a circle on the dank earth. I didn't even care that my white tennis skirt would surely be stained brown by the end of it. It felt good to sit. Predictably, we arranged ourselves in the same order we'd stood during the staring exercise. After a few minutes of hydrating and stuffing our faces, everyone looked a little fresher and more relaxed. Even Carol Ann's skin seemed to have regained some of its previous glow.

Shakti put down her bamboo plate and utensils and began the next activity.

"I'm going to challenge us all to listen respectfully in this next exercise. We are going to touch on our highs and lows from the retreat— our Parvati moment and our Kali moment. As you know, Parvati is the goddess of love and beauty. So she will represent your most positive experience from the trip. Kali, the goddess of death, will represent your darkest. If someone's Parvati or Kali moment relates to you in any way, I challenge you to listen without reaction. Can we all do that?"

We nodded, though it felt like an obvious lie. Shakti really loved to play with fire (no pun intended).

Barbara went first. As she stood, her tunic flowed in the light breeze and the moonlight glowed off her brownish-grayish hair. In lieu of speaking, she pointed to the sky and smiled. Her best moment, I assumed. Then she walked around the circle and patted each one of us on the head, as though we were her adored children. Sweet. Then, she frowned and gestured to the ground, stomping her feet. Her Kali moment. She pointed to each one of us angrily and mimed screaming and pulling out her hair. Yikes. Point taken, Barbara. She inhaled a deep breath, smiled, and sat down.

"Thank you, Barbara," Shakti said. "That was beautiful. Now Daniel."

He rubbed his hands together. "I don't know if I'd call myself a goddess," he said, laughing. "That term is reserved for all of you ladies. But, umm. My high moment was . . ."

I braced myself. Worried but also maybe secretly hoping it had something to do with me.

"Getting my press handstand! I've been working on that for a long time."

Ugh.

He continued. "Damn. Low point. I can't say I've really had one. Well . . ." He turned to Barbara. "Maybe not being able to hear your beautiful voice. For those of you who don't know, Barbie sings like an angel."

Literally fucking kill me right now. In that moment, I would have done anything to erase him from my body count. Barbara blushed and covered her mouth.

I was next. My head swam with everything that had happened that week. Feeling powerless. Becoming powerful. Fighting. Eating. Having bad sex. Feeling okay about it anyway. When I tried to distill it all into one thought, it felt like I'd lived a whole lifetime in less than a week.

"Yeah, so. My Parvati moment was stepping out of my comfort zone in a lot of ways. I can honestly say that I've grown as a person on this trip, and I really thank you all for that." Indira reached out and squeezed my hand. Shakti smiled serenely. "And my Kali moment was fighting with my best friend. But it's okay because I know we're going to get back on track. Because she's more than my best friend, she's my family. And that feels really great."

Indira and I looked at each other and smiled, squeezing our hands harder. "I'm sorry I called out your personal business in front of everyone when I was mad at you," I said.

She laughed. "And I'm sorry that I was such a raging bitch to you. I think some subconscious part of me always thought you secretly hated me for how my marriage ended. Since I'd done to someone else the shitty thing that happened to you."

The circle was completely silent, and I felt everyone around us disappear.

"Sometimes, I did hate you for it," I admitted. "But not as strongly as I love you for being my person." We held each other's gaze for an extra beat.

"Beautiful. Really beautiful, you two." Shakti looked relieved. "Let's remember that Kali doesn't mean bad. Kali is powerful. From her ashes grows life. Just like your friendship."

Indira wiped her eyes. "I'll go next. My Parvati moment was laughing and being silly with my best friend. But, sorry Jess, I also have to add getting my freaking freestanding handstand."

Barbara clapped.

"And my Kali moment," she continued. "I think we all know. And as Shakti said, we've risen from the ashes."

This time, I thought that Shakti was going to cry. Instead, she closed her eyes and nodded.

"Carol Ann," she said. "You're next."

She sat up straight and exhaled through her nose.

"Shakti, girl. You know I love you, but do you want me to be honest right now?"

"Yes," Shakti said. "We can take it. We are all adults trekking on the path to enlightenment."

Flies swarmed our empty plates. Something tickled my inner thigh, and I lifted my skirt. An earthworm was slithering up my leg. "Shit!" I yelled, plucking it off and tossing it into the grass.

Carol Ann closed her eyes, then spoke again.

"Okay, I'm gonna do this my way. My Jesus moment was meeting a spiritual teacher to help me put my life back where it needed to be." She stopped and looked at Shakti with glistening eyes. The evening had turned into such a freaking tearjerker session. On that account at least, it had been successful.

"And, of course," she continued, "nabbing that invasive python." A grin overtook her face, followed by a figurative dark cloud. "But my Satan moment, and there were many if I'm being honest . . ."

Indira scoffed. "Jesus." We all turned to face her.

Carol Ann's eyes blazed back at my friend. "Excuse me? Can I finish?"

"By all means," Indira said. "This should be good."

I wondered if Carol Ann's eye-gazing assessment had affected Indira more than I'd thought. My best friend isn't usually one to mince words, but that was aggressive even for her.

Carol Ann glared at me for some reason and continued. "My Satan moments were many, but I know they're just a reminder to stay in the light. Overall, the most disturbing moment this week was being forced to witness a man's nude genitalia on display for everyone to see."

I couldn't help it. I burst out laughing. In a weird way, Carol Ann wasn't even wrong. Daniel's naked butthole sunning was super gross and will forever live rent-free in my nightmares.

"What is so funny about that?" She turned to face me, her face rapidly reddening. "Do you enjoy seeing that kind of thing? I bet you do."

"What did I do?" I said, looking around the circle for allies. Daniel, as usual, seemed extremely amused.

He chimed in. "I'm sorry if I offended you, Carol Ann. I was just trying to harness the transformative power of the sun. You should try it some time." His expression was anything but apologetic. Barbara patted his knee.

"By dangling your balls and wiener around like a toddler who keeps taking off his diaper? It was disgusting, Daniel," Carol Ann said.

Indira smiled. "At least it wasn't my wiener."

On a scale of inappropriate things that could happen on a yoga retreat, this ranked pretty high. Poor Shakti. I was starting to feel bad for her. She looked shocked, and disappointed, and powerless. Eventually, she found her voice.

"Everyone, please. Let's come back to our breath. We are losing sight of our shared intentions. Our reasons for being here in the first place."

Carol Ann didn't seem to be hearing any of it. She looked like a woman possessed. "Make no mistake, *Indira*," she said. "You are in second place for my Satan moment. *You* are the lowest form of woman. An unapologetic adulteress."

It was a step too far. Indira's normally cool facade hardened, her jaw set, her shoulders squared.

"What happened to not judging lest ye be judged, huh? If your husband really loved you, Carol Ann, for who you are," Indira said, through her teeth, "why'd you need to turn yourself into QAnon Barbie? If you're so *all natural,* then why would you go cheap bottle blond and get giant fake tits?"

Indira had never been one to judge a woman for a little cosmetic enhancement. We live in Miami, after all. So I knew she was aiming to bruise.

Things were getting ugly, fast. And though I'm not a fighter, I knew I'd have my best friend's back if the situation took a turn for the worse.

Carol Ann's face was a contorted mess. She looked like she was about to stand up, but she just sat up straighter and leaned toward us.

"You take my husband's name out of your filthy mouth right now."

Indira laughed. "Or what?"

Shakti was frozen. Barbara was mute, as usual. Daniel was proba-bly happy to have the attention off him and his butthole. Somehow, it seemed like my turn to speak.

"Okay, I think that's enough trust workshop for one night. Should we cancel this thing and head to bed?"

Carol Ann twitched. "Cancel? I bet you'd like that, wouldn't you, Jessica? Is this conversation too threatening for your sensitive ears? Do you need a safe space?"

I reminded myself this woman had a gun and was an excellent shot.

"Actually, I would like a safe space right now. My bedroom. I think we're all tired and—"

"Listen, snowflake," Carol Ann interrupted, "I'm sick and tired of you people thinking that your precious feelings are the most important things in the entire world."

The comment was totally out of left field. This clearly wasn't going to end well.

"You people?" I asked. "Meaning liberal people or Jewish people or . . ."

"I mean it however it hurts you the most," she said.

She chuckled a little and I couldn't tell if it meant she was joking or not. But who jokes about that? Oh yeah, people like Carol Ann. The group went deathly quiet. Even the mosquitoes seemed to stop buzz-ing around my ears. How does one respond to such garbage?

The silence broke with the sound of sobbing. Shakti. She was bent over her legs in lotus pose with her hands covering her face. When she removed them, her eyes were wild, so different from the serene expres-sion she typically wore.

"Just stop!" she screamed. No singsongy voice. No faux Indian ac-cent. "You're all ruining it! You're ruining everything!"

She scrambled to her feet. Barbara tried to reach for her, but Shakti shook her off and ran barefoot toward her villa.

The rest of us sat in stunned silence. Barbara looked to be on the brink of tears. Daniel's face was twisted like a dog's who couldn't find his bone underneath the sofa. After a moment, he stood up and reached for Barbara's hand, helping her to her feet. Together, they walked off toward the villas, Daniel with his arm around her back. I'm pretty sure I saw him kiss her ear as they crossed into the darkness.

Indira turned to me and sighed. Carol Ann brushed her legs off and walked away next, without a word.

CAROL ANN

Back in my room, I poured some more electrolyte powder into my water bottle and shook it up. I couldn't blame dehydration for all the things I'd said, but honestly, it had probably played a role. Not that I'd said anything untrue. Maybe I'd been a little harsh with Jessica, but she'd just scraped so deeply on my nerves. The only thing I felt bad about was disrespecting Shakti's trust-building ceremony.

The previous night's cleansing had left me weak and raw, which Shakti had said was part of the healing process. I was building back up from scratch. And if we were being honest about our Satan moments, I'd *needed* to call out Daniel. So we could have had a mature conversation about what I'd seen and how it made me feel. Wasn't that the intention of the exercise in the first place? But those women couldn't help themselves. They just had to butt in and push my buttons. Bringing up my husband and my marriage! How freaking dare they. Of course I was going to explode.

I'd apologize to Shakti in the morning, but first I needed to calm down. Hydrate. Meditate. Pray. I settled into my bed to find my center.

Breathing in and out through my nose, I noticed there was zero trace of vomit smell in my room, which was really amazing considering what had gone down there the night before. Whenever Barbara started speaking again, I'd have to ask for her cleaning secrets.

After a full sixteen ounces of fluids and ten minutes listening to a guided relaxation on my ChillOut app, I began to feel like myself again. And there was something else, too. I was proud of myself. I'd spoken my truth without fear or hesitation. Yes, it went another way than Shakti would've liked, but that wasn't my fault. I was sure that everyone could pretty easily tell who the real villains were.

It reminded me of a phone call I received from school a couple years ago. I was in the middle of showing a house (a spectacular waterfront colonial on Ocean Road to a lovely Tennessee family), when I saw the school phone number pop up on my screen. Immediately, my blood started pumping. It was 12:30 P.M., and I knew the school wouldn't have been calling to let me know one of the kids had just done exceptionally well on a test.

I excused myself into the downstairs powder room and took the call. It was the principal. "Sorry to bother you, Carol Ann," she said. "And before you start to worry too much, let me tell you that the kids are okay. No one's been hurt. There's just a little situation."

My body relaxed and I thanked her for that opening disclaimer. Broken bones are harder to deal with than *little situations*. Then I heard Katie softly crying in the background and I thought, Okay, here we go.

Katie and Kam are both spirited kids, like their parents, but I'm big on manners and using our words properly. I don't condone nasty talk, or sassy talk, or talking back to elders. Not at all. But I do tell my kids that they can defend themselves if someone else is giving it to them. Don't be a bully, but don't be soft, either.

The principal wasn't even upset; it was more of an FYI call. Apparently, what happened was that some dingbat in Katie's class was saying, "When I grow up, I'm gonna be the first woman president! And I'm going to make a law that everyone has to eat cake for breakfast!"

Can we just stop with the faux feminist righteousness? I mean, women make all right politicians, but come on. President? Like Putin is going to share the stage with Marjorie Taylor Greene, as great as she is? Let's know our limits, people. Katie had learned from Beau and me not to suffer foolishness like what she was hearing, so she just responded, "Girls were put on this earth to honor their men! That's what's in the Bible. Women can't be president. And cake for breakfast will make all your teeth rot off. That's silly."

That should have been enough of it, agree to disagree, but this other child didn't let it go. She said, "Girls can do anything boys can do. Maybe even better! You don't even know anything! *That's stupid.*"

Like, excuse me? Is this poor child being raised on MSNBC?

My little fireball wasn't going to stand for the idiocy, and this other girl was being vicious.

Katie said, "You are a stupid little snowflake and your breath smells like diarrhea."

The little girl started crying because she could dish it out but not take it, like so many liberals, honestly. Then Katie stepped up to her one last time and said, "Go cry to your mama, stupid snowflake."

I don't condone the poop talk and I don't love how the whole thing went down, but I *understand*. Beau and I would have been more upset if she *hadn't* spoken up, so in a way we were proud. We took away dessert privileges for the night because of the language she'd used, but we also let her know she did the right thing for defending the truth. That's what the next generation so desperately needs—the courage to stand up for liberty. Because if they are silent, Lord, help us, the fascists will win.

And hadn't I really done almost the same thing with Indira and Jessica that night? I didn't let them take over and control the narrative. Maybe I was harsh and could have moderated my words, but you know what? I bet I got my point across.

The self-reflection made me sleepy. I texted Beau.

Two more sleeps until I'm home baby. Luv U.

He responded right away, making my heart leap when the notification popped up.

Two more sleeps babe.

BARBARA

Nothing helps us realize our universal oneness like when two bodies become one. That beautiful and ancient dance of love.

Daniel led me away from the Enlightenment Circle, where the lost souls were spreading their darkness, and I followed him because I needed the light. My heart wept for Shakti. I wanted to run to her. But I knew that she would be recharging in the comfort of solitude and meditation. My teacher is one who heals from within.

Instead, I let Daniel soothe me. He brought me to my bed and silently undressed me. Laying me on my stomach, he rubbed me with ayurvedic oil. My muscles became soft and pliant under his strong hands. Then he turned me over and we embraced in such a way that I didn't know where his hands ended and my body began. His touch lit up each of my senses. His lips on my neck, his tongue gliding down my breasts, my firm nipple greeting him hello. We breathed together in pure ecstasy. The language of lovers needs no words.

"I want to play something for you," he said. "Experts say that listening to the lovemaking of dolphins has therapeutic properties. Would you like to heal together?"

I nodded, my entire body aflame with want.

His body resembled that of a chiseled god, and I felt like a goddess in his embrace. We held each other's gaze, transmitting power from our eyes into our bodies. In the background, the dolphin lovemaking played. Loud, piercing, and full of mammalian desire. Then we pulsated together, slowly, my hands pulling gently at his shiny, chocolate-colored hair. At one point, it looked so delicious that I put a handful of it in my mouth. He rewarded me by tasting a lock of my own tresses.

In this way, we were perfectly blended as one body, one soul, immersed in the beauty of tantra. He whispered in my ear, "Teach me your ways," then tickled me on the sides of my rib cage. I laughed without sound, then pushed him down onto the bed and mounted him. This kind of play, where I embodied the male Shiva energy and he embodied the female Shakti, was thrilling in its subversiveness.

He growled playfully and then overtook me like a lion seducing his lioness. I let him pin my arms down on the bed, exposing my vulnerability through nakedness. He ate me first with his eyes, then with his mouth.

I was one woman and Daniel was one man, but in that moment, he was every lover I'd ever had. I saw the scores of men and women who have passed through my bed, the same hunger in their eyes, the same desire in their loins. Once mine in body, always mine in my soul.

Our night together could have been a day, a week, a month, an eternity. Entire lifetimes passed through us like air. Toward the end, he began to sing, *Sita Ram, Sita Ram, Sita Ram, Sita Ram.* His voice was as beautiful as an ocean wave, powerful, and rushing, and deep.

He finished on my stomach, and I spread the life force all over my skin, like a salve. Because why waste one of our most powerful bodily gifts? Daniel, I could tell, was surprised to see me bathe in his seed. But then he smiled and laid his face on my belly, rubbing the rest of it onto his cheek. Rarely, if ever, was I so in sync with another person. And all without words. *Jai!*

But still. There was so much I wanted to say, to know about Daniel. I bit my lip, knowing I'd brought something along in case I found myself in this kind of situation.

"Is everything all right, my goddess?" he asked.

I held a finger up to say *just a minute* and slipped out of bed and over to my suitcase. From there, I pulled out my mini whiteboard and dry erase marker. Perhaps using it wasn't perfectly keeping in the spirit of my vow of silence, but I allowed myself to treat it as a loophole.

Climbing back into bed, I uncapped the blue marker and scribbled on the slippery white surface. "What brought you to yoga?" I wrote. Something I'd been wondering since meeting Daniel back in Miami.

My lover sighed and reached over to squeeze my thigh. "Honestly, it's embarrassing," he said.

I shook my head vigorously. What is embarrassment? Just a useless tool of self-flagellation. A negative construct of the mind.

"Okay." He smiled sadly. "Well, a couple of years back, I lost my job at the tech start-up I cofounded due to what they said was 'inappropriate behavior.'" He swallowed hard. "Such bullshit, pardon my French. We were changing the world with our innovative approach to grocery store deliveries and, honestly, I think they just wanted me out. So, you know, they got all these ladies to *come forward* and *bravely* accuse me of making them uncomfortable or whatever."

I nodded along, my heart aching for the sweet, gentle man in front of me. Our culture has been going way too far in punishing men for being themselves. All it takes is one false accusation to ruin a good man's life. These are dark times we're living in.

"I lost everything. My company, my reputation. I hit rock bottom. Even thought about ending it all, you know?"

There were tears in his eyes, and I realized that I, too, was crying. I curled into his arms like a cinnamon bun.

He kissed my head and continued. "Anyway, I thought that my whole life was over and then one day I stumbled into one of Shakti's vinyasa classes and listened to her dharma talk. It was about letting go of outside noise and focusing within, on our essential truth. And it was like getting struck by lightning. It woke me up completely. Ever since that moment, I've been trying," he said, his voice breaking, "to be a better man than who I was."

I sat up and faced him, cradling his damp face in my hands. His eyes looked soft and almost frightened.

"You must think less of me now." He forced a little laugh. "I'm definitely not a Siddhartha. Not an enlightened man. Not even close."

How wrong he was. I squeezed his cheeks and then released them to pick up my whiteboard. On it, I wrote: "The best of healers come from troubled pasts. Even our dear Shakti. I believe in you."

His face registered confusion, and for a moment my stomach tightened. Had I revealed too much? Shakti hadn't told me her origin story in person, not directly. But I'd gleaned the details from cleaning her room. And just a little dive into her computer history. Maybe she wasn't ready to share the details. But she had nothing to be ashamed of. I knew that deeply in my heart.

"You are an angel," Daniel said, kissing my shoulder. "Truly. If there's anyone for me to learn from, I think it's you. That is, if you'll allow me to be your student."

I felt my cheeks grow hot, but nodded. Who am I to call myself teacher? But still, for Daniel, I would try. Later, while he dressed, I ripped a piece of paper out of my journal and wrote him a note. As he slipped out of my room, I folded it into a tiny square and pressed it into his hand. Inside, it read:

Dearest Daniel,

This is how we heal the earth. We fill our fingernails with dirt and plant the seeds of hope. We water our gardens with love. You are meant to be a source of life in this dying world. Use your able body to water, and plant, and harvest. Pull the weeds from the villa gardens as gratitude for this sacred space. Give yourself as service to the planet, and your spirit will soar above the clouds.

Love,
Barbara

When he left me, spent and satisfied, I fell into a deep, dreamless sleep. Om.

JESSICA

A knock on the door startled me out of my sleep. At first, I thought I'd heard it in a dream, but then it started again, insistent.

"Jessica. You up?"

Fucking Daniel.

"Just a second," I said, checking my phone. It was 2:30 A.M. In no universe was this appropriate.

"Is everything okay?" I asked, gauging whether I truly needed to get out of bed. If he was looking for a warm body, the answer was a hard no. But if something tragic had happened, I'd obviously want to help.

"You won't believe what happened!" Daniel said, his voice muffled through the door.

It seemed important, so I rubbed my eyes vigorously to make them focus, then flicked on the lamp on my nightstand. I'd fallen asleep in my SAVE FERRIS! T-shirt and a pair of Tom's old boxer shorts, so I was pretty sure he wouldn't be unintentionally seduced.

I walked slowly to the door, still waking up and trying to decipher if it was a good idea to open it in the first place. I did anyway.

Something seemed off about Daniel, and I quickly realized it was because he was wearing a shirt. A too-tight tank top over his balloon shorts, the latter revealing a full-mast erection. His hair was mussed and tangled out of its man bun, and I wondered if it was from a romp with Barbara. (Not because of jealousy, only a perverse curiosity.)

"What happened?" I asked, in lieu of a greeting.

He let himself in and sat on my bed. Presumptuous. Then proceeded to smooth out his hair.

"You were right, Jess."

"I mean, I love hearing that but what exactly are you talking about? Is everyone here okay? Is it Barbara? Why are you in my room at two in the morning?"

He spread his legs and I briefly debated tossing a throw pillow over his junk to conceal it from my tired eyes.

"Oh, Barbara is more than fine," he said, and I swear to god I threw up in my mouth.

He cleared his throat. "I left her room a little while ago and got to thinking about what you told me last night. About Shakti being a hustler."

I groaned. Not only did that seem irrelevant, but it also wasn't something to wake me up for in the middle of the damn night. I wish I'd never tried to gossip with him in the first place.

"Daniel, come on. She's harmless. Forget I said anything. Can I go back to bed now?"

"Wait, let me explain," he said. "We've all been following this girl like some kind of guru, right?"

Actually, I hadn't thought of her exactly like that. She was my yoga teacher, but I never considered her to be my holier than thou spiritual guide. I could compartmentalize—enjoy her classes without swallowing every word that came out of her mouth. Daniel kept going.

"Tonight, I noticed something strange inside her when she stormed off. Like she broke the fourth wall, you know? That's actor speak for breaking character."

I buckled up for a long story, cursing myself for answering the door.

"She's an actor?" I asked, not really caring what the answer was.

"No. Well, kinda." He sneered. "Tonight, when she stormed off, I caught a flicker of something. And it reminded me of our conversation. How you said something was off with her. It didn't hit me at first because I was . . . I was busy. But then I left Barbara's room and boom. I realized that nothing about Shakti was adding up. I sat out in the Enlightenment Circle and meditated on it. I mean, I've devoted myself to learning about the practice from this girl. I have a right to know what's up. Then I googled her Sanskrit name. But I only found the public-facing stuff. Classes, podcast, wellness shit."

I was tired of standing but didn't want to sit next to Daniel on the bed, so I took the desk chair instead.

"Please tell me you're getting to the point," I said, "of why you woke me up."

"Sorry, yeah," he said, looking a little sheepish. "I've been following this chick around like a trained dog and when I found out— Fuck. I had to tell someone. And I figured you'd get it."

"Get what?" I asked.

"That she's a total fraud," he said, throwing his hands in the air. "I looked her up using her real name, Alyssa Patterson. And our guru has a history that's anything but spiritual. Celibate, my ass. Homegirl was a full-blown porn star."

I gasped. This was a real fucking surprise. Maybe not a *wake me up in the middle of the night* revelation, but something I did not see coming.

"No fucking way," I said.

"Yes way. You wanna see?" Daniel smirked. God I was starting to hate him.

"No," I said.

"Suit yourself. Turns out she was like a big frat party slut in college and some of these guys were a little entrepreneurial and started filming her. They uploaded the videos to Collegegirls.com and she turned into one of their biggest hits. Like a million subscribers. Apparently, she specialized in spankings and cum shots."

There was an empty water glass next to me and I was tempted to chuck it at Daniel's smug face. This was dirty. Not what Shakti may or may not have done, but in how he was reliving it at her expense.

My face must have looked disgusted, because Daniel said, "Crazy right? She totally played us."

I shook my head. "No! Everyone has a past, Daniel. We all do. Who cares what Shakti did in college. That poor thing! It sounds like she was being manipulated or—"

"No, no, no," Daniel interrupted. "She consented. If that's what you mean. Collegegirls.com makes everyone sign a waiver."

He seemed to know way too much about the site.

"She was so young, Daniel. It sounds like she's a different person now. She found yoga and is on a spiritual path. Good for her. Not that there's anything wrong with porn."

He stood up suddenly and put his hands on his waist.

"Are you seriously defending her? You're the one who called out her bullshit in the first place."

My heart sank. It had been easy to poke fun at Shakti when she seemed like a self-important know-it-all. It didn't feel as good when I realized that her appearance might have actually been a meticulously painted mask. Maybe at her core she was scared and flawed on the inside, like I'd seen in her eyes earlier that night. Like I was, too.

Daniel seemed weirdly malicious about the whole thing. I couldn't imagine why he cared so much, especially since he was so blatantly sexual. Unless he was just pissed that he'd never had a piece of her.

"Why does it bother you so much?" I asked.

He grunted, pacing around my room. "Because she's a liar. She isn't enlightened. Shakti would give me all these lectures about going too far with my tantric philosophy, judging me for being too open with students. And all this time, it turns out that she's just a little whore. And I fell for it. It's embarrassing. Bottom line—it was unethical of her to bring us here and guide us and teach us about spirituality when she's the most fucked-up and lost of all of us."

If anyone was a fraud, I wanted to say, it was obviously him. Acting like a women-loving devoted yogi, when he was a fucking toxically masculine predator.

"I'd like you to leave now," I said.

He looked me straight in the eye and my blood froze. Something about his energy felt dangerously combustible.

"You know she didn't even graduate college? She always told me it was because she found the eight-fold path to be a better education. The truth is, she did two years of porn and then dropped out. Guess yoga teacher training was her only option when her film opportunities dried up. Helped that she could just change her name and assume a new identity. Virginal, celibate. Gimme a fucking break."

I tried to imagine myself in a hostage situation. How would I negotiate with the captor?

"This must be really difficult news to process," I said. "You respected her so much."

He stared at the ground and nodded.

"Maybe you should sleep on it," I said. "See how it looks in the light of day. You can always find a new guru to follow. So many of us have been disappointed by our teachers."

He was silent for a minute.

"I'd really like to get some sleep now," I said. "Can I walk you to the door?"

Daniel looked back up at me. "Yeah, sure," he said. Then, as I closed the door behind him, "Good night, Jess. I'll sleep on it, but I'm not going to let her get away with this."

SHAKTI

As an energy worker, I often absorb the vibrations of my students. That is why it's so important to keep people like Barbara close by, someone who radiates purity and goodness.

On the other hand, when those around me carry heavy and dark energy, it depletes me significantly. I slept fitfully after the unsuccessful trust-building exercise and woke up the next morning knowing I'd need to fill my own cup before serving the others. So I sent a message to all the students, asking them to please complete the morning hike on their own and help themselves to breakfast. I needed extra meditation and reflection time before I'd be able to lead them in our final yoga practice of the retreat.

INDIRA

When the pounding knock tore me out of sleep at 8:00 A.M., I was pissed. Quite intentionally, I'd deactivated the 7:30 A.M., alarm, telling myself I needn't attempt one last lake stroll, given all the floating crocodilians and Biblical serpents.

Jessica's voice sounded from outside.

"Indira! Open up!"

I stretched my arms taut over my head, enjoying the faint soreness from a week of consecutive yoga practices.

"One second. Keep your panties on," I said, slipping from underneath the covers.

I'd slept like a geriatric dog after a long walk. Last night had been weird, but only in the entertaining way of a reality TV show fight. Nothing that had happened concerned me in the slightest. If Carol Ann had been trying to get under my skin, she'd failed miserably.

"I'm really fine," I said, opening the door. "But sweet of you to check in."

Jessica pushed past me and sat in my unmade bed. She was in her yoga clothes for the day and freshly showered. I wondered how long she'd been up.

"It's not that," she said. "I mean. Wait. *Are* you okay?"

She had that frantic energy about her, like when she found out about the Allison Kent scandal. I closed the door and sat down beside her.

"Totally," I said. "What's going on? You're scaring me a little."

She leaned forward and put her hands on her knees.

"Sorry, I texted you when I woke up but couldn't wait any longer. Something . . . weird . . . happened last night. I have a bad feeling about it."

I scrunched my face at her. "Only one weird thing? It was a fucked-up night, Jess." An anxious jolt shot through my veins. "Please tell me this news isn't about Bougie Boho."

She shook her head.

"No, it's about Shakti."

Jessica told me how Daniel, the absolute creep, showed up at her door in the middle of the night with dirt he'd uncovered about our yoga teacher. She explained how he'd taken pleasure in her lurid past and threatened to *not let her get away with it*. Whatever the hell that meant.

"Oh no," I said, "that poor girl."

"That's exactly what I said." Jessica's eyes were shining. "It all makes so much sense now. Shakti must have gone through some sort of trauma and completely reinvented herself. I'm worried that he's going to try to destroy her reputation or something. This would be way worse for her than an Allison Kent scandal for us. I know I never super bonded with her in the past, but now I feel like we have to protect her somehow."

"Agreed," I said. "You know I always wondered if the reason you didn't like Shakti was that she reminded you of . . ."

"Don't say it," Jessica said. "But yeah. The Pilates instructor that Tom cheated with."

I didn't have Shakti as an ex–porn star on my retreat Bingo card, but I also couldn't have cared less. Far be it from me to slut shame. And also, she'd been so. Fucking. Young. Life was such a despicable double standard for women. Would anyone bat an eyelash at the frat bros who were featured with her on those videos? Would anyone call them whores and threaten them in some way? They were probably all making bank on Wall Street by now.

Jessica sighed.

"There's something else. I think it might be my fault. All week I've been cynical about her. And when Daniel and I were together . . ." We both shivered at the image. "I mentioned that I thought she might be a hustler. Of course, I didn't mean it like this. Just that sometimes all the yoga shit doesn't add up."

I put an arm around her.

"This isn't on you. Promise. But what do we do now?"

Jessica leaned into me.

"I think we need to talk to her and let her know that Daniel is angry, but we still support her. She's already said she's not coming to the hike or breakfast. Fuck. I hope he hasn't gotten to her already."

I agreed with Jessica's strategy.

"Let's see how she looks when we get to yoga. If she seems normal, we can pull her aside afterward. That way we won't throw her off her teaching game for the class."

I thought about my daughter, Tara. How I'd kill anyone who tried to take advantage of her, but also, how I'd never shame her for exploring her sexuality (once she was old enough). I won't saddle her with expectations and guilt, the way my parents had. I was an only child, and worse, a daughter. I had to watch while my male cousins were treated like princes, doted on, celebrated.

Meanwhile, I was taught to cook and dress appropriately, instructed to be obedient and receive exemplary grades. A good girl must maintain herself as pure and perfect for her future husband. Anything less for me would have been an unforgivable embarrassment.

One of my cousins, Manesh, committed the sin of getting his (white) girlfriend pregnant while they were still in high school. It was a scandal and an open secret. Of course, the family was furious. But they paid for an abortion and shipped him out east to boarding school, once again anointing him as prince, albeit a mischievous one, every time he came home with perfect test scores, and later, acceptances to Penn and Stanford.

The hypocrisy taunts me still. My marriage had been a felony offense for them, but I'd done everything perfectly up until that point. Well, technically, I'd lost my virginity to Greyson *before* saying "I do," but obviously my parents didn't know that. All they saw was that he wasn't a Brahmin prince, like my cousins, and that marked him as undesirable. But my cousin, who had premarital sex with a white girl while in eleventh grade, is now Manesh Chopra, CEO of Aviana Equities, LLC, pride and joy of the entire family.

Maybe Shakti loved being in porn or maybe she was coerced into it. Either way, that part of her life doesn't have to define who she is today. Jessica was right, we needed to have her back.

CAROL ANN

The dewy grass tickled my toes as I walked around the lake in my workout clothes and flip-flops. No one else had bothered to show up for the morning hike. Typical. The teacher asked us to do one thing on our own and people just didn't rise to the occasion. No matter, though; I was delighted to be away from the group and enjoying the grounds in peace.

It was the first cloudy day of the week, which is crazy for this time of year. Usually, it would be raining every single afternoon, instead of baking us with relentless sun. And it wasn't just overcast, it was dark and musty, with that prestorm energy that makes you wanna cuddle up in sweats and turn on Netflix all day.

The frogs were already out and croaking, ready for the coming rains. Ready to spill their little tadpole babies into the fresh water. I took a deep breath in through my nose. The air smelled like my husband after a hunting trip. Manly and powerful.

I circled the lake and counted my blessings with each step. One, for being married to the love of my life. Two, for the perfect children we brought into this world with God's love. Three, for the Father above who has blessed me in countless ways. And on and on for my health, my friends, my teachers, and even my enemies, for they are teachers, too.

When I reached the end, a fat droplet dampened my head, as though I were being baptized anew. *Hallelujah,* I said, under my breath.

A giant splash sounded in the lake. I turned back and a shiver overtook my entire body. That big fat bull alligator snapped its snout shut on a snow-white egret, feathers floating like angel wings from its teeth. It was beautiful. It was a sign. Of the natural order of things. How the predators must eat their prey to survive. How the brutal is beautiful. A sign to stay strong.

"Eat up, swamp puppy," I said to the gator. "You're the apex predator for a reason."

I picked up my pace to the Nourishment Pavilion, suddenly hungry. Inside, Barbara and Daniel were sitting at a table and sharing a plate of cut fruit and pastries. I couldn't say for sure what was going on there, but they made for the weirdest couple I'd ever seen. They waved when I walked in, so I said, "Hey there. Enjoy your breakfast."

The build your own parfait station was calling my name. I layered a bowl with Greek yogurt, house-made granola, manuka honey, and fresh mulberries, then sat down to enjoy it. Shakti was taking extra time to herself that morning, she'd said, and I wondered if it had something to do with all the arguing the night before. I hoped not. We still hadn't had the chance to talk about it.

"Hey, guys," I said to Barbara and Daniel. "Have either of you heard from Shakti this morning? I hope she's okay. I mean, after last night. Everything we all said was in the spirit of honesty. She knows that, right?"

Now that I'd gotten all that was bothering me off my chest, I felt much better about Daniel. Not that I liked him, of course. But at least my feelings were out in the open.

Barbara nodded and gave me a thumbs-up.

Daniel rubbed his possible girlfriend's back but made eye contact with me and said, "I don't think we need to worry about what Shakti thinks."

It was a bizarre thing to say. Barbara seemed to think so, too, because she looked over at him and tilted her head.

He kissed her cheek. Sweet, I guess. She might have been old enough to be his mom, but between the two of them, I'd say he was the lucky one.

"What I meant to say," Daniel continued, "was that Shakti is fine. She's probably just prepping for our last full day of activities."

Well, that made sense. Our teacher did everything to perfection and I'm sure she wanted to close the retreat out properly. I told myself I'd be along for the ride, for her sake, and even put aside my dislike for those awful jezebels, Indira and Jessica.

Shakti was waiting for us in the Active Room. She'd set up the space beautifully with tea candles around her mat and crystal sound bowls at her feet. She looked serene and peaceful, humming to herself quietly, and nodded to us one by one as we sat in our places.

As I laid out my mat, a calming aroma filled my nose. It must have been a blend of essential oils. I detected citrus, lavender, and a hint of peppermint. I folded my legs crisscross applesauce and closed my eyes. Shakti started playing the bowls, immediately giving me the chills, like the church organs on Sunday. Everything within the room vibrated, from the floors to the walls to the blood in my veins.

She rang one of the bowls and let its sound filter down to silence. A pause.

"Good morning, everyone." She said it almost as a song and I was glad to hear her sounding so grounded again.

Shakti opened her eyes. They were filled with love and patience. We waited silently for her to continue.

Thunder crashed outside, followed by the staccato drumming of raindrops on the roof. Like little tiptoes above our heads. These were the comforting sounds of my youth and they put a smile on my face. Even with the door closed, the air in the room grew thick and metallic, fogging up the windows. I never understood people who pout over rainy days; I love feeling the awesome power of nature. It makes my entire body feel electric and alive.

"As we know," Shakti said, "yoga isn't only about the poses, known as asana. Yoga is an eight-fold path that *includes* asana."

I actually hadn't known that, but I was listening.

"Yamas, niyama, asana, pranayama breathwork, pratyahara, dharana, meditation, and, finally, samadhi, which means peace. On our shared journey to peace, we've neglected so much of this path."

She made her biggest crystal bowl sing. The rain pounded harder over our heads. Tap dancers instead of tiptoes.

"Today we will forgo physical practice and do an extended meditation instead. You will each reflect on your intention from the beginning of the week and ask yourself if you've achieved it. If the answer is no, you will manifest your path to success. Now, lie down on your mats."

Oh, bummer, I thought. I'd been hoping for a decent workout for the last day since I hadn't been to the gym or lifted weights since leaving Vero. But I went along with it. Rest was kind of a nice treat, too. Especially with Shakti singing and playing her magical bowls the whole time.

The thunderstorm created a symphony with her instruments and voice, and part of me never wanted it to end. Like a good massage or a perfect meal. I lay back on my mat, spreading my feet hip-width apart and my fingers wide with my palms facing up.

I closed my eyes and let my mind drift to my original retreat intention. If I remembered correctly, it was something about being less judgmental, letting go of frivolous things, and learning to balance a handstand. Well, shoot. I'd gained a whole heck of a lot that week but wasn't sure if even one of those goals had been achieved. But maybe that was just because the things I'd thought I needed weren't *actually* that important. Since I'd been at Transcendence Week, my eyes had opened up to the real problems in my life and now I was working on solutions. So really, I'd *grown*.

What's the point of being less judgmental, anyway? Isn't judgment a positive thing? They don't call it *good judgment* for nothing. It's something we teach our children to have and to use. So why do some people act like it's a flaw we need to get rid of?

The bowls started singing louder, the rain matching their intensity. Shakti's voice floated in and out of my ears like a mother's lullaby. My body tingled from my nose to my fingertips to my toes. Little sparks of electricity.

It felt like being awake while inside a dream and I wondered if this was the closest thing to bliss I'd ever experienced.

Images of my children as babies appeared in my mind. Their faces glowing and laughing. I could almost feel the infant weight of them in my arms. Then, like a slideshow, they started growing in front of my eyes. Their baby chub melting into lean muscle and long limbs, their silky hair sprouting and growing out and tucking behind their ears. At one point, they held hands and danced in circles just behind my eyes. Hot tears spilled onto either side of my face as I tried to hold on tightly to their faces in each stage. Lord, how I missed them.

The sound bowls grew quieter. The rain slowed to thuds.

An ugly noise startled me out of the trance. "Beau?" I accidentally said out loud.

Then I heard it again. Snoring. I opened my eyes and turned my head to see Daniel with his mouth open and drool sliding down his cheek. Not very enlightened. Not at all.

Shakti banged on one of the bowls harder. Daniel gasped and suddenly sat up, looked around, and then lay back down on his mat. I'm pretty sure I saw Barbara shaking her head. By the end of the session, I was a boneless puddle melted on the floor. That's how relaxed I was.

"Let's start to wiggle our fingers, wiggle our toes," Shakti said, barely above a whisper. "Come back to our breath. Come back to our bodies."

I did as I was told, keeping my eyes closed to savor the moment a little bit longer.

"Reach your arms over your head, taking a nice, loving stretch.

Then roll over onto one side, like a baby, cradling your head on an elbow."

I opened my eyes and saw the rest of the group following along, all of us looking like giant cinnamon buns, curled into ourselves.

"And when you're ready, you can prop yourself up, little by little, and we'll meet in a seated pose at the front of our mats."

I folded one leg in for half lotus and noticed how the pose was so much more comfortable than it had been on the first day.

"This afternoon and evening," Shakti said, sitting with her hands on her knees, "we will share one final cocktail hour and one last dinner. Let us do so with love and light. Tomorrow, we will meet for breakfast and then part ways into the world. With joy. With gratitude. With peace. Thank you all for joining me on this journey of trust and openness. Namaste."

"Namaste!" I said, bowing to my feet.

We all stood up slowly, like we'd been drugged. I wanted to steal Shakti away for a minute to apologize about getting heated the night before, and also to chat with her a little about my growth, and where I saw myself going next. The tides were shifting so rapidly in my marriage, and I truly had her to thank.

But before I could get to her, Jessica and Indira cornered her and were speaking rapidly in hushed tones.

"Umm, excuse me," I said. "Can I just borrow her for a quick minute?"

Jessica tuned around and addressed me sharply. "Can it wait?"

I swear, that lady is lucky I am a woman of God. Part of me wanted to tell her that no, it could not wait, and she could hold her horses. But not wanting to argue in front of Shakti again, I decided to let this one slide.

"I'll come by your villa later then, Shakti, if that's okay?"

She smiled serenely. "Sure. That would be wonderful."

"Actually." Daniel wedged his body in front of mine. "I have something I wanted to discuss with you as well, dear teacher."

He sounded weird. Sarcastic. I recoiled from his sweating body in front of me. For Christ's sake, we hadn't even exercised. Something about that guy had always rubbed me wrong.

"Okay," Shakti said. "How about before cocktails then, Daniel?"

Outside, the steady whoosh of heavy rain continued. I lifted my unfurled yoga mat over my head and made a run for it back to my villa. In the time we'd been in meditation, puddles had filled in the gaps between the concrete walkways and the grass alongside of it on the way to the Enlightenment Circle, and they splashed up my legs as I ran.

The rain fell in cold drops onto my arms and slid down my body, soaking me through and through. Eventually, I gave up on the yoga mat as shelter and ran the rest of the way with it under my arm. By the time I reached my villa, I looked like a toy Pomeranian in the middle of a bath. The little hairs on my arms stood straight up on top of gooseflesh, and for the first time all week, I was shivering with cold.

It reminded me of being a kid. How my friends and I would be run off on summer mornings to play, our parents having only a vague idea of where we'd gone. And how sometimes we'd get caught in these kinds of showers or storms. We'd dance and laugh and let our clothes become heavy with rain and stay like that until our soaking socked feet couldn't take it anymore.

When I went inside my villa, the cool air making my teeth chatter, I peeled off my clothes and squeezed them out into the sink. Running in the rain was a thrill, but nothing felt better than the warm shower that followed.

I set the dial to the hottest setting. For having modest bathrooms with basic plumbing, the Namaste Club had pretty decent showers. I stepped in and let the steam fill my lungs. The water seared my skin with painful pleasure, and I closed my eyes to let it cover my whole face and body. It felt so good, I almost wanted to go out and run in the rain so I could warm myself up all over again.

I took my time. Lathering and rinsing my hair, letting a conditioning mask sit for an extra few minutes. Then I reached for the razor to shave the stubble off my legs. That's when something caught my attention in the strange little window that was affixed to the bottom of one of the shower walls. Movement. I knelt down to wipe off the steam and screamed, nearly falling back on my butt at what I saw. There was a man crawling in front of the window, his eyes on my naked body. It was Daniel.

JESSICA

Indira and I waited for Daniel to leave the Active Room so we could speak candidly with Shakti. He walked into the storm with zero protection, taking unhurried steps as if to prove a point. Barbara lingered, shifting her feet nervously. Had she sensed that we had bad news to deliver?

I watched Daniel's back disappear into the rain and turned to Shakti. "There's something I need to tell you," I said. "Well, actually, it's something *about* you. Perhaps you'd like us to go somewhere private?"

Her eyes briefly flashed with alarm and then settled back into her resting peace face.

"We are among trusted friends. Feel free to speak openly," she said.

Outside, the rain fell in sheets, making it hard to hear my own voice as I confessed what I'd heard the night before. I told her about how I'd accidentally planted a seed in Daniel's head. How he'd explored that kernel and scrounged up something from her past. The website. The videos.

Barbara listened with a hand over her mouth, her eyes sad and sympathetic.

Shakti was silent and stoic. Indira nodded me on.

"He seemed so angry for some reason," I told her. "When I kicked him out of my room, he said *She won't get away with this*. It seemed threatening. So I had to tell you. I won't let him destroy everything you've built."

Indira reached for one of Shakti's hands.

"We are here to support you. You're a great teacher and we respect you."

The facade broke. Shakti fell into racking sobs, her hands trembling over her eyes. Gently, Barbara guided her to sit on the floor and held her there, stroking her hair. Indira and I sat down, too.

For several minutes, she just cried and didn't look anyone in the eye. My stomach clenched. Seeing Shakti shed her teacherly authority was jarring, and part of me wished I could take back what I'd said. When she recovered herself a little, her voice sounded weak.

"Did you watch the videos?"

"No. But I'm pretty sure he did," I said, leaning over to take her hand.

"You must think I'm disgusting." She wiped tears and mascara from under her eyes.

"No!" Indira and I said in unison. Barbara shook her head vigorously.

"You won't get any shame from us," Indira said. "I may not have many good college stories but I more than make up for it now."

"And I'm certainly not one to talk," I added. "I slept with Daniel." I looked over at Barbara, who was still comforting Shakti. "No offense, of course." She waved it off.

"My point is," I said. "Our bodies, our decisions. You weren't hurting anyone. And you're allowed to have a past that isn't super yogi-ish. No one expected you to be born a Buddha."

"I really do believe in yoga," Shakti said. "In its transformative powers. It's changed my life." She whimpered again into her hands. "It saved my life."

I squeezed her hand. "Of course it has. And that's beautiful. It doesn't matter who you were back then. The only thing that matters is who you are today. Which is an amazing person and teacher."

"Old Shakti was probably amazing, too," Indira said.

"It's Alyssa," Shakti said. "Old me was Alyssa."

She caught her breath and swallowed hard.

"I skipped a grade in elementary school, so I graduated high school when I was seventeen. I was the youngest person in my freshman year college class."

Barbara handed her a bottle of water and she took a long drink.

"They called me baby Alyssa. I was the only girl in the dorms who couldn't get into the eighteen and over clubs. And no one wanted to socialize with the runt anyway. The only place where they actually wanted me to hang out was the Sigma Kappa frat house."

She squeezed her eyes shut. When she opened them again, they were cold and distant.

"They told me I was cooler than the other girls. That they preferred my company. Said the other girls were just jealous of me. They gave me beer and jungle punch and I started spending more and more time there.

"I wasn't a virgin, but I'd only been with my high school boyfriend at that point. Still, I didn't think of myself as naive at the time. And I didn't want to be one of those girls who made a big deal about sex.

"The first time it happened, we'd been doing keg stands at their Olympic-themed party. They cheered every time I went upside down and my skirt fell down. The attention was really nice, but as they got dirtier about it, I started to feel weird. One of the guys started spanking me with a rush paddle and then someone else had the bright idea to film me. I didn't want to be an uptight loser and make it a big deal. If they stopped wanting to hang out with me, I'd have ended up totally alone."

Barbara cradled Shakti in her arms. Indira and I sat shocked. I couldn't imagine how I'd react if someone had treated my daughter that way, but assumed it would probably end with me going to prison.

"You were a child," Indira said. "And they were fucking pigs."

Shakti smiled weakly.

"Anyway, it went on for over a year. Mostly me in schoolgirl outfits getting paddled, topless. The guys touching themselves in the background, but never showing their faces. The videos started getting more and more popular, and we were making money off them. Like, I was even able to make my car payments off the profits, so we just kept going. I can't pretend I ever asked them to stop. I knew what I was doing.

"Eventually though, I did want it to end. Creepy men were finding me on social media and sending me unsolicited photos and asking for all kinds of disgusting things. At that point, I just wanted out. All the other girls at school knew by then and would write 'whore' on the little whiteboard in front of my dorm room. It was humiliating.

"When I told one of the guys—the one I thought I was closest to—that I couldn't do it anymore, he flipped on me. He sent an anonymous email to my parents and linked all of the videos. That's when I hit rock bottom. The worst part was that I really thought he was my friend."

"Shakti," I said. "That is horrible. Absolutely horrible. The fact that you're sitting here today and leading these classes and retreats shows how strong you are."

Barbara and Indira silently agreed.

"I know you say you were in on it. But those guys took advantage of you." Indira was crying and I suddenly realized that I was, too.

Shakti shook her head. "I don't consider myself a victim," she said, her voice sounding stronger. "I really don't."

She straightened her spine and exhaled a slow, deep breath.

"After everyone found out, my parents disowned me. Everyone at school hated me, so I dropped out of college. I thought my life was over. Then my grandpa in West Palm Beach asked me to live with him and said he'd pay for any kind of education I wanted. That's when I met Guru Krishna-ji."

"Your teacher," Indira said.

"Yes. He showed me a new way to live and taught me that my past wasn't important. All that matters is now. It's not that I wanted to run from what had happened exactly. I just never told people because I didn't think they would understand."

Everyone in the room was crying now. I cleaned the smudged mascara from my cheeks with my sports bra strap and sighed. Even though she was vulnerable and in pain, it was nice to finally see the real Shakti.

"What can we do to help?" Indira asked. "You've worked so hard to become who you are today. We won't let some fake yogi douchebag take that away from you."

Barbara shifted in her seat, her eyes wide with worry.

The rain continued pelting the Active Room's roof like the feet of a thousand little subway commuters. Shakti pulled her hair back into a neat ponytail.

"He wants to speak with me privately. I told him to meet me before cocktails."

Mother's intuition buzzed in my ears.

"Don't let him in your room," I said. "Can you tell him to meet you somewhere out in the open?"

She bit her cheek.

"Yeah. I'll tell him to meet me by Shiva Lake."

Barbara chewed her fingernail, then stood up and kissed Shakti's head before turning to the door and running out into the rain.

The remaining three of us exchanged a look.

"We'll be on standby for you," Indira said. "Keep your phone out and call if you need us."

CAROL ANN

I screamed so loudly I almost popped an eardrum.

Without even thinking, I turned the water off, covered my breasts and privates, and ran out of the shower, soap streaming down my back.

I stepped quickly into my jumpsuit from the other day, which was sitting on top of my suitcase, and buttoned it all the way up. Then I grabbed my phone and ran the hell out of there. The rain had slowed down but was still insistent, depositing more drops on my warm skin.

Behind me, a male voice called out, "I'm sorry! Barbara told me that the villa gardens needed weeding!"

Yeah. Right. I kept running.

I'd almost made it all the way back to the Active Room when I noticed I was barefoot and my hair was soaking wet and full of conditioner. At least the rain was helping to rinse it out. My eyes stung badly, and as I patted my face, I realized that I was crying, loudly and with sloppy dripping tears.

It was like I was both in my body and out of my body. I didn't even know what compelled me to run, but that's also what animals do when they sense danger, so maybe it was my fight-or-flight response kicking in. My villa was no longer safe. It, and me, had been violated. In my manic state, I'd even forgotten to grab my gun. My safety. My protection. I'd just wanted to get the heck out of there as quickly as possible. But then, suddenly, I felt its absence like a phantom limb.

I must have been a sight walking into the Active Room. Partially washed hair, snot running down my face, jumpsuit soaked through with shower water and rain. Not that anyone was there to see it. My heart thudded in my ears and my hands were trembling. *This is a panic attack,* I thought, and decided to sit down and attempt to catch my breath. It brought me back to the day in my kids' school library, when I first saw the books those woke moms put there to taunt me, the wrongness of it, the impure intention. But this . . . this was way sicker. This man was probably planning on pleasuring himself later to the sight of me, naked. Without my permission. It was the scariest and worst thing that had ever happened to me.

I wanted my husband. I *needed* him.

After five slow, deep breaths, my hands stopped shaking enough to unlock my phone and call Beau. He didn't answer at first, so I called again. And again.

"Yeah?" he answered.

My voice came out strained. "Beau," I said, before breaking back down into tears.

"Carol Ann? What's wrong? What happened?"

I fought to catch my breath. He hit the button for FaceTime and I accepted the request.

As soon as he saw me, his body went rigid.

"What in Jesus's name . . ."

"There was a man watching me," I managed to squeak out. "In the shower. I was . . . washing myself."

I covered my face in shame and blew my nose into my hand, wiping it on my jumpsuit. Beau shouldn't have had to see me like this. I tried to fix my hair a little bit and twist it behind my back. It was no use. My image on the screen was a fright.

Beau's eyes just about popped out of his head.

"What did you say?"

It looked like he was in some kind of parking lot I couldn't recognize. Since it was Saturday, he must have been out running errands while my mother watched the kids.

"There's a window at the bottom of my shower," I said, steadying my voice. "And when I was showering just now, something caught my eye and . . ."

"Was this that fucking man who's on your trip?" Beau seemed to be pacing now. The phone was jiggling with his movements.

"Yes, baby."

"I had a bad feeling about him. I knew he'd be after you. I *told* you. Fucking perv at a ladies' retreat."

"You were right," I said, wiping my eyes again. Fresh tears kept spilling out, no matter how hard I willed them to stop. "As soon as I saw him, I got the hell out of there. I was so scared; I wasn't even thinking. Maybe I should call the police . . ."

"No police." Beau's eyes were as hard as I've ever seen them. "I'm coming up there right now. I'm gonna fucking kill this guy."

Warmth covered my body like a blanket. Even in the worst situations, my man was there to protect me. I wasn't alone. But fear pinched my stomach, too. I wanted Beau to rescue me, but what if he got hurt in the process? Or what if Beau hurt Daniel and then got in trouble? I worried that I had brought this on myself somehow. Beau had said from the beginning how it was fishy to have a male there in the first place. And I'd pretty much ignored the danger.

"Beau, I don't want anything to happen to you."

"Stop it, Carol Ann. It's too late for that. Someone violated my wife and there's only one way to settle that."

"But I can't risk losing you. Just please promise me you won't do anything crazy," I pleaded.

Beau spit on the sidewalk. "Don't worry. It will be self-defense."

I closed my eyes and nodded. "Thank you, baby. I'm sorry this even happened. I love you so much."

"I'll be there in an hour and a half. Stay somewhere safe until then."

He hung up the phone.

BARBARA

Tears drowned my weary eyes as I ran out of the Active Room to look for Daniel. I imagined the gods were cleansing me with their rains, making me pure again after what I'd done and heard.

Could it be true that Daniel would harm someone over their sexual nature? The same man who came alongside me just hours ago, crying in joy and ecstasy as he released his seed onto my welcoming body? This man who presented as so evolved, so advanced in his yoga and tantra?

Shakti is our teacher. It is our duty as followers to bow at her lotus feet. Not to harm or judge. She brings us light, strengthens our bodies and our minds. We are her servants, meant to be steadfast and loyal. How could he threaten her?

Given what we'd shared, which had felt like an otherworldly connection, I thought that maybe Daniel would listen to me. *Listen*. Should I break my silent vow? I'd promised myself two more days of not uttering a word. The thought of breaking that sacred oath squeezed my heart and shamed my soul. There had to be some other way. Shakti needed me.

I arrived at Daniel's villa, soaked to the bone and split open inside, and knocked on the door. *Tap, tap, tap, tap.* I pressed my ear to the wood and listened. Silence. So I tried again. *Tap, tap, tap.*

Nothing. I paced in circles in front of the door, thinking. Maybe I could leave a letter for him, explaining the error of his actions, begging him to reconsider, to come back to his teachings. *Ahimsa.* We must do no harm. He would listen. He would understand. Part of me still fully believed in his essential goodness.

I reached into my pocket for the master set of keys and let myself inside. Daniel is boyish in his messiness, a fact I once found charming. Sheets were strewn on the floor; clothes were littered on top of the various pieces of furniture. His laptop lay open on his bed. I pressed on a key to wake up the screen and typed in his password (I'd guessed it on the first day—1113, for his birthday).

The computer unlocked and revealed a paused still from an adult film. I recognized Shakti immediately, bent over but looking back at the camera, and so, so young. I studied the image on the screen, zoomed in on her vacant eyes. This was not a beautiful expression of sexuality. It was a girl being taken advantage of. I rushed to close the window, my hands shaking, my heart breaking. We've all been a girl who has been taken advantage of.

I squeezed my eyes shut and tried to moderate my breath. Maybe Daniel had just been curious, stumbled upon the video after I slipped that Shakti had a past. There had to be an explanation for why he was watching it. A spiritual one, to guide him on his path. I opened my eyes and stared at his computer screen, the little folders with labels like "Work" and "Mantra" blurring behind my tears. Then, with something tugging at my brain, I opened up his Finder app and scrolled to his iCloud folder. Call it intuition. I hovered the cursor over a file named "Personal."

"Forgive me, goddess," I said, like every other time I took the liberty of a little dive, and opened the file.

Immediately, the bile rose to my throat. Inside were a collection of videos, all named. "Karen." "Phoebe." "Jessica." "Barbara."

I opened the one with my name on it and gasped. It was a bird's-eye view of our lovemaking. When had he hidden the camera? The betrayal clawed at my heart as though a lion was eating me alive. Why? What was the purpose? All he had to do was ask, and I gladly would have consented to be filmed. To preserve a memory of what I had thought was beautiful and pure. But no, how wrong I was. Our love-making was tainted and rotten. Like that poor worm-infested pig.

I fell onto the mattress, gasping for air, trying to make sense of what I'd just seen, when my hands closed on a wad of sticky toilet paper. I realized it was drenched in Daniel's semen. My stomach churned at the realization. He'd enjoyed himself to Shakti's video, taken pleasure at her expense. That was wrong, and against our rules, and evil.

And then I remembered. Evil seduces. How could I have been so easily fooled? How could I have surrendered my body so willingly to a demon?

I gathered myself off the bed, knowing that there was no point in leaving a note. There would be no reasoning with that man. The only thing I had left to offer was a strong defense on behalf of Shakti, myself, and all the other women he'd victimized.

I threw the wad of toilet paper into the wastebasket, but something else caught my eye. A single-use plastic Zephyrhills water bottle. Eight ounces. I balled my fists together and squeezed my eyes shut, willing myself with all my might not to scream. Daniel had tricked me in so many ways.

Sometimes the path isn't as clear as good or evil, up or down, or left or right. Sometimes, one must choose a lesser evil to prevent a greater one. Daniel's room, my discoveries there, had illuminated the path. I knew what I needed to do. To take.

I ran out of his villa and straight toward Carol Ann's.

INDIRA

Jessica and I huddled together in her room, drying off with her still-damp bathroom towels. Outside, the sky was still smoky gray and foreboding.

I poured glasses of Enlightened Tequila into two water cups and handed one to my friend.

"To Shakti," I said, clinking her glass.

"May she find her peace, and may we protect her at all costs," Jessica said. She took a deep drink and slammed the cup back on the table. "What an absolute animal Daniel is." She contorted her face in disgust.

I felt bad for her. Not that she'd ever been in love with him, but even having been in lust seemed mortifying at that moment.

"Stop beating yourself up," I said, reading her mind. "You had no idea about her history. And you couldn't have predicted that Daniel would investigate it and then use it to hurt her."

She poured herself another glass and then looked up at me with a startle.

"I just realized that I never asked you," Jessica said. "I guess I didn't want to bring it up because I was afraid of starting another fight. But why *did* you bring Daniel to your room that night? If you weren't going to sleep with him? Because you knew he was a total tool?"

Shame burned hot in my gut, but it was time to come clean.

"I suspected his toolishness, maybe, but I had no idea he was this fucked-up."

I swallowed hard. The truth was embarrassing on every level, but my best friend deserved to hear it. Jessica never worries about being vulnerable with me, but unfortunately, I don't usually reciprocate on that front.

"When we were talking out at the Enlightenment Circle that first night, I mentioned how sore I was, and he offered me a back rub. Said he was 'one of the best in the world.' I was a little high on mushrooms and that sounded nice. But also, I was so pissed at you, and I knew it would sting if you saw us walking away together. I'm sorry. That was really horrible of me."

Jessica looked sympathetic, which was generous of her.

"There's more," I said. "I truly knew I wouldn't sleep with him. That would have been a step too far for you and me to come back from. And I'm not saying that to absolve myself. I was being a huge bitch. But anyway, the massage was incredible. I'd kept my clothes on, and he'd just pulled up the back of my shirt. I figured that he was probably doing it as foreplay and was totally prepared to shove him off me afterward, but . . ."

Confusion passed over Jessica's eyes. The next part was oddly hard for me to admit.

"He kinda just left. He didn't even try anything. Just said good night and winked on his way out the door."

Jessica's jaw dropped. She shook her head.

"You're telling me that horny Daniel the yoga douche didn't even attempt to hook up with the sexiest woman on earth?"

I laughed a little, but inside was relieved. It was such a silly insignificant thing now that it was out in the open, even though he had bizarrely bruised my ego.

"I guess I'm not his type. For all his faux-Hindu worship, I don't think he actually likes the brown girls."

"Further proof that he's an idiot," Jessica said. "I still can't believe I fell for his Casanova act, though. It feels like I've been making a lot of bad decisions lately. First, the influencer marketing fiasco and now him. At what point do I just have to accept that I'm the one to blame for all these mistakes?"

I hated watching Jessica punish herself for the sins of others, especially after I'd been so hard on her after the Allison Kent scandal.

"Not today," I said. "And anyway, we should focus on solutions. Like you so brilliantly pointed out back when that influencer spouted hate speech while wearing a ring named after my daughter."

Jessica winced. "Did you have to bring that up?"

Thunder roared somewhere in the distance, and I wondered if Shakti's meeting with Daniel would even still happen in this weather.

"I only bring it up because look how that turned out. There are ways to manage bad situations. And that is something you are very good at. Now, what's our plan for helping Shakti, in case things go south?"

Jessica dried her arms with her towel and chucked it on the floor.

"They're meeting at five right? Assuming the weather lets up. I say, if we don't hear from her by five thirty, we go down to the lake and check on them."

"You mean my favorite place?" I asked. "Let's make it five fifteen."

CAROL ANN

There was a brief lull in the storm when the torrential downpour slowed to a pitter-patter, so I used the break to visit Shakti's villa. As I crossed the path into the Enlightenment Circle, I pictured the little drops of rain cleansing the filth from my eyes. He'd tainted me, that man. And I hated him for it more than I'd ever hated anything in my whole life.

Back in junior year of high school, I briefly dated this lacrosse player named Chet from our rival school. He looked good on paper—youth group leader, good grades, athlete, etc. So my parents didn't mind if he took me out on dates here and there, as long as I got home by curfew. We kept things over the clothes, if you know what I mean, even though I felt the urges so strongly I thought my lady parts would explode. I was not about to disappoint my parents and ruin my marriage prospects over some teenage hormones.

One night, Chet picked me up to take me to the movies and stopped inside beforehand to have a quick chat with my father about a mission trip to Honduras he was going on. "Such a nice boy," my dad whispered to me as I walked out the door. And there's nothing like Daddy's approval. I smiled to myself as Chet held the car door open for me. He was a gentleman like that.

We were supposed to see *The Patriot*, with Mel Gibson. But instead of getting out and opening my car door when we arrived at the theater, Chet had pulled into the parking garage, put the car in park, and reclined his seat all the way back.

I remember feeling confused. "What are you doing?" I asked.

He didn't say a word, just smirked like we were sharing some kind of secret and unbuckled his seat belt. That's when the realization hit me. I froze, which he must have taken for compliance, because then he leaned back a little farther, undid his pants, and pulled out his erect penis. I'd never even seen one outside of a health textbook.

I covered my mouth. My eyes stung and my heart pounded. The whole thing was awful. I shook my head in disbelief. We'd been together for four months already and he absolutely knew my stance on abstinence, which I thought he shared.

"Come on, baby," he said. "Just give it a little kiss before the movie."

I shrieked like someone had cut me. Chet panicked and hastily zipped up his pants. He started explaining, but I jumped out of the car and ran to the garage's staircase, bolted down, and sprinted all the way to the theater. When I got there, I grabbed an attendant and begged for a phone to call my parents. My dad answered and I told him everything in between racking sobs.

"Stay right there," he said.

The theater was only five minutes from my house. By the time my father arrived, 12-gauge shotgun in hand, Chet had found me and was trying to downplay the whole thing. He thought I wanted it. What did I expect him to do when I'm so sexy? That sort of thing.

I was outside, barely listening to him, waiting to be picked up, when my dad pulled up to the curb. He jumped out and cocked the shotgun, fired one round into the air, and everyone outside of the theater froze. I will never forget the pathetic look on Chet's face. Terror. Shame. Regret. He stood there gobsmacked while my dad raged in his ear and didn't move a muscle, even when the trickle of urine down his leg had saturated his jeans.

That day, I learned so many things: that there are good guys and bad guys, that my father would always protect me, and that I needed to marry someone exactly like him. That's what I'd done with Beau.

I knocked on Shakti's door, still sopping wet with conditioner in my hair, and prepared myself to fall into her embrace. Earlier that day, there'd been so many things I'd wanted to discuss with her, but by the afternoon I couldn't remember any of them. Finding Daniel outside my shower window had become the Mason-Dixon Line of pre- and post-traumatic Carol Ann. At that point, I just needed love and a hug.

When she opened up, though, I gasped. The usually perfectly put together woman in front of me looked as crazed as I felt. Her face was streaked with tears and mascara, and she held a wad of crumpled tissues in her hand.

"Dear Lord," I said, letting myself in and closing the door behind me. "What happened to you?"

She broke down into convulsive tears. Then it hit me. What if this guy was a serial offender?

"Don't tell me it's about Daniel." My voice was screechy. I could feel my mama bear coming out of hibernation.

She nodded and I pulled her into a hug. *Daniel strikes again.* It's unbelievable what we women deal with sometimes. And to sully someone as innocent and sweet as Shakti seemed like an especially evil sin. We wrapped our arms tightly around each other, and I started crying again, too.

A few moments later, I pulled away and held her by the shoulders.

"When did he come peeping in on you?" I asked.

Her eyes searched mine. She wrinkled her eyebrows.

"Peeping? What do you mean peeping?"

"The shower," I said. "Didn't he sneak over to your shower to peep on you?"

She shook her head.

"No, he didn't." She stepped back and studied my face. "Carol Ann, was Daniel watching you shower somehow?"

Oh Jesus. So he'd done something different to her. I prayed it wasn't worse than what he'd done to me.

I nodded my head. "I caught him a little while ago. But don't you worry, Shakti. It will be handled."

She started crying again.

"I'm so sorry. I never should have brought him here. This is my fault."

"Don't you dare say that," I said, shaking her a little. "Everything you've done here is for love and light. You aren't responsible for that man's sins."

Her face softened.

"Thank you," she said.

"You're welcome. Now tell me what he did to you."

Now it was my turn to be strong for her. I had Beau as my bull gator, but who did Shakti have? Someone needed to protect her, and after all she'd done for me, I wanted to be that person.

Then she told me the truth. The awful, ugly truth.

"He found out something about my past," she said. "Something I'm not so proud of."

"Honey, you look ill," I said. "Do you want to sit down?"

She slouched down onto the floor, so I mirrored her. Something about her fragility was making me uneasy. Before, I'd seen only the strong, poised Shakti who was wise beyond her years. But before me sat a wounded girl.

"He found the videos." She reached back for the throw blanket on her bed and blew her nose into it.

I thought maybe she was talking about some early yoga classes she taught that weren't at her current level of mastery. Or maybe some evidence of her losing her temper and not appearing "enlightened." We all have those moments. But that's not what it was. What she told me was repulsive.

"It started in college," she said.

Shakti is no guru. She's no enlightened spiritual teacher. She's a dirty, lying, charlatan whore. My head got so fuzzy when she was telling me the story, I had to bury it in my hands. Frat party this and porn site that. I wanted to vomit right there on her sinful face.

When she'd finished talking, she looked at me expectantly, like I was going to applaud her bravery or give her a big hug. Shakti, or whatever her real name was, wasn't going to fool me twice.

Sure, maybe it was despicable that Daniel wanted to expose her for the world to see (talk about being a hypocrite), but honestly that's what she deserved. If Daniel was silenced, I'd go ahead and spill the beans myself. Her students had a right to know who they were following.

"You're a fraud," I said. "A no-good, lying, whoring fraud."

Shakti looked back at me like I'd slapped her, and honestly, she's lucky I didn't. I'd trusted this woman with my most intimate confidences. I told her about my sex life with my husband. I bet she was even getting off on all of it. How dare she betray me like that. I squeezed my palms into fists and thanked God that Beau was on his way. I needed to get the hell out of this sin-playground as quickly as possible.

"I'm s-s-sorry," Shakti stuttered, her true self finally shining through. "I never wanted to disappoint anyone." Crocodile tears rolled down her face.

"Tell it to Jesus," I said. Then I got off the floor and walked out of there, back into the storm, which wasn't nearly as threatening as everything I'd seen and heard at Transcendence Week. I slammed her door behind me, just as Barbara walked up with a tote bag wrapped under her arm. She startled when she saw me.

Another phony, I thought, as I stomped back to my villa to wait for Beau.

SHAKTI

NOW

A journey without bumps teaches us nothing, and Transcendence Week showed us this truth. After all our challenges, we ended the week with peace and light, as was the goal. We truly transcended. Everyone made meaningful strides on their spiritual journeys, having authentically waded through the darkness to reach the other side.

After taking the morning off, I had regenerated myself, and then taught double meditation practice and sound bowl healing with a full and open heart. The results were beautiful.

When the class was finished, everyone gathered at my feet to reflect on the week with joy and gratitude.

It was the perfect ending.

Sometimes the universe tells us when something is complete. In this case, it gave us the rains, which made our final planned meetings for cocktails and dinner impossible. What might have been disappointing ended up being the perfect sign. We'd completed the work that had brought us together.

I only wish I'd had the chance to tell everyone goodbye. Meditation practice was the last time I saw any of the students. It was also the last time I saw Daniel alive.

CAROL ANN

I was still barefoot, stomping through the soaking grounds, like some kind of cavewoman, walking aimlessly around the Enlightenment Circle. My toes sloshed through the mud and grass and were completely caked in filth. In another hour, Beau would arrive, and I just couldn't have him see me like that. He married a lady, not a backwoods trash girl.

There was no other choice. I had to go back to my villa. But make no mistake, before I passed through the door, I checked the entire perimeter for perverts. No Daniel. No anybody.

It had been raining for so long by then, the droplets on my body felt no different from a breeze on my back. I almost missed the rain when I entered my room, where the transition to a roof over my head and blowing A/C sent me into a shiver. No matter. After locking the door behind me, I quickly replaced the downpour with a new shower.

When I first looked at the stall, still wet and soapy from when I'd run out earlier, I shuddered, as if the walls itself had eyes that were hungry to see my nakedness. *It's just a shower,* I told myself.

Still, I covered the window with a bath towel, just in case Daniel was stupid enough to come back. Then I tiptoed to my tote bag on the little dining table, rooting around for the cool embrace of my Glock. An extra insurance policy, just in case. My stomach hitched a little. The gun wasn't there. But there was no need to panic. I vaguely remembered hearing something it about during my full moon fever dream when I was being put to bed. I must've put it in the safe, or maybe Barbara had locked it up for me.

I'd already turned the water to its hottest setting, again, and the inviting steam of the shower called me back. I rinsed the sticky conditioner out of my hair. Then I rinsed it through a second time with a fresh shampoo. I scrubbed the dirt from under my toenails, cleansed my face and neck, and shaved my legs all the way up the thigh. If I was a prize to fight for, I should look the part. An obsession took over me, the need to win my husband back. In my fit of passion, I'd forgotten all about the gun.

An hour is about how long it takes for me to get date-night ready, so that's exactly what I did: blowing my hair out and then curling it into a Marilyn Monroe swoop, making my face up in my signature daytime-out look, even giving myself an extra scrub *down there*. I finished off by patting scented lotion all over my body and stepped into the tangerine dress that Beau doesn't like me to wear for anyone but him.

I was ready for my man.

At 4:00 p.m., he texted saying he'd arrived at the Greeting Center, but no one was there. I responded with directions to my room. Then I spent the most nervous five minutes of my life pacing and checking myself in the mirror until I heard the knock on my door.

"CA?" he said from the other side. "You in there?"

I unlocked the door and flung it open, all but leaping on top of him. Beau caught me and held me tight as I buried my head in his neck. I'd almost forgotten how strong he was, the stubble on his cheek, the intoxicating smell of mustiness and steel. Before I knew it, I was sobbing again, and cursing myself for smudging my freshly applied makeup.

He pushed me away and gave me a serious look.

"Where is he?" Beau asked.

I can't explain it, but the authority in his voice sent a tingle down my legs. I wanted him. Badly. I'd missed him so much.

"I don't know," I said, reaching out to touch his face, to feel the warmth of the blood underneath his skin. "All I care about right now is you. I'm so happy you're here."

He shrugged me off and stalked around my villa, as though Daniel were hiding underneath the bed.

"It means so much to me that you came," I said, following him.

"What did you expect I'd do? Some simp comes on to my wife and I'm not going to retaliate? What kind of man would that make me, Carol Ann? I dropped everything to haul ass over here."

I noticed he did look a little mussed up, which made me feel awful. His hair was tousled, and his clothes were badly wrinkled. I wondered if it was from the stress of what I told him over the phone or because I hadn't been there to take care of the household for a week. He walked into the bathroom and pulled the towel down from the shower window.

"What the hell is a window doing here anyway?"

I shrugged. "I have no idea."

"Probably because this is a place for perverts." He threw the towel on the wet shower floor.

I nodded.

Beau's phone buzzed in his pocket, and he pulled it out to check the screen. He seemed so agitated, but I thought maybe I could help. When was the last time we'd been alone in a hotel room together? Probably not since our honeymoon. A rush took over my body and I wondered if he'd felt it, too.

I closed the gap between us and slid the phone out of his hand, tossing it onto the bed.

"What the hell, CA?" he started to protest.

I put a hand to his lips and slid down his body to my knees. Along the way, I loosened his buckle and slowly unbuttoned and unzipped his shorts. I pulled them down along with his boxers and looked up at him with a smile. He shifted a little but didn't say a word, watching to see what I'd do next.

While squeezing his thighs, I started kissing around his groin, waiting for him to wake up so I could take him inside my mouth. It was taking longer than expected, but I tried not to let it discourage me.

Maybe he just needed a more aggressive approach, so I started licking down onto his parts. Then I wrapped my hand firmly around him and slipped his tip into my mouth. Squeezing and sucking, squeezing and sucking. And because he likes when I'm a little noisy, I moaned a little with him inside my mouth.

Nothing.

My heart started racing. Was Beau not attracted to me anymore because another man had seen me naked? He was supposed to be starving for me.

I looked up at him again, but he wouldn't meet my gaze. He just reached down and put his shorts back on, pulling up on the zipper and reaffixing the button.

"What's wrong, baby? Haven't you missed me?"

He smoothed his hands down his pants and looked everywhere but my face.

"Course I missed you, but I'm a little riled up right now. A man almost molested you and now you're all turned on for some reason. Did you like him watching you or something?"

I jumped to my feet.

"No! I swear to my mother. I just missed you, Beau!"

He searched me up and down.

"Is this how you've been dressing every day?"

Hot tears burned my eyes again. I couldn't believe I still had any left to spill after everything that had happened that day.

"I just wanted to look nice for you. I'm sorry."

Beau punched the wall, and I jerked back.

"Is this a game to you?" His eyes were full of rage. I'd never seen him that angry at me. And here I'd been thinking about how far we'd come in the last week when really he'd just been slipping further away. I cursed myself for coming to the godforsaken yoga retreat. What had I been thinking?

"Carol Ann," he said, his jaw tight. "Where is this man who violated you, and where the fuck is my gun?"

I sat on the bed because my legs were shaking and pointed to the closet area.

"In the safe. And the pervert is probably in his villa. Two doors down," I said.

Beau marched over to the safe. "Code," he said.

"Zero five one four. Our anniversary. You aren't really going to shoot him, right? Just scare him a little?"

He punched the keys into the safe and I heard the door swing open with a beep. "Carol Ann, keep out of it." Then he slammed the safe door shut. "What the hell, CA? It's not here."

My hands were sweating, and a feeling of total dread washed over me.

"It has to be. I don't know where else I would've put it. I was just so sick and out of sorts the other night," I said, stumbling over the words and racking my brain. "I thought I'd left it in my tote bag but I just checked and . . . it wasn't there. It has to be in the safe!"

"Are you really and truly kidding me right now? Use your brain! What were you doing leaving a loaded Glock in a tote bag in the first place?"

He's a man who's seeing red because another male threatened his wife, I told myself. That's all this is.

"Maybe it's in my suitcase." I walked over to my luggage and threw all the clothing out, praying that the gun would materialize underneath my panties and leggings, even though I knew I hadn't put it there.

"Well?" Beau asked.

I shook my head.

"God damn it!" He kicked the table and marched into the bathroom again, throwing around my cosmetic bags.

It had to be in the villa somewhere. It just had to be.

I lifted the sheets and looked underneath, then shook out the throw blanket. Beau's phone fell on the ground with a thud, and I bent down to grab it and make sure I hadn't accidentally cracked the screen.

That's when I saw it. I hadn't been meaning to snoop. But a new message had lit up on Beau's phone and the heart emojis immediately caught my eye.

There was a string of messages.

Miss you and your big hard cock already

Wish you didn't have to run out like that. I can still taste you in my mouth . . . mmm

Hope everything worked out okay. Lemme know when you're ready for that rain check. ♡ U

My vision went red. If I wasn't already on the floor, I'm sure I would've fallen down. There was no way I could be seeing what I thought I was seeing. My eyes were playing tricks on me. Beau would *never* break his marriage vows like that. Never.

My thumb swiped the phone open to the chat. *Tammy Jean* was her name. I recognized it as a teacher's aide from school. My blood went cold. I needed there to be some rational explanation for what I was seeing other than my entire marriage being a lie. The whole foundation of my life. My everything.

As I scrolled up, romantic and lurid messages assaulted my eyes. And worse. Photographs. Mirror selfies of his little slut in cheap lingerie. Photos of my husband's nude genitals. If this was a bad dream, now would be the time to wake up. I forced myself to stare at the images to make sure they were real. Not tricks. Not a prank. Then I covered my mouth with my free hand, worried that I was going to be ill.

If you've ever heard the expression "my whole world came crashing down," well, that's what happened to me. Except instead of a crash, it was more like a nuclear explosion that blew my life as I knew it into smithereens.

I was coughing onto the wood floor when Beau came back in, pausing when he saw me. I held up the phone for him to see.

"Tammy," I said before dry heaving again.

He snatched the phone from my hand.

"Were you snooping through this?" His voice had a hard edge, like he was ready to hit me. But even with the new revelation, I knew he never would. Hitting a woman would make him look weak.

"You're cheating?" I pushed myself onto my knees and stared in his eyes.

It was the worst betrayal of my life, the embodiment of all my nightmares coming true. But if he'd just admit it, there could be some path forward. Somewhere for us to build back from. He could stop the bleeding if only he asked for forgiveness.

"You don't know what you're talking about. Don't tell yourself you saw something you didn't. Because you're being hysterical right now."

My old self left my body. My eyes became wide open. This man—my supposed king—was even more of a fraud than Shakti, even more depraved than Daniel, and more sinful than Indira. He was an unfaithful, lying bastard. And after I'd given him everything, he'd still betrayed me.

I found my feet underneath me.

"Adulterer," I said.

He put his hands on his hips and didn't speak for what felt like minutes.

"What did you expect?" he said, finally. "Getting me all hot and bothered on FaceTime like that? A man has needs, Carol Ann."

Lie, after lie, after lie.

"The messages go back way further than this week, Beau. Don't try to play me like that. I'm the mother of your children. I've spent half my life loving you!"

He didn't respond, because he's a coward. Weak and afraid. Beau was no alpha after all.

But maybe I was. I was the one who held everything in the household together. I made more money. I was the one who killed an invasive python with one shot.

Beau stood frozen and dumb, like a toddler caught with chocolate on his lips. It was pathetic. I hated the look of him, hated his stupid face. Hated that I'd been so blind.

I pushed my shoulder past him and reached for the lamp on the nightstand, pulling the cord out as I lifted it over my head. I paused for a moment to relish the fear in his eyes. Like captured prey. Then I threw the damn thing at his head.

He let out a girlish yelp and clutched his bleeding forehead, the sight of red immediately making me hungry for more.

"What the hell!" he yelled.

His words didn't have power over me anymore. I picked up one of the desk chairs. Beau backed away with hands up in the "don't shoot" position but I didn't care. I slammed it into his torso, again and again, until he finally grabbed one of the legs and ripped the chair away from me.

He shuffled a couple steps back.

"What are you doing? Huh? You're losing your damn mind!"

I picked up one of the water glasses from the table.

"Liar, cheater, sinner, asshole." It landed squarely on his jaw. The glass ricocheted off and shattered on the floor.

He doubled over and rubbed his face.

"What are you gonna do, Carol Ann? Divorce me? Come on, now. You sleep on this, and we can talk about it tomorrow. Emotions are way too high."

"I bet you'd like me to file for divorce," I said, reaching for the second glass. "That way I'd have to pay *you* alimony."

I knew that would do it. His expression melted into pure shame. What kind of man can't even provide for his family?

I cocked back the water glass and silently dared him to test me.

"You're a crazy bitch. You know that?" He hopped backward and out the door, leaving it open behind him as he turned and jogged back out into the rain toward the Enlightenment Circle.

He hadn't shown up there to protect me. He'd only been trying to validate his fragile male ego.

And I didn't need him anyway. *Run, boy, run.*

JESSICA

Our phones sat faceup on the bed, ringers on the highest volume, while Indira and I sprawled around them, staring. At 5:10 P.M., a message came in from Sky, the startle of which almost knocked me onto the floor.

> Hey mom. Dad made macaroni and cheese with hot dogs for dinner. Can't wait for you to get home. Hurry up.

They'd returned from the Universal Studios trip and Sky has settled back into a comfortable disdain for her dad. "My nerves are shot," I said. "What do you think Shakti and Daniel are even talking about?"

Indira picked her phone up and checked its Wi-Fi connection for the tenth time. The little lines around her eyes seemed somehow a tiny bit deeper than usual, and I wondered if she was worried or just late on making a Botox appointment.

She put the phone back down and sighed.

"I don't know. Maybe he's just telling her how he's disappointed that she kept her past from him, since he'd been such a loyal follower. She was kind of a guru to him, so I get that he might feel betrayed."

I wasn't buying it.

"Bullshit," I said. "He's no innocent follower. He's a disgusting man-whore. If he feels betrayed, it's only because he thinks the truth makes him look bad somehow. You should have seen him last night when he was telling me the news. He was almost giddy. Like he was happy to have found something on her."

"But why?" Indira asked. "Do you really think he would ruin her career? Blackmail her?"

I nodded. "Yeah, something bad like that."

A crash sounded from somewhere outside, then another one. Indira and I froze. Her eyes frantically searched mine.

"What the fuck was that?" She checked her phone again. Nothing.

I jumped off the bed and ran to the door, creaking it open and peering outside. It was still raining, but only lightly. Indira joined me and opened it wider. It sounded like the noise had come from Carol Ann's cabin. We leaned our bodies out to catch a glimpse.

A few moments later, her door flung open and a tall, bleeding man spilled out of the room, clutching his jaw. He half ran, half stumbled his way around the Enlightenment Circle.

"There's a special place in hell for adulterers, Beau! And you're gonna have your very own pew!"

Carol Ann's voice boomed through the air like a cannon.

Indira and I exchanged a wordless glance and slammed the door behind us. The adrenaline was making me dizzy. Between Daniel making veiled threats, gun-toting Carol Ann falling off her rocker, and strange injured men running around the Namaste Club, nothing about our environment was feeling safe anymore. I tried to recall for myself a moment when I felt powerful and unafraid, landing on my shooting practice with Margaret. I remembered how natural the rifle ended up feeling in my hands, how I could focus and breathe and hit my target, if necessary. I wasn't a helpless, defensive little lamb. I could protect myself and others if necessary. Maybe it was a reach, but it was the only affirmation that came to me at the time.

Indira walked back to the bed and picked up her phone.

"Five fifteen," she said. "What do you want to do?"

I was already slipping into my sneakers.

"Let's go to the lake."

CAROL ANN

I paced around my room feeling like a caged lion, hungry for blood with no food in sight. Over and over in my head, I replayed the last conversation between Beau and me. There were so many things I regretted not saying. My brain hadn't been working quickly enough, and it had all come out wrong. If I could've rewound time, I'd have been ready with the perfect speech. As soon as Beau fled my room, I fished my Bible out of my tote bag and unclipped the custom pink leather book jacket that cheating bastard bought me for Christmas.

Starting with Revelation 21:8, I'd remind him of the scriptures. "But as for the cowardly, the faithless, the detestable, as for murderers, the sexually immoral, sorcerers, idolaters, and all liars, their portion will be in the lake that burns with fire and sulfur, which is the second death."

And Deuteronomy 22:22. "If a man is found lying with the wife of another man, both of them shall die, the man who lay with the woman, and the woman. So you shall purge the evil from Israel."

There are so many more I could quote, but I'd have to search back in the Book for the good ones. The message of all of them is clear: Death was the biblical punishment for Beau's sins. Whether in this life or the next, he'd get what's coming to him.

But also, I wondered if I was being punished for *my* sins. For humming along while Shakti, the false prophet, sang about Krishna and

Durga and all the others. For fraternizing with sinners. Was I an idolator? I'd followed blindly, and maybe this was my curse.

I squeezed my eyes shut to hold back any more tears. There's nothing I despise more than a woman playing the victim. It was time to put on my big-girl pants. And also, I needed to find my gun.

My room was ripped to shreds, like the apocalypse had stormed through it, but there were still places to search: behind the curtains, underneath the bed, in the wastebins. Nada. Which could mean only one thing, that someone had taken it. I took a mental inventory. Every single person on the retreat could be a suspect, but why?

It didn't matter. I was going to get it back. Not a one of them could shoot like me, and I've known how to disarm a hostile since I was ten years old (jiujitsu).

Before leaving the room, I fluffed my hair in the mirror and swapped strappy sandals for tennis shoes. I didn't bother changing out of my dress, especially since Beau hadn't wanted me to be seen in public in it. I decided to wear it with pride while I defended my honor. No more peace and love and light or any of that junk. Not with that group. Not anymore. Not ever.

I'd just stepped outside the villa and was starting to make my way around the Enlightenment Circle when I heard it. The rainstorm had slowed to periodic drops but left behind dark gray skies and a thick blanket of humidity. Piercing through the thickness of it, a gunshot rang out from the lake. It was a sound I knew as clearly as my own children's laughter. It was *my gun*.

JESSICA

It was the kind of dark that made everything in the distance look like a shadow. Indira and I held hands and walked together toward the banyan trees.

Along the way, a frog leapt into our path. We startled and jumped back, clutching each other like a mother and baby possum.

"I'm not going to miss this part," Indira said. "Next time we do a girls' getaway, I'm booking us into the Four Seasons."

I urged her on toward the trees.

"You know, if I'm being honest, I'm really happy we came on this trip. As absolutely insane as it's been."

It felt strange to admit, after everything that had happened. Especially since we were on our way to defend our yoga teacher against a predatory male student who was potentially blackmailing her over past appearances in pornographic films.

"We'll be going home with some great stories," she agreed, squeezing my hand. "But why are you so clammy?"

"Involuntary nervous physical response."

The last time Daniel and I had spoken, he'd seemed unhinged. Unpredictable. Something about it twisted a knot in my stomach. The man who had shown up at my door late last night was completely different from the one I had slept with just days before. And the man in my bed that night was different from the one who led yoga adjustments in class. With someone like Daniel, who could shed skins as easily as most people get dressed in the morning, it was impossible to know what to expect. A real chameleon, that one.

We lowered our voices as we approached the banyans, my heartbeats pounding above the din. I tried to slow my breath, telling myself that everything was going to be fine. Then, right as we were passing to the other side of the trees, a shadow moved between the branches. I was about to scream when the apparition came into the light, and I froze. Barbara.

She was wearing one of her flowing white tunics, but the rain had rendered it completely see-through. Not that she seemed to notice or care.

Indira was breathing heavily behind me.

"My heart can't take much more of this," my friend whispered. "I thought Bubba the gator had come out of his swamp to meet us."

Barbara held a finger to her lips and pointed the other hand toward Shiva Lake. Her eyes looked equal parts frightened and exhausted. We all stopped to listen, hearing voices in the distance. At first, they were sharp but muted, but then they rose in intensity. Two voices: one male, one female. And then they were shouting.

Daniel and Shakti.

My heart pumped so forcefully that it was hard to make out the argument over the whooshing in my ears. *Remember to breathe*, I told myself again. The three of us wordlessly passed through the banyans and picked up our pace toward the lake.

We'd barely made it ten steps before it was all too late.

The shot tore through the distance. My knees buckled, but I stayed on my feet. Indira screamed. Barbara ran toward the lake.

By the time I reached the shoreline, Daniel's body was already covered in inky blackness, like an octopus was spreading out from his chest.

Shakti's hands were shaking. She looked at us with tears in her eyes, screwed up her face, and dropped the gun on the soaking grass. Barbara closed the distance between the two of them and pulled Shakti in tight.

Thunder roared in the distance. A few seconds later, a flash of lightning sliced through the sky, briefly illuminating the awful truth in front of our feet. Indira and I didn't move. I'd never seen a dead body before, assuming that Daniel was dead. The wound didn't look survivable. For all my newfound hatred of the man, I wasn't sure how I felt about seeing him lying limp and bloodied like that. But also, I wondered again if it was all my fault. Should I have let Shakti go down there alone? Should I have checked on her sooner?

My teeth chattered like a sudden fever had come over me. I'd have given anything, in that moment, to be transported back to my bed at home in Miami, under blankets, with my children in the next rooms and Netflix droning on the TV.

Shakti wailed into Barbara's arms, and Barbara was soothing her and humming like a baby nurse over a fussy infant.

Finally, Shakti looked up at us, her eyes cloudy and bloodshot. "He said he'd send the videos to everyone I knew if I didn't . . . if I didn't." She closed her eyes. "Pleasure him."

Indira reached out and took my hand. We looked at each other, sharing oceans of meaning without saying a word.

A rustling of wet footsteps approached from behind us. I turned around to see Carol Ann, her eyes wild. She was wearing a fancy dress with her hair and makeup done, and incongruously had on worn-out-looking sneakers. But I was too jittery and dizzy to linger on her odd appearance.

She walked right up to the body and knelt on the ground next to it, as though it were an invasive python or a wild boar she'd just hunted. Then she looked straight up at Shakti and said, "I'm calling the police."

CAROL ANN

It looked like I'd stumbled upon a Wiccan ceremony. I found a coven of witches all standing around a bloody sacrifice. I bent down to check the body, but he was *dead* dead.

"I'm calling the police," I said.

I didn't want any part in what they were doing. As far as I was concerned, I'd already been in way too close proximity to these people. And now someone had been murdered.

Shakti was trembling like a field mouse, and it was almost impossible to believe that she'd pulled the trigger. But there it was, my Glock, plain as anything, right at her feet. Not to mention the guilt painted all over her face.

"Please," she said, pitifully. "You know what he tried to do to you. He tried to do worse to me."

I winced. Daniel was no saint, and I might even have killed him myself, but not the way she went about it.

"You can't claim self-defense," I said. "Not with a stolen gun. That shows premeditation."

Shakti's face crumped. She fell to her knees and bawled into her hands.

"You're going to jail," I said. "There's no more hiding and moving on from your crimes. No more reinvention for you this time, *Shakti*."

Barbara flapped her arms up and down like a scared chicken, shaking her head. She was basically naked in her sheer dress, which was about as disturbing as the dead man bleeding out at my feet. How many crazy things did my poor eyes need to witness in one damn day?

"Oh, for Christ's sake. What is it?" Her silent act was really getting on my nerves. "Just speak!"

She started miming something. Pointing to me. Pointing to the gun. Mock turning a key. Pretend sweeping.

"I think Barbara took the gun," Jessica said. "She's saying she had a key. From cleaning your room. Is that right, Barbara?"

She nodded and mouthed, *I'm sorry.*

As if that made anything better. Of course, Shakti couldn't have pulled this off on her own. I wouldn't have been surprised if all four of them had been in on it. If they'd planned it from the beginning. I mean, even final relaxation in yoga class looks like a damn mass murder.

I looked around at their panicked faces. These women were God-less, but I had to admit it seemed unlikely that Shakti had intended to kill anyone. The girl looked straight-up traumatized, and the others were barely in better shape. They seemed more like the types to hire someone to do their killing than to wield the guns themselves. Or maybe they'd try their hands with poison, for a softer approach. From what I'd seen that week, Jessica practically wet herself every time she heard a gunshot.

"There has to be another solution," Jessica said. "Please, Carol Ann. She can't go to jail for this. Daniel wanted to ruin her life and . . . worse." She turned to Shakti. "Did he try to hurt you?"

Shakti slowly lifted her head from her hands and nodded. "He said he knew I liked it dirty and that I'd *profited* from it. That he'd been watching all my sponsorships and my life-coaching business. That if I didn't give him a piece of my body, he'd settle for just the money. He asked for fifty thousand to start, but said he'd prefer that I pay it off in 'favors.'"

I swallowed. He had been awful. Yes. A scoundrel. But that's what you get when you play with fire.

"Carol Ann," Jessica said. "She was only seventeen when she started making those videos. Daniel threatened to circulate them to people who knew her. To ruin her reputation."

My eye started twitching. He was even more depraved than I'd thought, which was saying a lot.

Jessica took a step toward me, her hands out like she was going to kneel at my feet. "She was just a child. She wasn't even an adult."

I sucked my teeth.

She put her hands together in prayer. "He was going to send the videos out to her students. That's distributing underage pornography. What would you do to a man like that?"

Something in my throat clenched. I looked Jessica in the eyes. We might have had almost nothing in common, but there was this. We were both mothers. Shakti wasn't my daughter, but if someone had done to mine what Daniel tried to do to her, there would be no question. Mothers protect their cubs from perverts and abusers no matter what.

Indira, Barbara, Jessica, and Shakti faced me with wide, unblinking expressions. They looked like a second-rate Spice Girls cover band, all staring and waiting for me to say something.

I opened my mouth to speak when a splash broke the quiet. We all turned in unison to the lake in time to see Bubba stalking the perimeter, his outline glittering like gems in the moonlight. Goddamn, he was a big boy.

I closed my eyes and exhaled all the air from my lungs.

Who was I to judge one sin over the next? To assume that righteousness, I'd be comparing myself to God. And I just couldn't do that. At the same time, though, sometimes man's laws aren't in keeping with God's laws, and as faithful servants it's up to us to bridge the divide.

There was only one thing to do, and I felt the path in my bones as deeply as I knew my own heart and my divine purpose on this earth.

"It's not in my name." I opened my eyes and smiled. "That gun is registered to Beau."

JESSICA

In the hierarchy of *things I never thought I'd do with my marketing degree,* covering up a murder is probably number one. But sometimes we surprise ourselves.

And anyway, I'm not sure I'd even label it a murder in the first place. Daniel's death was more like a public service. Of course, I realize how callous that sounds, given my brief interlude with him but, to be fair, that had happened *before* I knew exactly how depraved he was.

If anything, when I found out the fatal shot had come from Beau's gun, I thought that Carol Ann would be less likely to back down. But as it turned out, part of her wished her husband was lying there, lifeless, by the lake, along with Daniel.

Her exact words were "Beau was no alpha. He was an invasive species." Which was dark and weird, but, whatever, she was on our side. And since she was happy for Beau to take the fall, everything else seemed to fall into place. We wiped the gun off on Barbara's tunic and threw it into the lake. If the body was eventually found, we were sure the police would send divers out to find the weapon.

That's assuming there was any body left to find. We also hoped that nature would take its course and help us out a little, so we dragged Daniel's body closer to the lake, each of us taking a limb except for Shakti, who was still shivering on the ground, and let his arm dangle into the water.

American alligators aren't natural man-eaters, but they are opportunistic, and Bubba looked like he was in the mood for a snack.

Then we had to tie up our alibis, which was easy enough. It had been an absolute shit day, a real late hurricane season wash out, so a great excuse to have been in our villas. Meditating, or whatever.

"Shakti," I said. "We need you to focus."

She hugged herself and recited a mantra under her breath. *Lokah samastah sukhino bhavantu.* Her face was wan and streaked with tears. Without her poise and polish, she looked even younger.

I knelt beside her.

"I know you're in shock right now, but you need to know that we all understand why you had to do this. And now we need to work quickly so you can enjoy the rest of your life as a free woman."

She looked up at me with quivering lips.

"'Ahimsa' means *do no harm*. I took a vow."

Carol Ann cackled in the background.

"So did my husband! Sometimes, vows don't mean shit. Do you want to rot away in prison or not?"

"Here." Indira knelt next to Shakti and fished something out of her pocket. "Take this."

I shook my head. "You've got Xanax on you?"

Indira shrugged.

Shakti chewed on her cheek and nodded, taking the pill from Indira and swallowing it dry.

"What do I need to do?" she asked.

Everyone was looking at me, which made me uneasy. I wasn't used to being the leader. But I knew how to spin things and I had a plan.

"Okay, listen up everyone," I said. "We all need to memorize our roles and Barbara . . ." I shot her a direct look. "We're going to need you to speak."

MARTINA

NOW

Thank you for coming so quickly, Officers.

My wife and I have seen a lot of things working here, but dear Lord, never a body. I came upon the gentleman, Daniel was his name, while doing my morning grounds check. But by the looks of him, he'd been gone a long while. At least overnight. Didn't look like he had damn near any blood left in his body.

You'd have to talk to the ladies who are here for the retreat, but I can't think of any reason someone would want him dead. Not from what I'd seen, anyway. The women here seemed kind of cozy with him, if anything.

We have only the one security camera at the front gate and you're welcome to take a look at that, obviously. I took the liberty and sure enough did see an agitated-looking man drive in and then leave again about an hour later. I'm no detective but, if it were me investigating this case, I'd track that guy down.

With all the storms yesterday, my wife and I laid low at our residence after lunch service. The group leader, a young woman named Shakti, called in the evening to cancel cocktails and dinner on account of the weather. We took that as our cue to tuck in early. It had been a long week for us, looking after this group.

If there is anything my wife or I can do to be of assistance—anything at all—we are at your disposal. I do have one request, though. This seems like a clear case of murder to me, don't you think? This crime was committed by a man.

Now, I know how it looks with the bite marks, but I also know a bullet hole when I see one. If you could keep Fish and Wildlife out of this, sirs, I'd really appreciate it.

No need to euthanize an innocent for a crime he didn't commit.

SHAKTI

NOW

And that is all I can remember from yesterday.

When the storm refused to let up, I called Martina and Margaret to ask them to cancel cocktails and dinner. Everyone was satiated in their souls from meditation practice, and I thought it best we listen to nature's cues, which were telling us to stay in and reflect before parting ways.

I fell asleep with a full heart and woke up rested. It wasn't until I saw the police tape around the banyans on my way to the morning hike that I realized something had happened.

The news about Daniel is shocking. On a human level, I will miss his bodily presence. But I know, on the celestial plane, that his energy is still with us.

I chose my name, Shakti, because it is the Sanskrit word for divine feminine energy. If Daniel had lived to finish teacher training, I would have given him the opposite name: Shiva, which represents the divine male.

Even now, I can feel him chanting along with me: *lokah samastah sukhino bhavantu*. Which means—may all beings everywhere be happy and free. Wherever his soul is at this moment, I know that it is soaring high above the clouds, happy and free.

BARBARA

NOW

I'm sorry, Officers. I don't mean to be so emotional.

You see, the last time I saw Daniel alive it was, well, in the throes of romance. We'd begun as friends, fellow practitioners, and devout followers of our dear Shakti. And through that devotion, a spark formed.

He was a sweet soul, a tender lover.

After meditation today, he wanted to honor the end of his retreat experience in silence. I left him after the Active Room meditation and retired to my own private space as well. It is so important to self-reflect after these powerful and transcendent sessions. Little did any of us know that the end of his retreat experience would coincide with the end of his life's journey.

I'm going to have my family foundation, the Babbington Trust, donate one million dollars in Daniel's name to the Blessed Souls organization, which supports orphans in India. It's what he would have wanted.

May I chant three oms in dedication to his soul?

INDIRA

It was a washout, Officers. An absolute washout of a day. There was nothing to do.

My best friend, Jessica, and I signed up for this retreat as a girls' trip, so we spent the last evening in my villa streaming TV shows. If I'm being honest, since we were all cooped up, we did get a little tipsy off tequila and—I should mention I have my medical marijuana card for migraines—a little high. We ate all the gift-bag snacks in my room and were asleep together in my bed by 9:00 P.M.

I can't imagine what Daniel was doing outside, though he did seem incredibly connected to nature. Maybe that had something to do with it. Being among the elements. But what happened to him . . . I'm honestly just in disbelief right now.

He was a nice guy. Very devoted to his teachings and his yoga practice. And so young!

Never once have I felt unsafe here. If I had any idea something like that was possible on these grounds, I wouldn't have come in the first place. This is just so tragic.

Have you notified the family? I didn't know him well at all, but I would be happy to help in any way possible.

JESSICA

NOW

Daniel! Of all the people in the world, why would someone want to hurt Daniel? He was a nice, peaceful, spiritual man. My heart absolutely breaks for his family.

The last time I saw him was at meditation. He had a beautiful, serene practice. If you want to hear the truth, it was sometimes hard not to stare at him. He just exudes this beautiful energy, you know? I'm sorry—I mean *exuded*. Oh my god. I can't believe he's really gone.

The weather was terrible yesterday. Storms always make me want to stay inside, throw on some sweatpants, and watch TV, so Indira and I cuddled up in her villa for the night. We had a little too much to drink and I can't remember much of anything after 8:00 P.M. I woke up to a frantic knock on Indira's door from Shakti. Seeing the tears in her eyes, I knew something must have been very wrong.

CAROL ANN

NOW

Officers, I am so glad you're here. Thank God for y'all. I swear, I can recognize a gunshot as clear as my own mama's sweet voice, but the thunder was just so damned loud yesterday, I could barely hear the air-conditioning in my own room. I would've been the first to call, otherwise. The thin blue line is all that stands between us and whatever Godlessness went down here last night.

Let me explain to you everything that happened. I wish I could say I'm surprised that Daniel is dead. Well, he may have crossed a line calling me sexy, but he didn't deserve that.

This is extremely difficult to admit, but I can't stay silent. My man needs help! It's my husband, Beau. He's been slipping away mentally lately, but of course he's too proud to seek help. I never thought it would come to this, though.

I tell him everything, that's the kind of marriage we have, and he knew that I was having a tough time here. To be honest, I've been pretty homesick. I should have known that, in his mental state, he wouldn't be able to handle it. It drove him crazy that a man was here at a ladies' yoga retreat. He started making up these scenarios in his head that were just loony. Like out of nowhere. Thinking Daniel was violating me or acting inappropriate in other ways. Now, I should never have told Beau that Daniel called me sexy. The comment had totally caught me off guard and I accidentally let it slip when I was talking to my husband. But then Beau took it to a crazy other level. Said that Daniel was an agent of Satan who was sent to destroy our marriage. He fell into absolute delusion.

It's not the first time, either. A month ago, Beau had called me at work—I'm a real estate agent in case you guys are looking for anything—and he was shouting because the dog had pooped all over our living room rug. Officers, we don't have a dog.

I know. I know. I should have taken it seriously right there and then. But we've been sweethearts since we were twenty years old, and I just couldn't believe that I could be losing him. It breaks my heart! If you knew him the way I do, you'd see he's the most wonderful man. You'd want to invite him over for a Fourth of July barbecue, if you knew the real him. That man is still in there somewhere. And I've been over here enabling him by not speaking up.

Maybe this all could have been prevented.

I'm sorry, Officers. Can I have a tissue before we continue?

Breaking News: Florida Man Suspected in Yoga Retreat Murder Found Dead

A Florida man, who was also the prime suspect in a murder at the Namaste Club yoga retreat, has been found dead from a lightning strike. Identified as Beau DeFleur from Vero Beach, Florida, the suspect was matched to a murder weapon found at the bottom of the lake where Miami-based Daniel Rhine was found dead. Police have not released a motive, but sources say that DeFleur had recently suffered from serious mental delusions and thought that Rhine had made inappropriate comments to his wife, Carol Ann DeFleur, who was a student at the retreat.

Melbourne Police believe that DeFleur had left the Namaste Club facility in west Melbourne and was driving back toward Vero Beach when his truck hydroplaned and crashed into a utility pole.

"It appears that DeFleur exited the vehicle in the middle of yesterday's storm to assess the damage, and at that time he was struck by lightning," said Sergeant Rhonda Piper.

"I just can't believe it," Carol Ann DeFleur told reporters. "Beau was a loving husband and father. He's been struggling so much lately, but who among us can say we haven't experienced hard times? I can't believe that an act of God would take him from us so quickly."

Police had been trying to locate DeFleur in connection to Rhine's death but were unable to track him down. A Find My search for his iPhone eventually led authorities to the rural area where his body was found. It is believed that he died instantly.

In an initial report of Daniel Rhine's death, it was reported that his body had been mauled by an American alligator. According to the Brevard County Medical Examiner's Office, those injuries were sustained after the victim had already died. The official cause of death was a gunshot wound to the chest.

The animal involved in the postmortem maiming, known locally as Bubba, has been euthanized.

"They didn't need to kill Bubba," said Martina Shoenfeld, groundskeeper at the Namaste Club. "He was an innocent. He had nothing to do with the conflict between those two men."

All of the women involved with the retreat have been interviewed and released. According to police, they are not considered suspects in Rhine's death.

This is a developing story.

ACKNOWLEDGMENTS

When people ask me about this book, I usually describe it as an inside joke I have with myself. I love being a Floridian with all the idiosyncrasies that come with the title, and passionately believe that locals should be the first ones to point a finger at our diverse, nuanced, and sometimes problematic state. The thing with inside jokes, though, is that they don't always translate. That is why I am immensely grateful for the early readers who counseled me on when to rein myself in and when to let loose with my wilder ideas (like perineum sunning). This book would not be fit for publication without their wisdom.

Thank you to my brilliant agent, Helen Heller, who stressed to me the importance of one's second novel, while also proclaiming that this was mine. You will forever be the woman who made my biggest dream come true. It was incredible luck to work with my editor, Rachel Kahan, on my first book, and an embarrassment of riches to continue that relationship on this one. I am also grateful to the entire team at William Morrow, for their continued expertise and support: Kelly Cronin, Jen McGuire, Alexandra Bessette, Paul Miele-Herndon, and Rita Madrigal.

If I'm lucky enough to publish more books, I'm 100 percent positive that I will always need to thank Jennifer Close—for early reads, for providing space for writers like me to workshop, and for always picking up the phone when I panic about something book-related that seems monumental but ends up being trivial.

I workshopped this book with a talented cohort of writers, and their contributions are ever-present in these pages. Their names are Brigid Hogan, Valli Porter, Kari Pilgrim, Nancy Lee, Elizabeth Savage, Patrick Londra, Kate Leahy, and Rebecca Thienes. Special thanks are also due to my brilliant writer friend Catie Stewart, who is an incredible reader, a dedicated free therapist, and selfless pro bono publicist (for me, anyway).

Researching this book sometimes took me to dark corners of the internet, but more often was too fun to be considered *work*. Thank you to Bill Kearney for imparting me with your expertise on Florida invasive species, and for turning me on to many, many fascinating social media accounts dedicated to their hunting and capture. My algorithm will never be the same.

Jeff Costomiris, onetime CrossFit coach and lifelong friend, thank you for the hours of conversation about weird wellness trends. Your inspiration is all over this book, and certainly captured in the most entertaining parts. I'm only glad that this project was completed before you told me about the disturbing trend of fitness influencers massaging themselves with aged urine. That might have been one step too far for readers.

Zach Friedman, thank you for coining a term that I won't repeat here, but that you allowed me to steal. We both know what it is, and I still think it's genius.

To my tireless friends, Amy Stojanovic and Kirsten Vogel, who still agree to read my early draft manuscripts—I am fortunate beyond words to know you both. Dad, thank you for your help with yoga theory. Sorry about all the sex scenes. To my late mother, for whom yoga was so much more than a class, thank you for teaching me the mantras. I'll always miss your Ayurvedic cooking. Jamie Elias, thank you for still reading everything I write, for dragging our kids to book events, and for everything else, really.

To the wonderful people at Books & Books, with special thanks to owner, Mitchell Kaplan, and bookseller, Ed Boland, thank you for making the bookstore my *Cheers*, for championing my work to anyone who will listen, and for showing me the kind of community support you just don't find anywhere else.

And lastly, to my children, India and JJ, for being my endless sources of purpose and inspiration. I love you, I love you, I love you.